The Regency

LORDS & LADIES
COLLECTION

*Two Glittering Regency
Love Affairs*

Rosalyn and the Scoundrel
by Anne Herries
&
Lady Knightley's Secret
by Anne Ashley

The Regency

LORDS & LADIES
COLLECTION

Volume 7 – January 2006
Rosalyn & the Scoundrel *by Anne Herries*
Lady Knightley's Secret *by Anne Ashley*

Volume 8 – February 2006
The Veiled Bride *by Elizabeth Bailey*
Lady Jane's Physician *by Anne Ashley*

Volume 9 – March 2006
Perdita *by Sylvia Andrew*
Raven's Honour *by Claire Thornton*

Volume 10 – April 2006
Miranda's Masquerade *by Meg Alexander*
Gifford's Lady *by Claire Thornton*

Volume 11 – May 2006
Mistress of Madderlea *by Mary Nichols*
The Wolfe's Mate *by Paula Marshall*

Volume 12 – June 2006
An Honourable Thief *by Anne Gracie*
Miss Jesmond's Heir by *Paula Marshall*

The Regency

LORDS & LADIES
COLLECTION

Anne Herries & Anne Ashley

MILLS & BOON®

*MILLS & BOON and MILLS & BOON with the Rose Device
are registered trademarks of the publisher.*

*First published in Great Britain 2006 by
Harlequin Mills & Boon Limited,
Eton House, 18-24 Paradise Road, Richmond, Surrey TW9 1SR*

THE REGENCY LORDS & LADIES COLLECTION
© Harlequin Books S.A. 2006

The publisher acknowledges the copyright holders of the
individual works as follows:

Rosalyn and the Scoundrel © Anne Herries 2001
Lady Knightley's Secret © Anne Ashley 1999

ISBN 0 263 84423 4

138-0106

*Printed and bound in Spain
by Litografía Rosés S.A., Barcelona*

Rosalyn and the Scoundrel
by
Anne Herries

Anne Herries, winner of the Romantic Novelists'
Association's Romance Prize 2004, lives in
Cambridgeshire. After many happy years with a
holiday home in Spain, she and her husband now have
their second home in Norfolk. They are only just
across the road from the sea, and have a view of it from
their windows. At home and at the sea they enjoy
watching the wildlife and have many visitors to their
gardens, particularly squirrels. Anne loves watching
their antics and spoils both them and her birds
shamelessly. She also loves to see the flocks of geese and
other birds flying in over the sea during the autumn, to
winter in the milder climes of this country. Anne loves
to write about the beauty of nature and sometimes puts
a little into her books, though they are mostly about
love and romance. She writes for her own enjoyment
and to give pleasure to her readers.

Don't miss the brand-new novel from
award-winning Anne Herries:
Ransom Bride
is available from Mills & Boon Historical Romance™
in February 2006

Chapter One

Damn it! He must have been all kinds of a fool to come back to this country, thought Damian Wrexham. There was nothing for him here, except bitter memories. If he had the sense he had been born with, he would leave, return to India, or perhaps to a new life in Spain. At least it would be warm there. And yet he had undertaken the journey home for a particular reason. He had made a promise, and he did not break his word lightly.

He was standing with his back against a tree, brooding, staring at nothing in particular, when a flash of colour in the orchard caught his eye. His brow furrowed as he saw first the dog bounding towards him, and then, a little way behind, walking more slowly, the woman.

What a woman! She looked like a goddess of ancient myth, bestriding the Earth as her domain—Diana the huntress. Even in his misspent youth, Damian had not particularly admired the simpering Society misses he had met in the drawing rooms of London. Indeed, one of the sins for which he had been banished was—in his father's opinion—his unfortunate penchant for the company of older women: married ladies, who found illicit pleasure in the bed of a young, rather wicked and handsome man.

'Miss Eastleigh?' he wondered aloud. Damian's eyebrows

quirked in amusement. Surely not? This could not be the *old maid* he had been told was his nearest neighbour. Perhaps she had a young relative staying with her? His interest was stirred. 'It would seem that perhaps all is not quite lost…there may yet be some diversion in this place…'

Damian smiled to himself. He had begun to think he would have to go up to London to relieve the tedium, but now his mood of restlessness fell away like a second skin. Would the goddess have anything to do with him once she discovered his reputation? It would not be long before someone felt it their duty to tell her of his past—that he was, in fact, a scoundrel and that no decent woman should have anything to do with him. At least, if she valued her reputation, she would not. But until then it might be amusing to pursue her…a mild flirtation, nothing more.

What a wonderful morning! It made one feel so much better, thought Miss Rosalyn Eastleigh as she walked up through the orchard towards the back of her house. The buds had begun to burst, convincing her that spring had finally arrived after weeks of damp, miserable weather; the sun was warm on her head, for as usual she had discarded her bonnet and her glossy dark hair had been whipped into an artless tangle about her face.

It was a face that, though undeniably attractive, could not be called pretty—at least, it could not in Miss Eastleigh's own opinion. She knew her complexion was too dark to be generally admired: her grey eyes were wide and candid, expressing too openly her often controversial opinions, her mouth too big, her nose too long. She was also taller than most men of her acquaintance, and everyone knew that gentlemen preferred petite, pretty women who fluttered their eyelashes and looked helpless. Men did not spring to assist Miss Eastleigh to a chair when she walked into a room: she was only too capable of managing for herself.

Not that Rosalyn gave much consideration to either her

appearance or what the gentlemen might think of her. At seven and twenty she had spent too long on the shelf to bother about marriage. It was years since she had given the idea more than a passing thought.

'Come, Sheba!'

She whistled to the madcap dog her brother Freddie had foisted on her during his last flying visit to the country. Sheba was a black and white mongrel who, Freddie had assured her, was the *sweetest* little thing and would cause no trouble. At the time, the puppy had been no more than a ball of fluff, undeniably pretty and very affectionate.

She was still affectionate some nine months later, but had grown into a great, long-legged, boisterous dog, who was forever into some mischief. Hearing her mistress call, Sheba bounded towards her, jumping up and scrabbling at Rosalyn's gown with muddy paws.

'Down, you wretch!' ordered Sheba's mistress, brushing at her skirt in a vain attempt to save it. 'How did you get into such a state? This is the third clean gown you have ruined this week. I think you do it to spite me. I've a good mind to sell you to the gypsies—and, believe me, I would if I thought Freddie would ever forgive me.'

Sheba gave an excited yelp, understanding perfectly that her mistress did not mean a word of what she was saying. She lolloped off in pursuit of one of the kitchen cats, barking noisily.

'Disgusting animal!' Rosalyn said, smiling in exasperation. 'Sheba! Come back here.'

Sheba paid not the slightest heed. As a puppy she had developed an annoying habit of disappearing into the surrounding countryside for hours at a time, though so far she had always found her own way home eventually—usually wet and always hungry!

'You should teach that dog to obey you, or you may find she becomes impossible to control. Those half-breed collies can be a nuisance if they aren't properly trained.'

Rosalyn was startled by the man's voice. She had thought herself alone, failing until that very moment to notice him leaning against the trunk of an apple tree. Her eyes narrowed thoughtfully as she looked at him. This man was unknown to her—a stranger to the neighbourhood.

He was dressed plainly in a brown coat and cream riding breeches; his leather boots, though obviously well made, had seen considerable wear. Extremely attractive in a rugged, outdoor style, his skin looked tanned as if he had spent time in the sun, perhaps a much warmer climate than England's. Rosalyn noted that his raven black hair was cut short in a fashion she recognized as à la Brutus, which was a style much favoured by Freddie's friends; but, despite the haircut and the excellent fit of his coat, there was a carelessness about his attire that her brother would have frowned over.

'Forgive me…' Rosalyn realised she had been staring. 'I was startled. I had not expected to see anyone here. May I help you? Are you in some difficulty?'

Her neighbours usually visited at the front door. They came by carriage or on horseback, but never walked casually across fields and miles of open country, as this man must have, to reach her orchard.

Who was he—and what did he want here? She hesitated, a little wary, half-inclined to call Sheba to her.

'I have been watching you,' he said, a half-smile on his lips. 'Fair Diana, the huntress—come to earth in search of human souls.'

As compliments went, it was unusually apt. In all the illustrations Rosalyn had seen of the goddess, Diana was generously formed and looked capable of living up to her reputation. Which could just as easily be said of Rosalyn.

'I am sorry to disappoint you. No goddess, I am afraid, merely Miss Eastleigh taking her rather boisterous dog for a walk,' she replied, concealing her amusement with a wry look.

It was a long time since a man had paid her a compliment. Freddie's friends were too young to be interested in his spinster sister, and her neighbours were married, kind but incapable of paying such a tribute.

'Miss Rosalyn Eastleigh?' He seemed slightly taken aback as she affirmed it with a nod. He stood straight, bowing his head to her. 'I thought… Excuse my execrable manners. Miss Eastleigh, allow me to introduce myself. I am Damian Wrexham. Your new neighbour. At least, I expect to be residing here for the next few months.'

'Oh, yes, I remember now. Lady Orford told me her husband had let the Hall. I thought she said it was to an Indian gentleman, but I was obviously mistaken.'

'No, not at all,' Wrexham replied, a flicker of amusement in his eyes, which she had just noticed were very dark. 'My…pupil, Jared, is of Indian descent through his father, though his mother was an Englishwoman. A rather intrepid lady, I understand. Apparently, she went out to India with her own father, who was a missionary, and fell in love with…Jared's father. Despite all the difficulties and inevitable scandal, she married him and bore him a son.'

'How exciting.' Rosalyn's interest was fairly caught now. 'How brave of her to follow the calling of her heart and forget convention. I have often longed for adventure. India is very beautiful, I believe.'

'Yes. Very. Exotic, wild, dangerous—but undeniably beautiful.'

They had been walking as they spoke, he matching his steps to hers. Now, having reached the house, it seemed natural to invite him in. Rosalyn offered her invitation without hesitation, her manner exactly as it would have been with any other neighbour who chanced to call.

'I am about to have nuncheon, which for me is bread and butter, cold meat and tea. You are welcome to share it, Mr Wrexham, though it is but poor fare for a gentleman. I dare say we could find you some wine to make it more palatable.'

'Another day, perhaps.' He gave her an enigmatic look, which she found difficult to interpret. 'I came in the hope of persuading you to dine with us tomorrow evening, Miss Eastleigh. As I believe I mentioned earlier, Jared is my... pupil. His father wishes him to spend some time in England, and I am teaching him English ways and manners. However, I have no hostess and you...to be frank, I expected *you* to be older.'

The expression in his eyes was so full of wicked humour that she discovered the reserve she had first felt towards him had flown. Her brows rose and she gave him what could only be termed an *old-fashioned* stare.

'Indeed, sir. I wonder why?'

'No, do not look at me so,' he murmured wickedly. 'You cannot know what I have been told, ma'am.'

'Oh, I think I can guess.' Rosalyn was betrayed into a laugh. 'You were told I was an old maid. No, do not deny it, Mr Wrexham. It is quite true, you know. I am seven and twenty, and set in my ways. It would be a very brave—or foolish!—man who thought otherwise.'

'I am forewarned,' he replied, eyes gleaming. He raised one mobile brow. 'Forgive me, Miss Eastleigh, if I presume on your good nature. But you do see my problem? Ours is an all male-household, apart from the Orfords' excellent housekeeper, of course. Would it be quite proper, do you think, for a lady to dine with us? Even a lady of your advanced years...'

'Alone?' Rosalyn was amused. He was a shameless flirt, of course, but she liked his humour. 'Oh, no, not at all. Quite improper. That would not deter me, however—if it were not that to accept such an invitation would lacerate poor Maria's feelings.'

'Maria?' His brows arched. 'Tell me at once, I beg you! No, ma'am, do not laugh. It is of the utmost importance. I most ardently desire to know—who is *poor* Maria?'

'Miss Maria Bellows, my cousin, a very respectable lady

in her middle years. She lives with me. Has done so since Papa died three years ago.' Her own expression was little short of wicked, which made Damian chuckle deep in his throat. 'You *must* understand, Maria felt it her duty to devote herself to me. I could not refuse, of course, since she would otherwise have had to find herself a position as a governess—or some other equally unpleasant post—and, of course, it would not be proper for me to live alone. Indeed, it would be quite shocking—do you not agree?'

'Even at your advanced age? One would have thought that quite acceptable.' His brows rose once more. 'Unless you have an unfortunate propensity for wild orgies if not strictly watched?'

'Wretch!' Once again Rosalyn was betrayed into laughter. She decided she rather liked her new neighbour. If he was always so entertaining, he would enliven many a dull dinner party that summer. 'You deserve to have your ears boxed, sir—but I shall forgive you, providing you extend your dinner invitation to Maria as well as myself.'

'You *will* come?' She saw warm approval in his eyes and felt herself blush, something she had not done since leaving the schoolroom. 'You are generosity itself, Miss Eastleigh. I believe you will like Jared—and I am certain he will adore you.' He smiled at her, a smile so charming and full of warmth that it took her breath away. 'Tomorrow at six-thirty, then. We dine at seven. Late hours for the country, perhaps, but in India we have been used to dining in the evenings, because it was always cooler then. It will not upset you?'

'Not at all. We shall look forward to it, Mr Wrexham.'

'Until tomorrow, Miss Eastleigh.'

He bowed, then turned and walked back towards the orchard, obviously intending to return the way he had come.

Rosalyn stood watching him for a few moments. The chance meeting had lifted her spirits—if only because it made a change to converse with a man who was actually taller than she. No, that wasn't her only reason for liking him. She had found him amusing and he intrigued her, blowing away the slight cloud of ennui that had been hanging over her.

She sensed a slight mystery about him. Twice he had spoken of Jared as his pupil. Somehow Mr Wrexham did not strike her as being the kind of man who became a tutor. His skin had a deep tan, as if he had spent much of his life outdoors. She thought he looked too active—too physical—to be a teacher. He would have been more at home as a soldier—or some kind of a bodyguard, perhaps?

Rosalyn laughed at herself. Now what had made her think of that? Perhaps because he had been living in an exotic environment, where such guards were often necessary. She recalled reading recently a report in a newspaper of an Indian prince having survived an assassination attempt; it had only been a few lines, but had interested her more than all the usual stories of society events.

Her new neighbour could of course have had nothing to do with that infamous affair. Mr Wrexham was unquestionably a gentleman—but very different from the gentlemen she was accustomed to meeting in society. It was not just the casual way he wore his clothes, or his very direct manner of speaking…but a certain vitality, and an alertness she had sensed rather than seen. There was something out of the ordinary…unorthodox about him. One sensed that he would never bow to convention; he was too large a character, too bold to concern himself with the rules which governed others.

He was, she felt sure, a man who had tasted life to the full, no longer young—perhaps in his late thirties. He had spoken of India as being exotic but dangerous, and he too was a little like that. A man with a past. Yes, that description suited him very well.

Rosalyn was smiling at her own thoughts as she went into the house, to be met in the hall by a small, plump lady, who was wearing a grey gown and a lace cap over hair which even her kindest friend could only describe as mousy.

'Ah, there you are, dearest,' she said, giving a nervous little laugh. 'Has your headache quite gone? You are looking much better.'

'I feel better. The walk did me good.'

Rosalyn had forgotten the headache, which was merely an excuse to get her away from the house and her cousin's chattering for a while. Maria meant well, and she was devoted to her, of course, but sometimes she could be just the tiniest bit irritating. Oh, no, that was unfair! Rosalyn scolded herself for the uncharitable thought. But Maria would fuss so!

'Who were you talking to just now, Rosalyn? I couldn't help seeing you when I looked out of the parlour window. I do not believe I know the gentleman?'

'No, you wouldn't,' Rosalyn said, amused by her curiosity. Maria was such a busybody, but she could not help her nature. 'I met him for the first time this morning. He is Mr Damian Wrexham, our new neighbour. Or one of them, at least. His pupil is an Indian gentleman.'

'Oh, dear…' Maria looked uncomfortable. 'So unfortunate that Lord Orford should have let to strangers for the summer. Dear Lady Orford always gives such splendid dinners.'

'Well, she left her cook behind for the benefit of her tenants, Maria. So I'm sure you will be pleased to hear we've been invited to dine tomorrow night.'

'To dine…' Maria reached for her lace kerchief, dabbing at her lips. She was clearly disturbed by the news. 'But, Rosalyn, my dear…an Indian gentleman…do you think we should?'

'Maria! I am ashamed of you,' said Rosalyn with a look of mild reproof. 'Do not be a snob, dearest. Mr Wrexham is a very agreeable gentleman, and I am sure Jared will also be perfectly acceptable. Besides, I promised Lady Orford I would help introduce her tenants to the neighbourhood.'

'Oh, well, if you think…' Maria gave a little sigh of resignation. She had learned long ago that it was useless to expect Rosalyn to abide by her own very strict code of the behaviour proper to a lady. And she was only too aware that she was here because Rosalyn was too generous to turn her out. 'Of course it is not for me to object. I am here only as your guest. You must do exactly as you wish.'

Rosalyn ignored the opening.

'I am sure you will enjoy yourself, Maria. Besides, I did promise Lady Orford. You would not want me to break my word?' Maria silently shook her head. 'I am sure they are very respectable people. Lord Orford would not otherwise have let them the house.'

'No, of course not. You do very right to chide me, Rosalyn. I fear I am a foolish woman and I dare say I wear your patience to the limit.'

'I know that you act always out of affection and concern for me.' Rosalyn bestowed a careless kiss on her cheek. Despite Maria's unfortunate ways, she was quite fond of her cousin and was at some pains not to hurt her by speaking too sharply. 'Shall we have nuncheon, Maria? The walk has given me an appetite.'

It was late, past eleven. Rosalyn heard the long-case clock in the hall strike the hour and yawned over her book. Maria had gone to bed nearly an hour earlier, but she had stayed on to finish the last chapter. However, the ending had proved only too predictable, and she laid the book aside with a sigh of disappointment.

Sometimes…just now and then…she found her life a little tedious. Rosalyn was very attached to her home, a rambling old house, often draughty in the winter and filled with the clutter of years, but she was occasionally lonely. It was her own fault, of course. Aunt Susan had asked her to live with her in Bath, and Freddie would have welcomed her if she had taken up his offer to visit him at his London house. However, neither of the two alternatives would have suited her independent nature.

At Lyston House, she was her own mistress, free to come and go much as she pleased—to ride about the countryside unaccompanied, to walk bareheaded and visit only with the friends she had known and liked all her life.

She found society as it was lived in London and Bath a little too confining, too narrow. Rosalyn had a quick wit and rebellious spirit, both of which had been shamelessly encouraged by her father. While Sir Robert Eastleigh lived, his daughter had never known a moment's boredom. They had been friends and constant companions, delighting in each other's presence.

Oh, she did miss him so!

Tears stung her eyes as she recalled the last few weeks of her father's life. After having been revoltingly healthy for as long as she could remember, he had succumbed suddenly to a debilitating illness, which had left him bedridden. He had hated every moment he was forced to spend lying there, a prisoner of his failing body, and lost his temper with everyone who came near him—everyone except Rosalyn. Only she had been able to placate him, to make him smile at his misfortunes.

During those final weeks, they had drawn even closer. Rosalyn had been devastated by his death, and was not truly over it even now. All her family had tried to persuade her to go into society more now that she was free to do so, but she knew that she would never find a replacement for her beloved father amongst the gentlemen who frequented the drawing rooms of Bath and London. Sir Robert had been essentially a countryman, a huge man in both form and character with a bluff, good-natured manner...more alive and honest than most others she had met.

It was odd, she thought, as she got up and wandered over

to the window to look out at the moonlit night, but Mr Wrexham had reminded her a little of her father. No, that was wrong. She shook her head as she stood staring at the gardens, turned to silver now and more lovely than ever. They were not alike...except perhaps in their manner of speaking. Sir Robert had called himself a blunt man...too blunt for many, which was why he seldom went into society himself. Rosalyn had inherited many of her father's qualities, though perhaps plain speaking was not always considered a quality but rather a fault.

Her reverie came to an abrupt halt as she saw a shadowy figure lurking in the shrubbery. Someone was there! A man...at least, she was almost sure it was a man. Rosalyn felt a shiver of apprehension run down her spine. None of her own servants would be in the gardens so late. Besides, why would they need to hide in the bushes?

Suddenly, she heard a familiar barking. Sheba came running out of the shrubbery and a person followed...not a man's figure, much smaller...a youth of perhaps twelve or thirteen years. He ran after the dog, calling to her in a strange-sounding tongue. Because of the moonlight, Rosalyn was able to see the young man quite clearly. He was wearing a turban and his clothes were odd...Indian! Yes, of course, that was what they must be. He was the pupil Mr Wrexham had spoken of earlier.

He had caught up with Sheba. The dog stopped, its tongue hanging out, sitting back on its haunches and allowing the youth to stroke its fur. Rosalyn watched, smiling to herself as she saw the way her dog covered the youth's face in enthusiastic licks. She wondered whether she ought to go out to them. The young Indian lad was surely too young to be out at this late hour? What could Mr Wrexham be thinking of to allow it?

Her hand was reaching for the window latch when she saw another figure emerge from the shadows. A man this time, also dressed in those rather odd-looking clothes. He darted at the youth and had almost caught hold of him when he seemed to become aware of the intention. He gave a shrill scream, obviously startled by the sudden interruption of his play. Seeing the way he shrank back, Rosalyn unlocked the French windows, determined to investigate further.

At that moment two things happened simultaneously. The man glanced towards her and Sheba sprang at him. Rosalyn could never afterwards be sure whether the shock on his face was due to seeing her or to her dog's attack. He gave a cry of pain, clutching at his arm where Sheba had bitten him, then retreated a few steps. He was saying something in his own tongue, something addressed to the youth. Whatever it was made the lad shake his head and look fearful.

'Sheba, no!' Rosalyn called as she saw the fur rising on Sheba's back. The bitch clearly sensed menace towards her new-found friend and was prepared to defend him with her life. 'Who are you, sir? What are you doing in my garden at this hour?'

Her question was addressed to the man. He stared at her for a moment, clearly undecided what to do next. She believed he understood her. Something in his manner told her that, though he continued to speak to the boy in his own language.

Rosalyn had reached the boy and dog. She placed a restraining hand on Sheba's collar, standing so that she was between the youth and the man. She raised her head, defying him to attack the young man again.

'Please explain yourself, sir. What are you doing here— and why is this youth afraid of you?'

He stared at her in silence a moment more, then turned and pushed his way into the shrubbery. She could hear the sounds of his retreat, twigs snapping, leaves rustling. He had obviously been angered by her interference.

'He will not come back now,' the youth said behind her as the sounds died away. He spoke in English, his voice cultured but with a slightly foreign accent. 'You and the dog have saved me, *mem-sahib.*'

Sheba was still growling low in her throat. Rosalyn could not recall her ever having attacked anyone before. She rubbed her fingers at the back of Sheba's ears, shushing her.

'Who was that man?' she asked of the youth. 'Why were you afraid of him?'

'I am not afraid of him,' the lad replied proudly. 'I was merely displeased that he had followed me. I am not afraid of anyone.'

'I see…' Rosalyn hid her smile. He was certainly a very proud young man. She glanced down as Sheba stiffened, then barked. 'Be quiet, Sheba. You will wake the household.'

'Is she your dog?' The youth looked eagerly at Rosalyn. 'She followed Sahib Wrexham home this morning. He said she belonged to Miss Eastleigh, our neighbour, and sent her away—but she came back and I saw her in the gardens when I could not sleep. She ran this way and I followed her. I am sorry if I disturbed you, but I wanted to be sure she found her way home.'

The youth's voice had a high, sing-song quality, but his command of the English language was perfect, which it would be, of course, if he had an English mother.

'You must be Jared, I think? Mr Wrexham told me you were his pupil.'

The youth seemed to hesitate, then nodded. 'Yes, *mem-sahib*. I am Jared and Sahib Wrexham is my…I am not sure how to say it. Is the word tutor or teacher?'

'In Mr Wrexham's case, I should think tutor would be best,' Rosalyn said with a faint smile, 'since I do not imagine he teaches you the usual lessons, does he?'

'What are the usual lessons?'

'Oh, reading, writing, arithmetic…'

'I can do all those,' Jared replied, a hint of pride in his face. 'Mama taught me to read when I was a small child.'

'How old are you now?'

'Fourteen and three months, *mem-sahib*.'

Older than she had thought, but slight for his age. Rosalyn hid her smile. Jared was clearly very conscious of his dignity. He certainly had exquisite manners—manners that would be acceptable in any society. She thought it unlikely he needed to be taught English ways, even if it was his father's intention to send him to a public school in England. So what was the real reason they had taken a house tucked away in the Cambridgeshire countryside?

Rosalyn remembered that she had thought Mr Wrexham a very unlikely teacher. What was his true function—was he meant to be guarding the youth? And why had the man with the dark, resentful eyes tried to grab hold of Jared?

She gave him a meaningful look. 'Does Mr Wrexham know you are wandering about the countryside at this hour, Jared?'

'No, *mem-sahib*.' His expression became uneasy, anxious. 'Will you tell him tomorrow when you come to the house?'

'I do not think that will be necessary, do you?'

'He would be angry with me.'

'I think he would be very worried.' Rosalyn frowned. 'Who was that man just now? You were a little afraid of him, weren't you?'

'He would not harm me.' There was a scornful look in Jared's eyes. 'He would not dare. My father would punish him if he tried—but I do not like Rajib. Sometimes he looks at me so strangely…as if he hates me. I know he never liked my mother. So I do not like him, but I am not afraid.'

The boy lifted his head, a defiant air about him.

'You should speak to Mr Wrexham. Perhaps if he knew you do not like Rajib he would send him away.'

'Rajib is my servant.' Again there was a hint of hauteur in the youth's manner. '*I* may send him away if I choose—

but then Nessa would have no one to share her duties. She is old and it would be too much for her.'

'Who is Nessa?'

'She is my ayah. She was also my mother's friend and looked after her before she died.'

Rosalyn saw a suspicion of tears in his eyes. He was clearly still grieving for his mother.

'When did your mother die, Jared?'

'Last year.' He blinked hard but did not let the tears fall. 'Everything was better when she was alive—now it has all changed. I am no longer wanted in my father's house.'

'What do you mean?' Rosalyn's compassion was aroused by the hurt tone of his voice. 'That is a very odd thing to say. What makes you think your father does not want you?'

The youth's expression changed, as if a shutter had closed on his thoughts and emotions. 'I am not allowed to talk about that,' he said. 'I should go back now.'

'Will you let me walk with you?'

'I can go alone. There is nothing to fear.'

He was so proud, so dignified. Rosalyn's heart went out to him.

'I am sure you are right,' she agreed. 'But why do you not take Sheba with you? You can hold her collar as I am now. She knows her way…and you might get lost alone. If you let her go when you reach the house, she will come back when she is ready.'

'You are kind, *mem-sahib*,' he said, smiling suddenly. His teeth were very white and even against the dusk of his skin. 'I like you. I am glad Sahib Wrexham asked you to visit us. I *shall* take Sheba with me—but only because I am not sure of the way.'

'Of course.'

Rosalyn hid her smile. She watched as the boy set off, a tight hold on Sheba's collar. He turned his head to look at her; she waved, then went back inside the house and locked the French windows.

* * *

Damian Wrexham watched from the shadows of the shrubbery, a frown on his face. He had not been close enough to hear what Jared had said to her. It was a deuced nuisance that they should have met in such unfortunate circumstances. He could only hope that nothing had been said or done to arouse her suspicions. Miss Eastleigh was an intelligent woman—an unusual woman.

If she took it on herself to interfere…it could ruin his plans. And that could prove dangerous for them all.

Rosalyn was yawning over her needlework when Maria came into the parlour the next morning. She had spent a restless night, dreaming of menacing men hiding in the bushes—and Mr Wrexham. She could not recall just what she had dreamt, but she knew it had caused her to start up in alarm.

'Two letters for you,' Maria said, handing them to her. 'From Freddie and Mrs Buckley.'

'Aunt Susan?' Rosalyn was surprised. 'She wrote only last week. I wonder what…' She gave a cry of surprise as she broke open the wax seal and began to read. 'Oh, the poor child!'

'Is something wrong, dearest?' asked Maria. She seldom received letters of her own and looked forward eagerly to hearing Rosalyn's news. Rosalyn obliged her by giving her a resume of the letter.

'Cousin Celia's daughter has been ill with scarlet fever. She is over it now, according to Aunt Susan, but still poorly. Her doctor advises complete rest for at least several weeks. My aunt wonders if we could have her here for a while…' Rosalyn glanced at her cousin. 'You would not object to that, Maria?'

'I should hope I am not so heartless,' replied Maria, slightly wounded that Rosalyn should even think it. 'Write at once and say we should be happy to have the poor little lamb. You know how I love the dear children, not that I have met your Cousin Celia's little ones as yet.'

'I do not know what she is like now—her illness may have changed her—but when we last met, Sarah Jane was a horror,' said Rosalyn. 'All Celia's children are—to say the least of it!—over-exuberant.'

'Rosalyn!' Maria chided gently. 'What a thing to say about the little darlings. Of course, I know you are only teasing, the way you do sometimes—but you really ought not, my love.'

'I can assure you there is nothing amusing about being at the mercy of Celia's offspring. She has no notion of discipline—which is one of the reasons I do not choose to live with Aunt Susan. Celia and the monsters visit her far too frequently.' Rosalyn pulled a wry face. 'I cannot promise you it will be a pleasure to have Sarah Jane staying. Indeed, it may be quite the opposite, but I fear we must endure it. We can only brace ourselves for the ordeal and hope her stay will not last too long.'

'Rosalyn dearest!' Maria was truly shocked. She had never quite accustomed herself to her cousin's plain speaking, and could never be sure if Rosalyn was funning or not. 'I see what it is. You've worn yourself out with that mending. I've told you before, there is not the least need for you to trouble yourself. I can very well…'

Rosalyn slipped her brother's letter into her pocket. For some unaccountable reason she was restless, and her head ached.

'Are you going out?' asked Maria as she stood up.

'I have a little headache. I think I shall take a walk.'

'Yes, that is a very good idea,' said Maria. 'Leave that mending for me. It is always a pleasure for me to do those irritating little tasks for you.'

'You spoil me, cousin. I do not deserve it.' Rosalyn shook her head at Maria's protest. 'I may not be back for nuncheon. Do not wait for me, Maria.'

'Do not tire yourself, my love. Remember, we are invited out this evening—though to be sure, I should not mind if we did not go.'

Rosalyn was no longer listening. She took a warm shawl from the hall-stand, wrapping it about her shoulders as she went out into the back garden.

What on earth was the matter with her? She was surely not so selfish that she resented the idea of having her cousin's sick child to stay? No, no, it was not that; it would make little difference to her own life since Celia was sure to send the nursery maid. It was this strange restlessness that was making her have a fit of the sullens…the same feeling that had disturbed her sleep the previous night.

Her thoughts took an abrupt turn as Sheba suddenly jumped at her from behind, almost sending her flying.

'Heel! You stupid dog. Have you no sense?' The man's voice sent a shock of recognition through her. Rosalyn swung round to find herself face to face with her new neighbour. 'Forgive me, Miss Eastleigh,' he apologised. 'I was returning this wretched animal to you. She pulled at the leash when she saw you and I foolishly let her go. Are you hurt?'

'No, not really.' Rosalyn smiled, her spirits lifting insensibly. 'I am used to her ways. It was not your fault. She does this all the time.' She shook her head at the dog, who was playfully jumping about her, pulling at her shawl. 'Sheba! Bad girl. Sit!'

To her utter amazement, Sheba immediately sat, head up, tail wagging, alert and ready.

'Good gracious! She actually obeyed me. Did you teach her to do that, Mr Wrexham?'

He laughed at her astonishment. 'In this instance I cannot claim the credit. I believe it was Jared. I found them both curled up on the rug this morning, sound asleep. Jared does not like English beds. He told me you met last night, here in the gardens of your home.'

'Yes.' Rosalyn was surprised that boy had told him. 'I sent Sheba home with him. It seemed…unwise for a boy of his age to be wandering the countryside alone at night. Although I do not imagine he was in any real danger, I did not think you would approve. I believed Sheba would give him some protection, should he need it.'

'That was thoughtful of you, and I agree he should not have been out so late—but he is far more mature than you might imagine. Indeed, I believe he has been forced to grow up too soon. He needs to have some fun—to enjoy himself like other boys of his age.'

'Like other boys…' Rosalyn looked at him consideringly. 'Just who is he, Mr Wrexham? Last night I thought…I suspected…he might not be quite as you had described him. '

'Did you, Miss Eastleigh?' Damian nodded, his expression a mixture of vexation and amusement. 'Yes, I expected that. Rajib told me what happened. I came to explain—to set your mind at rest. Rajib was merely trying to watch over the boy, something which I am afraid Jared finds very irritating.'

'Yes, I imagined it must be something of the sort,' Rosalyn said. 'I would ask you in, but I have just escaped for a breath of air—and we can talk more freely if we walk for a while. If we went in, my cousin would be bound to join us, and then we should not be alone for a moment.'

'Poor Diana.' His eyes gleamed in appreciation. 'You were not meant for captivity, Miss Eastleigh. You should be free to live as you will…be it above in the heavens or here on earth. I fear domesticity irks you beyond bearing at times.'

How could he know that? He read her mind too well! Rosalyn gave him what was meant to be a quelling look, frowning as she saw the answering laughter in his face. Was he never serious?

'Tell me about your charge, Mr Wrexham. He is rather a special young man, is he not?'

'Very special. Forgive me if I do not give you precise details. There are reasons, believe me.'

'Yes, I see that. I imagine his father is a very wealthy man—perhaps an important man?'

'How clearly you see things. A virtue I have seldom found in your sex.' He gave her a wicked look as her eyes smouldered. 'No, do not defend them, Miss Eastleigh. I am a rogue and my opinion is of no account. I am sure all ladies have endless virtues, even if I am not quite sure what they are…'

She was amused by his outrageous statement, but shook her head severely to warn him that he was being frivolous.

'I shall not encourage you, sir. I am persuaded you know your own faults. You were telling me about Jared. Pray continue.'

Damian laughed. 'Indeed I was and I shall. For reasons I may not divulge, Jared's father decided it might be safer for him to live in England for a few months. Since Ahmed and I have long been friends…'

'Ahmed?'

'A name permitted only to a privileged few.' Damian gave her a straight look. 'It is best for all concerned that his title is not known here. As I was saying, Ahmed asked me to bring the boy back to England with me.'

Rosalyn nodded. 'It was your intention to return home at this time?'

'Yes. I have business of my own here. It enabled me to remove Jared from an environment that is not exactly welcoming at the moment.'

'He told me he was no longer welcome in his father's house.'

'Did he?' Damian's eyes narrowed. 'Did he say why?'

'Only that things had changed since his mother's death last year.'

Was that a look of relief in Mr Wrexham's eyes? Rosalyn could not be certain.

'Yes, that is unfortunately true,' he said. 'Jared's father took another wife—a rather young and pretty girl. There was some jealousy—on both sides, I believe.'

'Ah, yes. I understand.'

'So, as Ahmed had always promised his first wife that Jared would spend some years at an English school…he thought now was the right time to send him.'

Rosalyn turned to her companion. Why did she suspect that he was not quite telling her the truth? He could have no reason to lie, surely? And yet she had the distinct impression that he was keeping something back from her. Why? Why not be completely frank now that he had begun? Perhaps he did not quite trust her.

'So…' His dark eyes dwelt intently on her face. 'I hope what you have learned today has not changed your mind about visiting us this evening, Miss Eastleigh?'

'No, certainly not,' she replied. 'Quite the opposite. I liked your pupil, sir. He is charming, and I hope that we shall all get to know each other well over the summer.'

'Thank you.' His smile was lazy, his manner relaxed, giving nothing away. 'It will mean a great deal to us to have your friendship, Miss Eastleigh. We are both strangers in this place—and I would have Jared make friends here, if that is possible.'

Something more lay behind that statement. Rosalyn was intrigued. Her first impression of this man had not changed. She liked him—but she sensed that he had been forged in the fires of experience, not all of them exactly pleasant. He was a man with a past…and it might be interesting to discover the secrets he had left undivulged.

'Do not search too hard for answers,' he said, a meaningful look in his eyes. 'It is merely that Jared misses his mother very much. I believe it will help him to spend a little time with you—you are in some ways a little like Anna. If you took an interest in him, it might help him to recover from his grief.'

'I should be delighted to help in any way I can,' Rosalyn replied. 'Though I am not sure what I can do...'

'Just be yourself,' he said and smiled. 'What else?'

As Rosalyn stared at him, her heart suddenly starting to beat wildly, he took a step towards her, then bent his head and kissed her very softly on the mouth.

'I should not have done that,' he admitted as she moved back, clearly startled. 'It was irresistible—but wrong of me.'

'It *was* rather forward of you,' Rosalyn said. She was conscious of her flushed cheeks and the tumultuous racing of her pulses. What was the matter with her? She ought to be angry, but she was merely confused. He had surprised her. 'I should prefer you to give me warning another time; a kiss is something to be anticipated, sir...and savoured.'

For a moment he stared at her with a kind of disbelief, then he threw back his head and laughed...warm, natural laughter that made Rosalyn tingle deep down to her toes.

'When I was last in England, such an impertinence would have brought me a slap or a sharp setdown,' he said, entranced by her answer, which in its way was more outrageous than his own behaviour. 'I was right—you are a very unusual woman, Miss Eastleigh.'

'And you are unlike any gentleman of my acquaintance,' replied Rosalyn, her colour heightened. 'However, since you have been in India for some years, I dare say you might have forgotten the proper respect due to a lady?'

His laughter was so warm and infectious that she was unable to prevent a smile. Besides, she was rather flattered that he had been tempted to kiss her. It was a long, long time since anyone had shown her anything other than a rather tiresome respect. And she wasn't that old! Not so old that she could not be amused by a mild flirtation.

'That's done for me, hasn't it?' he said, eyes gleaming. He was enjoying their banter. 'How refreshing, Miss Eastleigh. You are even more like Anna than I first thought. I think a more intimate acquaintance with you will be good for me as well as my pupil.'

The reference to Anna was clearly meant as a compliment. Rosalyn was curious about the woman who had dared to marry an Indian gentleman—something that must have seemed beyond the pale to ladies of her own class.

'What was she like?'

'Jared's mother?' Damian looked thoughtful. 'Very beautiful...very determined to have her own way. She usually got what she wanted, though I never heard her raise her voice, nor did she nag. She simply seemed to assume that everyone would want to give her what she wanted—and they did. Her husband adored her and was devastated by her death: the reason for a rather hasty and unwise marriage was the grief he could not handle alone. You see, Anna was the strong one in that particular partnership.'

Rosalyn had never heard a man describe marriage in such terms. She was sure it was not the way most men would think of the marriage contract, but it sounded right to her: it should be a partnership but, in her experience, so often was not.

She smiled. 'Then I fear Anna and I are not so much alike, Mr Wrexham. I believe I do have a temper, which I try—not always successfully—to control.'

'I shall remember that.' His expression made her catch her breath. He was so very attractive! 'And now, Miss Eastleigh, I have business I must attend. I shall leave you—until this evening.'

'Until this evening...'

Rosalyn watched as he strode off across the fields. What a forceful personality he had! Despite his undeniable charm, there was something about him that made her wonder if it would be wise to become too friendly with Mr Wrexham.

Chapter Two

Rosalyn had forgotten her brother's letter, remembering it only when she was changing her gown for the evening. She read it quickly, with growing surprise. Freddie was coming down the next week and would stay for several days. He was bringing two guests. Female guests!

It was not often that Sir Frederick Eastleigh paid a visit to Cambridgeshire. He preferred his house in London or the estate in Devon. When he did come, his visit was usually unannounced and of uncertain duration. To write of his intention—and to bring female guests!—must surely point to something out of the ordinary.

Was Freddie thinking of marriage? The idea sprang to Rosalyn's mind immediately, though she wisely kept it to herself when she joined Maria downstairs in the hall a few minutes later.

'Freddie may bring some friends to stay next week,' was all she told her cousin as they left the house to set out on their visit to the new residents of Orford Hall, 'so we shall have a house full of guests.'

'How nice,' Maria replied, cheeks pink with excitement. 'We go on very comfortably, just the two of us, but I do so enjoy entertaining guests. Especially dear Sir Frederick. It must always be a pleasure to welcome him home, must it not?'

'Yes. I am always pleased to see Freddie.'

Rosalyn was engrossed by her own thoughts. Her brother was still only one and twenty, but having come into the title and his inheritance on his father's death three years earlier, had become quite the man about town. Freddie's sister had smiled to herself when he'd joined the 'Corinthian' set, a section of society much favoured by those gentlemen who enjoyed sporting pursuits. She knew Freddie spent his time indulging in the pleasures his not-inconsiderable fortune could provide—racing his specially made curricle, gambling, fencing, learning to box—but, since at heart he was a sensible young man, she had never worried too much.

She wondered that he should even think of marrying so young, but perhaps she was reading too much into his letter? Yet there must be a reason why he was bringing the Hon. Mrs P. Jenkins and Miss Beatrice Holland to meet her.

Rosalyn dismissed her vague worries as the carriage drew to a halt outside the rather grand façade of Orford Hall. It had been built in the previous century, was far more modern than Rosalyn's own home, and featured a rather splendid portico of white marble columns and long gracious windows.

She was helped from the carriage by a footman and welcomed into the house by Mrs Browne, the Orfords' housekeeper, who relieved both her and Maria of all the paraphernalia of cloaks, scarves, gloves and mufflers necessary for a cool spring evening.

'Mr Wrexham and Master Jared are in the drawing room, waiting for you, Miss Eastleigh—the vicar is also dining with us tonight.'

'Oh, is dear Mr Waller here?' Maria brightened. She was quite partial to the slightly deaf but agreeable Reverend Waller. 'That is nice. Thank you, Mrs Browne. I believe I shall keep my shawl. I feel the chill in the evenings still.'

'Very wise, ma'am. It doesn't do to invite problems at our age…'

Seeing that her cousin was content to indulge in a comfortable gossip with the Orfords' housekeeper, Rosalyn moved towards the drawing room. She had been a frequent visitor for years, and was almost as much at home in the Orfords' house as her own. On the threshold of the large salon, she stood for a moment taking in the scene of pleasant domesticity; the room was comfortable rather than fashionable, furnished in rich shades of crimson and gold, and had a welcoming atmosphere with a roaring fire, bowls of flowers and the faint smell of lavender.

Damian Wrexham was engaged in an amiable conversation with the vicar—wine glass in hand—but at her approach both gentlemen got to their feet and turned to her with a smile of welcome.

The Reverend Waller spoke first, 'Good evening, Miss Eastleigh. How nice to see you here this evening, m'dear. I have been meaning to call for a day or so now.'

'You are always so busy, sir.' Rosalyn smiled at the vicar, who had been a good friend to her at the time of her father's illness. 'But you know your visits are always welcome.'

'Oh, yes, yes, always a pleasure,' said the Reverend, nodding at her happily. 'The Orfords always set a good table.'

He seemed to have forgotten he was not dining with the Orfords, but, seeing the amused smile in her host's eyes, she did not believe any offence had been taken.

'Miss Eastleigh,' Damian Wrexham said, coming to greet her. He took the hand she offered, carrying it briefly to his lips. 'I am happy to welcome you to our—temporary home. Come, Jared, say hello to Miss Eastleigh.'

Rosalyn's heart fluttered as she saw how attractive her host looked in evening dress. She was sure that even Freddie could find no fault with the fit of his coat of blue superfine, or the extremely elegant neckcloth he had tied—and the high polish on his boots would make her brother envious.

'I am happy to be here,' she replied, smiling as Jared came to greet her. He too was dressed in formal English clothes—apart from a very splendid turban of gold cloth—and looked a little ill at ease. 'How are you, Jared?'

'Very well, *mem-sahib*.' His shyness was very different from his behaviour of the previous evening. 'You are welcome here.'

'Thank you.'

Rosalyn would have said more, but at that moment Maria came in and the youth retreated after introductions had been made. He stood by the window, looking out at the night, such a sad expression in his dark eyes that Rosalyn was moved to mention it to his tutor.

'Jared does not seem happy tonight, sir. Has something occurred to upset him?'

'I have for the moment been forced to curtail his freedom.' Damian glanced at his charge and frowned. 'He does not enjoy being kept a prisoner indoors.'

'A prisoner?' Rosalyn's brows arched. 'Surely not?' What could he mean?

'An unfortunate choice of words,' Damian said, his mouth twisting wryly. 'Do not imagine Jared is ill treated, Miss Eastleigh. Everything I am doing is for his own benefit.'

'Of course.'

Why would he speak of his pupil as a prisoner? Was there something sinister here, something Mr Wrexham was afraid to reveal? Her reflective gaze rested on the Indian youth, but she was not aware how much of her thoughts were betrayed by her expression.

'Sometimes circumstances dictate our actions, Miss Eastleigh. We are not always masters of our own fate.'

'I suppose not.' Rosalyn's attention returned to her host. She gave him a speaking look from her fine eyes. 'You will naturally make it your business to see that your pupil has regular exercise in the fresh air?'

'Naturally.' Damian's eyes gleamed with a secret amusement. 'Unfortunately, Jared does not always appreciate company—unless it is your wretched dog. She followed me home again and has been here for most of the day.'

'So that's where she went.' Rosalyn nodded. 'It seems she has attached herself to your household, sir. But I can assure you that Sheba will not harm Jared. Indeed, I believe she would protect him with her life if need be.'

'And you have no objection to her desertion?' His eyes quizzed her, bringing a faint flush to her cheeks.

'None at all. If having her here gives Jared pleasure, she is welcome to stay. Besides, Sheba has always had a mind of her own. As you may have observed, she takes very little notice of anything I say to her.'

A delightful little twitch of mirth touched her mouth, bringing an immediate response from the man.

'Then I shall not waste my breath in sending her home.'

'I fear Sheba is too independent to obey. Unless it suits her, of course.'

'As is her mistress, perhaps?'

'Touché!'

Rosalyn's laugh rang out joyfully. She gave him a look of playful reproach. This man read her mind far too well for comfort. She would have to watch herself in his company.

Her laughter caused both the vicar and Maria—who had been happily chatting to one another—to stare at her in some surprise. Although always good-natured, it was seldom that Rosalyn had been heard to laugh in just that way. Their curiosity, combined with the wicked look in Mr Wrexham's eyes, made her blush once more.

'Excuse me,' she whispered, feeling slightly flustered but unsure why. 'I believe I shall talk to Jared for a few minutes.'

She left her host to stare after her as she crossed the room, unaware of the whimsical expression her banter had brought to his eyes.

Jared looked at her uncertainly as she approached but, seeing her expression of warmth and approval, seemed to relax his guard.

'Sheba is in my room,' he confided in a low voice. 'I fed her before I came down. You need not fear she will go hungry while she is here, *mem-sahib*.'

'I had no such fear. I am perfectly certain she will be well cared for in your house, Jared.'

He grinned at her, his dark eyes glowing like wet coals. 'You do not mind her being here?'

'I have just told Mr Wrexham she may stay—if it pleases you?'

The youth nodded vigorously. Rosalyn noticed the huge emerald in his turban. It must surely be very valuable?

'You are generous, *mem-sahib*.'

'I see no reason why we should not be friends, do you? If you and Mr Wrexham would like to walk over to visit me, you will always be welcome.'

'Perhaps you would care to ride with us tomorrow?'

Rosalyn was startled, glancing swiftly over her shoulder as Damian joined them. He was bearing a crystal glass filled with champagne, which he handed to her.

'I hope you like champagne—or would you have preferred sherry?'

'This is wonderful. Thank you—for the champagne and the invitation.' She met the quizzing look in his eyes this time. 'Both are equally welcome to me. I ride most days before breakfast—alone, because my cousin does not care for it.'

'Our horses have just arrived,' Damian informed her. 'Jared is an excellent horseman and the exercise will do us both good. Would you not agree, Miss Eastleigh? Regular exercise in the fresh air, was that not what you recommended?'

'Oh, certainly!' She responded to his mocking look with an answering one of reproof. 'At what time shall we meet—and where?'

A time and place was agreed and almost immediately afterwards, Mrs Browne came in to announce that dinner was ready.

Placed between Jared and the vicar at table, Rosalyn was able to observe the way her host set himself to charming Maria. It was not by any means an easy task but, little by little, Maria thawed towards him. His gentle manner reassured her so that her smiles became warmer, reflecting approval.

Once, her host caught Rosalyn watching him and the expression in his eyes almost overset her. He knew she realised what he was doing and was sharing his amusement with her. His sense of humour was positively wicked! She had not been able to share a private joke like this with anyone since her father died. She raised her fine brows at him, but he merely smiled and renewed his assault on Maria's defences.

Maria responded by repeating most of the local gossip, telling him whom he ought to meet and offering to introduce him to everyone when he attended church on Sunday. By the end of the evening, she was positively glowing as she assured Damian that she would be delighted to welcome both him and the 'dear child' at any time.

'We are to have visitors soon, you know.' She gave Damian an arch look as they took their leave later. 'Sarah Jane is very much Jared's age. They will be company for each other.'

'You are very kind to take pity on us, ma'am.' He bowed over her hand, kissing it respectfully. 'I should be delighted to bring Jared for tea one day.'

'I am sure you will always be welcome.' Maria blushed as she saw Rosalyn looking at her, and recalled it was more properly her cousin's place to issue invitations. 'Would they not, Rosalyn dear?'

'Yes, of course.'

Rosalyn wondered why Mr Wrexham had gone to such lengths to win her cousin's good will. Her gaze was drawn irresistibly to his face, and the wicked, quizzing look she discovered there made her want to laugh. She frowned, suppressing the desire. Just what was in his mind? She felt his care with Maria was more than just kindness. Once again, she suspected there was something hidden here—some motive that was not immediately apparent.

The long-case clock was striking ten when Jared accompanied them into the hall to say goodbye. He had been allowed to stay up late as it was a special occasion, but, hearing his name called, Rosalyn turned to discover he was being urgently beckoned by a woman, quite an elderly woman with greying hair and dark eyes.

Rosalyn realised she must be Jared's ayah, and she was aware of curiosity in the other woman's gaze, curiosity and perhaps a slight hostility. But no, she believed that hostility was directed at Mr Wrexham, for it was when he touched Jared on the shoulder that her eyes flashed with jealousy.

'Come,' Nessa said in English. 'Time for you to sleep now, my lord.'

'Goodnight, *mem-sahib*,' Jared said, giving Rosalyn a formal bow. 'Nessa calls me. I must go to her.'

'I shall see you tomorrow.'

Rosalyn watched as the youth ran to his ayah, and as she saw the loving way the woman greeted him, she realised that Nessa was merely possessive of her charge. No doubt she was feeling out of place, and uneasy in a strange country. But why had she called him *my lord*? Could it be that the young Indian boy was even more important than Rosalyn had thought?

There was some mystery here!

'Until tomorrow, Miss Eastleigh. I shall look forward to our ride.'

Rosalyn turned to her host. She offered her hand. He kissed it briefly as he had Maria's, but his eyes swept up to meet hers in such a wicked, teasing look that she was caught off balance and her heart did a rapid somersault.

'Thank you for this evening,' she replied with a prim nod of her head to hide the flood of emotion. 'It was kind of you to invite us, and I shall look forward to seeing both you and Jared tomorrow.'

His mouth twitched at the corners. He was amused by her formal society manners. Good gracious! Had he read her mind? Did he know she found him attractive? Or was he laughing at her, hiding something from her? There was certainly more to this rather odd household than met the eye!

Rosalyn felt her cheeks flush as she followed her cousin out to the waiting carriage. It was cooler now and she hugged her cloak about her, feeling a shiver run through her. The English climate could be so treacherous, promising spring one moment and reverting to winter the next.

'What a truly charming man Mr Wrexham is,' sighed Maria contentedly as their carriage began to move off. 'As you know, Rosalyn dear, I was not sure about the wisdom of dining with a single gentleman—but with the dear vicar there, it was perfectly respectable. Besides, Mr Wrexham has such exquisite manners. He is such a pleasant gentleman, did you not think so, my love?'

Rosalyn made no comment. Perfect manners perhaps—but what kind of a man was he really? Why had he come here to this quiet corner of England? She sensed something secretive, something perhaps not quite as it ought to be.

Was there something sinister going on? Why was Jared being kept almost a prisoner? She had thought there was apprehension in the youth's manner once or twice when his tutor spoke to him…and yet she could not think him in any danger from Mr Wrexham. No, surely not! The memory of his smile made her pulses flutter—but she was not such a fool as to be taken in by his charm. Or was she?

Maria continued to chatter for the remainder of their journey home. Since she required no more than a murmured yes or no at appropriate moments, Rosalyn was able to let her thoughts wander at will.

Rosalyn had seen the challenge in Mr Wrexham's eyes. She was sure he had sensed the doubts filling her mind. He was a man she could like, she had known that from the beginning—but was he a man she could trust? Her instincts told her to be wary, even as her heart urged her to throw caution to the winds and accept what fate was offering.

But what was she being offered? A mild flirtation perhaps...with a man she knew nothing of—except that his smile could make her heart beat very fast, which perhaps made him a dangerous man to know.

Rosalyn's thoughts went round and round like fallen leaves in a storm.

Just who was Mr Wrexham? She had sensed from the start that he was a man with a past...but what kind of secrets was he hiding? He was definitely hiding something!

'I have seldom enjoyed an evening more,' Maria said happily as they went into the house. 'You must give a dinner party next week, Rosalyn—and invite Mr Wrexham.'

Rosalyn made no reply. She was not sure she would be wise to continue the acquaintance, and yet already her mind had begun to race on, to their next meeting. There might be something a little dangerous about her new neighbour, but of one thing she was quite certain...he was the most interesting person to come into her little world for an age.

Damian was thoughtful as he took his customary turn about the garden before retiring. It was a damned nuisance that Nessa had disobeyed his orders not to come down until the visitors had left. She had been warned not to address Jared by his title, but she could not bring herself to abandon the habits of a lifetime. Devoted as she undoubtedly was to the boy she had nursed since he was a baby, she could, if she were not careful, ruin all Damian's carefully laid plans. And then all their lives might be in danger.

Miss Eastleigh's expression had left him in no doubt of her suspicions—and if she were to voice them aloud, they could force him to look elsewhere for a safe place to keep Jared hidden.

Would it be better to look for a different house immediately, somewhere nearer London, perhaps—somewhere he would find plentiful opportunities to accomplish his rehabilitation into the society that had rejected him years ago?

Damian sighed inwardly, cursing the need for his return to this damned country. Left to himself, he would have been happy to continue his life in India. He'd had everything he wanted or needed there—but the tenuous ties of his past had drawn him home. He had come because he needed to put things straight, and because he was needed here.

And there was Jared, of course. He had given his word to the youth's father, and he would not break it. He was aware of Nessa's resentment at his authority, over her and Jared. It was a nuisance, but it could not be helped.

Hearing something behind him, Damian turned sharply. Someone was behind him, in the bushes. His hand instinctively reached towards the pistol in his pocket.

'Who is there?' he demanded. 'Come out, damn you! Or I'll break your scurvy neck.'

'It is I, *sahib*,' said Rajib, emerging from the shrubbery. 'Jared has run off again with the dog. I came out to look for him.'

'Damn!' Damian frowned. 'That stupid animal. It is a pity the bitch ever followed me here. I dare say Jared would not have wandered so far without it.'

'I could get rid of it,' Rajib suggested. 'No one need ever know.'

'You harm that dog and I'll send you back to India

quicker than you can blink! Do you hear me? The animal is a nuisance, but it belongs to Miss Eastleigh. She has allowed Jared to share it—and I have no intention of paying her back by killing her dog.'

'Perhaps you should lock Jared in his room at night?' Rajib gave him a look that made Damian's blood run cold. 'Unless you want him to wander the countryside?'

The meaning behind Rajib's words made him angry. He took a step towards him, eyes glittering in the moonlight.

'Perhaps you should mind your own business and leave me to mine?' he muttered. 'While Jared is in my care he will not be locked in during either the day or the night. It would disturb and frighten him—more than he is already. I shall talk to him, make him see he must stop this wandering at night.'

'If anything should happen…'

'Why should anything happen here?' Damian's eyes narrowed. 'At home he was not safe, we both know why. Here there is no reason to fear another attack on his life—is there?'

The Indian's dark eyes fell before his burning gaze. 'No, *sahib*. Jared should be safe here—but still it is wrong that my master's son should wander alone at night.'

'I shall look for him,' Damian replied. 'Go to bed, Rajib. You may safely leave this to me.'

Rajib put his hands together and bowed his head, but not before Damian had seen the resentment in his eyes.

He watched the Indian walk back to the house, then sighed. If only he had been sure enough of his suspicions to speak out before they left India. And yet was it not always best to have the enemy where you could see them? Besides, he could not be sure if Rajib was Jared's enemy or only his; it might just be that he was merely jealous of the trust Ahmed had placed in him. He and Nessa considered the boy their property, and resented the fact that Ahmed had placed so much trust in him.

Turning away, Damian went off to search for his charge. It was unlikely that Jared would come to much harm with that great dog in tow. As Miss Eastleigh had said earlier, Sheba would probably defend the boy with her life if need be.

A smile touched Damian's mouth as his thoughts returned to that particular lady. He had been misled by Lord Orford's agent's information. She was certainly not young, but neither was she a dried-up old maid. Her cousin had proved easy enough to win over, but what did Miss Rosalyn Eastleigh think of him?

He believed she did not quite know whether to trust him or not. She had shown plainly that she felt the restrictions placed on Jared were not quite fair. And Jared's own manner towards him was, to say the least, prickly, which might make anyone suspect him of being unkind. Yet Miss Eastleigh could not think him capable of harming the boy?

He was annoyed to discover it mattered to him. He would not like to have her think him too stern a guardian, that he might actually abuse the youth.

What a fool he was to let such considerations weigh with him! His duty was to keep Jared safe, no matter what. If the boy was unhappy with his situation, that was not his fault. Besides, what should he care for the opinions of a woman who could mean nothing to him?

There could never be anything between him and Miss Eastleigh—he would be foolish to let himself think otherwise.

Damian had no time for flirtations, and certainly no intention of a deeper relationship. Marriage was not on his agenda. He had far too many problems as it was! And yet she intrigued him. She was a most unusual woman.

He chuckled softly to himself as his mood changed and he imagined suggesting a more intimate relationship to Miss Eastleigh. In other circumstances, he would have enjoyed pursuing her…tempting her into his bed.

What a delight she would be! He had already caught glimpses of a passionate nature, though she did her best to hide it. It must irk her no end to be forced to live the restricted life of a maiden lady. She was an Amazon, fearless and brave, and more rightly belonged in another age.

Catching sight of Jared playing with Sheba in the bushes, he called to them. The dog responded at once, and Jared followed reluctantly. Damian studied his rebellious face. The trust Ahmed had placed in him was proving more of a burden than he had first thought; nevertheless, he was determined to carry out his promise.

'Have I not told you to stay in the house unless I am with you?'

'Yes, *sahib*.' Jared kicked at the grass stubbornly. He had taken off his English clothes and was dressed in the loose Indian trousers and tunic he preferred. 'I was only in the garden—and Sheba was with me.'

'I know that.' Damian frowned. 'Do not force me to be stricter with you, Jared. I do not want to restrict your freedom completely—but if I have to, I shall. Do you understand me?'

'Yes, *sahib*.' The dark eyes looked up at him. 'You won't send Sheba away?'

'No—but you must obey my instructions, Jared. You know why.'

'Yes…' For a moment anger, rebellion and fear showed in his face, then the shutter came down. 'Yes, *sahib*. I know.'

Damian watched as he went up to the house, the huge dog lolloping about, barking and leaping at him.

It would be no better anywhere else, Damian decided. He would just have to pray that Miss Eastleigh was discreet enough not to voice her doubts to others. If gossip became rife, he would simply have to move on.

Rosalyn's heart leaped as she saw them riding towards her, the man and the youth, both so at home in the saddle…both riding horses she recognized as being pure Arab and mettlesome creatures.

'Miss Eastleigh.' Damian reined in, sweeping off his hat in greeting. 'I am delighted you managed to keep our appointment.'

'Did you imagine I would cry off?' Rosalyn gave him a direct look. 'I am not such poor stuff, sir. Besides, I wanted to invite Jared to tea this afternoon. My cousin is to bring her daughter to stay with us next week. You will both be invited to take tea with us then, of course—but I should like to have Jared to myself first.'

Jared was looking at her oddly.

'That is if you would like to come, Jared?'

'Very much, *mem-sahib.*'

'Good—that is settled, then.' She smiled at Damian. 'Shall we ride towards the river? It is the boundary between Lord Orford's estate and that of our other neighbours—the Sheldons. Have you met Sir Matthew yet?'

'No, we have not been so fortunate as yet.'

'You must attend church on Sunday morning. That is the best way to meet everyone,' Rosalyn said. 'Either I or the vicar will be pleased to introduce you to your neighbours.'

Damian brought his horse to a gentle trot beside her while Jared raced on ahead. It was obvious the youth had an excellent command of his mount, so Rosalyn was surprised when her companion shouted to warn him not to venture too far ahead.

'He seems quite capable of managing his horse,' she remarked. 'And we shall not be far behind him. Jared seems to resent restrictions. Do you not think it may make him more rebellious still if you hold the leading strings too tight?'

'Jared is my charge,' Damian replied seriously, his eyes meeting hers without flinching. 'I have no wish to hold him on too tight a rein. Perhaps we could increase our pace so that I do not lose sight of him?'

Rosalyn agreed to it, spurring her own mare to a canter. It meant they were no longer able to converse, but she gave herself up to the pleasures of the countryside, gradually increasing her speed until she was able to reach Jared's own horse and even race him for a while. She glanced over her shoulder, realising that Mr Wrexham was holding his own mount in check and seemed content to watch over them.

Once again, she was aware of a mystery, of something slightly sinister hidden beneath the surface.

Surely he could not imagine any harm could come to Jared in this peaceful corner of England?

Once again, she was intrigued by the situation at Orford Hall. Just who was Jared—and why did Mr Wrexham need to keep such a careful eye on him? It was often necessary to guard the children of wealthy or important men—but Mr Wrexham seemed particularly vigilant.

They rode for almost an hour, alternating between a thrilling gallop and a brisk trot, before Damian insisted on accompanying to her own stables. She invited them to stay for some breakfast, but Damian refused, dismounting and coming to help her down.

He stood for a moment longer than necessary with his hands about her waist. It was a rather pleasant sensation to be held thus, Rosalyn discovered. So pleasant that she allowed it to continue until she suddenly realised that he was staring at her very oddly. She drew away at once and he let her go, immediately catching the reins of his own horse.

'Jared will be here at three this afternoon,' he said as he looked down at her. 'Rajib will accompany him, but he will not come into the house.'

'Will you not take tea with us yourself?' Rosalyn frowned as he shook his head. 'Perhaps I did not make myself clear? The invitation was to both of you, of course.'

'Thank you, Miss Eastleigh. Perhaps I shall avail myself

of your kindness another day—but today I have other business, so I must ask you to forgive me.'

'Very well.' She smiled at Jared. 'I shall look forward to your visit, sir.'

'I shall bring Sheba with me,' the youth promised. 'Then Rajib need not wait for me.'

'There is not the least need for him to wait,' agreed Rosalyn. 'I shall be very pleased to walk home with you myself.'

The satisfied expression on the youth's face told her that her suggestion had found favour.

'Until later, Jared.'

'We must leave,' Damian said, frowning slightly. He tipped his hat to her. 'Your company this morning was much appreciated, Miss Eastleigh.'

'I enjoyed myself.'

She stood watching as they turned their horses and rode away, Jared leading at first but gradually caught by the man as they disappeared over the rise.

Rosalyn discovered she was a little disappointed that Mr Wrexham had business elsewhere that afternoon, though she scolded herself for allowing it to matter. During a restless night, she had decided that she would not cut the connection, even though she suspected that everything was not quite what it seemed up at the Hall.

Mr Wrexham could never be more than a slight acquaintance, of course. Just a stranger who had come to stay for a few months and would move on when summer was gone.

Like a migrant swallow, she thought, watching a bird swoop beneath the eaves of the stables to a neat mud nest which seemed to be defying the laws of gravity and looked terribly vulnerable.

In the autumn the swallows would be gone and so would Mr Wrexham.

As she went into the house, Rosalyn heard voices. Good gracious! Could that be Aunt Susan? She had written to invite her aunt to bring her granddaughter Sarah Jane to stay, but she could not possibly have received the letter so soon.

Going quickly into the parlour, she discovered that it was indeed her aunt. Maria was still wearing her dressing robe and looked flustered, though she had had enough presence of mind to ask for tea to be brought to the small parlour.

'How lovely to see you,' Rosalyn said and went to kiss her aunt's cheek. 'I wrote yesterday to tell you to bring Sarah Jane, but did not expect you for several days.'

'Forgive me for descending on you like this,' said Susan Buckley, pulling a wry face. 'I was sure you would not mind my bringing Sarah Jane, so I did not wait for your reply. Tommy has gone down with the measles and Celia was at her wit's end to know what to do. She was terrified that, even though we kept them apart, Sarah Jane would take it from him—and on top of her last illness, that might be too much for the poor child. She really was very poorly with the scarlet fever, you know. It quite pulled her down.'

'Oh, I am so sorry,' Rosalyn said, immediately sympathetic. 'You did very right to bring her straight to us. Where is she?'

'Maria took her to rest upstairs, because she complained of a headache,' Aunt Susan replied. 'Sarah has always been so full of life. It upsets me terribly to see her like this.'

'Yes, of course. It must—and you must be worried about poor dear Celia and little Tommy,' said Maria. 'You mustn't worry, we shall take very good care of Sarah Jane—shan't we, Rosalyn?'

'Yes, certainly we shall.' Rosalyn smothered a sigh. She remembered Sarah Jane as being a very dominant personality, and thought she would not be an easy guest, especially if she was feeling unwell. 'How long can you stay, Aunt?'

'I must leave again tomorrow,' Mrs Buckley said regretfully. 'Celia cannot cope without me. Besides, she is increasing again and ought not to go near Tommy while he has the measles. He cried so when I left, the poor darling. I would not have left him at all if it had not been so urgent.'

'Must you leave so soon?' Maria was horrified. 'You will wear yourself out with all that travelling.'

'I have no choice,' replied Mrs Buckley. 'Besides, I shall not rest until I know how Celia and Tommy go on.'

'You must take the journey steadily, Aunt,' Rosalyn said, agreeing with Maria for once. 'It will not help either Celia or Tommy if you are ill yourself.'

'Good gracious, my dear,' her aunt said. 'I am as fit as a fiddle. Travelling is nothing to me. When I was first married I did the Grand Tour, you know. I sometimes think I should like to travel now—but not until Celia's children have grown up a little.'

She put down her teacup and patted the sofa beside her, encouraging Rosalyn to sit with her.

'I have done nothing but rattle on about my own affairs since you came in, my love. Maria tells me you have a new neighbour—and his pupil is an Indian boy. It sounds very exciting.'

'Mr Wrexham and Jared have taken the Orfords' house for some weeks,' Rosalyn said with a smile. Goodness, Maria had been busy! 'If you could stay longer you might have met them both. Jared is coming to tea this afternoon, but Mr Wrexham has business elsewhere.'

'Wrexham…' Susan Buckley wrinkled her brow in concentration. 'Now where have I heard that name? I suppose he is no relation to the Oxfordshire family? Sir Robert Wrexham was a cousin of Earl Marlowe. I almost became engaged to Sir Robert when I was a gel…but the Earl did not approve of me. Neither my fortune or consequence was large enough to satisfy his pride—and naturally his word was law.' An odd expression came to her eyes. 'I always thought it served him right a little when his eldest grandson was sent away in disgrace. Now, what was the boy's name? I cannot recall it…something odd, I believe.'

A tingling sensation started in the nape of Rosalyn's neck. 'Why was he sent away?'

'Oh, I never did know that,' replied Mrs Buckley. 'I was married and had a child of twelve years by then; my husband would not have sullied my ears with scandal—he was always so protective of me. Dear George.' She sighed and looked sad for a moment as she thought of her dead husband. 'But I do know it was thought very bad. Marlowe's grandson could not have been more than seventeen or eighteen at the time. Oh, it must be all of twenty years ago.'

'So he would be about seven and thirty now?'

'Yes, I should imagine he must be.' Rosalyn's aunt looked at her. 'How old is your Mr Wrexham?'

'About that age, I would suppose.'

'Has he spent the last few years in some outlandish place abroad?'

'In India…' Rosalyn shook her head as her aunt's eyes lit from within. She had clearly scented an intrigue. 'No, you are wrong, Aunt. I very much doubt if it is the same man.'

'What is his first name—is it Damon or something similar?'

'Damian, I believe.'

'Yes! Yes, of course. Damian.' Her aunt was clearly intrigued. 'The scandal was over a woman, of course. There was more to it—but I cannot quite remember the details. I think someone may have been killed. No, I am not sure of that. I do know that his father disowned him, said he would never allow him to return home while he lived, which he isn't—living, I mean. Poor Lord Edward died soon after from a fall while out hunting. Not that I ever liked him. He was much like the Earl, a cold proud man as far as I can remember. Lord Jacob, his brother, was so much kinder—

and their cousin, of course. I was quite attached to Sir Robert, I recall.'

Rosalyn felt a little shiver down her spine. What could Mr Wrexham have done to make his father disown him? She carefully kept her voice level as she asked, 'Do you still keep in touch with the family?'

Susan Buckley stared at her. 'Sir Robert died some years back. I haven't spoken to Lord Jacob in years—but I know his wife. We speak when we happen to meet, which is once or twice a year, when Lady Ruth comes to Bath to take the waters. She has been an invalid for years.' She hesitated, observing Rosalyn's heightened colour. 'Would you like me to ask her about her nephew Damian?'

'Oh, no, of course not,' Rosalyn cried. Suddenly, she did not want to learn that Mr Wrexham was a man she ought not to know. 'It would be embarrassing if he heard...no, it is nothing to do with me. Besides, it all happened so long ago. If he has come back to England, the scandal must surely have been forgotten?'

'I am not so sure about that,' her aunt replied, frowning. 'Some things are never forgotten or forgiven. If the tale was remembered...well, it might be awkward for you to know him.'

'Mr Wrexham could not possibly be the man you are thinking off.' Rosalyn was surprised to hear Maria's instant defence of their neighbour. 'He is a perfect gentleman. There must be some mistake.'

Rosalyn hid her smile as her aunt's brows rose.

'Yes, Aunt Susan,' she said. 'I am sure there is a mistake. And if there is not...it is a very long time ago. I do not think we should stir up trouble where none exists, do you?'

'No, perhaps not,' Mrs Buckley agreed, making a mental note to do a little research on the mysterious Mr Wrexham when she returned to Bath. 'Besides, as you say, it is not really our business.'

It was not their affair. Rosalyn was determined not to let

the old rumour disturb her peace of mind. Whatever Mr Wrexham had done in the past, it could not affect her or her way of life.

She would put it from her mind. She would not give it another thought.

Damian Wrexham looked about him as he paused outside the inn on the outskirts of Cambridge. He was tempted to walk away, wishing now that he had never agreed to meet his uncle—that the letter had never reached him in India. Or that he had not been fool enough to respond to the desperate appeal it contained.

He sighed and pushed open the door of the sixteenth-century inn. His memory of Jacob Wrexham was one that could not be denied. Of all the family, Jacob was the only one who had lifted a finger to help him. If it had not been for his uncle, he would have been forced to leave England without a guinea to his name. How could he refuse a request for help from the man who had stood by him all those years ago?

A musty smell of stale ale and neglect met him as he went inside. Surely they could have met somewhere decent? Damian glanced round, searching for the man he remembered. There was no one…no one but a rather tired-looking man in the corner. Surely that could not be his uncle?

The man was standing up, smiling, walking towards him.

'Damian?' he said, a look of relief spreading over his face. 'I was afraid you wouldn't come.'

'I gave you my word, sir. Whatever you may believe of me, I do not break a promise.'

'No, Damian,' Lord Jacob said. 'I never believed a half of what was said at the time. I knew you were not capable of murder. Reckless, headstrong—but not a villain.'

A wry smile flickered over Damian's mouth. 'Then you are the only one, sir. My father and grandfather both died believing it.'

'No, Damian. Not the old man. Your father…' Lord Jacob sighed. 'He never forgave you, but Henry did…towards the end. He wanted you to come home. We tried to find you but, by the time we discovered your whereabouts, it was too late. He died with your name on his lips. He wanted your forgiveness, Damian.'

'He had nothing to be forgiven for—except his stubborn nature.' Damian's mouth set hard. 'He believed what he was told and acted on it, nothing more. My father always hated me…as you know. The old man seemed fond of me when I was a boy, but he refused to listen when I tried to explain. The fight was forced on me, Jacob. I killed Roderick Harrington, but it was a duel. I had to face him…' He shuddered at the memory. 'Well, you know. I told you in confidence, though you do not know the whole—no one knows the extent of it.'

'I know that you did not deserve what happened to you.' Lord Jacob took his arm. 'Come and sit down, Damian. We have much to talk about.'

'Could it not have been left to the lawyers?' Damian was more disturbed than he cared to admit by this meeting. Cast out by his family, he had put his memories aside, throwing himself into the life of exile that had been forced on him. 'I never expected to inherit anything. Why can I not simply sign the estate over to you?'

'Can't afford to take it off you,' replied his uncle with a rueful smile. 'Your father gambled away a fortune before he died—and the old man let the place go to rack and ruin. He seemed not to care after you left. I tried to help, but he would never listen to me.'

'No…I remember.' Damian smiled wryly. 'What do you want me to do—pay the debts?'

'Could you?'

'Perhaps—if I thought it was worth it.'

'I'd heard you'd made money.' His uncle looked uncertain, awkward. 'Is it any use appealing to your feelings for the family name?'

'Good God, no!' Damian laughed. '*That* means nothing to me. When I was younger perhaps…but now, nothing. I came because I owed *you* something—if you are in trouble yourself?'

'I had expected the old man might leave what was left of it all to me. But his will is quite clear. I can only inherit if you are dead. Besides, there is only that old barn of a house—and debts. The land was sold or mortgaged long since.'

'If I paid the debts, what would you do with the house?'

'Sell it,' his uncle replied promptly. 'Without the land it is nothing more than a millstone around anyone's neck. I wouldn't want to live there—and nor would my son.'

'So what do you want me to do?'

'I can't sell without your signature,' his uncle said. 'And the debts will have to be paid eventually. If I have to find the money it will put a great strain on my personal finances—and I do not care to leave such a burden for my own son.'

'And I am the heir, so I am responsible.'

His uncle made no reply, but his expression showed that he did feel it was Damian's responsibility.

'Yes, of course,' Damian murmured, nodding to himself. 'Leave it to me, Uncle. I'll have a look at the house one of these days, and in the meantime I'll arrange for the debts to be settled—providing a proper accounting can be made.'

'What do you mean?' Jacob looked startled. 'I have already agreed them with the lawyers. You can't want to be bothered with all that?'

'I most certainly do,' replied Damian. 'I am aware that it is not quite the thing to take a healthy interest in money in your world—but my fortune was not easily earned and I do not intend to throw it away. I shall not pay anything that cannot be proven.'

'You must do as you think best, of course.'

'I intend to, sir.' He saw the shocked expression on his uncle's face and laughed. 'If that is all, I believe our business is finished.'

'Damian…won't you even consider setting up a home in England? You could restore the house, buy back the land, take your rightful place in society.' Lord Jacob looked at him oddly. 'Won't you visit us…discuss the situation?'

'There is nothing to discuss,' Damian replied. 'I came back for a purpose. When that is done, there will be nothing more to keep me here.'

Yet even as he spoke, he knew that he was not speaking the whole truth. He had believed that he would never wish to live in England again, but now he was not so sure.

Chapter Three

Rosalyn had hoped to have Jared to herself when he came to tea. She had guessed that he was feeling lonely, missing the warmth and colour of India, and the people he loved— perhaps his family most of all. Now that her aunt had arrived, she accepted her hopes of a tête-à-tête were at an end.

To her credit, Aunt Susan behaved exactly as she would with any other youth of her acquaintance. She pressed a dish of little, sweet almond cakes on Jared, together with the lemon barley water Rosalyn had herself prepared, as she began to quiz him.

'How do you like England?' she asked. 'Are you going to school here?'

Jared's manner was polite but formal as he fended off her questions, though clearly uncomfortable to be the object of her curiosity. Rosalyn cursed the misfortune which had brought her aunt's visit forward. Especially when Sarah Jane decided to put in a belated appearance.

The girl was pretty in a fair, insipid way, her pink dress too frilly and ornate for Rosalyn's taste. Sarah looked like a dressmaker's mannequin—delicate, precious and unnaturally tidy.

'Ah, there you are, dearest!' her loving grandmother said,

smiling on her indulgently. 'I am glad you have decided to come down for tea. Are you feeling better?'

'A little…' Sarah Jane's large blue eyes regarded Jared with a mixture of curiosity and hostility. 'Who is he? His skin looks a funny colour.'

'Sarah!' Rosalyn admonished sharply. 'Jared's skin is a very nice colour. He comes from India, where the sun is extremely hot.'

'Hasn't he got a parasol?'

Rosalyn was about to answer her, but Jared got there first.

'My father has a thousand parasols,' he replied scornfully. 'Some of them are bigger than this room. You are an ignorant little girl. My father's people are all dark-skinned. It is your people who are strange with their red and white skins that burn quickly in the sun.'

Sarah Jane's mouth opened and closed like a fish out of water. No one had ever spoken to her in that way in the whole of her life. She was not sure how to reply; however, there was something about him that seemed to command her respect, so she reached for a cake and ate it in silence.

Mrs Buckley and Rosalyn stared at each other, both struggling against a desire to laugh, though Maria was clearly horrified, but wise enough on this occasion to keep silent. Before anyone could think of the right words to ease the situation, the door was thrust open and Sheba came bouncing in. Sarah eyed the dog uncertainly, but Jared called to her and she obliged him by jumping all over him and licking his face thoroughly. It was then that Rosalyn had an inspiration.

'Jared,' she suggested. 'Why don't you and Sheba take Sarah Jane into the gardens? She has never been here before so you could show her around the grounds.'

'I'm not sure—' began Mrs Buckley, but before she could finish, Sarah Jane was out of her chair, obviously eager to take up the suggestion. 'Well, if you feel up to it, dear. I dare say a little air will not hurt you.'

Sarah Jane ignored her grandmother, her eyes firmly fixed on Jared. 'Come on, then,' she said with an imperious lift of her head. 'I want to see the gardens.'

For a moment mutiny flared in Jared's dark eyes, then he turned to Rosalyn, his manner clearly that of someone struggling to maintain his dignity in the face of severe provocation.

He inclined his head to her. 'Since it is your wish, Miss Eastleigh, I shall take the...child into the gardens.'

He was fourteen, Sarah Jane thirteen and a half—but of course he was male and therefore superior.

Neither Rosalyn nor her aunt dared to so much as breathe until the pair had departed, Sheba enthusiastically following at their heels. Once the children were safely out of range, their eyes met in shared amusement.

'Oh, dear,' Mrs Buckley said, dabbing at her wet cheeks when she had stopped laughing a little later. 'I just hope she will not suffer a relapse. But indeed, I think the fresh air may do her good. Celia does tend to be a little...overprotective of her children at times.'

It was the closest Aunt Susan had ever come to admitting that her beloved grandchildren might possibly be spoiled.

Rosalyn nodded but refrained from comment. The French windows were open and occasionally they heard the sounds of laughter—both Jared's and Sarah Jane's—mingling with Sheba's barking.

Rosalyn, her aunt and Maria enjoyed a comfortable half an hour over the teacups, and when a slightly less immaculate Sarah Jane came rushing in with Sheba and Jared following behind, it was immediately apparent they had come to no harm.

'Can I go to tea with Jared tomorrow?' Sarah demanded impetuously. 'May I? Please say yes, Grandmama!'

'It is Rosalyn you should ask,' replied Mrs Buckley. 'I must return home in the morning. Your mother needs me.'

Sarah Jane turned her large, very bright eyes on Rosalyn.

'Please may I? Jared has promised to show me all sorts of things. Please do say I might!'

'If Jared has invited you…' Rosalyn glanced at him. He had assumed his rather haughty expression, but the gleam of anticipation in his eyes betrayed him. 'Then I see no reason why not. And now I must walk home with Jared as I promised his tutor.'

Sarah Jane's instant demand to be allowed to accompany them was firmly denied by her grandmother. She *was* still recovering from a severe illness, and too much exercise might undo all the good playing in the garden had obviously done.

The afternoon was pleasant as they began their walk, a cloudless sky and a bright sun warming the air. Rosalyn was pleased to have the opportunity of some time alone with Jared.

'You were very good with Sarah Jane,' she told him as they left the orchard behind and started to climb a grassy bank. To the right was a small copse, to the left open fields in which horses grazed. 'She can be thoughtless at times— but she has been ill. It will be nice for her to have someone of her own age to talk to now and then.'

Jared's teeth were very white, gleaming against the dusk of his skin as he grinned at her. 'She is not bad for a girl,' he said. 'At home the other children would not dare to talk to me as she does. But I do not mind it.'

Something in his eyes touched Rosalyn's heart. She suspected he had been very lonely. She did not pursue the subject he had raised, understanding that anything he wished to confide must come naturally, without prompting.

'I am sure Sarah Jane will be safe with you, Jared. Perhaps you could teach her some manners? I fear she has been indulged more than is good for her.'

They had almost reached the Orfords' house now. Rosalyn's heart took a flying leap as she saw the man coming to meet them. He was wearing riding clothes, but his coat was dark blue and he had taken more care with his appearance than on the first time they had met.

'Miss Eastleigh,' he said. 'I returned earlier than I expected. Will you come in and take a glass of wine?'

'Thank you, Mr Wrexham, but I must not stay. My aunt arrived sooner than we thought, but she is to leave again in the morning. I should go back now or she will think I am neglecting her.'

'Then allow me to walk part of the way with you?' Damian glanced at Jared. 'I shall see you later. We have neglected our studies today and must make up for it.'

'Yes, *sahib*.'

Rosalyn wondered at the change in Jared's manner. Did he resent his tutor? He seemed subdued—but not frightened. Surely not frightened?

Sheba seemed uncertain when Rosalyn turned back, whining a little as if torn between two loyalties. Rosalyn ignored her and she ran after the boy.

'You have lost your dog,' Damian said. 'Shall I purchase a similar animal for Jared and send Sheba back to you?'

'No,' she replied, glancing thoughtfully at him as they began to walk back the way she had come. Could he really be the man Aunt Susan had mentioned earlier? What was the truth of the scandal which had caused his exile? 'I do not think that would serve. Jared has become attached to Sheba. Another dog would not be the same. Let him keep her for the moment.'

'You are generous, Miss Eastleigh.'

She shook her head. 'You must not imagine it to be a great sacrifice on my part. I am fond of Sheba, but she was foisted on me by my brother and has always been prone to roaming at will. I can spare her for a while. Besides, I have an ulterior motive...'

Rosalyn gave him a wicked look and went on to explain about her cousin's daughter, particularly the way she had suddenly thrown off her sickly air after being with Jared in the garden.

'I believe it may do them both good,' she confided, raising her candid gaze to Damian's face. 'Jared has not led an exactly normal life, I think?'

'It was not so bad while his mother lived,' Damian replied. 'His mother—Anna—did her best to give him some freedom, but when she died…circumstances changed.'

'Yes, I see.' Rosalyn sensed there was much more he was not telling her. She did not look at him as she asked, 'Is it your intention to stay in England beyond the summer, Mr Wrexham—or shall you return to India?'

'I have not yet decided.' Damian frowned. 'My business may take longer than I had imagined. Why do you ask?'

'Oh…no particular reason.' They had reached the orchard. Rosalyn stopped walking. She raised her head, giving him a challenging stare. 'You need come no further, Mr Wrexham. I shall be perfectly safe—and I am sure you must be wanting your dinner after having been out for most of the day.'

He caught her arm, detaining her as she would have walked away, swinging her back to face him. His expression was harsher than she had previously seen it, his eyes angry.

'What is it, Miss Eastleigh? What have you heard?'

Rosalyn hesitated, then breathed deeply. She supposed it was best to have it out in the open. 'Nothing certain, sir—merely some gossip concerning an old scandal.'

'Damn!' Damian cursed aloud. 'I had hoped to avoid this—it was so long ago. It seems I should have told you at once. I was sent away in disgrace by my own family.'

So her aunt had been right!

'There is no need to explain. It is entirely your own affair.'

'Is it? Are you not angry with me for concealing it from you?'

'No, not at all.'

'Indeed?' His brows rose in disbelief, but as he gazed down into her eyes he saw that she meant every word. 'You are indeed a remarkable woman, Miss Eastleigh. Are you not outraged?'

'By something that happened twenty years ago?' She shook her head. 'I think not, sir. Besides, I do not truly know what happened—only that there was a scandal and you were cast out by your family.'

'It was nineteen years and three months to be exact,' he replied, his face reflecting bitterness, anger and, she thought, regret. 'I killed a man, Miss Eastleigh. I have never tried to deny that—but it was a duel, and fairly conducted with witnesses to testify that I behaved properly. However, the circumstances…there were reasons why my family decided to disown me. Reasons I do not wish to discuss, even with you.'

'You have no obligation to do so.'

'Not yet…but under certain circumstances…'

He was going to kiss her again! Rosalyn felt suddenly breathless, her heart beating madly. She realised that she wanted him to kiss her, to hold her close to his chest, to make love to her. Her body was melting in the warmth of the wonderful new sensation flooding through her.

So this was desire! She had often wondered, but had never before come close to experiencing passion. It shocked and yet excited her to discover that she was capable of such strong feelings, for until this moment she had not thought it possible. She had never felt in the least inclined to welcome a man's kisses before. Without her being aware of it, her mouth softened, parting invitingly as she gazed up at him.

'Do not look at me like that,' Damian said harshly. Her response had surprised him, even though he had guessed her capable of passion. 'You can have no idea of the danger you risk at this moment, Miss Eastleigh. Remember! I have lived abroad too long to respect English customs. In India when a woman looks at a man that way…he knows how to react.'

Rosalyn felt the hot colour flood her cheeks. Goodness! She was inviting his embrace. What must he think of her? Indeed, what was she thinking of to allow it?

'You do not need to remind me of your lack of English manners,' she replied crossly. 'If you will let go my arm, sir, I shall cease to look at you at all.'

Her obvious annoyance at being reminded of the impropriety of her own behaviour—and the fact that she had not denied it—broke the tension in him. He laughed and released her.

'Forgive me, Miss Eastleigh. I am not usually such a brute—but you tempted me. I did want to kiss you. In fact, I wanted to do very much more. So you have no need to be embarrassed or to imagine yourself at fault. It was entirely my own decision. I beg you to show mercy. I fear I am a barbarian and do not deserve all the kindness you have already offered me.'

'There is nothing to forgive. I was as much to blame as you—though it was very wrong of me. You must be thinking me shameless?'

When he smiled at her as he was doing now, Rosalyn was unable to maintain her anger against him. Something warned her she would be wise to cut the connection now while she could, that she was skating on thin ice and would pay the penalty for her foolishness—but deep inside her there was a feeling which would not be denied. It was almost as if she had been waiting for this moment, for this man, all her life.

'Sarah Jane has been invited to tea with Jared tomorrow,' she said. 'I shall send her in the carriage at about three. You will permit Coachman and Nanny to wait for her?'

'Will you not come with her yourself?'

Rosalyn shook her head. 'Not this time, but we shall meet again soon, Mr Wrexham. At church tomorrow, perhaps—

and you must come to dine with us when my brother arrives.'

She walked away then and he let her go.

She was a remarkable woman. She deserved much more than he could give her. He had thought to while away a few weeks by a mild flirtation, but he had suddenly discovered that his feelings toward Miss Eastleigh were anything but mild.

Rosalyn sat gazing out at the moonlit gardens. She had tried sleeping but was restless and found it impossible. Her strange thoughts had forced her to rise, but she was still unable to resolve them.

Why had she let Damian Wrexham turn her calm, pleasant world upside down?

Surely she had not fallen in love with him? No, of course not! They had only met three or four times. People did not fall in love just like that—did they?

Rosalyn sighed, twisting a strand of her long hair about her finger. She suspected that was exactly the way it happened. Oh, what an idiot she was! She had rejected so many offers of marriage when she was younger—all of them from very respectable gentlemen. Men of consequence, who had offered her a life of ease and luxury. Never once had she been tempted to accept—so why was she in such turmoil now? To fall for someone like Damian Wrexham was madness—foolish beyond belief!

Nothing could come of it, of course. Marriage was unlikely—even if it was possible. He might have a wife in India. No, no, she did not believe so ill of him. He must have mentioned it if he were married.

He would have had a mistress, of course. That was only natural. She would not expect him to have lived like a monk.

Rosalyn got up to return to her bed. It was wrong of her to allow her thoughts to take this route. If Mr Wrexham wanted a wife he would have married years ago. Besides, the very idea was out of the question. Not to be considered in the circumstances! Her family would all be against it. And anything else was impossible, of course.

Yet there had been a moment when she might have been willing to surrender all she held dear for love.

Rosalyn's cheeks burned in the darkness. Mr Wrexham had sensed how near she was to capitulation. That was why he had drawn back, of course—acting the part of the gentleman he claimed he was not—but why? Why would he do that? Because he respected her, or because he did not wish to become involved?

Did he think her an old maid? He had laughed at the idea when they met, but it was not so very far from the truth. Rosalyn had given up all idea of marriage when her father died. Her grief had left her feeling empty, drained, willing to settle for the comfort of her home and the friends she had gathered around her. But now…now she was aware that the dissatisfaction with her life had been growing for a while.

Even so, she had not considered marriage as a way out of her situation. Until now… Oh, dear! Rosalyn laughed at her own thoughts. She really must not let her dreams run away with her.

Mr Wrexham was not here to find a wife.

Just why was he here? Rosalyn pondered the mystery as she lay watching the dawn slowly creep over her windowsill, quite unaware that, as the light strengthened and he rose from his bed, Damian's thoughts were also far from easy. He too had spent a restless night chasing unwanted dreams—dreams he had imagined long dead.

Rosalyn saw him as soon as she entered the church the next morning. He was standing looking about him as though he wondered where he ought to sit. She hesitated, then touched his arm, smiling up at him as she whispered, 'You may sit with us if you wish. I am sure Maria will not mind.'

'Thank you. I did not wish to take anyone's special place.'

Rosalyn went into the pew reserved for her family, Maria following behind. Mr Wrexham came after her. From the corner of her eye, Rosalyn saw him bend his head, his lips moving in silent prayer. She had not been sure he would come. Or that he had retained the faith he had been born to—but it seemed he had despite the years spent in a foreign land.

Rosalyn said the usual prayers for her family and sat down. She carried her own Bible, which was covered in white leather. Mr Wrexham had none of his own, but Maria offered him hers and recited the prayers she knew by heart.

The Reverend Waller's sermon was as usual long and slightly muddled, but Rosalyn felt uplifted by it in a way she had not for some time. Perhaps it was the very pleasant tenor voice of Mr Wrexham which seemed to bring the familiar hymns alive for her?

Afterwards, she filed out of church, pausing to speak to the vicar for a few minutes. Several of her neighbours were looking at Mr Wrexham curiously. She introduced him to Sir Matthew and Lady Sheldon, and their two rather pretty daughters, smiling to herself as an instant invitation to dine that day was issued. The Sheldons had three more daughters at home to see settled, and Mr Wrexham was looking very presentable that morning.

Rosalyn had been thinking of issuing a casual invitation herself, but reserved it for another time.

She nodded farewell to Mr Wrexham, then began to thread her way through the small group who still lingered, leaving him to make the acquaintance of his neighbours in his own manner. By taking him into her family's pew that morning, she had given him all the credit he needed and she had no doubt he would soon be in great demand.

Rosalyn stood at the open landing window, gazing out. She could hear Sarah Jane's squeals of laughter and won-

dered at the extraordinary change in the girl. In just six days
she and Jared had become almost inseparable. They visited
each other every day, not just for tea but for hours at a time.
There was no doubt that it was doing the girl a great deal
of good. One had only to look at Sarah Jane to see that she
was happy, thought Rosalyn.

She, on the other hand had not seen Mr Wrexham since
their meeting after church. Rosalyn sighed. How fortunate
the children were! They had no need to consider anything
but their own amusement. While *she*…was being very foolish again!

She looked up at the sky, noticing that it was becoming
overcast. The weather had been kind these past few days,
but it looked as if they might be in for a storm. If it threatened to rain, she would send Jared home in the carriage. In
the meantime, she must not dawdle here.

Freddie was due to arrive at any moment. He had sent a
groom ahead to warn them, which was so unlike him that
his sister had begun to suspect that his guests were even
more important than she had imagined.

Rosalyn glanced at herself in a heavy, gilt-framed mirror
on the wall, patting a stray hair into place. She had drawn
her thick hair back into a neat chignon, allowing a few ten-
drils to fall about her face. It was perhaps a rather severe
style, but it suited her as curls and ringlets would not, fram-
ing a face that had its own special beauty but was not pretty
in the accepted sense. Her pale grey gown clung lovingly
to her statuesque figure in a way that, had her likeness been
taken at that moment, would have made her a perfect model
for Queen Boadicea at the reins of her war chariot. There
was something bold and fine about Rosalyn, something that
was at odds with her status as a spinster.

Of course, none of this was apparent to Rosalyn herself.
She saw a woman who was dressed plainly, not in the first
stare of fashion, but certainly respectable, which was all she

required. She turned her head as she heard running footsteps and Maria came rushing up the stairs.

'They have just arrived,' Maria said, a little breathlessly. 'I saw them from the parlour window and thought you would want to know.'

'Yes, thank you,' Rosalyn said. For some reason her heart had started to beat rapidly and she was nervous. 'I was about to come down. Take your time, Maria, get your breath back.'

'I shall follow you at once,' said Maria. 'I should not want to be backward in any attention to dear Sir Frederick. Besides, I dare say you have not thought, dearest—but he may have a special reason for bringing guests. Two ladies, you know.'

She gave Rosalyn such an arch look that it was all she could do not to make a cutting remark. A mere irritation of the nerves, of course. It could make no difference to Rosalyn if her brother married. After their father's death, Freddie had agreed that the Cambridgeshire estate would always be his sister's home.

'I've never particularly liked the place, as you know,' he had said, grinning at her. 'It suits me to have you live here, Ros—and it is what Father would have wanted.'

Her father ought, of course, to have made some provision in his will, other than the trust fund he had set up years earlier to give her financial independence. If he had expected to die he would no doubt have made it plain that he wanted Rosalyn to have a life tenancy of her home, but his illness had struck so suddenly, and he had been in such distress, that he must have forgotten that everything would to go to his son.

Such arrangements were quite normal. Daughters were expected to marry and leave home—or live as dependents in the house of a brother or close relative.

Rosalyn could not imagine having to live as the dependent relative of anyone, even her brother, whom she loved very much. She was used to running her household to suit herself, for she had done much as she liked even before her father's death.

But Freddie would not want to bring his wife here! Rosalyn reassured herself. Of course he wouldn't. If he was thinking of marriage—and that wasn't sure yet—he would continue to live in London and Devon as he did now. He did not particularly care for the country, except during the hunting season.

Rosalyn shook off her vague doubts. She was halfway down the stairs when Freddie and his guests entered the house, which gave her a moment to study the ladies before they noticed her.

The younger of the two was a tiny little thing, very delicate and fragile in appearance, with golden ringlets and a perfect rose complexion. She was, Rosalyn thought, the prettiest young lady she had ever seen. Her companion, however, was a rather stout, cross-looking woman with a fussy hairstyle more suited to a young girl and frosty grey eyes.

Those eyes were staring up at her, Rosalyn realised, and they were distinctly hostile.

'Freddie!' she cried and hurried down the last few stairs. 'How lovely to see you, dearest.'

'Ros!' Her brother took two huge strides towards her, embracing her in a bear hug. 'It's been too long, I know. Forgive me?' His grey eyes looked into hers. 'I shouldn't have neglected you.'

'You haven't,' she replied, smiling at him. 'But you *are* neglecting your guests. Pray introduce me.'

'What an idiot I am!' Sir Frederick turned to the older woman, a flicker of something in his eyes…something his sister thought might be a mixture of both respect and dislike. 'This is Mrs Jenkins, Ros—ma'am, my sister, Miss Rosalyn Eastleigh.'

'We have heard so much about you,' the woman said in

a high, false tone. 'We have been longing to meet you—isn't that so, Beatrice?'

'And this…' said Freddie, ignoring her as he took the young lady's hand and drew her forward. 'This is Miss Beatrice Holland. Say hello to Ros, dearest.'

'Miss Eastleigh.' Miss Holland blushed and curtsied, giving Rosalyn a shy smile. 'We are so very happy to be here. I do hope we have not caused a great deal of trouble for you?'

'Of course not—' Rosalyn began but was interrupted by Mrs Jenkins.

'Of course it is no trouble, Beatrice,' she said. 'Miss Eastleigh must always be happy to entertain her brother's guests in his house.'

'Aunt Patricia…' Beatrice said, her colour deepening in acute embarrassment. 'Please…'

'Mrs Jenkins is perfectly right,' Rosalyn said easily. 'I am always happy to entertain Freddie's guests.' She turned her steady gaze on her brother. 'Freddie, I think perhaps you have something important to tell me? But we should go into the parlour.' She frowned, then looked back at the older woman. 'Mrs Jenkins, you must be tired from your journey. My cousin will take you up to your room at once. Maria, please look after Mrs Jenkins for me! We shall all meet again very soon.' She smiled at her brother and the pretty but nervous child, whose hand he was clutching with such determination. 'Freddie, won't you bring Miss Holland into my parlour *now*?'

From the indignant expression in Mrs Jenkins' eyes it was clear that she thought Rosalyn's behaviour high-handed, but Freddie was quick to respond, giving his undivided attention to Beatrice as the housekeeper helped her off with her pelisse and bonnet. Seeing that she could not count on his support, Mrs Jenkins went away with Maria, who was fluttering around her and trying very hard to soothe the feathers Rosalyn had so clearly ruffled.

'So you guessed at once,' Freddie said, looking at his sister in some apprehension. He had always been slightly in awe of his elder sister, who was his equal in height and, he sometimes thought, his superior in everything else. 'I suspected you might. I suppose I should have told you, but—'

'There was no need,' Rosalyn cut short his apology. 'I am delighted to welcome Miss Holland here—and though you still have not told me, I suspect you mean to marry her?'

'Oh, Freddie.' Beatrice looked at him with big, reproachful eyes. 'You did promise to tell Miss Eastleigh before we came down. I am so sorry…he did promise, honestly.'

'Well, now he has done so,' Rosalyn said giving her a warm smile. 'And I am delighted, of course. You are very welcome here, my dear Beatrice. I may call you that, I hope?'

'Yes, of course.' Beatrice dimpled, looking shy. 'You really don't mind, Miss Eastleigh?'

'Only that you call me Miss Eastleigh, when I would prefer us to be friends…Rosalyn, please.' Rosalyn moved towards her, taking her hands and kissing her cheek. 'So pretty. You are very lucky, Freddie. I hope you appreciate your good fortune?'

'Rather,' Freddie replied with such a besotted look at his fiancée that Rosalyn knew he was head over heels in love with her. 'They were all after Bea—all the fellows in town—but she preferred me. I can't imagine why. I'm not much of a catch compared to Lord Hamilton or Devonshire.'

'You silly thing!' cried Beatrice and immediately endeared herself to Rosalyn. 'I wasn't in love with either of them. Aunt Patricia did think I ought to have accepted the Duke…but I really couldn't. Not once you had shown a preference for me.' She gave Rosalyn a shy smile. 'I wasn't sure Freddie even liked me at first.'

'You must have known?' Freddie said, looking incredulous.

She shook her head. 'No, not at first…not until the masked ball when we went on to the balcony and…' She blushed and looked uncertainly at Rosalyn. 'You will think me very forward to have let Freddie kiss me before we were engaged, but I had been wishing he would give me some sort of a sign and—'

She broke off as her aunt came bustling into the room, Maria trailing unhappily behind her. It was clear that Mrs Jenkins was not willing to be denied any longer.

'So, my dear?' She turned her baleful eyes on Beatrice. 'Is it all settled then? Miss Eastleigh knows you are to marry Sir Frederick?'

'Yes, Aunt.'

'Good…' Mrs Jenkins gave Rosalyn what could hardly be called anything other than a glare. 'I wanted to announce it before we left London, but Sir Frederick insisted you must be told first.'

A cold dislike for the woman settled in Rosalyn's breast. There was surely no need for her belligerent attitude?

'There was no hurry for that, surely? You do not imagine that my brother would cry off at the last moment, I hope?' She had the satisfaction of seeing Mrs Jenkins turn pale. 'I am very glad Beatrice and Freddie came to tell me themselves. I admit I should have been distressed to read of it in *The Times*. And I fear Freddie has never been much of a letter writer.'

'I thought we could give a few parties, Ros?' Freddie was looking at her gratefully. 'Introduce Beatrice to the neighbours—'

'An excellent idea,' Mrs Jenkins put in before Rosalyn could answer. 'Since Beatrice will be living here after you return from your honeymoon, it will be much better if she makes a few friends first.'

Rosalyn saw the look of discomfort in her brother's face. He was clearly angry with Mrs Jenkins for coming out with the news in such a way, but his guilty expression told her that it was indeed his intention to bring his bride here. Rosalyn's heart sank, though she tried not to show she was disturbed.

'Then it will obviously be best for us to give some dinner parties and perhaps a dance,' she said, keeping her voice light and unconcerned. She would speak to her brother later—alone! 'As it happens, I have already sent out some invitations for a dinner tomorrow evening, just a few of my closest friends—but I shall make immediate preparations for something more elaborate. An engagement dance, I think.' She glanced at Freddie, who had been frantically trying to catch her eye. 'When is the wedding? Have you decided on a date yet?'

'We thought the end of next month,' Freddie said. 'I shall take Bea to Paris for three weeks afterwards and—'

Rosalyn gave him a warning frown. 'We do not need to discuss this just yet, Freddie. Later, perhaps...' She welcomed the arrival of a maid with the tea tray. 'Ah, here we are. I am sure we can all do with some refreshment. Maria, please pour if you will. I must just speak to Mrs Simmons. Excuse me, please. I shall not be a moment. Do not wait for me, I beg you.'

'Yes, of course, Rosalyn dear.'

Maria gave her a nervous look as she got up and went from the room. Of course, Rosalyn thought, she must be worrying about *her* future. If Freddie and his new wife were to live here, Maria would not be needed as Rosalyn's companion.

Rosalyn felt a flush of anger. What had Freddie been thinking of to let all this come as such a surprise? But of course he had not thought at all! He had merely carried on as he always did, expecting everyone to fall in with his plans. It was so like him that his sister could not feel as angry with him as he deserved.

'Ros—wait a moment!' Freddie had come out into the hall after her. 'Please, let me explain...'

Rosalyn turned to look at him. 'Later,' she said. 'You have no need to explain anything: this is your house. You are perfectly entitled to do as you wish with it.'

'I could strangle that woman!' Freddie said wrathfully. 'I had hoped to talk to you about this in private—to explain why Beatrice would like to live here.'

'Can it not wait until later?' Rosalyn asked. 'I have to make arrangements to send Jared home in the carriage. It has just started to rain and I do not want him to get a soaking.'

'Jared?'

Freddie looked puzzled, so she gave him a brief explanation.

'Jared and his tutor are renting Lady Orford's house. We have Celia's daughter staying. They are much the same age, and Jared and Sarah have become friends.' Her smile was a little strained. 'I'll tell you more when the others have gone up to change for dinner. Excuse me, Freddie, this will not wait.'

She walked off and this time her brother did not try to delay her, merely standing in the hall and staring after her with a look of frustration on his handsome face.

'Of course I have no objection to your bringing Beatrice here,' Rosalyn said when she and Freddie were alone an hour or so later. 'It *is* your house and you have a perfect right to do as you wish.'

'I don't want us to quarrel over this,' Freddie said, his expression a mixture of shame and determination. 'I promised this would be your home for as long as you required it, and I haven't changed my mind. Beatrice won't mind at all—and she is such an adorable goose that she will be glad to have your help with running the house. You need not fear that she will want to be interfering in your arrangements—and of course we shall still spend much of our time in London. At least until we have a family. Bea wants a large family, that's one of the reasons she would prefer to live here—for the children's sake. I told her this house was much larger than the one in Devon and she said she would like to see it—to share it with you.'

'Any woman would prefer this house,' Rosalyn said, frowning slightly. 'The one in Devon was meant only as a summer retreat—and is much further from a decent-sized town. Here, she would be near enough to Cambridge to go shopping when she pleases. I have always found it a perfect combination, living in the country but with a town nearby.'

'I'm sorry, Ros,' her brother said again. 'I know this must have been a shock for you.'

'I should certainly have preferred to have been told sooner,' Rosalyn said. 'It would have given me more time to think about the future.'

'I've told you, there is no need for you to move away.'

'What about Mrs Jenkins?' Rosalyn lifted her gaze to meet his. 'Are you planning to include her in your household?'

'Good God, no!' said Freddie, looking horrified. 'I would not stand for it even if Bea wanted it—and she certainly doesn't. That woman has made Bea's life a misery for months on end, hounding her to make a good marriage. It is because Bea wants to get away from her that we've arranged the wedding so quickly.'

'I can understand that,' Rosalyn said, giving him a rueful look. 'Is she Beatrice's only relative?'

'Yes—since her mother died.' Freddie frowned. 'Bea is an heiress—or she will be when Mrs Jenkins dies. She made quite sure I knew how much Bea will inherit. If it weren't for Bea's sake, I would tell her to take herself off—but I cannot be the cause of Bea's losing twenty thousand pounds, can I? She would not thank me for it, you know.'

'You don't care about the money?'

'I would have married her without a penny—but it's

Bea's inheritance. I cannot deprive her of that, even if I don't like the old battleaxe.'

'Freddie dearest!' Rosalyn pulled a face at him. 'You must not speak so disrespectfully of your fiancée's aunt. Let us hope she won't visit too often when you are married.'

'Unfortunately, her own estate is in Huntingdon,' Freddie said with a gloomy look. 'Too close for comfort. I dare say she will descend on us several times a year.'

Rosalyn laughed at his expression. His words had made it plain to her that she would have to think very hard about the future. She might just have managed to live for a while with Beatrice—who was a sweet girl and would need help if she was to run this huge house efficiently—but not if Mrs Jenkins were to become a frequent visitor.

'Well, you must try to keep on terms with her if you can for Beatrice's sake,' she said. 'And now, Freddie, we should both go and change or we shall keep our guests waiting for their dinner.'

'Are you very upset, Ros?'

Freddie looked so anxious that the last remnants of Rosalyn's anger melted away. 'No, of course not,' she said and went to kiss his cheek. 'I think I shall like Beatrice very much—and I am naturally happy for you.'

'And you won't run off and leave us?'

'Not immediately,' Rosalyn promised. 'In time I shall probably want my own house, but not just at once—and of course I shall visit you several times a year. I do hope my visits will not cause either of you to quake in your shoes?'

'As if they would!' Freddie looked relieved. 'But I really do wish you would continue to think of this house as your home. There is no need for you to leave. Unless you marry, of course.'

Rosalyn shook her head at him, but would not be drawn further. As they parted, each going up to their own rooms, she allowed herself a moment of regret. She *had* been happy here, and there were so many memories. She would miss the life she had known here when she was forced to leave.

But leave she would, that was beyond question. It would not be fair to Beatrice if she remained here, because she would always be the mistress. At least until the girl became more assertive, and that might eventually lead to tension and quarrels.

No, it would not do, Rosalyn decided. She could not consider it. She must find herself a new home.

At least she was financially independent—her father had seen to that years ago. She would not be able to afford a house like this, of course—but she might buy a medium-sized cottage or even a house in Bath.

Either would be preferable to living with Aunt Susan or her brother. The trouble was, of course, that she was far too independent. Perhaps that was why she had never married.

A picture of a man's face flashed into her mind and she sighed. There was no point in thinking of Mr Wrexham. She had not met him on any of her walks or rides these past days, which seemed to indicate that he might be avoiding her.

She had sent him an invitation to her dinner for the following night, but so far he had not answered. It was her own fault. She must have shown her feelings too plainly the last time they met. Since he did not wish to become more involved with a woman who was too old to be thinking of marriage, Mr Wrexham had clearly decided to stay away from her as much as possible.

Chapter Four

Damian threw off his capped travelling cloak as he entered the hall. He greeted the housekeeper with a nod, answering her kind inquiry about his journey pleasantly, before striding into the study where a cold meal and wine awaited his coming. There was also a roaring fire in the large open hearth, which was welcome after a long, hard ride.

He had made a brief, angry inspection of the property left to him by his grandfather, and returned to the Hall almost immediately. He was tired and frustrated by what he had seen—the neglect of a once great estate—and did not immediately bother with the small pile of invitations awaiting him on his desk. When he did, he discovered the invitation from Rosalyn and a smile came to his lips.

Damian relaxed as he sat before the fire with a glass of wine, letting the tiredness and the frustration seep out of him. He glanced at the invitation again; it was very formal. Miss Eastleigh was simply repaying his hospitality.

He had hoped for this when he had first invited her to the Hall. If two respectable ladies like Miss Eastleigh and her cousin showed they were willing to be his friends, he would soon be accepted by the whole county. That had, of course, been his aim when he'd first heard of the spinster living nearby...but that had been before he met Miss Eastleigh. Now his feelings were very different.

He recalled the way Miss Eastleigh had looked into his eyes the last time they had talked. He had known she wanted him...really wanted him, as he wanted her. There was nothing of the milk-and-water English miss about Miss Eastleigh! No, indeed there was not! She was a goddess come to Earth, Diana the huntress, beautiful, brave and passionate. He felt desire stir inside him, burning its way to the centre of his manhood as he thought of her—and the resolution it had taken to let her walk away the afternoon he had accompanied her to her home.

She would have come to him in love if he had asked it of her, though, having heard the old scandal, she must surely be aware that a marriage between them was impossible. He could never ask her to share the shame attached to his name. He had hoped it might be possible to rehabilitate himself into English society, to make a new life here in England— but now he had begun to think it would never work. There would always be someone to point the finger and whisper behind his back. He could not ask Rosalyn to share that, even if she would. He would be a fool to let himself hope— to wish for the moon. He had learned long ago that to hope for too much brought only despair.

Besides, his business was unfinished. He had come back to England unaware of the true situation. Now, after his shocking discovery, he knew that he must settle an outstanding debt. Something that should have been done long ago. As yet he was not quite sure how his objective was to be achieved, but he would discover a way—and when he did, his disgrace would be complete.

Rosalyn had asked if he meant to return to India, and he had told her he was not sure. But things had changed. He had a score to settle, and when he had, there would be no question of his remaining in England.

* * *

She had been tossing and turning for ages! Rosalyn could not understand why she was so restless. She sat up and yawned, then reached for her dressing robe and slipped it on. It was impossible to sleep! Her thoughts were chasing themselves round and round in her head like fallen leaves swept up in a gale. Yet surely she was not letting her brother's imminent marriage distress her? Why should it? She could put up with Mrs Jenkins for as long as necessary, even if it meant biting back the angry words that sometimes leapt to her tongue.

The woman was both rude and careless of the feelings of others, but Rosalyn could cope with her. She would find the strength from somewhere. Not like poor Maria, who had been almost in tears when she went to her room before retiring for the night.

'I am sure I don't know what I shall do when Sir Frederick marries,' she had told Rosalyn, sniffing mistily into her kerchief. 'Mrs Jenkins has made it clear I shall not be welcome here.'

'It really has nothing to do with her,' Rosalyn said gently. 'Cheer up, Maria. I shall not stay here for ever, and I do assure you—you will always have a home with me. Indeed, if I decide to set up a house of my own I shall need you more than ever. You must know that I would not allow you to be turned out without a feather to fly?'

Maria had brightened a little at that, though it was obvious she was greatly distressed at the way their lives were about to change.

Of course she could not desert her cousin, Rosalyn told herself as she walked over to the window to gaze out at the night. Yet the idea of them both settled in a country cottage was somehow very lowering. The purchase of a house would naturally eat into her capital, and that meant she might not be able to live in quite the same style as she had here...but, she scolded herself, if all she had cared for was consequence she might have married long ago and none of this would have arisen.

Rosalyn took a branch of lighted candles and went down to the parlour she had always thought of as her own. She had left a favourite book of poems lying on the sideboard and thought perhaps it might help to lift her spirits. However, when she reached the parlour, the book had mysteriously disappeared and, having set down the candlestick, she wandered towards the French windows, unlocking them and venturing out into the gardens.

Perhaps a little fresh air might help to ease the headache that had begun soon after dinner. Mrs Jenkins had such a loud, harsh voice. Rosalyn truly pitied her brother if he was forced to play host to her too often, and wondered if even the considerable fortune she was intending to leave to her niece was worth having to put up with her company.

Money had never meant a great deal to Rosalyn, but she was beginning to realise she *had* taken it for granted. Her father had never questioned what she spent, never allowing her to use one penny of her own money for household expenses. All that would change now. She would not be poor, but she would have to learn economy.

A shadow moved from out of the shrubbery, making her start with fright. For a moment her heart beat so madly that she could scarcely breathe, then, as the clouds obligingly moved away, she was able to see him clearly in the resulting moonlight.

'Did I startle you, Miss Eastleigh?'

'Mr Wrexham,' she said, a note of welcome in her voice. Her spirits leapt gladly. It seemed such an age since she had seen him, but she tried not to show how pleased she really was by this surprise meeting. 'I was startled for a moment. What are you doing here?'

'I brought Sheba for a walk,' he replied. 'She ran into your gardens and I was forced to follow. I'm afraid I seem to have lost her for the moment. I was looking for her when I saw you.'

'She will find you when she is ready,' Rosalyn said, smiling in understanding. 'It is such a lovely night, do you not think so? I came out because I could not sleep. I thought the fresh air might do me good—take away my headache.'

'I am sorry you are unwell.'

'More like out of temper,' Rosalyn said with perfect truth. 'Perhaps we could walk together for a little, sir? You must take Sheba back with you, or Jared will wake and miss her. I believe she usually sleeps at the bottom of his bed. Or so he has told us.'

'Yes.' A smile lifted Damian's mouth at the corners. 'I know. She was there when I looked in on him on my return this evening. She must have followed me downstairs, and when I went out for my walk, she decided to come with me.'

'Do you often walk at night?' Rosalyn glanced at him as he fell into step beside her. 'I have not seen you for some days…' She blushed at what she had said but did not apologise for it: it was, after all, only the truth. 'Have you been away?'

'Did Jared not tell you?'

She shook her head, her eyes dwelling intently on his face. He had such strong features and, she suspected, a character to match. Those broad shoulders would be such a comfort to lay one's head against in times of stress, even for someone as independent as she. An inquiring look came into his eyes as she continued to gaze at him, and, blushing, Rosalyn looked away. He seemed always to read her mind, and that might be embarrassing when her thoughts were so confusing.

'No, he did not mention it.'

'I dare say he was relieved to have no lessons for a while. Yes, I was obliged to leave him for a few days…on business.'

So that was why she had not met him out walking! He had not been avoiding her after all. Insensibly, her spirits lifted, banishing the cloud that had shadowed her for days.

'I see. So he will not be so free to spend all his time with Sarah Jane now you are back? They have fallen into the habit of visiting each other every day—not just for tea, but for most of the day. I think they have become great friends. She will miss him if he does not come so often to the house.'

'She will be welcome to share his lessons,' Damian replied. 'She may find it boring, of course. Jared studies world affairs, fencing, shooting—and politics.'

'Does he? Good gracious!' Rosalyn was surprised. 'That is rather a demanding schedule for a youth of his age. I had no idea. I imagined you might teach him some manly sports for when he goes to school here—but not world affairs.'

'It is important for him to know these things. It is very possible that he will have an important role to play one day.'

'Who is Jared's father? Or should I not ask?'

Damian hesitated for a moment, then sighed. If he could not trust his instincts now, he was lost. Besides, his inclination was to share his thoughts with her—to open his heart to her—as he had not to another person since he was sent into exile.

'Ahmed is a prince. One day, when his own father dies, he will be the ruler of a mountain state in India. Jared is Prince Ahmed's oldest son—but there has been dissent over his right to step into his father's shoes, because his mother was not Indian.'

'I see…that might pose problems with religion and other things, I suppose.' Rosalyn began to understand the need to keep a close watch on the youth. 'It could well cause unrest amongst fanatics, I think?'

'Particularly in the matter of religion, though Prince Ahmed always insisted his son should be brought up in his own faith. Anna did explain to Jared that there were other religions, but she was not allowed to take him to her church.'

'Did her husband allow her to keep her own religion?'

'In private, yes.' Damian frowned. 'I hesitated to tell you the truth at first, Miss Eastleigh, because it may shock and disturb you. We came to England because there was an attempt on Jared's life.'

He did not add that it was only his own prompt action that had saved the boy, that in doing so he had been wounded and come close to losing his own life.

'It was merely chance that saved him. Ahmed was terrified the next attempt would succeed and begged me to bring the boy to England with me.'

'Oh, no! That is terrible.' This was much worse than she could ever have imagined. 'The poor child—no wonder he seemed so sad and frightened when I first saw him. But who could want to kill Jared?'

'Enemies of his father,' Damian replied, looking grim. 'Many people—including Ahmed's own father—think the prince should disinherit his eldest son in favour of the son his new wife has recently given him. So far he has stubbornly refused to consider it. His obstinacy was the cause of much unrest, which is why Ahmed desired me to bring his son to safety in this country.'

'And why you have been forced to stop him wandering all over the countryside alone—to keep such a strict watch over him.' She understood perfectly now what had seemed harsh before. Her intuition had been right, and she had been wrong to allow herself to doubt this man's integrity even for a moment.

'Yes, that is exactly my dilemma.' Damian smiled at her. 'Jared would be quite safe with Rajib, of course—but he does not like him. Neither do I, as it happens. I have begun to think I would have done better to leave both Rajib and Nessa in India.'

'Oh…' Rosalyn looked at him curiously. 'Surely Jared is fond of Nessa, and she of him?'

'Yes, he is,' Damian said. 'I was thinking of my own comfort. Unfortunately, both Rajib and Nessa resent my authority. They disobey my orders whenever they dare—and their influence on Jared makes him disinclined to listen to me.'

'That must make things difficult?' Rosalyn remembered Jared's sulky looks the evening she had dined at the Hall, and that it had made her wonder if Mr Wrexham was treating his pupil as he ought. 'Perhaps you should send them back to India?'

'Only if Jared wishes them to go. If things change, settle down, his father may send for him.'

'And will you go with him?' Rosalyn could not quite prevent the catch in her voice. 'You must have so many ties in that country…it must seem more your home than England after so many years.'

Damian looked at her, seeing the faint flush in her cheeks.

'What exactly is it you are asking?' he said. 'What do you want to know, Miss Eastleigh…whether I have a wife or a sweetheart waiting for me in India, is that it?'

'No…of course not,' Rosalyn replied quickly, but she could not look at him. 'It would be impertinent of me to ask such questions. I have no right…'

Damian caught her arm, swinging her round to face him. He seemed very intense, almost angry. His reaction was unlike the behaviour she had come to expect of him, and startled her.

'No right?' he said. 'Why are you lying, Miss Eastleigh—to yourself and me?'

'I am not lying.'

'I think you are,' he replied, an odd, machiavellian light in his eyes. 'Well, have you no comment to make? Will you not ask why I think you are lying?'

Rosalyn's mouth was dry. She swallowed hard, her heart beating madly as she looked up at him.

'It doesn't matter,' she whispered. 'I...Damian...'

Before she could say anything more she was in his arms; his lips were on hers, soft, persuading...demanding. Rosalyn melted into his body, yielding her mouth and her whole self as the kiss sent her senses spinning into space. It was the most wonderful feeling of her life, so wonderful that she wanted it to last forever and she sighed with regret when he let her go.

'There, my sweet girl,' Damian said and stroked her cheek with his fingers. 'That is why you have the right to ask any questions you like—and the answer to them all is no. There is no one else.'

'Oh, Damian,' she murmured. 'I don't know what has happened to me. I have never felt this way in my life...never wanted to...' She stopped and dropped her gaze in confusion. What had she been about to say? That she wanted him to make love to her? Surely she could not have been on the verge of saying anything so scandalous!

'Wanted to what?' he asked teasingly. 'Are you telling me you want me to make love to you?'

'No—yes!' Rosalyn could not deny the urgings of her own body. She laughed as she saw the wicked gleam in his eyes, her natural honesty making her say, 'Of course I want you, Damian. I should hardly have allowed you to kiss me like that if I did not.'

'Was it your first real kiss?'

'There have been others,' she confessed, a mischievous smile tweaking the corners of her mouth. 'But none that I truly wanted—none that made me feel the way you did just now.'

'But what?' He gazed deep into her eyes. Her naughty, teasing look enchanted him. 'There is a but, isn't there, my dearest Rosalyn? You are not sure that you can give yourself to such a wicked man as I—is that it?'

'You are not wicked,' she replied, laughing. 'No, it is not that, Damian. I have never thought myself missish, but…'

'But you are not quite ready to cast the world off for love?' His eyes teased her gently. 'To become a fallen woman in the eyes of your contemporaries?'

'I am not sure,' Rosalyn said. Her heart and body clamoured for him, knowing no caution, yet her head told her to wait, to take care. What did she really know of this man who had shot into her life like a comet passing across the sky? 'I know it is foolish of me to hesitate. At my age I ought to be grateful for the chance of knowing love, for however brief a time—and I am not making demands, not asking you to marry me. I know you have no thought of taking a wife.'

'Do you, indeed?' Damian's mouth quivered. He struggled to contain his amusement as he realised she was giving serious consideration to becoming his mistress. Something that for her would be a huge step. She was unique, beyond price. More than anything, he wanted to sweep her up in his arms and run off with her—but he too was aware of the need for caution. 'I admit I have no right to ask you or any other woman to share my disgrace—but that does not mean I have not thought of it.'

'Your disgrace?' Rosalyn gazed up at him in surprise. 'You mean the old scandal?'

'There is—or will be more,' he said. 'I cannot tell yet how much, or what will happen in a few weeks' time. Until I am sure, I could not offer you marriage, Rosalyn. Any intimate relationship between us would be of uncertain duration.'

'Yes, I see.' She had known it instinctively, but it still hurt her to hear it from his lips. She blinked back her tears, looking bravely up at him. 'Give me a little time, Damian. I must be certain.'

For answer, he kissed her again. Such a tender, loving kiss that her resolve was almost broken, her body racked with a sharp longing for the pleasure she had never known but sensed she would find in this man's arms. Why wait? For what? She was seven and twenty, unlikely to meet another man she could love. She would be a fool not to take her one chance of happiness while it was offered, regardless of how long it might last.

'Damian,' she began breathless. 'I think—'

'No, do not say it.' He placed his fingertips to her lips, halting the reckless words she would have spoken. 'Not tonight,' he said, smiling at her puzzled look. 'To take such an advantage would be unfair of me. You must have time to consider, my love. I shall be at your dinner party tomorrow evening. You can give me your answer then.'

As if to underline what he had said, Sheba came bounding up to them, barking and leaping around them as if she had made some miraculous discovery at finding them together.

'I must go in before that wretch wakes the household,' Rosalyn said and reached up to kiss his cheek. 'Goodnight, Damian. I want you to know that I do care for you and always shall…whatever happens between us.'

He seized her, holding her pressed hard against him as he kissed her once more. He felt her surrender, felt the way her body moulded to his, the need and vulnerability in her— and he let her go, giving her a little push to send her on her way before it was too late.

'Go, my Amazon,' he murmured huskily. 'While I still have the strength to let you.'

He watched as she walked away from him, fighting the fierce desire leaping in his blood and cursing the sense of fair play that was forcing him to let her leave. If she came to him…if she gave herself to him…it must be right for them both. He wanted her so desperately tonight, but cared for her too much to take her when she was so vulnerable.

As he turned, he caught sight of a face at an upper window of the house. Rosalyn had only just gone inside the parlour so it could not be her. Someone must have been watching them—but who?

Damian cursed his own carelessness as he called the dog and began to retrace his steps through the shrubbery. He and not Sheba had determined their course tonight. Something had drawn him here, tugging at that inner core…the part of him he had thought dead long ago.

He had hardly believed his eyes when he saw Rosalyn come out into the garden wearing only a flimsy dressing robe, almost as though his spirit had called to hers. He doubted she had even been aware of the way the lovely shape of her body was revealed by the silky material, of the sensuous perfume of her warm skin…of what it had done to him. The temptation to hold her, to kiss her, had been overwhelming—but if someone had seen them together? Had jumped to the wrong conclusions!

He knew only too well what certain minds—and tongues!—could make of an innocent kiss, how cruel gossip could destroy a tender soul. It was in defence of a woman's honour that he had called out Roderick Harrington. Only after the man was dead had he discovered that another man had been most to blame.

Roderick Harrington had enticed the girl, snatching her as she walked alone down a country lane and bundling her, screaming and terrified, into his carriage—but it was his brother who had raped and shamed her. It was Mr Bernard Harrington who had broken her heart, causing her to take her own life because she could not face the scandal she feared would shame her family.

And it was also Mr Bernard Harrington who had ruined Damian's father at the card table, and hastened his death. It was because of him that an old man had died alone, lonely, regretting the loss of his eldest grandson. It was Bernard Harrington he was determined to bring to justice…by challenging him to a duel, if he could find no other way.

* * *

Rosalyn did not expect to sleep after her chance encounter with Damian in the gardens, but once her head touched the pillow, she fell into the sweetest dream. Although she could not recall the details on waking, she knew she had dreamed of being with Damian—and that it had made her feel very secure and happy.

She was relaxed as she took her mare out for a brief gallop across the fields, before returning to the breakfast room to find Maria and Mrs Jenkins already there.

'Has Freddie come down yet?' she asked, then turned to Mrs Jenkins. 'I gave instructions that Beatrice should have breakfast carried up to her room. You need not have come down, ma'am. Maria and I prefer it, but you are welcome to have your tray upstairs if you so choose.'

'I do not care for the habit of sleeping in late,' Mrs Jenkins said, giving her an odd look. 'As it happens, I sleep very little. I always keep a book at my bedside. Last night I borrowed a book of poems, though I do not approve of Lord Byron's work. I believe he shows a lack of propriety, both in his work and his morals. Scandalous!'

Such a forbidding stare accompanied her words, that Rosalyn was at a loss to understand her meaning.

'I am sorry you do not care for Lord Byron's poems, ma'am. However, I am sure my father's library contains much that will please you.' Rosalyn turned to her cousin, who was looking decidedly dejected. 'Will you walk down to the greenhouses and beg a few flowers for the house from Tom, Maria? I am not sure what he has, but I am certain he will find us something—and you always arrange them so beautifully.'

'Yes, of course.' Maria glowed at her praise. 'I shall go at once.'

'Only if you have finished your breakfast.'

Maria assured her she had, and seemed in a hurry to leave. She had clearly been upset. What could the odious Mrs Jenkins have been saying to her earlier?'

'Maria is always so obliging,' Rosalyn remarked after her cousin had gone. 'She has been such a help to me since my father died.'

'I imagine you could not have continued to live here alone,' Mrs Jenkins remarked sourly. 'Though whether it was wise for you to have done so, with only Miss Bellows as your companion, remains to be seen. You might have protected your reputation more securely had you lived with a married lady—someone with a little more standing in society.'

'Protected my reputation more securely?' Rosalyn stared at her, too astonished to think what she could mean. 'I really do not understand you, ma'am.'

'Do you not?' Mrs Jenkins gave her a false smile. 'I shall say no more for the moment, but you would be unwise to think me a fool. You may not care what others think of *you*, Miss Eastleigh—but my concern is for Beatrice. I shall do all I think necessary to protect her good name.'

Rosalyn was struck dumb. What on earth was she hinting at? Unless she had seen…? A horrid thought struck her. Mrs Jenkins's bedchamber overlooked that part of the garden in which she had chanced to meet Damian the previous night! Had she seen them together? Had she seen them embracing? If she had been unable to sleep…it was quite possible that she had been at the window.

Recalling that she had been wearing a flimsy wrapping gown over her night-chemise, Rosalyn could not help blushing. It must have seemed to a casual observer that she had gone out on purpose to meet her lover.

'You have no need to be concerned either for Beatrice's or my own good name,' she replied with as much dignity as she could muster. She stood up, knowing that she must escape before she lost her temper and said something rude. 'If you will excuse me, ma'am, I have guests coming this evening and must speak to Mrs Simmons urgently.'

Rosalyn walked from the room with dignity, head high,

back straight. Of all the unfortunate things! Naturally a woman of Mrs Jenkins's order would assume the worst. She would think that Rosalyn had gone out deliberately to meet a lover—and in her night-clothes!

She felt very angry at having morality preached at her in her own home, but knew she was to blame. Living alone for years, she had become accustomed to wandering about the house in her night-attire. And she *had* given into temptation the previous night. Indeed, if Damian had not shown restraint, she might have given herself to him there and then.

Last night in the moonlight, her reputation had not seemed to matter very much. Now she realised that any relationship between her and Damian would have to be discreet. She would not want to cause a scandal that might reflect badly on Freddie and his young wife.

How unfair it was! If Rosalyn had been born male she could have taken as many lovers as she chose without causing a ripple of scandal—and as the firstborn she would have inherited this house!

A little worm of resentment worked inside her. She did not care about the title or the money, but it was upsetting that she could no longer call this house her own—that she must think of leaving her home.

Rosalyn's thoughts went round and round in her head, chasing each other like a puppy dog after his tail. She longed to be in Damian's arms again, yet knew how much she risked. If she gave herself even once without marriage, she would have no chance of making a decent match—and if the affair became public knowledge, she would be finished in the first rank of Society, despised by all decent women.

Yet what did she care for any of these things? She had never needed more than a few close friends, nor had she met anyone else whom she would wish to marry—so what would she really be giving up?

She felt frustrated and uncertain, unlike her usual positive self, perhaps because she had never been faced with such a conundrum before. Oh, bother! She had too much to do to think of this now. Once her brother was married, she would be in a better position to decide.

She would in any case be leaving this house. If she were to leave England, perhaps the scandal would not be so terrible. Rosalyn had always longed for travel and adventure—and since she must leave her home, why should she not follow her heart?

Would Damian be prepared to take her with him when he left the country—to share his life with her?

She would be his mistress, something she had been taught was beneath contempt for a respectable, unmarried lady—but if he loved her she might find something precious, something that made the sacrifice of her reputation worthwhile.

It was a frightening proposition, because she would be cut off from all that she had ever known and loved—and yet, what was the alternative? To sink into a lonely and disappointed old age? No! No, her rebellious heart cried. She wanted so much more. She wanted Damian Wrexham.

Rosalyn's pulses raced wildly. Suddenly the future held many possibilities. She felt recklessly alive. She would tell Damian they must be patient for a while—and then, if he still wanted her, she would go away with him.

Rosalyn's dinner guests were surprised but pleased to learn of Sir Frederick's betrothal. His bride-to-be was such a shy, pretty child that her arrival in the neighbourhood was thought to be a definite asset. She and Sir Frederick would naturally entertain more frequently and more lavishly than a spinster lady, and that was generally welcomed.

Rosalyn was aware of Damian's dark eyes watching her from across the table. She smiled at him, ignoring the narrowed, hostile stare of Mrs Jenkins. She could not possibly have seen Damian clearly enough the previous night to be certain of his identity, though she might suspect it.

Rosalyn hardly cared. Mrs Jenkins would surely say nothing of what she suspected outside this house, if only for her niece's sake. And once the wedding was over, it would not matter. Besides, she had gone beyond caring. It was an age since she had felt so excited…so alive!

Rosalyn's wide, clear eyes shone as she met Damian's quizzing gaze. She was sure that he had read her mind—that he could guess her thoughts. Now that her decision was made, she felt as light as air, floating on warm currents like a bird.

In a month she would be free to go to him!

'You look extremely well this evening, m'dear.'

Rosalyn turned to the vicar, who was placed at her left. She smiled at him, seeing the kindness in his eyes. He was a good man, genuinely caring but not overly critical of his parishioners' failings, being all too human himself.

'Thank you, sir. I am feeling very well.'

'It is good news about Sir Frederick, is it not?'

'Yes, certainly.'

The vicar looked thoughtful. 'I hope you and Miss Bellows will not be leaving us?'

'Not immediately,' Rosalyn replied. 'Lady Eastleigh will want to be mistress of her own house in time, of course. I have assured Maria she may be sure of a home with me— wherever I go.'

'Oh…' He seemed concerned at this. 'So you might not be living near by. I see… Dear, dear me, that would be a sad loss. Miss Bellows has always been a tireless worker for the church. We shall miss her very much—and you too, Miss Eastleigh, of course.'

Clearly he was most distressed by the thought of losing Maria's help. Rosalyn was struck by his expression. She had known Maria often helped at the church bazaars, of course, but until now she had not believed it was anything other than a way of passing the time. Now she wondered if there was more to her cousin's devotion to church matters than a desire to be of service to the community.

Later that evening, when she saw the two of them talking earnestly together, her suspicions began to harden into certainty. How blind she had been! Why had she never noticed how much more animated Maria became when she was with the vicar?

'A penny for your thoughts?'

Rosalyn felt the warmth of Damian's breath on her bare shoulder as he leant across the arm of the sofa to whisper in her ear. She glanced back at him, pulses racing as she met his challenging gaze and the message he was sending her. How she wished they were alone! Her eyes sparked with mischief and her lips parted slightly, revealing far more of her feelings for this man than she knew.

'I was thinking it would be nice if I could push Maria and the vicar into declaring their affection for each other before I leave here.'

'Are you thinking of leaving?' Damian looked at her intently.

'Yes, I believe I shall—after the wedding. I could do nothing before then, of course.' She smiled as she saw understanding in his eyes. 'I had thought of finding a country cottage, or perhaps a small house in Bath—but now I think it might suit me better to live abroad. I have often wished to travel, you know. And after the wedding, I shall be free to live my own life.'

'Ah!' Damian's eyes seemed to smoulder with heat: the heat of desire. She could almost feel his lips on hers, almost taste them. If he continued to look at her that way she would grow faint with longing. 'Yes, I understand. After your brother's wedding? Many things may have happened by then. I too may be thinking of leaving England.'

They understood each other perfectly. Rosalyn's heart fluttered. She had given her promise. There was no going back now. Indeed, she had no wish to retract. She yearned for the moment they would be together as one.

'Mr Wrexham?' She was jerked rudely back to the present by the strident voice of Mrs Jenkins. 'Are you by any chance a relative of Lord Edward Wrexham?'

Damian looked at her, and by instinct moved away from Rosalyn. Something in the older woman's manner alerted him to danger. He had met her type in the past, and knew what to expect.

'Yes, ma'am,' he replied in a cool, steady tone. 'He was my father.'

'Your father?' Mrs Jenkins gave a shriek of outrage. 'Then you are Damian Wrexham—the devil who murdered my youngest brother! Deny it if you dare! You killed Roderick! You are a murderer!'

The accusation was made in such a shrill tone that it attracted the attention of every person in the room. Damian was silent, his eyes flicking to Rosalyn as if in apology, but his expression did not change, nor did he give any sign of being disturbed by Mrs Jenkins's charge.

'Do you deny that you murdered Roderick Harrington, sir?'

'I do not deny that he died from a wound I inflicted,' Damian replied, not a flicker of emotion in his face. His body was stiff with pride, his eyes colder than the northern sea in winter. 'It was, however, a fair fight.'

'A fight you forced on him,' Mrs Jenkins accused. Her large bosom swelled with indignation, her face going puce with temper so that she resembled a large, purple-clad toad with popping eyes. 'I do not know how you have the effrontery to force yourself on decent people. Had I known you were a welcome visitor in this house, I should not have brought Beatrice here.' She turned her baleful gaze on Rosalyn. 'I can only think that you were not aware of this man's shameful past, Miss Eastleigh.'

Silence had fallen over the room. Rosalyn was so angry

she could have struck the woman's spiteful face. How dare she? Oh, how could she create such a scene? The malicious expression on Mrs Jenkins's face sent a shiver down her spine. What a truly unpleasant woman she was!

'Well, have you nothing to say?' demanded Mrs Jenkins as Rosalyn remained silent. 'Will you kindly request this person to leave—or must I take Beatrice and return to Huntingdon?'

'Take Bea—' Freddie was stung into life. He took a protective step towards his fiancée, a look of alarm in his eyes. 'What's all this? I don't understand. Rosalyn...Wrexham, is this true?'

'Damian...' Rosalyn whispered, her face pale with shock. She felt unable to do or say anything, torn between her love for him and loyalty to her brother. 'I...' Words failed her— only her eyes conveyed her distress.

'It is true that I killed Roderick Harrington in a duel,' Damian said, his eyes narrowing to contemptuous slits as he recognized the weakness in Freddie's character. It was clear that he would not stand up to his fiancée's aunt, would not defend his sister. 'There were, however, reasons—which I shall not go into at this moment.'

'It was murder,' insisted Mrs Jenkins, addressing the room at large. 'The charge was quashed, of course. He got away with it because his grandfather was the Earl of Marlowe, but it was murder. Either he leaves this house now or I shall take Beatrice—and the wedding will be cancelled!'

'Freddie!' Beatrice looked at him with frightened eyes. 'Oh, please do not let her...' She lapsed into silence as her aunt glared at her, clearly terrified that she would carry out her threat. As indeed she would, Rosalyn saw that at once.

'Do not distress yourself, Miss Holland.' Damian bowed stiffly in her direction. 'I shall, of course, leave at once. Had I known, I should not have burdened you with my presence. There will be no need for further communication between us. Rosalyn, forgive me. I must leave.'

'Damian!' Rosalyn could not be certain whether she said the words aloud or merely in her heart. 'Please do not go…'

She watched as he walked from the room, head up, back straight and stiff, and she longed to run after him but knew she must not. If she gave the odious Mrs Jenkins any reason to destroy the happiness of Beatrice and Freddie, she would never forgive herself. She must let him go, though her own heart felt as if it had shattered into a hundred tiny pieces.

'Aunt Patricia,' Beatrice said, breaking the awkward silence after he had left. 'Surely you cannot think Rosalyn knew who that man was? He has but recently come to the district—is that not so, Freddie?'

'Yes. Of course Ros did not know what he had done,' he said, giving his sister an odd, defensive look. 'No one did. Good grief! He would not have been invited if any of us had guessed…'

Maria opened her mouth and closed it, clearly thinking now was not the time to defend Mr Wrexham. Rosalyn was silent, her stomach churning with both nerves and anger. She had been forced into an impossible situation. For the moment she was unable to speak her mind as she would have liked—for Freddie's sake. Yet not to do so was unbearable.

'Mr Wrexham's past has never been of any concern to me,' she said at last. 'Naturally I should not have invited him this evening had I known…of the unfortunate tragedy in your family, Mrs Jenkins.'

The glitter in the older woman's eyes told Rosalyn that she was neither convinced nor satisfied, but for the moment she seemed prepared to let it go.

'I was sure you could not have known,' she said with a cold smile. She fluttered her fan, glancing about her as if to apologise. 'You must all forgive me for causing a scene— but I really could not bear to stay under the same roof as that wicked man. Not once I was certain it was indeed he.'

There were embarrassed murmurs from the guests, several

of whom had rather liked Mr Wrexham and, though shocked by what they had learned that evening, were not certain of their own feelings on the matter. Mrs Jenkins had found herself in an unfortunate position, of course, and there was a great deal of sympathy for her; but a duel was not necessarily murder—in the eyes of the gentlemen at least.

Rosalyn turned away. How could she bear to stay in the same room as Mrs Jenkins? Her nerves were stretched to breaking point and she felt like screaming aloud in her rage, yet she knew she must remain calm—she must pretend to accept the woman's apology, for Freddie's sake. She curled her nails into the palms of her hands, willing herself not to speak, not to say something that would ruin everything. She must do nothing that would harm her brother or Beatrice.

'Rosalyn dearest.' Maria was at her side as the tension eased and people began to talk and laugh in an effort to cover their embarrassment. 'That dreadful woman! Really, I cannot think what she was about. It is bad enough that she thinks she owns the house…'

Rosalyn's chin went up, anger and pride warring for supremacy. 'Do not let her upset you, Maria. We must think of Freddie and Beatrice. It is only for a few weeks, after all.'

'How brave you are,' Maria replied, with a warm look of approval. 'If I had been you, I should have said something extremely rude—and not simply because of what she did this evening. I tell you frankly that I cannot like her. Nothing would persuade me to remain in the same house as Mrs Jenkins—if it were not that I know you need my support, I should leave immediately.'

Maria's fighting words conjured up such a comical picture in her mind that Rosalyn suddenly found herself smiling.

'You know my wretched tongue,' she said. 'It was with the greatest difficulty that I held back this evening. Under any other circumstances, I should have been delighted to show her the door.'

'And I should have locked it after her,' declared Maria stoutly. 'The dear vicar was horrified. He likes Mr Wrexham—says he is a true gentleman in every sense of the word. Indeed, we both felt he behaved very creditably throughout it all.'

'The vicar is very right,' Rosalyn replied. 'I have always respected his judgement. I believe him to be a good man. Kind, considerate and sensible. A man to be relied upon in times of anxiety.'

'Yes. He is all that and more.' Maria looked thoughtful. 'Oh, our guests are leaving, dearest. You should say goodbye to them.'

'Yes, of course.'

Rosalyn had recovered her composure by now and was able to accompany her friends to the door, where they took an affectionate leave of her. She could see concern in several of their faces, but none of them were willing to speak of the embarrassing incident openly. It was best brushed under the mat and forgotten.

When they had all gone, Rosalyn went immediately to her own room without returning to the parlour to wish her family goodnight. She did not feel like talking to either her brother or Mrs Jenkins, so when someone knocked at her door just as she was about to undress, she sighed in resignation.

'Yes. Come in.'

It was Freddie. He looked at her awkwardly, his colour heightened. She sensed that he was feeling both ashamed and ill at ease—as indeed he ought!

'Ros…' he began, dropping his gaze as she met his eyes. 'I'm not sure what to say.'

'Then say nothing. I understand your position.'

'You could not expect her to welcome the presence of a man who…killed her brother?'

'No, of course not. It was unfortunate that neither of us were aware of it. However, she might have spoken to you privately. There was surely no need to make a scene in front of our guests—to force Mr Wrexham to leave like that?'

'Good grief, no!' Freddie said. 'It was a wretched thing to do. Most embarrassing for everyone.'

'She is an unpleasant woman,' Rosalyn said quietly. She gave him a direct look. 'I am sorry but I cannot like her, even for your sake. I hope she will not ruin your marriage, Freddie. You will have to be careful or she will make your lives miserable.'

'You know how I feel. If it were not for Bea—I would have liked to throw her out.' He relaxed a little as his sister was betrayed into a smile. 'I am sorry. Truly, I am. I would not have had you placed in such an abominable position for the world. Do you…do you like Mr Wrexham, Ros?'

'Yes. Very much, as it happens.'

'I thought you might.' Freddie played with his watch chain, clearly feeling both guilty and awkward. 'You weren't thinking of marrying him, were you?'

'Would it matter to you if I was?'

'Not personally. Seemed a decent enough chap to me—but you know how things stand at the moment.'

'Yes, of course.' For a moment Rosalyn was angry. Did he not realise how selfish he was being? 'If it will set your mind at rest, Freddie—I have no plans to marry Mr Wrexham, and I shall not invite him to this house again while Mrs Jenkins is here.'

'Ros…I know I have no right to ask, but will you promise not to see him until after the wedding? She's such an awful woman. She might refuse her permission if she heard gossip about…the two of you.'

'Oh? What kind of gossip?' She gave him a frank, direct stare. Freddie could not meet her eyes. Obviously, Mrs Jenkins had reported what she'd seen the night Rosalyn had met Damian in the garden! 'There is nothing for anyone to gossip about, Freddie. No matter what anyone has told you. Believe me—there has been nothing more than a kiss.'

'Good grief! I didn't think there had,' Freddie said at once. 'I know you, Ros—but people always like to believe the worst. And you have been living here practically alone—' He quailed at the look in his sister's eyes. 'Forgive me. That was very bad of me. I should not have said it.'

'No, you should not.' Rosalyn glared at him. She was very angry now. 'I am my own mistress. My behaviour is my own affair. I believe I am capable of deciding what is or is not proper for me to do. You should leave now, Freddie, before I lose my temper and say something we shall both regret. I promise not to shame you—at least until after you are married!'

'Ros…' He realised she was very angry and stopped. 'Sorry…I've made a mess of this. I did not mean to upset you. '

Rosalyn did not answer. She waited until the door closed behind him before throwing a cushion at it. The action did little to relieve her feelings. Losing one's temper was never an answer in itself. But she was very angry. How could her own brother say such things to her? It was all the fault of that wretched woman!

Oh, why did she have to come here? Why was the situation so awkward?

Rosalyn was restless, so frustrated and incensed that she longed to scream. Why did everything have to be so complicated? Why could she not simply follow her heart? Do as she wished? Yet her own good sense told her that she would have to be very careful. She must do nothing to cause a split between her brother and the girl he loved.

Yet she had to see Damian! She had to see him alone, to explain to him that Mrs Jenkins's revelations had made no difference to her feelings—or her intention of going away with him once the wedding was over.

She must and would see Damian, but she must contrive to keep it a secret from everyone in this house. Particularly the odious Mrs Jenkins!

Chapter Five

'Why may I not visit Sarah Jane?' Jared demanded. Mutiny flared in his dark eyes as he faced his tutor across the room. He looked every inch a prince, his manner haughty and proud. 'Why can she not come here any more?'

'Because I say so.' Damian sighed inwardly as he saw the stubborn set of Jared's jaw; he recognised the all-too-familiar signs of rebellion and knew he must explain more fully. 'Your father would not approve of your becoming too attached to the girl—and there are other reasons. Neither of us will be visiting that house again, nor any other in the area, I dare say.'

'Why? Are you ashamed of me? Ashamed of the colour of my skin?'

Anger flashed in Damian's eyes. 'Where the devil did you get that idea? You know I have never cared for such things. You have always been as a younger brother to me, Jared. I was your mother's friend as well as the prince's. I care only for your safety and well being. You must know that? Surely you cannot believe me capable of such prejudice?'

Jared looked uncertain. 'Nessa said you would turn against me now you are amongst your own people—that you would find me a nuisance.'

'If Nessa told you that she is either lying deliberately or

mistakes the matter,' Damian said, his mouth thinning in annoyance. 'Believe me, Jared. I shall always care for you. The only thing I find a nuisance is that I am forced to curtail your freedom all too often. I do not enjoy making you stay within the grounds—nor do I wish to stop you making friends, believe me.'

'My father has cast me out.'

'Only for your own safety.'

'He will never allow me to return to India. I am the cause of too much trouble amongst the people. I do not belong there—or here.'

There was both pain and anger in the youth's face, reminding Damian of the feelings he had experienced years before, when he too had been forced to seek a new life in exile.

'You belong with me, Jared.' Damian pulled a wry face. 'I too am a social outcast—so we are two of a kind. Where I go, you go; I'm afraid you're stuck with me until your majority. Then you will be free to tell me to go to hell if you so choose.'

His words brought a smile to Jared's face. 'Do you mean it? Shall I always belong with you, *sahib*?'

'Have I not said it? You have reason to know I do not say things lightly, have you not?' Damian grinned as Jared looked rueful. 'Come, there is no need for anger between us. You are no longer a child, Jared.'

'Some treat me as if I am,' Jared replied, a flash of hauteur in his eyes.

'Then I shall not be one of them, unless you force me to it. Act like a man, Jared, and I shall respect you as one.' Damian moved towards him, laying a hand on his shoulder. 'My name is Damian. Why do you not begin to use it? We are not in India now. It may be that neither of us will ever return. Perhaps it would be best if you left the old ways behind now, Jared. Your mother was English—a very intelligent, lovely lady. You have no reason to be ashamed of carrying her blood, though I know some of your father's people would have you think so. In certain cosmopolitan societies people of mixed race adopt European ways and are accepted, even admired for their differences—and their talents. You are intelligent and knowledgeable. You could find a place for yourself in such a society, Jared. You are very like your mother, more like her than your father, perhaps. If it had been otherwise, you might have been more accepted at home.'

'My mother loved me.' Jared's eyes were shiny with the tears he was too proud to let fall. 'You do believe she loved me?'

'Always.' Damian offered his hand and after a moment the youth took it. 'If I thought it best that we should go away—disappear, perhaps even change our names—would you trust me?'

Jared was silent for a few seconds, considering, then he smiled. 'Yes, Damian,' he said. 'I shall trust you—but I would like to see Sarah Jane once more. She is my friend, perhaps the only true friend I have apart from you. I want to give her a present…so that she will not forget me.'

'I'll do what I can,' Damian promised. 'Be patient, Jared. It will not be easy. I cannot risk going to the house at the present, for Miss Eastleigh's sake. Nor can I let you go. But I shall find a way. I promise.'

'Why can I not see Jared?' Sarah Jane stamped her foot, her face pink with temper. 'He is my friend. I hate you. You are mean to stop me seeing him. I shall see him, I shall!'

Rosalyn sighed. She could not approve of Sarah Jane's tantrum, but she understood completely how the girl felt. It *was* unfair. No one was more aware of that than she.

'I'm sorry,' she said. 'Please do not be cross with me, Sarah Jane. Believe me, I really do not want to stop you seeing Jared. I have no choice for the moment. It is just as difficult for me. I would like to see Mr Wrexham but I may not—not just yet.'

'It's because of that horrid woman, isn't it?' Sarah Jane said, her face sulky. 'I heard her saying things to Beatrice this morning—about you and Mr Wrexham. Beatrice tried to defend you from her insinuations and she made her cry.'

'Mrs Jenkins does not like Mr Wrexham because of something that happened a long time ago.' Rosalyn explained without going into precise details. 'She has threatened to stop Freddie marrying Beatrice if Mr Wrexham comes here again…and that would make both her and Freddie very unhappy. You must see that we have to consider their feelings as well as our own? At least for the time being.'

'I like Beatrice. I do not want her to be unhappy—but Jared could come,' Sarah said, her face mutinous. 'Or I could go there. That horrid woman need not know where I've gone.'

'That would be deceitful,' Rosalyn said, crossing her fingers behind her back. It was wrong of her to deny Sarah Jane the very thing she was planning for herself. 'Besides, your mother will be wanting you home soon. Her letter says your brother is on the mend.'

'I must see Jared before I go home,' Sarah Jane pleaded, her large eyes filling with tears. 'I want to give him something…something to keep so that he will always remember me.'

Rosalyn nodded. Sarah Jane had made a friend. She did not want to forget him, nor was it right that she should be forced to give him up when her own grandmother had approved the friendship.

'I might be able to arrange a meeting,' she said. 'Be patient, Sarah. I'll try my best. I promise. Now go downstairs and find Maria, there's a good girl.'

Sarah Jane went reluctantly, clearly still feeling the injustice of what had been imposed on her. Rosalyn crossed

over to the window and looked out at the view. It was driz-
zling with rain. She could hardly pretend she was going for
a walk in this weather. And if she ordered the carriage,
everyone would want to know where she was going. Mrs
Jenkins would probably ask to go with her in order to spoil
any plans she might have for meeting Damian.

It was no use. She would have to wait until it was fine—
until she could be sure that Mrs Jenkins was safely out of
the way.

The opportunity to escape did not present itself for three
days. Three long, wet and gloomy days in which Sarah Jane
grew ever more obstinate and Rosalyn found it almost impossible to sleep at night. During this time her resolution
hardened. Why should Mrs Jenkins dictate who she and
Sarah might know? She was determined to find a way for
them both to see their friends, but without causing harm to
Beatrice and Freddie. When at last the chance came, however, the weather could not have been kinder. It was a warm,
dry day with scarcely a cloud in the sky.

A luncheon party had been arranged at the vicarage. Mrs
Jenkins had asked to look at the church before deciding
finally whether the wedding should be held there or in London.

'There will be nearly two hundred guests,' she announced
grandly. 'I am not sure a village church will be large
enough. Our own in Huntingdon is certainly not suitable.'

Beatrice had looked anxious, having previously declared
that she would prefer a smaller wedding if it could be held
here. She was obviously a country girl at heart, and did not
care for all the fuss and consequence of a large society wedding.

So the visit to the church had been arranged for the Friday
morning, followed by a cold collation to be prepared by the
vicar's housekeeper. When Rosalyn announced that Sarah
Jane had been sick and she must stay behind to care for her,

there were cries of disappointment from Beatrice and a suspicious glare from her aunt.

'Let me stay with her, Rosalyn,' begged Maria. 'I should
be the one to remain behind and nurse poor Sarah.'

'You are needed at the church,' Rosalyn replied. 'You
know more about the flowers and the music—besides, I
have a little headache. I shall sit quietly with Sarah and have
a nice rest. No one is to worry about me, I shall be quite
content to stay home.'

'You do look a bit pale,' Freddie said, settling the matter.
'Poor Ros. You do look tired. I dare say we have worn you
out these past few days. You are not used to so many people
visiting at once. Stay here and read a book or something.'

Did her brother imagine she was at her last prayers? Rosalyn murmured her thanks, hiding a wry smile. She did not
feel in the least guilty at deceiving them all. If her brother
had supported her—if he had stood up to Mrs Jenkins in
the first place—there would have been no need for deceit.

She waited until the carriage had rumbled out of sight,
then called to Sarah to come down.

'We have to be quick,' she said, catching the girl's hand.
'No one must realise where we've been. If anyone asks you
later, we just went for a little walk in the orchard.'

Sarah Jane nodded, her cheeks pink with excitement. It
was a real adventure, made all the more thrilling because
she was being asked to tell white lies by an adult. Sarah
knew the difference between real lies and fibs—and this was
on the borderline. They were being very wicked, but she
liked her cousin Rosalyn all the more because of it.

They slipped out of the house by a side door, making
their way casually towards the orchard. Once out of sight
of the house windows, they increased their pace. It was
when they began to cross the pasture land behind the orchard that they saw the two horsemen coming towards them.

Rosalyn knew at once who the riders were, as did Sarah
Jane. The girl gave a cry of pleasure and started to run to

meet them. Only a great effort of will on Rosalyn's part prevented her from doing likewise.

'Jared!' Sarah Jane cried, her face lighting up with pleasure. 'We were coming to see if you were at home. Oh, I have missed you so! It seems ages since I saw you last.'

He leapt from his horse's back and caught her hands as she reached him, so obviously thrilled to see her that any doubts Rosalyn might have had about the wisdom of this meeting were forgotten. She watched as the two walked a little way off, the horse following behind, then stopping to graze the rich pasture. The young people's pleasure in each other was plain to see, and made her feel a little sad that they must part again so soon.

Damian had not dismounted. She glanced up at him, her heart catching as she saw his stern expression. Was he angry with her? Had she offended him by seeming to take her brother's part the other evening?

'I shall not get down,' he said. 'We may be seen even here. We have ridden this way every day in the hope that you might choose to walk in this direction.'

'I could not come sooner. Sarah Jane wanted to see Jared, but it was difficult.'

'So I might imagine.' His dark eyes studied her intently, reading so much that she had not been able to say. 'And you? Have I placed you in an impossible position, my love? Do you wish we had never met?'

'No, of course not!' She gazed up at him, willing him to see the need in her, the longing her upbringing forbade her to express in words. 'I wish I could come away with you now. If I were free...' She blushed hotly as she saw the sudden blaze of desire in his eyes. 'Damian...you know. You *must* know how I feel?'

His look seemed to embrace her, holding her as closely as his arms ached to do, caressing her so that she could almost feel the softness of his lips on her.

'Will you really come with me? Follow me to some

strange, foreign land—knowing you can never return to your family? That you are forever lost in their eyes? A scarlet woman…forbidden your own kind for as long as you live.'

'Yes. Yes, I shall. Only duty holds me here now. I do love Freddie—but he doesn't deserve it. I was so upset that you were forced to leave the other night, that Freddie did nothing to make things easier. He should have refused to be bullied by that woman.'

Damian's eyes lit with laughter. 'You are too severe on him, my Amazon. Beside you, most men would fare no better than Sir Frederick. He has not your courage, my love. And it was better that I left immediately. I might otherwise have said things I ought not—revealed a secret that is not mine to share, even with you.'

'The reason why you fought that duel?' Rosalyn asked. She gazed up at him, sensing a long-remembered grief and wondering what it was that still held the power to hurt him after all this time. 'You had good reason to kill him, didn't you?'

'I believed so.' His expression was grave, eyes darkly reflecting his inner turmoil. 'Perhaps I shall tell you one day, but not unless there is need—and not in front of that woman.' He glanced towards Jared and Sarah, calling out a reminder. 'We must go soon, Jared!'

'Must you go?' Rosalyn wanted to beg him to stay. She could not bear to be parted from him again so soon, knowing it might be for some weeks. 'It seems an age since… since we were in the garden together.'

Damian smiled, reaching down to touch her hand briefly. 'We ought not to risk being seen together just yet, for your sake—and Miss Holland's. I must go to London for a few days. When I return, perhaps we can meet again? '

'I will send a message when it is safe,' Rosalyn promised. 'There is a groom I think we can trust. How long will you be away?'

'A week…two at most.' Damian frowned. 'There is

something I must settle. Afterwards…I must take Jared somewhere else, but I shall see you again first. And when your brother is married…'

'I shall come to you,' Rosalyn said without hesitation. 'We shall go abroad somewhere, Damian. The scandal will not touch us there, nor shall we harm others by what we do.'

'I love you,' he said, his dark, expressive eyes seeming to caress her. 'Remember that, whatever else you may hear.'

'What do you mean?'

'I am not certain…perhaps nothing.' He looked at the boy and girl once more. 'Jared!'

Jared pressed something into Sarah Jane's hand, then turned to his horse, put a foot in the stirrup and mounted. The girl stood staring after him as he and Damian rode away, then turned to smile when Rosalyn came to stand beside her.

'He said we shall always be friends, no matter where we are,' she said, looking a little dazed as she showed Rosalyn what he had given her. 'I gave him a smooth pebble I liked—but he gave me this. He said I should keep it and one day we would meet again.'

'That is a beautiful pearl,' Rosalyn said as she saw Jared's gift. It was as large as a pigeon's egg and slightly pink. 'It is very valuable. You must take great care of it, Sarah.'

'Yes, I shall,' she replied. 'One day I may have it set as a pendant. I shall wear it when I meet Jared again—when we are both older.'

Rosalyn said nothing. She thought it unlikely the two would meet again. Jared would return to India, to his own people—and Sarah Jane would find new friends. Yet perhaps she would never quite forget the sunny days of an English summer when she had made friends with a young Indian gentleman.

'We should go back, now,' she reminded the girl gently. 'I'm sorry we could not stay out longer.'

'Oh, it does not matter,' Sarah Jane replied, hiding a little smile as she turned away.

There was no point in telling Rosalyn that she and Jared had devised a way of sending each other messages—that they planned to meet as often as they could—because it would mean a disagreement between them. Sarah did not want to quarrel with Rosalyn, she liked and admired her—but nothing was going to stop her seeing Jared, at least until his tutor took him away or she herself was sent home.

When the others returned from their luncheon party, Sarah Jane was sitting on the sofa in Rosalyn's parlour, reclining against a pile of pillows, and looking for all the world like an invalid. She managed a wan smile for Maria in reply to her tender inquiry, replying that she was feeling a little better and might even attempt to eat something later.

Sarah Jane was a consummate actress, Rosalyn decided, feeling slightly guilty that she had encouraged it, and even worse because she was forced to continue the lies.

'And you, Miss Eastleigh,' asked Mrs Jenkins with a hard stare in her direction. 'I trust you have recovered from your headache?'

'It was only a little one,' Rosalyn replied. 'I feel entirely well again now, thank you.'

The look Mrs Jenkins gave her would have curdled milk straight from the cow, but Rosalyn was able to smile. Now that she had seen Damian, had settled things between them, nothing could hurt her.

Beatrice began to chatter and the atmosphere lightened as she declared she adored the village church, that she wished with all her heart to be married there and nowhere else would do.

'I have told Aunt Patricia that it is quite large enough to invite all those friends I really wish to have at my wedding,' she said with a sweet smile that embraced them all. 'And she has agreed to have the wedding here. We have arranged it with the vicar for three weeks on Sunday.'

'So we shall have the reception at the house,' Rosalyn said. 'Do you wish me to engage more staff for the reception, Freddie? Or will you bring in outside help?'

Her brother was considered to be something of a gourmet amongst his acquaintances, and she knew he would have preferred a London wedding with all the trimmings, but he had given Beatrice her wish without a murmur of protest, as he would probably do for the rest of his life.

The arrangements were discussed at length. Freddie decided he would bring his own Monsieur Maurice down from London ten days before the wedding and that they would hire as many women from the village as were needed to help in the house.

'We shall also need refreshments for the dance,' Rosalyn reminded her brother. 'And that is arranged for two weeks before the wedding itself.'

'Then I shall return to London tomorrow and beg Maurice to come at once,' Freddie declared. 'He hates the country, but I dare say he will make an exception to oblige me this once.'

Freddie's chef was very temperamental and inclined to throw tantrums if everything was not to his liking. Rosalyn shuddered to think of the chaos he was bound to bring to her household, but there was no denying he was an artist in the kitchen. His sauces had to be tasted to be believed, and even Rosalyn admitted that his wonderful food seemed to melt on the tongue.

'And I need another fitting for my wedding gown,' Beatrice said, turning to Rosalyn with a pleading look. 'Why don't we all go up to town for a few days?'

'I really ought to stay here,' Rosalyn said doubtfully. 'There is a great deal to do—and Sarah Jane to think of; she cannot be left alone for several days, that would be too unkind.'

'Surely Maria can see to anything that needs be done in the house?' Freddie said, frowning at her. 'I should like you to come with us, Ros. And you will want to purchase a new gown yourself for the wedding—and the dance also, will you not?'

'Please do go,' Maria added her voice to the others. 'Give me a list of all you want done and I shall be pleased to attend to everything. It will give me pleasure to think of you having a little trip to town, dearest. It is an age since you went anywhere. And Sarah and I will be quite comfortable together, shall we not my dear?'

'Yes, of course.'

Rosalyn was outnumbered. She could not refuse when Beatrice's soft eyes pleaded with her. Besides, why should she? It would be quite pleasant to stay in town for a day or so, and she did need some new clothes. She had not bothered with anything stylish since the summer before her father's death, making do with the services of a local seamstress.

Mrs Jenkins had a hard suspicious look in her eyes. No doubt she thought Rosalyn had a reason for wanting to stay behind.

'Very well, if it will please you, Beatrice. I shall come,' she said, giving in with a good grace. 'It is very true that Maria can look after things here.' She glanced at Sarah Jane, who was taking an interest in the conversation though remaining silent. 'I hope you will not be too lonely?'

'No, of course not,' Sarah replied. It would be much easier to slip away from the house with only Maria around, she thought with satisfaction. 'Will you bring me a present from town, Cousin Rosalyn?'

'Yes, of course. What would you like?'

'A riding habit,' Sarah replied without hesitation. 'I want to learn to ride. Papa always said I ought, but I did not want to—until now.'

'If that is what you would like, of course you shall have it.'

Rosalyn thought she knew why Sarah had changed her mind about riding. She could still hardly believe the change in her cousin's daughter. Sarah Jane had grown up tremendously these past two weeks, and was much the better for it.

'Now if you will all excuse me…' Rosalyn glanced at her brother. 'If we are to leave in the morning, I think I had better speak to Mrs Simmons immediately.'

The wedding was going to make a great deal of extra work for their housekeeper and her staff, and the sooner Mrs Simmons was prepared for it the better.

Rosalyn could not help smiling to herself as she left the room. She did not really mind going to London at all. Damian would be there. It was just possible that she might meet him somewhere—that she might be able to contrive to see him alone. Her heart lifted at the thought and she began to think that a shopping trip in town would suit her very well. Very well indeed!

'It is lovely to be alone with you like this,' Beatrice said, her arm tucked through Rosalyn's as they strolled together in Regent's Park. They had spent the morning at the dressmaker's and were enjoying the warm sunshine rather than returning home immediately. The lovely weather had brought a great many people to the park, and they were able to watch and admire the sight of several smart carriages bowling along the roadways. 'Aunt Patricia scarcely ever lets me go anywhere without her.'

Surprisingly, Mrs Jenkins had cried off from accompanying them at the last moment, saying she would remain behind and write her letters—a circumstance that both of them had found agreeable.

Rosalyn gave the younger girl a sympathetic look. 'It cannot have been easy for you since your mama died, to be tied so to your aunt. That will all change soon,' she said. 'When you are married you need not see her too often—indeed, Beatrice, I think you should begin to stand up to her. If you do not, she may make your life intolerable.'

'You cannot know how I have longed to escape from her,' Beatrice said on a sigh. 'My aunt—and her odious brother Bernard.' Her cheeks flushed as Rosalyn looked at her in surprise. 'I dislike Bernard Harrington so very much. He frightens me sometimes. Indeed, I have thought—' She stopped as if what she had been about to say was too shocking to be spoken aloud. 'No, I cannot say it! But I take good care never to be alone with him.'

'Beatrice!' Rosalyn was startled. 'Has he ever done anything...touched you in a familiar way?'

'Only once and then it was done when he was in his cups, but I confess I have been afraid of him since,' Beatrice confided, her cheeks pink. 'I dare not tell my aunt. She dotes on Bernard and will not hear a word against him. I suppose it is because of what happened to Roderick, because he died young...' Beatrice looked awkward. 'I rather liked Mr Wrexham. I do not believe he would murder anyone.'

'Nor do I,' Rosalyn replied and smiled at her earnest look. 'But you had better not let your aunt hear you say that, my dear. I fear that your hopes of an inheritance would then be at an end.'

'I have Mama's money in trust—some five thousand pounds, I think. Aunt Patricia's money means nothing to me. Indeed, I wish I need never see her again once Freddie and I are married.'

'Have you told Freddie that?'

'No...no, I have not.'

'Then I think perhaps you should mention it.'

Beatrice looked struck by this. 'Do you think I should? Yes, perhaps I shall. I certainly do not care for the money if he does not.'

'I think you will find that Freddie cares only for you.'

Rosalyn squeezed her arm affectionately. Beatrice had a lovely nature. She was already very fond of the girl and, despite all the problems her engagement to Freddie had caused, she was very glad they were to marry. She suspected that there was far more to Beatrice than her brother yet dreamed, and that she would be very good for him when she had had time to grow up herself.

Turning to glance to her right, Rosalyn caught sight of two men standing together a short distance away. Her heart began to beat very fast. As the path they were following wound in that direction they would have to pass them. The men were talking earnestly and had not noticed them—but one of them was Damian, and he was bound to see her if they continued in the same direction.

'Oh…' Rosalyn did not realise she had spoken aloud. Her pulses were racing wildly. She wanted to speak to Damian, but believed it would embarrass her companion. What ought she to do? To turn away might cause him to think she wished to avoid meeting him.

'Is that not Mr Wrexham?' asked Beatrice, her cheeks a little pink as she too noticed the men.

'Yes. Shall we turn away?'

'Why? I should like to have the opportunity to apologise,' Beatrice replied. 'In any case, it is too late. He has seen us. He is looking this way.'

'Yes, so he is.'

Damian's companion was walking away. He hesitated, seeming uncertain of what to do, then came towards them.

'Mr Wrexham,' Beatrice said, before he could speak. 'I have not had the chance to apologise to you, sir. I was most distressed by what happened that evening.'

He swept his hat off, bowing to her. '*You* have nothing to apologise for, Miss Holland. I was sorry to spoil your evening.'

'*You* did not,' she replied and smiled at him.

'You are very gracious.' His dark eyes met Rosalyn's. 'I was not expecting to see you here, Miss Eastleigh.'

'We came up for a last fitting for Beatrice's wedding gown and a little shopping. We have been here two days and return home at the end of the week.'

'Ah…' Damian nodded. 'I myself expect to be here several more days. My business is taking longer than I had hoped.'

'Then we shall be back in Cambridgeshire before you,' Rosalyn said and glanced at the pretty silver watch pinned to the lapel of her gown. 'I see it is past noon. I suppose we ought to be thinking of returning home. Beatrice and I have been out all morning. Besides, we have an important engagement this evening. Lord Renshaw's ball…'

'Renshaw's ball?' Damian nodded, his eyes intent on her face. 'I believe it will be a sad crush.'

'But that means it will be a success, you know,' said Beatrice, laughing at him. 'If there was actually room to move freely, it would be counted a failure.'

'Yes, I believe you are right. It is years since I attended such a function,' Damian admitted. 'However, I do seem to recall something of the sort. I wish you both a pleasant evening.'

Rosalyn sighed inwardly, as he tipped his hat once more and walked on. She had hoped Damian might have said he too would be attending the ball, but it had been a forlorn hope. It was to be a sparkling society affair, one of the most important balls of the new season. She could hardly expect Damian to be on the guest list. He had spoken of himself as a social outcast, though she imagined most people would have long forgotten the old scandal. Even so, it was unlikely he had been invited.

It had not been possible to arrange another meeting with Beatrice there, but perhaps it was for the best. She would be returning to the country soon enough.

* * *

Damian walked into the select gaming club. He had not bothered to put his name forward for membership, but was able to come and go at will as his uncle's guest. It was just one of the several clubs he had visited in the hope of finding Bernard Harrington. So far, that particular gentleman was proving difficult to track down. It seemed he must have reformed his old habits, for Damian had been told he was definitely in town.

He must seek him elsewhere. Perhaps Harrington's degenerate ways had given him a taste for low dives and gaming hells. Since he had not visited any of the exclusive clubs he had been used to frequent, he must be gambling at less respectable haunts. Damian was about to leave in search of him when someone laid a hand on his shoulder.

'Good lord!' a cheerful voice exclaimed as he turned to find himself staring at a man he had not met for years. 'Is it really you, Damian? I had heard you were in the country—why didn't you call on me?'

A slow smile spread over Damian's mouth, bringing genuine warmth to his dark eyes. His friend had put on weight over the years, but he was still the same honest, decent fellow he had always been—and there was real pleasure in his greeting.

'Renshaw,' he said and laughed as he found himself heartily embraced in a bear hug. 'I meant to call, but you know how things stand…' He shrugged expressively. 'I wasn't sure…'

'You must have known you would be welcome?' Lord Hugh Renshaw's brows rose. 'My house is always open to you. No matter what anyone else thinks, Damian! After what you did for Helen. You must know I would never turn my back on you.' He frowned at the memory. 'It should have been me. I should have been the one to call that devil out!'

'With your reputation as the worst shot in England? You could never hit a barn door from ten paces,' Damian replied, chuckling at his friend's affronted look. Then his smile faded, his expression becoming serious. 'Besides, we both loved her, Hugh. It only mattered that she should be avenged.'

'You did that,' Renshaw said grimly, and there was anger now in his gentle eyes. 'But suffered for it. It was a terrible price you paid—exile from your home and everything you loved.'

'If you think that, your wits must be addled,' Damian replied with a wicked grin. 'It was the best thing my father ever did for me, sending me to India.'

'You ain't a nabob?' Renshaw's eyes widened. 'Made your fortune, did you?' Damian nodded and he laughed, the old grief returned to its habitual place in a tiny corner of his heart. His friend slapped his thigh in high humour. 'Well, if that ain't the best thing I've heard in a month of Sundays. Have you come home to rub their noses in it? All those damned idiots who cast you out? Serve 'em right if you have!'

'Grandfather left everything to me. I had to come back, to sort out the mess. It seems there are quite a few debts. Jacob can do nothing without my help.'

'Leave 'em to sink in it, I would,' said his friend robustly. 'Pack of rascals, the lot of them! Begging your pardon, Damian, but there ain't one of your family worth the saving. Not one of them lifted a finger to set the record straight. It was my father who did that—and was glad to do it. Can't thank you enough for keeping quiet all these years. No one outside our family has ever known that my sister was...' He stopped, choked with emotion.

Damian saw the pain, still so raw after all this time, and gripped his shoulder. 'She was as dear to me as she was to you,' he said gruffly. 'The sister I never had.'

'I always hoped she would be more to you one day,' Hugh said and sighed as he remembered the lovely, innocent girl, hardly more than a child, who had died of shame.

'I must tell you something,' Damian said. 'Something I discovered too late…'

'Something to do with Helen?'

'Yes.' Damian looked grim. 'It seems we have some unfinished business, Hugh—and perhaps you can help me?'

'Yes, of course. Whatever you need,' Hugh assured him. 'Come and lunch with me. Tell you what, Lady Renshaw is giving a small affair this evening—why don't you join us?'

'A small affair?' Damian's knowing eyes mocked him. 'I have it on the highest authority that it is bound to be a sad crush and therefore a success.'

'Lady Renshaw's ball always is,' murmured Hugh and sighed in a melancholy way that did not deceive his friend for a moment. Hugh was proud of his lovely wife, and her extravagance. 'Between us, old fellow, I sometimes think Jane is set on beggaring me—but think of it like this, amongst so many, one more cannot make the slightest difference.'

Damian chuckled and promised to consider his friend's invitation. He was not particularly interested in attending a society ball—and yet Rosalyn would be there. Perhaps he might be able to snatch a few moments alone with her.

Chapter Six

'You look lovely,' Rosalyn said and kissed the younger girl's cheek. It was early evening; they were in Rosalyn's bedchamber and Beatrice had come to show her her gown before they went downstairs. 'That shade of blue particularly becomes you, dearest.' She held up a choker of pearls to show the girl. 'Could you please fasten these for me? The clasp is a little awkward at times.'

'Of course.'

'Thank you,' Rosalyn said, patting the necklace on her neck as Beatrice fastened the tiny diamond clasp. 'Papa gave me these. I am very fond of them and do not wish to change the fastening, because I think it particularly pretty, though difficult to secure.'

'It is pretty—and you are beautiful,' responded Beatrice. 'I could never wear such a rich shade of green. On you, it is magnificent.'

'Thank you. Emerald has always been a favourite shade of mine, though I would not call myself beautiful.' Rosalyn glanced at the small gilt-and-bronze clock on her dressing chest. 'Perhaps we should go down? Unless you—' She had been about to ask if Beatrice thought she ought to go to inquire if her aunt was ready, but turned her head as someone knocked at her bedroom door. 'Yes, come in.'

A maid entered, giving her a rather flustered curtsy. 'Miss Eastleigh...Mrs Jenkins bade me tell you she is laid on her bed and too sick to leave it this night.'

'Aunt Patricia is ill?' Beatrice cried, looking anxiously at Rosalyn. 'Does that mean we may not go to the ball?'

'Wait here,' Rosalyn said, frowning. 'I shall speak to her. I see no reason why we should not go—unless she is very ill, of course.'

It was the second time Mrs Jenkins had cried off that day. Rosalyn hurried along the landing to her room, knocked and, being invited to enter, did so. Mrs Jenkins was lying against a pile of pillows and looking quite unwell, her complexion slightly yellow.

'I am sorry you are feeling poorly,' Rosalyn said. 'Shall I send for a doctor?'

'No, thank you. I am occasionally prone to these bouts of nausea. I shall be well enough soon. All I need is rest and quiet.' Mrs Jenkins sighed and held a lavender scented kerchief to her nose.

'Then I shall leave you in peace,' Rosalyn replied. 'If you need anything, you have only to ring and someone will come.'

'You mean to attend Renshaw's ball, then?'

'You would hardly wish Beatrice to miss such a prestigious affair?'

'No—no, I suppose not,' Mrs Jenkins said, reaching for her little silver vinaigrette, which was rather pretty and engraved with leaves and vines. 'I dare say she will be safe with Sir Frederick—and you.'

Rosalyn allowed herself a smile. 'Yes. I am convinced she will always be safe in my brother's care. Do not hesitate to ring if you need anything, ma'am. Forgive me if I leave you now: Beatrice is waiting.'

Mrs Jenkins waved her away. Rosalyn scolded herself for feeling as if a weight had been lifted from her shoulders as she returned to Beatrice. It was very unkind in her, but she could not help thinking the evening would be so much more enjoyable without Beatrice's disagreeable aunt watching every move she made!

Beatrice's prediction was proved correct the moment they entered Lord Renshaw's large and impressive house in Mayfair. The very handsome rooms were overflowing with richly dressed ladies and gentlemen, their jewels flashing beneath the light of brilliant crystal chandeliers. Despite the size of the rooms and the high ceilings, it was extremely hot and the ballroom windows had been opened to let in some air.

Rosalyn accepted a glass of cold champagne and made her way unhurriedly towards the windows. She was in some part Beatrice's chaperon that evening and imagined she would not dance very much, if at all—though she had already noticed several gentlemen she knew: friends of Freddie and some older men who had occasionally called on her father before his illness.

She stood watching for a few moments, her foot tapping in time to the music, absorbing the atmosphere. It was a long time since she had attended such an affair and she found she was enjoying the experience.

'Are you not dancing this evening, Miss Eastleigh?'

Rosalyn's heart jerked as she heard the familiar voice behind her. She turned, her expressive face reflecting her great surprise and pleasure at seeing him.

'Damian!' she cried. 'I hoped—but you said nothing earlier and I supposed you would not be here.'

'Renshaw insisted on it,' Damian replied, a gleam of mischief in his eyes. 'I am not quite without friends—even though I do not choose to impose myself on them.'

'You cannot imagine a true friend would consider it an imposition to have you as a guest? If it were not for Freddie's situation, I should have requested Mrs Jenkins to leave the other evening.'

'Would you, my dearest Miss Eastleigh? How very brave you are.'

Rosalyn flushed. 'Do not mock me. I have no intention of allowing Mrs Jenkins to dictate to me once the wedding is over.'

'A veritable Amazon,' Damian murmured wickedly. How lovely she looked tonight! Especially with that faint flush of pride in her cheeks. 'Brave enough to dance with me? I wonder.'

'Yes, though I must confess Mrs Jenkins is not here to censure me.' Rosalyn caught his mood. Her eyes sparkled with a naughty sense of humour. 'No, no, you must not look so! It is unkind of you. She suffered a most unfortunate bilious attack and was unable to accompany us. However, in the circumstances, I see no reason why we should not dance, sir.'

'Then I am rewarded for having allowed Hugh to persuade me into coming this evening.' He bowed to her. 'Shall we see if I can remember how to dance, Miss Eastleigh?'

She laughed, taking his hand as the musicians struck up a popular melody and groups began to form on the dance floor. It was a country dance, which meant that Rosalyn passed from her own partner to others, returning after certain moves had been executed. She clasped his hand, smiling up at him for a moment before being claimed by the next gentleman.

'It is nice to see you in town, Miss Eastleigh,' the young man said. 'I do not suppose you remember me?'

'Of course I do, Mr Carlton. Freddie brought you down to stay with us two years ago. I remember very well.'

'Grown up a bit since,' he said. 'I was still a bit wet behind the ears then. Dare say you thought me an idiot? Must have done—Freddie and me both, larking about when you were wishing to be quiet.'

'Not at all,' she replied and smiled at him. 'You gave me

a copy of Lord Byron's poems. I often read something from it before I retire. It is quite a favourite with me.'

'Really?' Philip Carlton went pink with pleasure. 'Perhaps you would stand up with me later?' he asked as they were obliged to part company.

'Yes, of course.' She smiled again and passed on.

'One of your admirers?' Damian asked, mouth quirking at the corners as she took his hand once more. 'Tell me— do I have a rival for your affections?'

'Foolish man,' chided Rosalyn. 'He cannot be older than Freddie.'

'A case of calf love, then,' Damian murmured. 'Do you know how lovely you look this evening? I should like to kiss you.'

Rosalyn gave him a speaking look. He was wicked to tease her. Surely he knew how much she longed to be in his arms?

'We should spoil the formation if we left now,' she said softly. 'But I declare it is so hot in here I can scarcely breathe.'

They parted again, but his eyes relayed a message of understanding. She knew that sooner or later he would find a way of being alone with her.

It was not to be immediately, however. Rosalyn thanked him when their dance was over; she turned, intending to go out on to the balcony for some air, but was not allowed to leave the dance floor.

Her willingness to dance had been noted and she was besieged by gentlemen wishing to enter their names on her card, which she was obliged to allow or be thought churlish.

Rosalyn was a little surprised at her own popularity. She had not taken particularly well in her come-out season, and, not being in the least inclined to vanity, could not be aware that she had come later to her full potential. As a girl, her height had made her awkward and tongue-tied; but now her beauty shone out like a beacon, drawing old and young alike to her side, her ready wit finding her many admirers.

Damian watched with a wry smile on his lips. It was not to be expected that others would not see what had struck him so forcibly at their first meeting. Rosalyn exuded sensuality and charm. She outshone all the pretty young ladies at the ball, promising so much that any red-blooded male would wish for in a woman. Such promise was not often met with amongst the young ladies on the marriage mart; it was more usually found in a mistress—a lady who had been married for some years to a man she did not love.

Rosalyn's life had been odd for a woman of her class. She had poise, beauty, intelligence—and a high degree of independence. This evening the various ingredients had blended into an irresistible whole, making her a target for every unattached male in the room.

Damian frowned as he recognised some of the men being drawn into her net. The young fools he dismissed as irrelevant, but there were others…at least three with old titles and spotless (comparatively speaking) reputations.

He reviewed them in his mind. Davenport had been a bit of a rake in his time, but was nearly forty and looking to settle. Marksby had recently become the Earl of Salter and was reputedly on the catch for a second wife, his first having died without giving him an heir—and Sir Edward Forster was quite simply a decent man, though slightly pompous in his manner. Any one of them could offer Rosalyn a secure future and an enviable position in Society. Far more than Damian could offer!

He was suddenly assailed with doubts. What was he doing here? Why on earth had he imagined he had the right to claim such a woman for his own? He was a fool and should have remembered he had other business to settle. He turned away. It was time he was leaving—time he followed the various leads Renshaw had given him earlier and sought out his quarry.

'Not going already?' Renshaw stopped him at the ball-room door. 'I quite thought you were enjoying yourself with Miss Eastleigh. She's a beauty, ain't she? Can't think where she has been hiding herself all these years. If I wasn't madly in love with Lady Renshaw, I'd have joined the hunt my-self.'

'She is certainly very lovely,' Damian said, cursing him-self for a fool as the pain tore at his insides. 'Any one of them would be better for her than me, Hugh. What right have I to drag her down to my level?'

'Rise to hers,' advised his friend with a lift of his thick brows. 'If you are thinking of this other business…it was a long time ago, Damian. You cannot bring Helen back. For-get your plans for revenge and marry the lovely Amazon.'

'Take my rightful place in Society, you mean?' Damian laughed harshly. 'Yours is the only invitation I've received since I've been in town, Hugh. What kind of a life would that be for a woman like her? Look at her—she deserves her chance to shine. She deserves someone like Forster or Davenport.'

'You would condemn her to choose between a rake and a bore?' Hugh scowled at him. 'Shame on you, sir! You are a better catch than either of them. At least allow her to make her own choice. I am sure she is perfectly capable of doing so.'

'Perhaps you are right.' Damian relaxed and smiled wryly. 'I'm a stiff-necked fool at times. Too much pride, I dare say.'

'Miss Eastleigh looks warm,' his friend said. 'She looks as if she needs a breath of air. If you do not offer her the chance to escape, someone else certainly will.'

Damian laughed. 'You are too persuasive, Hugh. How-ever, I shall take your advice.'

He returned to the crowded ballroom. Rosalyn had ceased to dance and was clearly headed towards the balcony. He waited, following discreetly.

Her back was towards him and she did not immediately notice he had come after her. She had moved away to the shadows and was fanning herself, staring out into the gardens. He watched her for a moment, thinking she looked sad. He had sensed it before, understood that she too had known loneliness—that her life was not all it might have been. It was this that had first made him think she might be willing to step out of her world into a very different one.

'Rosalyn…'

She spun round at once, her lovely face suddenly alight with pleasure. 'Damian! I thought you were leaving?'

'I was—but Hugh stopped me.' He moved towards her, his eyes dwelling on her face so intently that her heart caught with fear. 'It might have been better if I had left. Better for your sake.'

'Why? Why do you say that? You know I love you…want you.' She spoke from the heart, bravely, with such a devastating honesty that he felt humbled, unworthy of so fine a woman. 'I have loved you almost from the first moment you came into my life. You challenged me, Damian, brought me to life—made me want to feel again.'

'Did I, my love? I am not sure it was well done of me. In the country I thought perhaps we had a chance of finding happiness…but tonight I have seen you as you ought to be. You shine like one of those stars above us, too bright to have your light dimmed by such as me.' He stepped closer, reaching out to touch her shoulder, his fingers straying up to caress her neck; his touch sent little shivers winging their way down her spine. 'You deserve so much more, my darling—so much that I can never give you.'

'This?' Rosalyn glanced back towards the ballroom, a look of dismissal on her face. 'Do you think I care for such things? You misjudge me, sir. Had I wished for a life spent in Society, I might have married a duke when I was eighteen. I have remained a spinster from choice, not necessity.'

She raised her head, her face proud, angry. 'I may be seven and twenty—but I am not at my last prayers!'

'Indeed you are not.' Damian laughed. 'Tonight you are magnificent. I dare swear there are at least a dozen gentlemen in there willing to offer their hearts and fortunes to win you. And I did not mean to insult you. I just wanted you to be quite sure—to understand what you would be giving up if you came to me.'

'Foolish, foolish man! As if I was not already aware of what I shall lose—and what I may gain.' Her eyes glittered with the sheen of tears she would never let fall. 'Do you think me a vain, silly creature—that my head would be turned by a few compliments?'

He saw that she was not quite won over by his apology. Smothering his conscience, he reached out to draw her into his arms. For a moment he gazed down at her, letting her nearness and the musk of her perfume seep into his senses, filling him with sweet desire; then he lowered his head, his mouth taking hers in such a gentle, tender kiss that she swayed into his body, surrendering herself in a way that almost made him lose control.

'Do you not know how much I want you—need you?' he breathed huskily. 'The thought of you torments my dreams. I have struggled against this feeling for your sake, Rosalyn—but I cannot fight you. You are too strong for me, my love.'

'I have given my promise,' she said, a hint of reproach in her eyes. 'I shall come away with you after my brother's wedding—if you still want me.'

'I shall never cease wanting you,' he murmured against her throat. 'I adore you, Rosalyn. I shall try to deserve your trust. Believe me, my love, I shall never hurt you…though I know I am not fit to worship at your feet.'

There was such an odd look in his eyes then that she wondered at it. Just what mystery lay in this man's past?

Why did he look so bleak at times? What inner torment drove him?

'Oh, Damian—'

Rosalyn broke off as she saw her brother come out on to the balcony. She moved away from Damian, into the light.

'So there you are,' Freddie said. 'Beatrice thought… Oh, Wrexham! Didn't realise you were here.' He looked awkward, embarrassed. 'Should it be Marlowe? I heard you'd inherited your grandfather's title…'

'Wrexham will do,' said Damian. 'I've no use for titles or any of that nonsense.'

'No, I suppose you wouldn't have after…' Freddie cleared his throat. 'Sorry about the other evening. Bit difficult…hands tied, if you see what I mean?'

'It was unfortunate for everyone,' Damian said. 'I am sorry, but you will excuse me, I have an appointment I must keep.' He glanced at Rosalyn. 'Forgive me. I really must go.'

'Damian…when?'

'Soon,' he promised. 'Soon now, my love. Eastleigh, I must bid you goodnight.'

There was a strained silence after he had left. Freddie looked at his sister, eyes narrowed, searching.

'So you are determined to have him, then?'

'You need not worry that we shall make things uncomfortable for you, Freddie. Nothing will happen until after your wedding.'

'Bea tells me she doesn't care about her aunt's money.' Freddie sounded ashamed. 'Once we're married—I don't give a damn. At least, you know what I mean. Best to keep things discreet—but if it's Wrexham you want, you will have my blessing.'

'Thank you, dearest.' Rosalyn smiled and kissed his cheek. 'We shall be living abroad. You won't be forced to acknowledge us.'

'Ros…' Freddie protested, cheeks burning. 'I ain't such

a damned snob. Wrexham might have…well, you know the
story better than I, no doubt. But his family…at least, his
grandfather was a decent sort. Earl Marlowe. Wrexham inherited the lot, you know: title, crumbling mansion somewhere near Hastings, I believe—and a load of debts. If you
should need money…'

'I'm sure we shan't,' Rosalyn said. 'I have my own trust
and I dare say Damian has what he needs. Money has never
meant that much to me. I can be happy anywhere with the
right person.'

'Yes, I know.' He smiled at her with affection. 'I haven't
been much of a brother to you, Ros—but I do care about
you. I would stand by you…if things didn't work out. You
could always come home. Bea loves you—and that aunt of
hers can…well, you know!'

The look of disgust on his face made her laugh. 'Freddie,
dearest!' she admonished. She had been angry with him but
was no longer. He had been afraid of losing Beatrice, and
she could understand that. 'Please, there is no need to worry
about me. I know exactly what I want and I am not frightened of the consequences.'

'No. You never were,' Freddie said, offering her his arm
as they returned to the ballroom together. 'You should have
been a man, Ros. You were always braver than me.'

Mrs Jenkins had recovered from her sickness by the next
morning, but said it had been caused by too much racketing
about town and declared her intention of returning to the
country at once. At first she was determined to spend a few
days at her home in Huntingdon before bringing Beatrice
back to Cambridgeshire for the pre-wedding dance.

She was persuaded to relent after some tears from Beatrice, and a promise from Freddie that she could invite her
brother to stay with them.

'Bernard wrote to me,' she told him in confidence when
they were alone. 'He has some small difficulty with his fi-

nancial affairs. I must discuss the problem with him in private.'

'I understood Mr Harrington was in town?' Freddie was surprised. 'Would it not be easier to ask him to call here, ma'am?'

'No, it would not. He can come down to the country if he wishes for my help!' she snapped, causing Freddie to bite his tongue and count to twenty lest he reply in like manner.

What Mrs Jenkins did not reveal was that her brother was a committed gamester, incapable of staying away from the tables for long. In the past, he had often won huge fortunes, but somehow they had slipped through his fingers. Of late, his talents, or luck, had seemed to desert him—perhaps because he had taken to drinking too much. She suspected that he frequented the kind of places she would think disgraceful, and was determined to drag him away from town if she could.

'Your brother is welcome to stay with us, ma'am. Pray write to him immediately.'

Freddie gave his promise easily, entirely unaware that his beloved Beatrice detested her aunt's brother—or that he was stirring up a hornets' nest.

'Ah, there you are,' Maria said, coming to kiss Rosalyn as she entered the house. 'Goodness! How bright you look, dearest. Have you had your hair trimmed at the front? It suits you very well.'

'No, I haven't had it cut,' Rosalyn replied, feeling amused by her cousin's expression. She knew that she was looking very much more the thing now that she had bought herself some fashionable clothes. 'It's just the way the wind has blown it. We had the carriage window down for miles. Mrs Jenkins was feeling unwell.'

'What a shame,' Maria said. 'Is that why she went straight to her room? Never mind, we can have a comfortable coze together. Just like old times.' She tucked her arm through Rosalyn's as they went into the parlour. 'It is so nice to have you home again.'

'You seem very cheerful,' Rosalyn said. She had taken off her pelisse and bonnet in the hall and, as Maria released her arm, glanced into an ornate wall mirror to tidy her hair. 'How is Sarah Jane? Where is she, by the way?'

'Oh, out with that dog, I expect.' Maria seemed uninterested. 'She has taken quite a liking to the wretched thing. She says it needs lots of exercise—and I must admit she is a different girl these days. Always helpful and polite. Her grandmother will hardly know her when she arrives next week.'

'Is Aunt Susan coming to fetch her?'

'Her letter said she would be staying for the dance but not the wedding. Unless Celia and her husband decide to come—in which case they will all be here for two weeks.'

'Goodness me,' Rosalyn said. 'I am not sure how we shall squeeze everyone in. Mrs Jenkins has invited her brother too.'

'I can always stay with a friend,' Maria offered and blushed. She hesitated a moment before making her confession, 'You will be amazed, Rosalyn. I was myself—but dear Mr Waller has...' Her colour deepened even further. 'He has asked me to be his wife and I have said I will... providing it does not upset you too much.'

'Upset me? Maria, you goose! I am delighted. I had thought you might quite like him. It is the very thing for you, and I do wish you happy, my very dear cousin.'

'Well, I think I shall be,' Maria said looking extremely pleased with things. 'But there is not the least hurry. I shall not leave you in the lurch. When you are settled I shall think of myself, but not before.'

'You need not worry about me.' Rosalyn laughed. 'No, I may not tell you just yet, but my own plans are almost set.'

They were prevented from talking further as first Beatrice

and then Sarah Jane arrived. Gifts were exchanged, tea poured and everyone settled down to enjoy themselves.

'Where is Sheba?' asked Rosalyn when she had a moment to talk alone with Sarah Jane. 'Maria tells me you have been looking after her for me. That was very kind of you.'

'Oh…it was just taking her for walks and things,' Sarah replied, avoiding her eyes. 'Thank you for the riding habit. I've been out on one of the horses several times this past week, but now I shall be able to dress properly.'

'Your grandmother will be surprised when she comes to visit next week.'

'Yes, I expect so,' Sarah said. 'We can stay for the wedding, can't we? Beatrice has brought me such a lovely dress. She says I can be one of her bridesmaids if I like.'

'In that case you will have to stay,' Rosalyn said. 'I had better write and urge your whole family to come, though they had thought they would not wish to travel so far.'

She was thoughtful as she went away to write her letters. Everything was working out quite well. Maria was to be married, and Sarah Jane's family would take her home after the wedding.

And then, at last, Rosalyn would be free. She smiled as she remembered her last meeting with Damian, the way he had kissed her and told her he loved her.

Where was he now? Had he completed his business at last? How soon would he be returning to the country—and would she find a way of seeing him when he did?

Chapter Seven

Damian entered the gaming hall, glancing about him with distaste. It was the kind of place that attracted the worst types: hardened gamesters, ruthless sharps out to fleece any young idiot willing to be parted from his fortune—and worse. There *was* a sprinkling of respectable men, men with old titles whose dull, comfortable lives had driven them to find new experiences to enliven their routines. These were the men that might also be found at the Hellfire Club, another place of dubious reputation and frequented by the wilder elements of Society, but here there were also other men—men with desperation in their hearts who were close to destruction.

Had Bernard Harrington sunk to their level? Hugh Renshaw had spoken of debts and wild drinking bouts that had led to Harrington being excluded from the more select clubs where he had once been a member.

'He's had a run of terrible luck,' Hugh had confided when they spoke of Damian's quest to find the man. 'I've heard it said he's close to ruin. Davenport holds several of his notes, I believe. Not many will accept them now, so he has been forced to play elsewhere. His estate is mortgaged to the hilt—there can't be much left.'

The notes Davenport held were now with a firm of lawyers. Damian had purchased them for the sum of ten thousand pounds.

'Why do you want them?' Davenport had asked with careless interest, when requested to sell the notes at a private interview. 'I doubt Harrington can cover a half of that sum.'

'It is a personal matter,' Damian replied. 'One that should have been settled long ago.'

'Killed the wrong man, did you?' Charles Davenport arched his brows. 'I ain't a slowtop, Wrexham. You kept your mouth shut and that was damned decent of you, especially when you consider the way your father behaved towards you—but anyone with a grain of sense understood why you called Roderick Harrington out. We all knew you were like a brother to Renshaw—and, though they hushed it up, his sister's death was obviously a suicide. Add two and two and the reason for that duel becomes obvious.'

'Roderick and his brother were both involved, as it happens, but at the time...she named only one.' Damian frowned. 'I trust you will not speak of this to anyone? Ever?'

'You need not ask. I ain't one to gossip where a lady is concerned, but I have always felt you did the rest of us a service by ridding the world of that filth.' Charles Davenport smiled. 'Yes, I will sell you the notes. My fervent wish is that Harrington will oblige us all by doing the decent thing and blowing his brains out—but I must tell you I doubt it.'

'Then perhaps I shall do it for him.'

'Planning on spending the rest of your life in India? He's hardly worth the sacrifice.' Davenport toyed with the intricate gold watch fob attached to his waistcoat. 'If you ever decide to assume your title and place in Society, I believe you would find yourself more welcome than you might think.'

Their conversation had taken place earlier that day; now it was evening. The gaming tables were full of hard-eyed, ruthless men, the air thick with the stench of sweat, stale smoke and spilt wine.

What an awful place! Damian was about to turn away when he heard the rumpus begin at the far end of the room. It was apparent almost immediately what had happened. Someone had been accused of cheating! The cardinal sin, even amongst these men. There was a lot of shouting and one of the tables was overturned.

'Damn you!' A man was on his feet. From his manner it was clear he had drunk too much wine. 'Call me a cheat, would you? You're the cheat, sir! No one has such luck as to win every hand.'

'By God! I'll have your apology for that or you will meet me for it. Name your seconds, Harrington.'

Damian's eyes narrowed as he studied the man swaying unsteadily on his feet. Was that Bernard Harrington? He could scarcely believe what he was seeing. No more than ten years Damian's senior, the man looked old, fat, his face puffy from too much drinking, late nights—and perhaps worse.

The room had gone silent, tense, as everyone waited to see what Harrington would do. He seemed to hesitate, blinked and shook his head as if suddenly realising what was going on, then he turned and stumbled away, knocking into tables and a waiter. The waiter's tray was sent flying, spilling its load of glasses on to the floor with an almighty crash.

'Damned fool,' muttered the man who had challenged Harrington. 'Won't come up to scratch. He's a coward and always has been.'

'I agree with you there,' Damian said. He had approached as the overset table was being righted. 'May I have a word with you, sir?'

The man stared at him for several seconds, then nodded. 'You're Marlowe's heir, ain't you? Someone pointed you out at Renshaw's affair the other evening. Sit down, sir.'

'Thank you. I don't believe I've the pleasure of having met you before?'

'No, we ain't met.' He offered his hand. 'Tamworth's the name. So, what can I do for you, sir?'

'I believe you may have something I want,' Damian said. 'Would you perhaps have taken Harrington's notes in lieu of coin?'

'Too damned many of them,' Tamworth said, a note of indignation in his voice. 'Tried to fob me off with another this evening. I already hold five thousand pounds—more than his entire estate is worth, I dare say.'

'And I now hold another ten thousand,' Damian said with a smile. 'Far more than Bernard Harrington could ever hope to pay. What do you imagine the outcome would be if I were to buy your notes and present the entire holding to a magistrate?'

'He would be arrested and taken to the debtors' prison until he could pay—which he couldn't, as far as I can tell.'

'Exactly.' Damian smiled wolfishly. 'What is the precise sum you are owed, sir? I shall engage to cover it and relieve you of the burden.'

'What has Harrington done to you?' Tamworth shook his head as Damian's mouth hardened to an uncompromising line. 'No, no need to tell me. I dare say he deserves it. Five thousand I'm owed.' He took some scraps of paper from his coat pocket and laid them on the table. 'Not worth a penny to me—but perhaps to you?'

'If you will furnish me with your address, sir, I shall send you a draft on my bank in the morning.' Damian pocketed the notes, shook hands once more, then hesitated. 'In the unlikely event that Harrington does name his seconds, my advice is to hold your fire until he discharges his own pistol, especially if you mean to fire into the air. Turn your back while he has a loaded pistol and…well, I leave the rest to your own good sense.'

He nodded and walked away, leaving Tamworth to stare after him.

'Well, what do you make of that?' he asked as an interested observer sat down on the chair Damian had vacated.

'Don't you know the story?'

Tamworth shook his head.

'Wrexham killed Harrington's younger brother in a duel years ago. He waited until Roderick had fired, then turned his back. Must have decided he didn't want to go through with it, I suppose. Roderick had another pistol inside his coat…tiny thing but powerful enough to nick Wrexham's arm as he walked away. Wrexham turned and shot him, put a ball dead between his eyes from thirty paces. It was pretty to see, so they said, took his time as he was entitled to do…and then fired.'

'Good grief!' Tamworth ejaculated. 'And now he's after the other one. What do you suppose they did to him?'

'It was all hushed up, but there was talk of a woman being abducted and raped. The thing was, Wrexham went after the wrong brother. Everyone knew Roderick might have had a hand in it—he was completely under Bernard's domination, always did as he told him—but he wouldn't have raped the girl. Not his style; tastes in a different category altogether, if you see what I mean.'

'So it was Bernard who raped the girl…and now Wrexham knows about it?' Tamworth nodded. 'Sounds as if debtors' row is too good for Harrington.'

'That's if he ever gets there. He has a sister. She was left a considerable fortune by her husband. Harrington will wheedle the money from her if he can.'

'He might be better off going to prison,' Tamworth remarked as he recalled the look on Damian's face. 'Unless he fancies a ball between the eyes.'

'Oh, Rosalyn,' Beatrice cried as she entered the parlour, 'he is *here*. I cannot imagine why Freddie told her to invite him. It will spoil everything.'

'Why, what can you mean?'

Rosalyn looked at her in surprise. Beatrice was obviously agitated. She paced about the room in distress for some seconds, before turning to face Rosalyn.

'Bernard Harrington is here! Aunt Patricia invited him without telling me. It seems he is in some financial difficulty. Oh, I do wish he had not come!'

'You cannot believe he would dare to embarrass you in *that* way?' Rosalyn said. 'Not now that you are to marry?' She saw the fear and revulsion in the girl's face and moved towards her instinctively. 'If he dared to lay a finger on you, Freddie would take a horse whip to him. You have only to tell him what you fear and—'

'It would cause a terrible scene,' Beatrice said, biting her bottom lip to stop it trembling. 'I really cannot tell Freddie—but you must promise never to leave me alone with Bernard. Please, Rosalyn. I should die if he tried to kiss me again. He makes me go cold all over. He is the most detestable man I have ever met. Truly he is.'

'Do you not think you might be overreacting?' Rosalyn asked, looking at her flushed cheeks. 'Could it not be that you have allowed a small incident to play too much on your mind?'

'No!' Beatrice shuddered. 'It is the way he looks at me as if… Oh, I cannot tell you. You must believe me! You must.'

Rosalyn could see she was nearly hysterical. She took her hands, holding them, calming her.

'I do believe you, dearest,' she said, 'and I shall do everything in my power to protect you.'

Rosalyn still felt it would be best if Beatrice were to confide her fears in Freddie, but she realised that would be too painful and embarrassing for the girl. Perhaps it would be better if nothing were said just yet, but if she considered Beatrice to be in danger, she would tell Freddie herself.

Rosalyn had thought Beatrice might be overreacting until she herself met the man later that morning. He was without doubt a repulsive creature, his face a pasty white and bloated, with dead, reptilian eyes that seemed to strip a woman naked.

No wonder Beatrice was frightened of him! Rosalyn was conscious of some apprehension herself, despite his many efforts to ingratiate himself with her.

'I have heard so much about you,' he said, bowing over her hand as they were introduced. 'You are far more lovely than the rumours…which I assure you are rife in town. They say Davenport and Forster were at each other's throats over you at Renshaw's ball.'

Rosalyn removed her hand from his moist grasp, barely repressing a shudder as she surreptitiously wiped it on her gown a moment or so later. It took all her resolution not to betray her extreme dislike of him, but for the time being she had no alternative other than to show him the politeness she owed to her brother's guests.

'You flatter me, sir. I am sure it was nothing but a friendly rivalry—a jest for the evening, no more.'

'I do assure you it is true, Miss Eastleigh. Do not tell me that neither of them came up to scratch? Can they be such fools?'

His attempts to flirt with her made Rosalyn's skin crawl. She saw Mrs Jenkins watching with a complacent smile. Good gracious! Could she be condoning his pursuit of a woman she had almost accused of having fallen from grace—of having consorted in the garden with a lover? Surely not! She would not consider Rosalyn a fitting wife for her brother, would she?

And yet there had been a subtle change in Mrs Jenkins's

manner towards her. She was not exactly friendly...more watchful, wary. What could she be thinking?

Rosalyn's fortune was not exceptional. Her trust provided her with a comfortable independence, but she imagined her capital could not be more than five or six thousand pounds. She had never bothered to go into details, but supposed it would be released if she married.

Surely the brother and sister could not be considering the idea? No, no, it was quite ridiculous! Rosalyn dismissed the thought...and yet an uncomfortable suspicion lingered as the days passed and he continued to pay her fulsome compliments.

Rosalyn did her best to ward off his unwanted attentions without being rude. She was better able to cope with his advances than poor Beatrice, who stayed as close as possible to Freddie and barely opened her mouth when Bernard Harrington was in the room.

Even Maria confided she could not like him, and Sarah Jane could not be brought to stay in the room if he was there.

'He is so ugly,' she told Rosalyn with a shudder. 'And those eyes—ugh! *You* have to be polite to him, I suppose, but I don't. I am only a child. I'm not expected to understand Society manners.'

The look on her face was pure wickedness. Sarah Jane was not above claiming to be grown up when it suited her. However, she was seldom in the house these days. If she wasn't taking Sheba for a walk, she was out riding with one of the grooms. Her new regime of exercise suited her, bringing a fresh bloom to her cheeks.

Freddie's manner towards Harrington was at best brusque.

'I wish he would take himself off,' he confided to Rosalyn in a private moment. 'But I cannot ask him to leave.'

Only Harrington's sister seemed pleased to have him staying, so it surprised Rosalyn to hear them having harsh words when she came in from the garden the day before Beatrice's dance.

She paused outside the door of her parlour, not liking to enter when they were so obviously having an argument.

'I've told you before, Bernard,' Mrs Jenkins was saying. 'I am willing to pay any reasonable debts from tradesmen— but not your losses at the card tables. You must find some way of paying them yourself.'

'I would if I could,' he replied. 'Damn it, Patricia! I would not have come to you if there was any other way. I've mortgaged my land to the hilt. Even if I sold everything, I could not pay a third of what I owe. Now this damned lawyer is pressing me to settle my notes.'

'I thought you said they were owed to gentlemen who would give you time to sort out your affairs?'

'I thought they would, but apparently the notes have been sold on and the new creditor is determined to be paid. It is a damned nuisance, but perfectly legal. I am obliged to pay—or face the consequences.'

'Could you not see this person, ask him to be reasonable? Even if I were to pay a part of what you owe, I could not release the money for some weeks.'

'The lawyer has given me two weeks. After that, they will apply to the courts…and I'll be finished. I've given notes on property that no longer belongs to me, Patricia; land I have already mortgaged to the bank. That's fraud; I shall go to prison for it.'

'Then you must do something about it,' his sister said sharply. 'Marry Miss Eastleigh. Her capital is nearly fifteen thousand, though I doubt she knows it. I saw the papers in Sir Frederick's desk when we were in London. She can dispose of the money as she pleases once she is married.'

'She wouldn't have me. I dare say she could take a pick of half-a-dozen fellows if she cared to—but they say she does not wish to marry.'

'Then think of some way to persuade her…'

Rosalyn turned away in disgust, having heard more than enough. Mrs Jenkins should be ashamed of herself for trying to foist her brother on an unsuspecting victim—except that Rosalyn was neither unsuspecting or a victim. She would not in any case have married Bernard Harrington, and now she would take good care never to be alone with him.

Rosalyn was in her bedroom changing for dinner that evening when Sarah Jane burst in. Her hair was hanging loose about her shoulders, her gown had been torn and there was a scratch on her cheek.

'What has happened to you?' Rosalyn cried, terrible thoughts chasing through her mind. Had the girl fallen from her horse, or was there something more sinister behind her dishevelled appearance? 'Are you hurt, dearest? Did someone try to harm you?'

Sarah Jane was fighting for breath. 'No, I'm not hurt,' she managed to gasp out. 'It isn't me, it's Jared—they are trying to kidnap him. Two men…enemies of his father…'

'What?' Rosalyn laid down her hairbrush with a clatter. 'Tell me more details, Sarah. Two men, you say—where are they?'

'In the field behind the orchard,' Sarah said, recovering her breath. 'Sheba is with him, fighting them, but Rajib is hurt and I think they may kill Jared. He told me to run away, but I came to fetch you. We must help them. We must!'

'We shall certainly try,' Rosalyn said. 'And we must hurry.'

Her long hair was hanging loose about her face and she was still wearing her blue silk wrapping-gown over her chemise. She did not stop to bother with her clothes. Instead, she went over to her dressing chest and took out one of a pair of pistols that had belonged to her father, which she had kept by her after his death. She had recently cleaned and loaded it, in case someone tried to pay an unexpected and unwelcome visit to her room. Picking it up, she looked at Sarah Jane.

'Find Freddie, if you can—but stay here in the house. Do not follow me. It may be dangerous.'

'What are you going to do?'

'Whatever is necessary,' Rosalyn said. 'Tell no one else but Freddie—and stay here.' She did not wait to hear the girl's answer.

It took only a few seconds to run down the stairs. Maria called to her, but Rosalyn did not look back as she left the house and ran across the lawns towards the orchard. Later, she would ask Sarah how she had happened to be with Jared when he was attacked, but for now all she could think of was that she might be too late. Damian had told her the youth's life had been in danger in India, but she had not dreamed there were would be another attempt on him here—and in broad daylight!

She ran faster, lifting the skirt of her dressing gown so that it did not impede her, heart pounding, lips moving in fervent prayer: let her be in time. These men must not be allowed to snatch Jared, for it would mean almost certain death for him. Please, God! Let her be in time!

Had it not been for Sheba, Rosalyn might very well have arrived too late. The terrifying scene that met her eyes as she left the orchard and began to run up the pasture land beyond was something she would always remember in her nightmares. Sheba was defending her friend with all her strength, growling and snapping ferociously.

Rosalyn saw the bitch jump at one of the men, biting his leg and shaking her head as if he were a rabbit. She heard the man's scream of pain. A second man carried a long, curving sword which he was using to try and fight off the brave animal. Before Rosalyn could reach them, she saw the blade flash out and suddenly Sheba lay still, her coat stained with the blood that was draining out of the deep wound in her neck.

Rosalyn saw one of the men try to grab Jared, who seemed stunned and could only stare at the lifeless body of the animal he had loved. Lying face down on the ground a few yards away was another man—a man Rosalyn imagined must be Jared's servant Rajib.

She did the only thing she could think of and fired in the direction of the second assassin, who was holding his leg and leaving the capture of Jared to his companion. Her ball went wide, as indeed it must, for she was not near enough, nor sufficiently skilled to hit him. However, her shot had a powerful effect on both the men. They stared at her as she took aim more carefully this time, then the injured one started screaming something in his native tongue; he began to hobble away as fast as he could, and was followed a few seconds later by his companion.

Rosalyn reached the top of the rise, steadying her right hand with her left as she aimed the pistol and fired once more. Her shot was close enough to cause a scream of fear as the ball whistled past the nearest man; it terrified him and both men fled as if the devil were after them. Her momentary feeling of elation faded as she turned to see Jared cradling Sheba in his arms. He looked up at her, tears streaming down his cheeks.

'She saved me,' he said in a choking voice. 'They would have killed me—but Sheba saved me and now she is dead.'

Rosalyn's eyes filled with tears as she saw it was true. Sadness swept over her. She had loved the noisy, tiresome creature—but not as Jared had, not with a love that hurt as his so plainly did. He stared up at her pitifully, his dark eyes reflecting the depth of his pain and anger.

'Sheba loved you,' she said, laying her hand on his bowed head. Her heart went out to him in his grief and loneliness: the bitch had been all he had to love. 'She was a brave dog and died as she would have wanted, saving her beloved master.'

'She was your dog, *mem-sahib*.'

'No, she was yours,' Rosalyn replied. 'She chose you— and I was happy with that choice.'

Hearing a moan behind her, Rosalyn turned and then went over to where Rajib lay on the ground. His clothes were heavily stained with blood. He had been stabbed several times in the chest and arm, having fought valiantly to prevent the kidnappers taking his master's son. She knelt beside him as he opened his eyes.

'It is all right,' she said. 'Jared is safe. But you are badly hurt. We must get you home.'

'My master's son...' Rajib looked beyond her, then sighed with relief as he saw Jared still kneeling by the dog; he closed his eyes again. 'I heard the shots. You came in time, *mem-sahib*. I owe you a debt of honour. If you had not come, if they had taken him, I should have died of shame.'

As Rosalyn had always suspected, he spoke perfect English, but until now he had not chosen to speak to her. She understood now his presence in her garden the night Sheba had attacked him, and his resentment at her interference: he had been merely doing his duty, trying to protect a wilful, unhappy boy.

'It was fortunate that Sarah found me so quickly,' Rosalyn said as she realised he was trying to rise. 'Can you walk if we help you? Or shall I send for someone to carry you on a gate?'

'I think I can walk...'

He groaned as he flopped over to one side and managed to kneel, then, clearly in great pain, forced himself to stand upright. Rosalyn took his uninjured arm, helping to support him, and he muttered his thanks.

'Come, Jared,' Rosalyn said. 'We shall send someone to fetch Sheba later. She will be buried in the gardens of my home—but you can visit her grave whenever you wish. You must help me with Rajib. He needs urgent attention or he may bleed to death.'

'Yes.' Jared stood up. His manner was quiet and dignified as he came to stand with her as she helped Rajib to remain on his feet. He looked apologetically at his servant. 'You almost gave your life for me, too,' he said. 'Damian was right. I should not have disobeyed you. I should have stayed close to the house as you bade me. Will you forgive me, Rajib?'

'It was my duty to protect you,' Rajib said. 'I knew it made you angry—but my master bade me watch over you.'

'Thank you. Please lean on me, Rajib. Miss Eastleigh will help you if you put your arm over her shoulder.'

'It is not fitting, *mem-sahib*.' Rajib hesitated. 'You will get blood on your clothes.'

'Then I shall buy a new dressing gown,' Rosalyn replied. 'Please do not waste your breath in arguing, Rajib. We must get you home before you bleed to death—and before those assassins can return.'

'They will not come back,' Rajib said. 'To run from a woman will shame them. They will not return—but others will come in their place. Jared is not safe here. He will not be safe until his father takes a new heir.'

'Damian will take me away,' Jared replied. 'As soon as he knows what has happened…he will take me somewhere they cannot find me.'

It was a long, difficult process getting Rajib back to Orford Hall, but somehow they managed it between them. Rosalyn was less worried by the weight of his body, which almost caused her to stumble once or twice, than by her very real fear that he was losing too much blood and might die. However, when they were nearly at the house, a man came striding out to meet them, and she breathed a sigh of relief as Damian took the burden of the injured man from her.

'Rosalyn! My God! Let me help you,' he commanded. 'Rajib, lean on me.' He shouted and servants came running from the house to help. 'This man is badly injured. Take him inside and summon Nessa to tend him. I shall come in a moment.'

'I have failed you, *sahib*,' Rajib gasped weakly. 'I should have protected Jared. You should dismiss me—send me away.'

'You did all you could and almost lost your life in the process,' Damian said grimly. 'Do not talk now. Go with the others, Rajib. Your wounds must be dressed before you bleed to death. We shall speak later and decide what must be done to protect Jared.'

Rajib was silent, his head bowed in shame. In his own estimation he had betrayed the trust placed in him, and owed his life to the prompt action of an Englishwoman. Something that would not sit easily with his pride, but he held his tongue and allowed himself to be led away by the servants.

'Thank goodness you are back!' Rosalyn said when Rajib had been borne into the house by willing hands. 'I shall feel safer knowing you are here to watch over Jared.'

'What has happened?' He looked at her anxiously. 'Are you hurt also? And Jared? What has been going on?'

'After Rajib was wounded, Sheba tried to protect me— but they killed her and it was Miss Eastleigh who saved us,' Jared told him. 'It was my fault, Damian. I have disobeyed you by leaving the grounds every day. They knew where to find me. I made it easy for them.'

'That does not make it your fault,' Damian said grimly. 'It was my duty to protect you. I should not have stayed away so long.' He looked at Rosalyn's pale face. 'Will you come up to the house and let me give you something for the shock?'

Rosalyn hesitated, glancing down at herself. 'I ought to go back,' she said, realising all at once how she was dressed. 'I must see to poor Sheba—and explain to my family. They will be wondering what has happened.'

'I shall come with you—you cannot walk home alone.'

'You are needed here. The men who attacked Jared have fled. I shall be safe enough.' She lifted her hand, showing him her pistol. 'I believe I can protect myself if need be.'

'It seems you have already proved it.' His smile was so tender it almost overset her. 'Go then, if you wish. I shall come to the orchard tonight,' Damian promised. 'If you can slip away, meet me there. We must talk.'

'At half past eleven,' she replied, giving him a fleeting smile. 'Take care of them, Damian. Jared needs you now. Stay with him.' Then she turned and began to run back the way she had come, before she weakened and gave into the prompting of her heart.

Rosalyn did not want Damian to realise she was on the verge of an attack of nerves. Her thoughts on hearing of the danger threatening Jared had been solely for him, and afterwards she had known she must help the injured Rajib. Only now did she begin to think of her own situation. She was wandering the countryside improperly dressed. If any of her neighbours chanced to see her, they would think she had gone mad!

More worrying was what Mrs Jenkins would make of it! Rosalyn could only hope that no one would see her return. What must she look like? Her wrapping-gown was stained with blood, her hair blown into a tangle by the wind—and she was still clutching her father's heavy pistol!

The picture that presented itself to Rosalyn's mind was so funny that she laughed, and then the tears came. For a moment she was shaken by a storm of grief and delayed shock. Poor Sheba was dead. Rajib might yet die of his wounds—and she was beginning to feel decidedly odd. Oh, how very foolish of her! This really would not do: she must stop immediately.

She found a kerchief and wiped her face, smearing it where some of Rajib's blood had mingled with her tears, then she took a deep breath and lifted her head. There was nothing to cry about: it was all over! What a very silly woman she was to be sure, and how fortunate that Damian was not there to see her give way to weakness.

She blew her nose, feeling much restored, then slowed her pace to a walk as her home came in sight. There, she was almost home and could now put the whole incident from her mind.

It was not to be expected that she could reach her own room unobserved. Freddie was in the hall surrounded by servants, who were all making a lot of noise but doing nothing.

Maria was with them. She gave a shrill scream as Rosalyn entered.

'You have been hurt!' she cried as she saw the dried blood and thought the worst. 'Oh, I knew it—and it is all that foolish child's fault. If she had gone to Freddie as she ought...'

'Stop talking nonsense!' Rosalyn commanded. 'What is going on here? Freddie—Sheba is dead. Send someone to fetch her from the pasture, please. I shall have her buried in Mama's rose garden. I must go and change. I dare say dinner is already ruined.'

'Sheba has been found and I've had her brought back to the stables,' Freddie said, sounding relieved to have his sister returned apparently none the worse for her adventure. 'What happened, Ros? We thought you must have been kidnapped.'

'Thanks to Father's pistol I wasn't, nor was Jared,' she replied. 'The Indian servant—Rajib—was injured. Jared and I took him home. He could barely walk so it was a long and awkward journey. I am sorry if you were worried—but did you have to tell everyone, Freddie? I meant you to keep it to yourself.'

'Freddie was worried when he found the body of that poor dear dog,' Maria said, completely forgetting all the times she had called Sheba a wretched animal. 'We were wondering how best to search for you.'

Rosalyn nodded. She glanced beyond her cousin to where Mrs Jenkins and her brother were standing, watching the commotion in silence. Rosalyn saw disapproval in the other woman's face, and a look in Bernard Harrington's eyes that sent a cold shiver down her spine.

'I must apologise for my appearance,' she said, addressing the older woman. 'I was dressing when Sarah Jane came to me—and there was no time to finish. I had to act immediately. Had I wasted even another second, I believe I must have been too late. I fired at the assassins just after they killed Sheba—I dare not think what might have happened had I delayed.'

'You should of course have informed Sir Frederick,' Mrs Jenkins said, her mouth screwed up into a sour look. 'However, if what you say is true, it would seem you have acted bravely and with no thought for yourself. We can only hope that no harm to your reputation is sustained from roaming about the countryside in…what is hardly suitable attire.'

'You are too harsh, Patricia,' objected her brother, a gleam in his eyes. 'For myself, I admire Miss Eastleigh. I take it you scared the ruffians off, ma'am?'

'Had I been closer I should not have hesitated to shoot them,' Rosalyn assured him. 'My father taught me to protect myself. He gave me a small pistol to take with me when I ride out alone—but I thought this would be more useful today.' She showed them the gun, which was an odd-looking thing with multiple chambers. 'You see, it fires more than once.'

'I have one of Mr Wheeler's contraptions myself,' said Bernard Harrington. 'An ingenious tool, but seldom reliable. You were brave to use such a weapon, Miss Eastleigh. It could have exploded in your face.'

'As you see, it did not.' Rosalyn was made uncomfortable by the look in his eyes, and very aware that every line of her body must be visible to his gaze through the soft silk of her wrapping-gown. 'Maria—please inquire if some kind of a dinner can be rescued. I must change, but I shall be down in fifteen minutes.'

She hurried away. If she could have followed her own inclination, she would have liked to lie down for an hour, but there had already been too much disturbance. The sooner everything was back to normal the better because, once they had all retired for the night, she would be able to slip away to meet Damian.

Chapter Eight

'Will this cause more trouble for you, my love?' They were in the orchard, alone in the moonlight. Damian stood with his arms about her, gazing down into her eyes. 'I ought not to have asked you to meet me, but it was such a shock when I saw you come back with Rajib: realising what a risk you had taken—what might have happened to you. You could have been killed, my darling.'

He looked so concerned that Rosalyn reached up to kiss him. His arms tightened about her, the kiss deepening to one of such intense passion that it shook them both.

'I love you too much to lose you now,' Damian murmured. 'I want you so badly—need you in my life. Come with me now, my darling. This very night. Soon, I am going to take Jared somewhere safe. Somewhere his enemies will not find him. You could come with us, then we need never be apart again.'

'I wish I could come with you tonight,' Rosalyn said, her voice soft and full of longing. 'If it were not for Freddie and Beatrice, I would—but I have given my promise. Mrs Jenkins is capable of cancelling the wedding even now. At the moment she is being polite to me, perhaps because she hopes I will marry her brother. Of course I shan't, but...'

'My God!' Damian exclaimed, startled. His eyes narrowed, becoming angry. 'Is that man here? You do not mean to tell me that Bernard Harrington is actually staying at your house?'

'Yes. Yes, he is—why?' She saw the expression of anger and disgust on his face and her skin prickled with goose bumps. 'What is it, Damian? Please tell me.'

'He is evil,' Damian said in a voice thick with emotion. 'You must be very careful, Rosalyn. Take care never to be alone with him. Promise me, you will be very careful.'

Rosalyn's gaze became thoughtful. 'Beatrice told me he has made her afraid of him. I dislike him very much—but what has he done that you should call him evil?'

Damian hesitated, then inclined his head. He had kept the secret for so many years, but now he must speak out—for her sake.

'He raped a young woman. She was not much more than a child, only seventeen. A shy, delicate, pretty girl—very much like Miss Holland.'

'I thought it was his brother who did that? I have heard the old rumours, Damian—was that not the reason why you fought a duel with Roderick Harrington, over a woman?'

'It seems I have kept silence to no avail. You are not the only one to have guessed what I have tried so hard to keep secret. Yes, my darling, the duel was over a young woman. Helen was like a sister to me,' Damian said, his expression showing both remembered grief and outrage. 'We lived within a few miles of one another and I visited my friends often. One day, I found Helen weeping bitterly in the garden of her home. At first she shied away from me, would not tell me what was distressing her so much—then, because she had always trusted me, at the last she told me what had happened. Roderick forced her into his carriage when she was walking back from the village to her home. She fought him but he was too strong for her and she was so frightened that she fainted. Something unspeakable happened to her later that day; she would not tell me all the details, but I believed I knew.'

'That was wickedness indeed,' Rosalyn said, feeling sickened by the tale, 'but what has it to do with Bernard Harrington?'

'Nothing, or so I thought then. I comforted Helen, promised to avenge her and left her sitting there in the sunlight…by that evening she was dead. She had taken something poisonous…some plant or berry she had found growing in the garden.'

'Oh, that is terrible!' Rosalyn cried. She had not realised the extent of the tragedy until this moment. 'The poor, poor girl…to take her own life! How unhappy she must have been.'

'She was ashamed,' Damian said grimly. 'I think she regretted telling even me. It was more than she could bear and so she took her own life. When I heard how she had died, I went after Roderick and forced a duel on him. I was young then and hot-tempered. I wanted to make him pay for what he had done. He tried to tell me he had not himself abused her, but I would not listen. It was only later that I learned the truth.'

'It was Bernard?' Rosalyn's face went white with shock. 'That is what you are saying, isn't it?'

'Apparently, he boasted of it to one of his cronies, and my father heard the story. He told me I had killed an innocent man, accused me of murder, then banished me. He did not tell me he knew Bernard was guilty. I learned that only a few weeks ago, from papers my father left when he died. All these years I have been tortured, not knowing for sure…wondering if I had mistaken Helen's meaning.'

'That was not kind of him.' Rosalyn sensed Damian's pain—and the guilt he must have felt when he discovered that he had forced a duel on the wrong man. Roderick was not innocent, but there was another more to blame. 'You must have been out of your mind with grief and guilt.'

Damian's expression did not change. 'Father never cared for me, and he had lost a great deal of money to Bernard Harrington at the card tables. He blamed me for his losses.'

'How could it be your fault?'

'He said he could not refuse Harrington's challenge, because of what I had done, and that he had been cheated. He was angry, blaming me for having become embroiled in a matter that did not concern me.'

'Your father said he was cheated—did you believe him?'

'I was never sure, but now I think it may well have been the truth.'

Rosalyn asked what he meant, and he explained about the incident he had recently witnessed at the gaming hell.

'What are you going to do?' she asked, gazing up at him fearfully. 'Will you take revenge for what he did to Helen—and for your father's sake?'

Damian saw the anxiety in her eyes. He touched her cheek, marvelling at the softness of her skin, at the sweet perfume that seemed always to cling about her. There had been other women in his life over the years, but none had ever aroused such feelings in him before.

'Do not distress yourself,' he said, smiling at her. 'Mr Harrington will be brought to book for crimes other than rape—or cheating at the tables. I have purchased notes far above the worth of his estates. He will in time be arrested for debt and probably spend some time in prison. I believe he deserves at least that—and it will close the door on the past for me. I do not require revenge for myself, only that he should receive some punishment for his crimes.'

'I am glad you do not mean to fight a duel,' she said softly. 'I could not bear it if you were killed.'

'If we had not met, I might have thought it worth the risk,' Damian said in a voice caught with emotion. 'But now…' He drew her to him, kissing her tenderly once more. 'When I asked you to come away with me just now it was in a moment of madness, because I want you so much, but it was wrong of me. If you will have me, my darling, I should like to marry you.'

Rosalyn's face lit up with joy. 'Oh, Damian! You know I will. I would have lived with you as your mistress, but to be your wife is all the happiness I could ask of life.'

'We may have to go away for a time—to live abroad. I am thinking of adopting Jared as my own, of giving him my name. You would not object to that—to what others might think or say?'

'Of course not.' She touched her fingers to his lips, smiling at him with love in her eyes. 'I am already very fond of him. I am sure I shall come to love him as if he were my own. Besides, he needs to be loved—and I know you care for him.'

'I imagined you might say that.' Damian trailed a finger down her throat, letting it rest for a moment on the tiny pulse spot at the base. 'You are so generous. Because of what happened today, I may have to take him away before the wedding—but, once he is safe, I shall return to claim you.'

'Must you go at once?'

'We cannot leave for a few days. Rajib is too weak to move just yet—but as soon as he is well enough, I shall leave. Perhaps without telling you. Do not fear that I have deserted you. I would never leave you—unless you told me to go.'

Rosalyn felt her love swell and grow within her. She could not imagine ever wanting him to leave her side.

'Shall we meet again before you leave?'

'It is Miss Holland's dance tomorrow evening, is it not? You will be too tired to meet me afterwards—but perhaps the following day? In the afternoon. I do not like the idea of your wandering about alone at night. Particularly as Harrington is a guest in your home.' He drew her close, kissing her again. 'Promise me you will be careful. If he harmed you—I *would* kill him!'

'Do not say such things.' Rosalyn laughed up at him. 'You are worrying for nothing. He saw Papa's pistol earlier this morning. He knows I am capable of firing it. You must not be concerned for me, Damian. Mr Harrington will not dare to harm me.' She leaned towards him, pressing herself against his body, offering her mouth for his kiss. 'How I long to be with you, my dear one, to know the sweetness of your love. Kiss me one last time, then I must leave you.'

Her honesty, her sensuality, was almost too much for him. He held her close to him; his need to have her, to know the intimate secrets of her lovely body, was overwhelming. Only his sense of honour, the caution that told him it was she who might suffer if he lost control, held him back. He wanted her so desperately, burned for her, but knew their plans might falter, be delayed. No matter how much he needed her, her safety came first. He must be strong now, because her love was so natural, so trusting, that she would willingly give whatever he asked of her.

'You must go back,' he murmured against her throat. 'I shall come with you, to make certain you are safe.'

'It is best if no one sees you. Come only as far as the shrubbery, Damian. You can watch over me from there.'

'Sheba was a better guardian than I thought,' he said, frowning. 'I wish you had her still.'

'Poor Sheba,' Rosalyn replied sadly. 'She was often a trouble to me, but she died bravely. Had it not been for her, I should surely have been too late. You must buy Jared another dog when we are settled, Damian. He needs something of his own to tend and love.'

'I have thought the same,' he said. They were walking with their arms about one another. 'It is a nuisance that I must take him away from here, but I have no choice. It is both my duty and my earnest wish to protect him from his enemies.'

'We shall be together soon,' she said and turned to him, reaching up to kiss him on the lips. 'Come no further, my love. Mrs Jenkins is an uneasy sleeper. She saw us in the gardens once before, and though I am decently dressed this time, I would prefer her not to see us together again—at least for the moment.'

'I shall watch until you are safely in the house,' Damian said, releasing her reluctantly. He did not want to let her go, was frightened that something would happen to part them—that he would lose this woman he loved with a passion that was so intense it shocked even him. 'Until the day after tomorrow—at three?'

'Wait for me in the orchard. I shall come to you as soon as I can.'

With that, they parted. Rosalyn ran across the lawn towards the house, but though she paused to glance back before entering through the French windows, she resisted the temptation to wave.

Damian was watching her. He would make certain she was safe inside the house. What neither of them could know was that someone else had seen her run across the lawns.

Bernard Harrington hid behind the curtains as Rosalyn locked the French windows after her. He could not be certain, but he believed he had caught a glimpse of a man standing in the shadows out there.

Why had Miss Eastleigh been walking alone at night? Had she been meeting a lover? His curiosity was aroused. Patricia's suggestion that he should marry her had perhaps held more merit than he'd imagined. Her fortune was not large, but it would stave off his ruin for a while—and his luck at the tables must surely change! Until the last year or so he had won almost as often as he lost, without resorting to cheating too often, though there had been times when he had considered it worth the risk.

With Miss Eastleigh as his wife, he could regain the respectability he had lost. He would be welcomed in the best houses again—and might soon recoup at least a part of his fortune. He had thought his cause impossible. The haughty Miss Eastleigh would dismiss an offer of marriage from him with the contempt it deserved—but if she had a lover there was hope.

She would have married the man if it were possible. He must be married—one of her neighbours, almost certainly. How long had it been going on? Harrington's thin lips parted in an unpleasant smile. It would cause a fine scandal if it all came out. She would do almost anything to prevent that—Miss Eastleigh and that pompous brother of hers. Harrington had seen the way they looked at him, known he was on sufferance only because he was Patricia's brother.

It would humble their damned pride if he threatened to expose Miss Eastleigh's little affair. From now on he would keep his eyes open—and if she slipped off on her own again, he would follow her.

Unaware of the plot being hatched against her, Rosalyn went swiftly up to her own room. She locked her door—something she had never thought necessary before—and began to undress. Her head was full of dreams as she sat brushing her hair before the dressing mirror. She had never felt so alive, so full of anticipation in her whole life.

In little more than a week, the wedding would be over. Once all the guests had gone, her life would be her own again, to order as she wished. She might have to wait for a little while for Damian to fetch her—but then she would go with him.

She had been willing to follow her heart, to live with Damian as his mistress, but now he had asked her to marry him. Her body felt as light as thistledown as she went to bed, leaning across to blow out the candle beside her bed.

She was smiling as she fell asleep.

'Are you enjoying yourself, Beatrice?' Rosalyn asked as the young woman came up to her. Her face was flushed from dancing a rather energetic polka with one of their neighbours. He was a hearty country squire, red-faced, good-natured but not an accomplished dancer. 'You look warm. Why don't you ask Freddie to take you outside for a few minutes?'

'Yes, perhaps I shall.' Beatrice looked nervously across the room. 'Mr Harrington asked me to dance with him next—but I really do not want to. His touch is unpleasant to me, Rosalyn, but I did not know how to refuse him.'

'Tell Freddie you are feeling over-warm,' advised Rosalyn, 'and tell him you do not want to dance with your aunt's brother. He will protect you. He will know how to handle it. You must let him do that for you, Beatrice—now and in the future. It will make things much easier for you.'

'*He* is coming this way,' Beatrice whispered. 'Oh, there's Freddie looking for me. I shall go to him.'

Rosalyn frowned as she hurried away. What had Bernard Harrington done to make her so nervous of him? It had surely been more than an attempt at a kiss?

Was it time she had a private word with her brother? After Damian's revelations, it was clear that Mr Harrington was more of a danger than she had supposed. It might be wise to put Freddie on his guard. Indeed, it was her duty to do so.

'I was about to claim Beatrice for this dance,' Harrington said as he came up to Rosalyn. 'Why did she run off like that?'

'She felt too warm,' Rosalyn replied, avoiding his eyes. 'I believe Freddie is taking her out for some air.'

'She was always a nervous girl, excitable and prone to fancies,' he said, a scowl of displeasure on his face. 'I dare say all this excitement and fuss has been too much for her.'

'Perhaps—though I would not have called her exactly nervous. No more than other young ladies of her age.'

'You, of course, are more worldly,' Harrington said, a

sudden gleam in his eyes. 'I admire that in a woman, Miss Eastleigh.'

'I am older,' replied Rosalyn, wishing he would go away and leave her in peace. His next words told her that her hopes were doomed to disappointment.

'May I hope that you will do me the honour of standing up with me, Miss Eastleigh?'

Rosalyn would have liked to refuse, but she had no prior engagement for the dance now starting, and felt it would seem rude to refuse. He was a guest in her home, and she must try to be polite to him, little though she relished it. And, since it was a lively country dance, she would not be condemned to his company the whole time.

'Thank you, sir,' she said, allowing him to take her hand.

His grasp was moist, unpleasant to the touch, but Rosalyn was able to bear it for the duration of the set pieces she was obliged to perform with him. Afterwards, he thanked her and wandered off in the direction of the library, where card tables had been set up for some of the older guests who did not care to dance.

Rosalyn breathed a sigh of relief. Now that there was no further need to see or speak to Mr Harrington, she could give herself up to the pleasures of the evening.

'Rosalyn, my dear.' She turned as Mrs Buckley came up to her. 'You look very handsome this evening—that dress becomes you. Indeed, I have scarcely seen you look so well. I declare there is quite a new sparkle about you, my love.'

'That is because I am happy, Aunt.'

'You are in love!' Her aunt quizzed her with her lorgnette. 'At last! You cannot imagine how often I have longed for this. Tell me, who is the lucky man?' She laughed and tapped Rosalyn on the arm with her long-handled spectacles. 'No need, my dear. Unless I much mistake things, it is Mr Wrexham—or the Earl Marlowe, as he ought properly to be called. Where is he? Point him out to me. I am anxious to meet him.'

'Damian isn't here, Aunt.'

'Not here? Am I wrong?' Rosalyn shook her head. 'Why has he not come this evening?'

'Mrs Jenkins objects to his being in the house while she is staying. It was her younger brother—the duel all those years ago. One cannot blame her, it is a most unfortunate circumstance—and very awkward for us. You recall telling me something about the old rumours?'

'Yes, most certainly I do. I have discovered the truth of it, Rosalyn—and I must tell you that I consider Mr Wrexham—as he then was—to have been unjustly treated by his whole family. They cast him out, when they ought to have honoured him for ridding society of a disgraceful rogue.'

'It was actually worse than you might imagine,' Rosalyn said. A shiver went down her spine as she recalled the dance she had been forced to share with Mr Harrington. 'I dare say you do not know the whole story. Indeed, I did not learn it myself until yesterday—and now is not the time to speak of such things.'

'No. You are very right to remind me.' Mrs Buckley frowned. 'Here comes Freddie, and Beatrice. She is a delightful girl—though I do not care for her relations. That woman is beyond bearing, so odiously top-lofty. Who does she imagine she is? I dislike the way she speaks to both Freddie and Beatrice.'

'She has been in the habit of having her own way,' Rosalyn said. 'Her husband left her very comfortably off, I believe, and Beatrice's mother left her to Mrs Jenkins's care when she died—so I suppose she thinks she has a perfect right to dictate to her.'

'If one has enormous wealth, one does not need to puff one's consequence in that way. She is very rude, Rosalyn. If she does not mend her manners, I may be forced to give her a set down.'

Knowing her aunt was capable of doing so, Rosalyn laughed. 'I am so glad you have come, Aunt Susan,' she said. 'At least I have an ally in the house, and that makes me feel much better.'

'Have they been upsetting you, my dear?' Mrs Buckley studied her. In her opinion, Freddie had not always behaved as he ought towards his sister. 'You should not have let them, even for Freddie's sake. He has always done as he pleased. He should consider you more.'

'I am quite happy as things are, Aunt,' Rosalyn said and smiled at her. 'When we are alone, I may have some news for you.'

'Indeed?' Mrs Buckley arched her brows. 'If it is what I hope for, it will be good news.'

She turned her attention to Beatrice as she and Freddie came up to them, taking her hand and talking to her kindly.

'Will you dance with me, Ros?' Freddie asked. He frowned as she gave him her hand. 'You were dancing with that fellow Harrington earlier. I should not do that too often if I were you. I do not like him—nor the way he looks at Bea.'

'Neither Beatrice nor I wish for his presence here,' Rosalyn replied. 'I think she is afraid of him, Freddie. I am not exactly sure why—though I can guess. He does have a rather unpleasant way of looking at females. Especially young ones. Even Sarah Jane has complained of it.'

'Damn his impudence!' Freddie said, a glint in his eyes. 'If I thought for one moment—'

'I am sure nothing has happened which ought to disturb your peace of mind,' Rosalyn assured him hastily. Her brother could fly off the handle without warning sometimes. 'Nothing serious—but I believe he is capable of vile behaviour. The very worst. And you should make sure he never has a chance to be alone with Beatrice.'

'What?' Freddie glowered down at her. 'What do you know of Harrington? Why have you not told me this before?'

'Keep your voice down,' she cautioned. 'Now is not the

time to discuss this, Freddie. Stop glaring at me. I have said nothing because I did not want to cause more trouble for you. Mrs Jenkins is fond of her brother. Had I not wanted to avoid another quarrel, I should have refused to dance with him this evening. You know how unpleasant Mrs Jenkins can be, dearest.'

'You do not imagine I would let that deter me?' Freddie saw the look in her eyes and flushed. 'No, no, you wrong me, Ros. This is a very different case. Had I been aware…I shall request Harrington to leave tomorrow.'

'And cause a breach with Mrs Jenkins? She may very well decide to leave—and take Beatrice with her.'

'Mrs Jenkins has given written consent. It would cause a scandal if she withdrew now, and I should make sure everyone understood why. I doubt she would risk it. She may disown Beatrice if she chooses—neither of us cares for that.'

'Do not quarrel with her without speaking to Beatrice, Freddie—and do nothing this evening, please. You do not want to spoil the dance for Beatrice?'

'No…' He was still frowning, though the first flush of anger was abated. 'No, of course not. I wish you had spoken to me sooner about this, Ros. It was very wrong of you not to confide in me—but I dare say no harm has been done. I'll think things through and speak to Bea tomorrow.'

Rosalyn said no more. It was not quite fair of him to blame her. Until Damian revealed the truth to her, she had not known anything of substance. Beatrice ought properly to have confided her fears to her fiancé, but Freddie would not think of it in that way. *She* could do no wrong in his eyes, and he found it easier to blame his sister.

Rosalyn was a little saddened by his thoughtless attitude, but it was not the first time it had happened. Besides, what could it matter? She had only to be patient for another week or so—and then she would be with someone who did care for her feelings.

* * *

For once in her life, Rosalyn decided to spoil herself and have breakfast in bed the next day, so it was well past noon when she finally emerged from her own bedchamber.

The house seemed very quiet, as if it were recovering from the rush and tear of the previous day. When Rosalyn went downstairs, she found Maria removing dead flowers from a vase in the parlour.

'Working again?' Rosalyn chided her with a smile. 'You should have slept in as I did, Maria. I am sure you must be tired. You did so much to make the dance a success last night. I am sure both Freddie and Beatrice are grateful for all your efforts.'

'Yes, it did go well, did it not?' Maria smiled in a contented way. 'Mr Waller—that is to say, Edward and I have decided we shall be married the week after your brother. It will be a very quiet affair, of course, but I should like you to be there if you will.'

'If I can,' Rosalyn promised. 'I am going to tell you something, Maria, but you must not tell anyone—no one at all. Please give me your word?' Her cousin nodded, eyes wide with curiosity. 'I am going away with Mr Wrexham. We shall be married, but not before we leave England, and not until after my brother's wedding. Damian is anxious to settle Jared in a place of safety first, and then he will return to fetch me.'

She had expected Maria to look shocked, but her cousin surprised her by coming to kiss her cheek.

'I have thought there was something, dearest. You seemed so much happier than you had for a very long time. I am exceedingly glad for you—and I wish you happiness. I hope you will keep in touch—write to me now and then?'

'Yes, of course I shall,' Rosalyn said. 'You have been a good friend to me, Maria. Indeed, I do not know what I should have done without you.' She kissed her cousin again. 'Have you seen Freddie this morning, by any chance?'

'He went out half an hour ago,' Maria said, giving her

an odd look. 'He was most unlike himself, Rosalyn. Seemed to be in a bad humour. I asked him what was wrong and he told me it was not my concern—quite sharply. I was a little upset, though I am sure he did not mean to be harsh.'

'Oh, dear.' Rosalyn was disturbed by the news of her brother's ill temper. 'I know he has things on his mind just now, but he should not have been rude to you.'

'Oh, he was not exactly rude,' Maria said. 'At least, I do not mind that; it was just a careless moment, and Sir Frederick does sometimes…well, you know, my love. I was merely concerned that he seemed upset over something. I do hope he has not quarrelled with Beatrice.'

'He was not really annoyed with you,' Rosalyn said, excusing her brother. 'I expect it is all this fuss over the wedding. Men do not enjoy it in their hearts.'

'Yes, perhaps that is so…' Maria glanced up as the housekeeper entered the room. 'Did you want me, Mrs Simmons?'

'It is Mrs Jenkins,' the housekeeper replied, her mouth twisting wryly. 'It seems she has been ill in the night—in pain and vomiting. She says she does not want a doctor—but she looks proper poorly to me, Miss Eastleigh. I wondered if you would take a look at her?'

'Very well, I shall come and see her now,' Rosalyn said. 'It might be wise to send for the doctor—but I shall hear what she has to say.'

She ran hurriedly up the stairs. This was the second time Mrs Jenkins had suffered such an attack—or had it happened more often?

Rosalyn was shocked by Mrs Jenkins's appearance. She had dark violet patches under her eyes and they had an unnatural staring look. It was clear that she was quite ill. Very sick, much more so than she had been in London.

'I am sorry to be so tiresome,' she apologised in such a fading voice that Rosalyn was alarmed. 'I am prone to these attacks. I have my powders, but of late they seem not to help—indeed, I have wondered if they make me worse.'

'You must rest,' Rosalyn insisted. She sat on the edge of the bed and reached for Mrs Jenkins's hand, patting it soothingly: it felt moist and over-warm. 'You are no trouble to us. I am only sorry you feel so unwell at this time.'

'You are…generous.' Her eyes dropped before Rosalyn's clear gaze. 'I am sorry…' She turned away to press a handkerchief to her mouth. 'Forgive me. I feel sick again.'

Rosalyn reached for a small china bowl and held it for her; she waited patiently as she vomited several times, then handed her a damp cloth to wipe her mouth.

'I shall leave you to rest, ma'am,' she said after emptying the bowl into the waste bucket in the pot cupboard and fetching a glass of water. 'A sip or two of this may help. But I think we should have the doctor. He may be able to give you some different powders, which will ease the nausea.'

Mrs Jenkins was too demoralised to protest. The woman she had treated as an enemy, had insulted and threatened, had just shown her more compassion than she could have expected. She felt embarrassed and slightly ashamed, turning her head away as the tears filled her eyes.

In all her life, Patricia Jenkins had only ever loved one person: her brother Roderick. She had done her best to love Bernard. God knew, she had paid enough of his debts—but she could not love him as she had her beloved Roderick. *His* death at such a young age had almost killed her, turning her into the sour woman she now was.

Rosalyn could, of course, know nothing of the older woman's thoughts. Her sympathy had been aroused when she'd seen how unwell Mrs Jenkins was, and she had acted instinctively. She did not consider herself to have been particularly kind. Indeed, she had given no thought to anything other than her guest's comfort.

The stable lad was sent to fetch a doctor. Mrs Simmons was instructed to give every attention to the invalid, and Beatrice was told not to worry.

'It is probably best that you do not go up to Mrs Jenkins for the moment,' Rosalyn advised. 'I do not believe your aunt's illness is infectious, but we must be careful. You would not want to take an infection so close to your wedding.'

'No, of course not.' Beatrice looked anxious. Her face was pale and Rosalyn suspected she might have shed a few tears. 'Have you seen Freddie? He—he was so cross with me earlier. I have been looking for him, but I cannot find him. He is not in the house, or the gardens. Where can he have gone?'

'Maria said he went off earlier. He may have taken one of the horses out.' Rosalyn saw the girl was in a state of acute distress and frowned. What could have happened to make her so upset? 'She said he was in a temper—surely he did not quarrel with you?'

'He…asked me about Bernard,' Beatrice said in a faltering voice. She bit her lip and tears started to her eyes. 'He does not like the way Bernard looks at me…so I told him.' She drew a shaky breath. 'I told him everything, Rosalyn. It was terrible! I was so embarrassed and Freddie was furious. He shouted at me. He has never done that before. He said I ought to have told him all this at once—and that he would not have such a vile creature in his house.'

'I am afraid it is my fault,' Rosalyn said regretfully. 'He said something particular to me last night, and I felt obliged to tell you were nervous of Mr Harrington, but not why. Indeed, I do not know, for you have never said exactly what he did to upset you.'

Beatrice told her in a shame-faced whisper. The words came out haltingly and obviously caused her pain in the telling.

When she had heard the girl's story to its end, Rosalyn was not surprised her brother had flown into a temper: it was far worse than she could ever have imagined. How could Mr Harrington have behaved so badly towards a girl who was a guest in his own sister's home? Yet had he not done something far worse to another young girl? Perhaps Beatrice had been lucky to escape with a fright.

'He actually came into your bedroom and tried to get into bed with you? He put his hands on you? Oh, Beatrice, my dear! That must have been a terrible shock. What did you do?'

'I called for my maid. I had asked her to sleep in my dressing room because I was afraid he might...' Beatrice blushed for shame. 'Alice rushed in and hit him on the shoulder with a hairbrush. He ran off then, but the next day he threatened to tell Aunt Patricia that I had enticed him. He said she would believe him instead of me and I think...I think perhaps she would have.'

'Oh, my dearest girl,' Rosalyn said. 'Surely she could not be so prejudiced—or so stupid? It was a terrible experience for you. And you had no one you could tell, no one to comfort you. No wonder you cannot bear to be near him.'

'I was too ashamed to speak of it,' Beatrice said, smothering a sob. 'I felt that I must have done something wrong, though I could not think what. I never once gave him cause to think me willing, I swear it. It has hung over me like a black cloud—and now Freddie is angry with me.'

'Leave him to mull things over,' Rosalyn advised. 'You have done nothing of which to be ashamed, Beatrice. Freddie is angry because he unwittingly allowed you to be exposed to danger and he feels guilty. He does not blame you, I am sure of it.'

'I really did not give Bernard encouragement to think I might welcome his advances,' the girl said, her lip trembling. 'Not ever. You must believe me. You *must*!'

'I do,' Rosalyn replied and smiled at her encouragingly. 'I have no idea where Freddie has gone, but when he returns I shall tell him something he ought to know.'

'Good God! I can scarcely believe it.' There was revulsion in Freddie's eyes as he looked at Damian across the drum table in the library of Orford Hall. Beatrice's story had shocked and angered him. Furious, and afraid of doing something he might regret, he had rushed out of the house and ridden hell for leather to the Orfords' house, knowing that one person could tell him for certain what he needed to know. 'Do you mean to tell me that I have been harbouring a rapist in my house? And no one told me!' He banged the table with his fist. 'This is monstrous. I had a right to know! Rosalyn should not have kept this from me.'

'You have no reason to blame your sister,' Damian said, frowning. 'Rosalyn did not know herself until the night before your dance. She was shocked and distressed herself. I imagine she wanted to tell you—but was not sure of your reaction.'

'What do you mean? Not sure of my reaction…' Freddie glared at him, expressions of anger and shame warring for supremacy in his face. 'You are thinking that I would have ignored this for the sake of peace? Damn it, Wrexham! I am not such a fool. This cannot be brushed under the carpet. It is too serious, too dangerous. Besides, no matter what her aunt does, Beatrice will marry me. Even if we have to elope. She has assured me of it several times.'

'I am very glad to hear it.' Damian allowed himself a smile. 'You would soon have found Mrs Jenkins had too much influence in your matrimonial affairs had you let her continually have her way.'

'I was concerned for Beatrice's inheritance,' Freddie admitted, looking ashamed. 'But she does not care a fig for it and nor do I. All I want is to be left in peace with her. I'm damned if I'll have that fellow in my home another night. To think that Beatrice has been forced to be polite to him! I can tell you, it turns my stomach, Wrexham. The man ain't fit to live. If I had my way I would take a horse whip to him.'

'He will be punished, you may rest easy on that—but perhaps not in quite the way you suggest.'

'I don't care what happens to him once he's out of my house!'

'I confess I shall feel easier in my mind if he has gone,' Damian said. 'It is my intention to meet Rosalyn in…' he glanced at the gold pocket watch which hung from a chain attached to his waistcoat '…just about an hour's time. After that I shall not be able to see her for some days. The attack on Jared makes it important that I move him to another location—but when I return I shall claim your sister. We shall be married, but not until we have reached our destination. You have my word that my intentions are honourable, and that I shall do my best to make her life as comfortable and happy as possible.'

'And where will you live?' Freddie looked sceptical. 'Some outlandish place abroad, I suppose? Why can you not wait and marry her here? A proper wedding with all her friends about her. Do the decent thing, Wrexham. You cannot expect her to give up everything she knows and loves for your sake?'

Damian hesitated before he answered. 'I believe Rosalyn is well able to make her own decision, Eastleigh. I have a duty to Jared and it may be some years before I could return to this country to live. I do not imagine it would suit her to be kept waiting that long. Indeed, she has told me that she has often longed to travel.'

'I suppose if it is what she wants…' Freddie reluctantly offered his hand '…then of course you have my blessing. But I do not like it. I tell you frankly, sir, it ain't what I want for my sister. She belongs here amongst her friends and family.'

Damian inclined his head, accepting his hand. Sir Frederick was right, of course; what he had to offer was not good enough for a woman like Rosalyn, but he believed he could make her happy. She would have his name, his fortune and his love. It was all he could give her.

Would it be enough? Only time would tell.

Chapter Nine

Rosalyn was detained by her aunt just as she was about to slip away from the house to meet Damian. Mrs Buckley was in high spirits and kept her talking for several minutes, so it was almost a quarter past the hour when she reached the orchard. She had hurried, fearing that Damian might be gone, and was breathless. When she saw him leaning against an apple tree, waiting for her, her heart took a flying leap. How handsome he was—and how very much she had come to love him!

'I am late,' she said as he reached for her hands, holding them and gazing into her face, before bending his head to kiss her lips. Her pulses raced with excitement as he caught her to him. She smiled, looking up at him. 'Forgive me? My aunt had so much to say that I thought I should never manage to get away.'

'Did you not know I would wait?' His eyes teased and challenged her. 'Did you think I should fly into a temper because you were a few minutes late and leave without seeing you?'

'I was not sure. No, of course I did not think that, but you might have been in a hurry to start on your journey.' Rosalyn recovered her breath and laughed at herself. 'I should have known—but I was eager to see you. No, do not laugh at me! You must know I have been longing to see you—that my haste was because I was eager to be with you.'

'No more eager than I to see you,' Damian said, looking deep into her eyes as if he sought her very soul. His wicked smile had gone and now he was serious. 'It will be the last time for a few days. I wish I did not have to leave you, my love—but I fear I must. Jared grows impatient at being almost a prisoner in the house, and who can blame him?'

'No one. Of course you must think of his safety first. It must be almost unbearable for him to stay closed in—especially when the weather is so fine,' she said. 'Where will you take him?'

'To France for the time being—and perhaps we shall all travel on to Spain in a few weeks. Jared will be happiest in a warmer climate. I too have grown accustomed to the heat from my years in India...'

'And I have always loved the sunshine,' Rosalyn said, answering the question in his eyes. 'How exciting it will be, Damian. To see places I have only read of in books, to experience new cultures and meet new people. I have often thought I should enjoy travelling.'

'I believe it will suit you,' he replied with a strange little twist of his lips. 'You are no pale English rose to wilt in the heat of summer, but a more exotic bloom—one best suited to growing wild.'

'How well you know me! Perhaps too well. I shall never be able to have secrets from you.'

Rosalyn's laughter rang out. She went into his arms willingly, lifting her face for his kiss. It felt so right, being held close to him. She had never known such sweetness, such content. Her body swayed into his, melding with his in the heat of their desire.

'I want you so much, my darling,' he whispered huskily into the softness of her fragrant hair. 'I shall always love you. Always want and need you.'

'And I long to be yours.'

Rosalyn felt as if her heart was being drawn from her body as they kissed. She was no longer a separate being, but a part of Damian: without him, she would wither and die like a vine in arid soil.

'You will come back soon?'

'The journey there and back should take me no more than a week,' Damian promised, his thumb smoothing the lips he had just kissed so thoroughly. 'Look for me in the gardens on the eve of your brother's wedding. If I do not come then, I shall the following night or without fail the next.'

'It does not matter. I shall be ready when you come,' she promised. 'Once Freddie is married, there will be nothing to hold me here. We can leave the moment you are ready.'

'It cannot be soon enough for me,' Damian said, drawing her into his arms once more. 'Take care of yourself, my dearest. And remember, I love you. No matter what anyone says to you—I love you and I believe we shall be happy together.'

What did he mean—no matter what anyone said to her? Rosalyn would have asked, but he was kissing her again, kissing her with such tender passion that she let it go. Damian must know that no one could say anything which would make her change her mind about him.

'And now you must go,' he said as he released her. 'You will be missed—and I have work to do if we are to leave this evening.'

'This evening? You mean to travel by night?'

'Jared and I leave on horseback after sunset,' he replied. 'Rajib and Nessa will follow by coach in the morning—that way I hope to avoid being seen and followed by anyone who might try to harm Jared.'

'Do you think the men who attacked him are still around, waiting for another chance?'

'No, I think they have been frightened off—but it is best to be careful. There may be others willing to take their place.' He smiled as he saw her anxious look. 'Do not worry, my love. Nothing will happen to us, I promise you. Jared was attacked because I was not there to protect him. In India I was known for the accuracy of my shooting—a skill much appreciated by villagers being attacked by renegade tigers, I assure you. You need have no fear for my safety.'

'No, of course not.' She smiled at the picture his words conjured up, realising there was so much she did not know of him or the life he had led in India. She reached up to brush her lips over his in a farewell kiss. 'I must go now, but I shall be thinking of you until we meet again.'

From somewhere high above in the branches of an apple tree, a blackbird trilled its song. Rosalyn stood back, gazing at him for a moment longer, then turned resolutely.

She began to walk away, looking round to wave once more before leaving the orchard. Damian was still standing there, feet apart, eyes intent, watching her—as if he were reluctant to leave even though they had said their farewells.

Rosalyn knew an urgent longing to run back to him, to tell him she did not care about her brother's wedding and would go with him that very moment. She fought the urge down, telling herself that she was being very foolish. In a week, Damian would return to her. She could not break her promise to Freddie, nor must she do anything that might spoil Beatrice's wedding day. That would be extremely selfish of her, and might lay heavy on her conscience. No, no, she must be patient a little longer.

Lost in her own thoughts, Rosalyn walked slowly through the shrubbery that led towards the back lawn which in turn led up to her parlour. If she could gain the house without being seen, she might be able to snatch a little time for herself…time to dream, to think of Damian and remember what it felt like to be in his arms, what it would be like when they were married.

Because she was wrapped up in her plans for the future,

she was completely unaware of Bernard Harrington until he suddenly stepped out in front of her, blocking her path.

'Oh!' She was startled to see him. 'Mr Harrington. Where did you come from?'

There was such an odd expression in his eyes! It made her uncomfortable. Why did he look so very pleased with himself?

'I have been watching you,' he said, a sneer of mockery on his lips. 'I saw you meeting your lover in the orchard...'

'You have been spying on me!' Rosalyn was shocked, a feeling of unease going through her as she looked into those cold, merciless eyes. He was so evil! 'That was impertinent of you, sir. What gives you the right to follow me?'

'I saw you alone in the gardens the other night,' he said. 'I guessed then that you had a lover—and so I followed you this afternoon when I saw you slip away. I saw you meet him. Who is he...the husband of one of your neighbours? What a deceitful little slut you are to be sure, the haughty Miss Eastleigh throwing herself into the arms of a man like any common bitch on heat.'

'How dare you!' Rosalyn's hand shot out, striking him across the face. 'How dare you insult me, sir?'

'Whore!' he snarled, catching her wrist. 'I'll teach you to respect your betters! You looked down your nose at me. I saw the disgust in your eyes, as if I were beneath you, some kind of filth from the gutters—and all the time you were sneaking out to meet a lover.'

'You had no right to follow me,' Rosalyn cried, twisting and turning furiously as she tried to break free of his grasp. 'Take your hand off me, sir. What I do is not your affair.'

'I have made it so,' he said, his grip tightening on her wrist, bruising and hurting her as he swung Rosalyn round so that her back was to him. She cried out as he twisted her arm, pressing it hard up against her shoulder blade. He put his other arm about Rosalyn's waist, so that she could not move as he pressed his face close to her ear, spewing out his spiteful threats. 'I have decided you will make me a fine wife. I like women with spirit—and I need your inheritance, my dear. Marry me, and you need never reveal your shame—refuse me and I'll ruin you.'

'I would as soon wed a snake,' Rosalyn spat at him. She kicked out hard at his shins, making him curse and let her go. She retreated but, instead of running, from a safe distance she turned to face him, her eyes bright with anger. 'Do your worst, sir. I care nothing for your blackmail or your threats. I shall be married as soon as Freddie's wedding is over. Damian is coming for me and—'

'Damian...' His eyes narrowed to dangerous slits. 'You mean Wrexham—that murderer? Patricia told me she had seen him here in this house...that you had invited him.'

'Damian is not the murderer,' Rosalyn cried shrilly. 'You were your brother's murderer, sir. It was you who raped that girl—you who drove her to take her own life because she was so ashamed...ashamed of what you had done to her. Your brother kidnapped the girl, but you were the instigator of that foul deed. Damian killed your brother fairly in a duel—but it should have been you, not Roderick, who died that day. You let him die in your stead rather than confess your guilt. You killed your brother, sir—his blood is on your own hands.'

'What do you know of this?' Harrington's voice was a dry rasp. 'What lies have you been spreading, bitch?'

'I have spread no lies,' Rosalyn said, lifting her head proudly. 'You will be brought to book for your crimes, sir. If not for rape, for—' She broke off as he snarled and lunged at her, retreating before the fury in his face. 'When I tell my brother of your attack on me, he will request you to leave our house at once. You are no longer welcome here, sir. Besides, Freddie knows that you tried to abuse Beatrice—that you went to her room and attempted to get into her bed. Her maid drove you off, but you threatened to tell your sister that Beatrice had encouraged you, thereby ensuring she would not dare to speak out and accuse you. You are everything despicable, sir. Everything any decent woman would revile and refute.'

Bernard hesitated, staring at her in frustration. How dare she defy him? He would have liked to take the bitch by the throat and break her neck, but her screams would rouse the household. Besides, he had other more important business for the moment. He had known when the lawyers began to press for payment that he must have an enemy, but had not suspected the man's identity until this moment. He needed to confirm who held the notes that would send him to the debtors' prison, and to teach that person to keep his nose out of his affairs—time enough to take care of this woman when he had dealt with the instigator of his troubles.

'There is no need for your brother to ask me to leave,' he said with a curl of scorn about his mouth. 'I cannot wait to shake the dust of this accursed place from my boots. Be damned to you and your brother, Miss High-and-Mighty Eastleigh! I came here only because Patricia commanded it, but for all the help she's given me I might as well have stayed in London. She clings so tightly to that damned money of hers, I doubt I'll see a penny of it until she's dead. And the sooner that happens, the better as far as I'm concerned.'

He walked off, fuming. Be damned to the bitch and to his own sister! Patricia could have given him the money and not missed it, but she was too tight-fisted. He needed to cool his temper before returning to the house or God only knew what he might do!

Rosalyn stood where she was for several seconds after he had walked away from her. She discovered she was trembling; the encounter had upset her more than she cared to admit. When he'd held her imprisoned in his grasp, she had feared what he might do. His strength was such that he could have killed her if he had chosen to do it, and she could feel the imprint of his steely fingers on her flesh. She would no doubt have bruises to show for his rough handling of her.

Taking a deep breath to steady herself, Rosalyn lifted her head and looked up at the windows of the house. In that moment, she saw something move. Someone had been watching and—since the window had been opened slightly at the top to let in air—they could also have heard every word she had exchanged with Mr Harrington.

It was the window on the landing at the top of the stairs, not one of the bedchambers—so it could have been anyone: a servant, Maria, Freddie…any one of them. Rosalyn went quickly into the house. She must hurry. Her most urgent thought was that she must stop whoever it was from speaking of this if she could…but when she reached the top of the stairs whoever had been standing there had gone.

She was too late. She had hoped to prevent any gossip reaching Mrs Jenkins's ears, but there was nothing she could do about it now. Any mention of that unpleasant scene in the garden to other members of the household would only bring about that which she hoped to avoid.

Who could it have been? Rosalyn looked about her. It had taken her a few seconds to come in from the garden, plenty of time for the person who had been observing her quarrel with Mr Harrington to have gone downstairs or into one of the bedrooms.

What a nuisance! She frowned in annoyance. If only she had been in time. She must simply pray that whoever it was, would have the sense to keep what they had seen and heard to themselves.

Rosalyn sighed. The damage had been done. She dare not think what Mrs Jenkins would make of it if she learned of the unpleasant incident. She was bound to blame her—or Damian, of course. Beatrice had spoken of her aunt's fondness for her brother, so it was unlikely Mrs Jenkins would believe a word of what Rosalyn had said, even after his harsh words concerning his sister—but it could still cause trouble. She would be very angry that the accusation had been made, and might even call off the wedding as she had threatened once before.

Thinking of Mrs Jenkins made Rosalyn remember how sick the poor woman had been. The doctor had visited earlier, but perhaps she would just look in and see how she was now. She glanced at herself in a wall mirror, smoothing her gown and a few stray wisps of hair, then she went down the hall and knocked at Mrs Jenkins's door.

Several seconds passed and she was about to turn away when she heard something and then the door was opened. Mrs Jenkins was dressed and, although her skin still looked slightly yellow, seemed better, more like her usual self.

'I am sorry to disturb you,' Rosalyn said, startled by the look of anger in the other woman's eyes. She was clearly very disturbed about something. 'I just wondered how you were feeling—if you needed anything?'

Mrs Jenkins gave her a cold, proud stare. 'Thank you, no,' she said. 'I am much recovered, Miss Eastleigh. I believe I shall come downstairs in a little while.'

'I am very pleased to hear that,' Rosalyn said and hesitated. 'Without wishing to intrude, may I ask what the doctor said was the cause of these unfortunate attacks?'

'He said the powders I have been using for my indigestion had a peculiar smell to them and might have gone bad,' she replied, a very odd expression in her eyes. 'He took them away with him and gave me something different to use.'

'Then I hope you will find an improvement in your health,' Rosalyn said. 'It would be a shame if you were ill and we had to postpone the wedding. Beatrice would be so upset.'

'You need not fear that,' Mrs Jenkins said, surprising her. 'I am determined that nothing shall stand in the way of Beatrice's happiness.' She saw Rosalyn's expression and smiled strangely. 'I dare say you may find that difficult to believe, Miss Eastleigh—but I happen to be very fond of my niece, regardless of what either she or anyone else may think.'

'I am sure…' Rosalyn found it almost impossible to answer. 'I am sure she knows it, ma'am.'

'No, do not lie to me,' Mrs Jenkins said. 'I have come to appreciate your honesty, Miss Eastleigh. I know I am a difficult woman, but I do care for Beatrice and I shall do nothing that might harm her. She will be happy and safe with your brother, and that is all that I desire for her.'

Rosalyn smiled, making no comment; it was best to leave the conversation there for the moment. She merely repeated her hope that Mrs Jenkins would soon be fully recovered and said that she was about to take tea in her parlour.

'We shall all be very happy if you were to join us, ma'am.'

'Thank you. Perhaps a little later…I have something I need to do for the moment.'

Rosalyn went away. She was thoughtful as she walked down to the parlour. What had changed Mrs Jenkins? She had seemed very angry when she first opened her door, but her manner had softened as they talked—and she had so far unbent towards Rosalyn as to become almost friendly. Her promise that she would do nothing to spoil the wedding was reassuring.

At least one thing seemed clear: she could not possibly have been at the window to witness the quarrel between Rosalyn and Mr Harrington. No, that must have been someone else. Who? Rosalyn wrinkled her brow. One of the servants—or Maria? Perhaps it did not matter. Providing no one said anything to annoy Mrs Jenkins, the wedding would go ahead without any further upsets.

Rosalyn sighed as she recalled her brief meeting with Damian that afternoon. How she wished she had been able to go away with him at once. She felt a coldness pass over her skin, a premonition of something frightening making her shiver.

Now she was being silly. Nothing was going to happen. Damian would only be away for a few days, and then they would be together for the rest of their lives.

Very early the next morning, Rosalyn woke suddenly. She had been dreaming, a dream so clear and vivid she could recall it as if it had been real. She had been lost in a mist, running, trying to find…Damian.

Her cheeks were wet with tears. In her dream, she had seen him but she had not been able to reach him. He had been somewhere in the mist, so near that she knew if she just reached out she could touch him, but something was stopping her, holding her back. Invisible chains…the chains of duty.

Rosalyn got out of bed and went to the window, looking out at the garden, which was shrouded in a fine morning mist. A shiver went through her. She longed for Damian, wished that she had gone with him when he asked.

'Damian, come back to me, my darling,' she whispered. 'I love you so—and I am so afraid…so afraid of losing you.'

What a very foolish woman she was, to be sure! Rosalyn laughed at her own fears as the sun began to break through the mist. It was just a dream…nothing terrible was going to happen, nothing that could prevent her leaving with Damian when he came for her.

It seemed that Mr Harrington had departed without a word to anyone, except perhaps his sister. He did not come in for dinner that evening and Rosalyn took it for granted that he had left as he intended. As no one asked her, she did not speak of the incident in the garden, preferring to put it out of her mind as though it had never happened. Beatrice and Sarah confided privately that they were glad he had gone, and Freddie seemed distant from everyone except his fiancée.

Mrs Jenkins made no mention of his departure to anyone, so if he *had* taken leave of his sister, whatever had passed between them could not have included a revelation of the quarrel between him and Rosalyn. Indeed, Mrs Jenkins seemed to have made a remarkable recovery—of her health and her manners. She went out of her way to be pleasant to Rosalyn and her aunt, revealing a side of her that no one had previously guessed was there.

'You might almost think her a different woman,' Mrs Buckley remarked in private. 'Now, what do you suppose could have brought about such a change?'

Rosalyn laughed. 'I have no idea. I am just glad of it for Beatrice's sake, and Freddie's, of course.'

The next few days passed so pleasantly that Rosalyn was able to forget her fears of exposure and enjoy all the celebrations leading up to the wedding itself. The only altercation was when one of Mrs Simmons' staff upset Monsieur Maurice and caused the great artist to throw a tantrum in the kitchen, as well as several heavy copper-bottomed pans, which were aimed at the unfortunate maid who had aroused his wrath, but happily they missed and caused nothing more than a few tears.

His threats to resign immediately threw Freddie into a panic, for how could the wedding reception go ahead without him? Rosalyn was called, and, after several minutes spent soothing feathers and tending injured pride, was able to restore a smile to the chef's face.

'You understand me,' he said, placing a hand on his heart. 'You understand what a great chef must suffer in the cause of his art—and if that stupid woman does not understand when I say the onion must be chopped just so, she has no soul.'

'She is young and silly,' Rosalyn said to placate him.

'You who are so much wiser must find it in your heart to forgive her.'

'So beautiful and so wise.' He bowed over her hand, kissing it and sighing. 'If only you did not live in the country, Mademoiselle Eastleigh—what a joy it would be to serve you.'

'Sir Frederick would be devastated if he lost you,' Rosalyn said, smiling inwardly as she imagined his reaction if the chef transferred his loyalties to her. 'You must not think of deserting him. Besides, you will have far more opportunity to practise your art in his service than you could in mine. No, no, you would be wasted here.'

As Monsieur Maurice nodded over the wisdom of this, Rosalyn made her escape. No matter how wonderful his food was, she thought she could not have put up with his tantrums for very long. She apologised privately to the kitchen maid, and told her she could have the afternoon off to recover from her fright.

'You should be the mistress of your own home,' her aunt told her when they laughed together over the incident in the privacy of her parlour later that day. 'I wonder how Beatrice will cope with the *artiste*'s tantrums when she is mistress of Freddie's household.'

'I dare say she will manage better than you may imagine,' Rosalyn replied. 'I think there is more to her than any of us yet guesses. Poor Freddie may well be in for a surprise.'

'Yes, perhaps…' Her aunt smiled and nodded. 'Well, tomorrow is the big day. It will soon be all over.'

Rosalyn smiled happily. Every day that passed brought her closer to the moment Damian would return to claim her.

'Yes, tomorrow is Bea's wedding day. I was sorry Celia did not feel up to coming—but I am glad you and Sarah stayed on, Aunt Susan.'

'I wanted a little time with you,' her aunt replied. 'I know we do not often visit one another, but I shall miss you. It would have been much nicer if you had married Mr Wrexham here amongst your friends and family, my love—but I do understand how you feel. I hope you do not mean to desert us altogether? You will visit from time to time?'

'I shall write, of course,' Rosalyn said and touched her hand affectionately. 'But I am not sure whether we shall visit England again. I dare say it may not be for some years.'

Rosalyn hugged her thoughts to herself. Damian had told her to meet him in the garden that night. He would come if he could, and if not he would be there the following night or the next. There was not long to wait now. Soon she would be with him, and then they would never part again.

'Freddie has some visitors,' Sarah Jane announced as she came into the parlour just before tea, and flopped down on the sofa. 'They looked very odd when they arrived, very serious and grim, as though something unpleasant had happened.'

'Oh, dear,' Rosalyn said. 'I do hope it isn't bad news.'

'No, I'm sure it isn't,' her aunt reassured her. 'What could possibly go wrong? Unless they have come to arrest Monsieur Maurice for attacking the kitchen maid?'

'Oh, Aunt,' reproached Rosalyn with a smile. 'How can you make a jest of…?' Her words died on her lips as the door opened and her brother walked in. One look at his face told her that something was very wrong. She rose to her feet, her heart beating very fast. 'What is it, Freddie? What has happened?'

'Sarah Jane,' he said, his expression that of a man struggling against his emotions. 'Would you be kind enough to go and find Beatrice for me, please? I believe you will discover her in the garden picking roses.'

'Must I?' Sarah Jane hesitated. It was obvious to her that she was being sent away because Freddie had some important news to impart—news he did not want her to hear. However, the unusually stern look on his face made her obey without further protest. 'Oh, all right, if you like…I'll go, I am going now.'

Rosalyn waited until the door had closed behind the girl. 'Tell us,' she said, sitting down next to her aunt on the large sofa because her legs had begun to shake. 'Something awful has happened, hasn't it? It is bad news, isn't it, Freddie?'

'I have just received a visit from an officer of the law, Rosalyn,' he said and she saw his hands clench at his sides. 'It appears that…there has been a murder.'

'A murder!' Mrs Buckley cried, her face draining of colour. 'Who has been killed? For goodness' sake, Freddie. Explain yourself. Who has been murdered and why did those men come here? What can this possibly have to do with us?'

'The body was found yesterday by a man walking his dog along a seldom-used country lane between the village and the boundary of our estate,' Freddie said, a flicker of something that might have been disgust…or fear…in his eyes. No, surely not fear, thought his sister, dismissing such a ridiculous idea immediately. 'It was the body of a man who had been shot at close range…at least two or three times. There was no doubt it was murder; it could not have been anything else.' Freddie seemed to look at Rosalyn in a very strange way as he paused.

'Who was it?' she asked, but the coldness seeping through her was already warning her that she would not like the answer. 'Please tell us, Freddie. Who has been murdered?'

'Bernard Harrington,' Freddie replied hoarsely. 'It appears he has been dead for several days…perhaps since the day he left here. They cannot be sure, naturally, but he has been dead for some time.'

'How do you know?'

'Apparently…' Freddie looked sick and avoided looking at her or their aunt. 'This *is* the countryside, Ros. We *have* foxes. I shall not go into details. Sufficient to say that it was not a pretty sight for those who had to deal with it. Identification was only possible from certain personal items—

which I was able to say quite positively belonged to Mr Harrington.'

'So he was shot after he left here…' Rosalyn stared at her brother, her face white. 'And they think it could have been that very day…'

'But who would want to do such a thing?' Mrs Buckley asked, looking puzzled. 'I know he was not a very likeable man, but murder…that is horrid! I can hardly believe it.'

'Do they have any idea of who might have done it?' Rosalyn said. Freddie looked down, refusing to meet her questing gaze. 'Were there any clues—any witnesses?'

'None as far as I could tell,' replied her brother. He was clearly disturbed and did not know how to answer her. 'Robbery would be the usual motive for such a crime—but he still had his purse and his watch. Which makes it difficult to know why he should have been attacked—and so close to our estate.'

'What are you thinking?' Rosalyn's hand crept to her throat as she realised why he was looking at her so strangely. He could not think…but she could see by his face that he did! 'No, Freddie, you are wrong. Damian left for France that same night. He would not have had time to do it. Besides, he would never had killed Mr Harrington in such an underhand way. If he had wanted him dead, he would have challenged him to a duel.'

Rosalyn remembered her nightmare, and she felt cold all over. She had sensed that something terrible might happen. No, no, she must not let herself be frightened. Damian was not a murderer. Nothing could part them.

Freddie could not look her in the eyes. 'I did not say it was him… Indeed, I told the officers that I had no idea who might want to kill Harrington—that it must have been a stranger. A gypsy or some other itinerant passing through the county.'

'But you thought it! I can see it in your face,' Rosalyn cried, jumping to her feet as the anger rose in her. 'How

can you, Freddie? How can you! There was no reason...'
her voice died away as she recalled the scene in the gardens,
the moment when Bernard Harrington had attacked her. If
Damian had seen that, there was no telling how he might
have acted! 'No, no, he wouldn't...I was not harmed. I
know Damian would not, could not have done this terrible
thing.'

'What did Harrington do to you?' Freddie's eyes narrowed as he saw her expression. 'Did he attack you—or
Beatrice?'

'He tried to blackmail me into marrying him,' Rosalyn
said slowly, her throat tight with emotion. 'He had seen me
with Damian, and he called me a...whore. I slapped him
and he twisted my arm behind my back. For a moment I
thought he might attempt to...but I managed to break away
from him, and I accused him of his crimes. I told him you
would not tolerate his presence in this house another night,
and he said he did not wish to stay—that he had come only
to ask his sister for money and, since she would not give
it, was leaving of his own accord. Now I think of it, he did
not go towards the house, but past me towards the orchard—
and could have found his way to the lane from there.'

'Did you speak to him again after that?'

'No, Freddie, I did not. I assumed he had left...why?'

'His things are still in his room,' her brother replied. 'Mrs
Simmons told Maria apparently, but she assumed he would
be returning for the wedding so said nothing of it to anyone.
As far as I can ascertain, he told no one but you of his
intention to leave.'

'You think he was killed soon after the attack on me?'
Rosalyn felt cold all over. Her skin prickled with goose
bumps as she saw the expression in her brother's eyes. 'You
do believe Damian killed him, don't you?'

'What I believe does not matter,' Freddie said, refusing
to meet her eyes. 'The man was undoubtedly a menace. Had
I known what he had done, I should never have invited him

here. I cannot pretend to be sorry he is dead—my only fear
is that it will bring scandal on the family. For heaven's sake!
I am supposed to be getting married tomorrow. This could
ruin everything…if it gets out. If it is known that my own
sister is meeting the man who killed Harrington's brother,
that she intends to go away with him—what do you imagine
people will say? They will think it odd Harrington was murdered here—and assume Wrexham left the country because
he was guilty. Our name will be dragged through the mire
with his. Especially if you—'

'You need not fear that,' Rosalyn replied, her face revealing more of her feelings than she realised, making Freddie flinch at his sister's scorn. 'Damian will be coming for
me very soon, and I shall go with him. You can always
disown me.'

'You will still go with him—knowing that he may be a
murderer?' He stared at her in disgust. 'Surely this changes
things? You must see you cannot marry him now?'

Rosalyn felt the sting of tears. How could Freddie say
such things to her? She lifted her head, looking into her
brother's eyes.

'No, I do not see it,' she said. 'I would go to him even
if I believed him capable of murder—but I do not. I know
Damian would never kill a man in the way you describe,
Freddie.' She stood up, her expression stiff with pride. 'I
am going to my room. Please excuse me.'

'Ros…' The cry was wrung from her brother as she left
the room. 'I'm sorry…but it all points to him, you must see
that?'

She stood in the doorway and looked back at him, her
scorn making him turn pale. 'Does it, Freddie? I think there
are others who might feel anger against him…others not far
from where I stand. Where did you go that day, tell me that
if you can?'

She knew the accusation was unfair even as she made it,
but could not help herself. How could Freddie point the

finger at Damian, knowing as he must that she was in love with him? Any consideration for her must have forced him to keep silent, even if he suspected Damian of wrongdoing.

Freddie was stunned to silence. He stood staring after her as she closed the door. Was she saying that he…? Be damned to that! He would not stand for her insults in his own house! But his aunt was speaking to him, claiming his attention.

'You had no right to make such accusations, Freddie. You owe Rosalyn a great deal, and you have not always treated her as you ought. This house was her home and you have forced her from it without a thought for her feelings. I think you should go after her, apologise. Ask her to forgive you. If you do not, I fear it will create a breach between you— one that may never be healed.'

Freddie turned to stare at his aunt, the fury beginning to mount inside him. 'Apologise after what she just said to me?' he cried, his face white with temper. 'I think you much mistake the matter, Aunt. I shall leave her to think better of things and then she may apologise to me if she wishes.'

With that he turned and left the room, slamming the door behind him.

Mrs Buckley frowned. She would have done better to keep her silence, but she had been provoked into making what she felt was a well-justified comment. Freddie had jumped to conclusions—conclusions that besides being very unlikely had been hurtful to his sister.

Did he not understand that Rosalyn had fallen in love for the first time in her life? And so deeply that she was not likely to recover from it if forced to give up the man she loved. He could not expect her to do so simply for the sake of what people might say? Freddie should have thought things through more carefully before making such a statement…unless Rosalyn had hit upon the truth and he was hiding his own guilt.

Was Freddie capable of such wickedness? For that was

what it was if he had blamed Mr Wrexham for his own deed.

Rosalyn had told her in confidence of the reason why Beatrice stood in fear of the objectionable Mr Harrington. It was just possible that, knowing the man had once attacked his fiancée, Freddie had come back from his ride that afternoon and seen the quarrel between Harrington and his sister…and his fury had been such that he had followed the man and, possibly, in a rage, killed him.

Upstairs in her bedchamber, Rosalyn paced the floor in a turmoil.

'Damian…oh, my love,' she whispered, her face pale and distressed. 'I know you are innocent of this crime…I know it.'

But someone had killed Harrington. Someone had seen the quarrel between her and Bernard Harrington that afternoon. Someone had heard every word that was spoken—and that person had killed Harrington because of something that had been said or done.

Could it have been Damian? Had he decided to follow her through the orchard…he had seemed to linger as if unwilling to leave her, had still been standing there when she looked back. He had once said he would kill Harrington if he harmed Rosalyn…but she had not been harmed, apart from a few minor bruises.

For a moment Rosalyn was racked with agony. Was the man she loved so much capable of murder?

No, she would not believe it. Damian would have called the man out, as he had Roderick all those years ago—so someone else had followed Bernard as he left the estate that afternoon. Someone else had taken a gun and killed him, leaving his body lying on the ground to be discovered by anyone who chanced to find it.

Who would do that? The lane was seldom used because it led only to the estate and the body had lain undiscovered for some days, covered in part perhaps by the hedges that grew thickly there.

Why had no attempt been made to hide the body? Had a grave been dug it might never have been found.

Rosalyn tussled with the problem, then dismissed it—it was not important. She felt sickened that her brother had not hesitated to blame Damian. How could he say such things to her? How could he expect her to give up her only chance of happiness?

Unless he had done so in order to cover his own guilt? She had seen something in his face which had made her wonder if he was frightened. No, surely she was mistaken? Freddie would not… She shook her head, feeling sickened by the thought. Even if he had been driven into an act of violence, he would not seek to cover it by blaming someone else—or would he?

Rosalyn paced the floor of her bedchamber. She was distressed by the idea, but could not quite rid herself of it. Freddie had always been selfish and inclined to think first of his own comfort, but surely he would not do anything so wicked?

It was as difficult for her to believe ill of her brother as it was of Damian. She could not think that either of them would murder in cold blood. Her brother might have carried out his threat to take a horsewhip to Harrington, and Damian might in anger have challenged him to a duel…but murder? No, she did not, would not believe it of either of them.

Oh, Damian, she thought, I wish you were here. Here to defend yourself—and to hold me. I need you so much!

All at once Rosalyn stopped her pacing. What was she thinking of? This was so selfish of her. Her own distress at what had happened could be nothing compared to what Mrs Jenkins must be feeling. Had anyone thought to tell her? Freddie was hardly likely to do it, might even wish to conceal the facts in case she demanded the postponement of the wedding, as was her right—but it could not be kept from her. She must be told immediately, and in the kindest way possible.

Rosalyn splashed her face with cold water and dried it on a towel. She tidied her hair, squaring her shoulders as she prepared to go down the landing and speak to Mrs Jenkins, but even as she turned to leave, there was a knock at her door.

'Come in,' she said, expecting Freddie and preparing to meet her brother's recriminations. He had no doubt come to argue with her again. She was surprised as the door opened and Mrs Jenkins entered. 'Oh…I was just about to come to see you, ma'am.'

'Forgive me for disturbing you,' the older woman said. 'Mrs Buckley gave me the news of…' Her voice almost failed her, but she lifted her head, meeting Rosalyn's sympathetic gaze with determination. 'I have been told of my brother's unfortunate accident.'

'Accident…' Rosalyn was surprised by her calm manner. She had expected something very different. Anger, indignation, distress—but not this iron control. 'Oh, I am so sorry. I meant to speak to you myself. My aunt has told you how he died?'

'He was shot by a poacher or some such person, I dare say,' Mrs Jenkins said, a tiny nerve flicking in her throat. 'Or perhaps one of his many enemies followed him from town. My brother did have enemies, Miss Eastleigh. I believe several threats have been made against his life at various times. I regret to say it, but he had recently begun to mix with very low company. Although it may have been a poacher. Bernard would have remonstrated with anyone he saw shooting your brother's game; he was very strict with poachers on his own land at one time…before he took to gambling so much.'

'I…' Rosalyn stared at her, uncertain of what to say. She had not thought of such a solution, but she saw at once how much better it would be for everyone if it were true. 'I—I believe you must be right, ma'am. It was most unfortunate. Especially at this time. I do understand that you are very upset—and if you intend to postpone the wedding I shall support you.'

'No, no, not at all,' Mrs Jenkins said. 'I do not wish to cause distress for Beatrice or your brother. It is not yet generally known that Bernard has...met with an accident. Therefore, I believe the wedding should go ahead as though nothing has happened. Later, I shall insert a brief notice of my brother's death in *The Times*. I think that should suffice.'

'That is generous of you—and very brave.'

'I have caused enough grief in this house, and so had Bernard,' Mrs Jenkins replied in a dignified tone. 'The least I can do is allow the wedding to go ahead.' She hesitated, then said, 'If my brother importuned you with his attentions, I must apologise. I suggested that he might solve his financial problems with your fortune—that was wrong of me. Please forgive me. I was not thinking properly at the time.'

'It...does not matter.' Rosalyn frowned. There was something very odd here. Why had Mrs Jenkins changed so much of late? 'I am glad you have come to me, ma'am—and I am sorry that such a terrible thing should have happened to your brother.'

'Please do not...' Mrs Jenkins held up her hand. 'I have been aware for some time that Bernard...' She paused, took out her kerchief and blew her nose. 'I loved my brother Roderick very much. When he died, I was devastated. It made me bitter. I have tried to love Bernard, but could not—not as I had loved Roderick. I am sorry it has come to this, of course, but you must not imagine I am suffering too much grief, Miss Eastleigh. Let me assure you I am not.'

'I see...' Rosalyn felt chilled for some reason she could not decipher. 'Then we shall say no more of this, ma'am. Have you told my brother the wedding is to go ahead?'

'I thought perhaps you would do that for me,' Mrs Jenkins said. 'If you will excuse me, I shall stay in my room this evening—though I shall of course attend the ceremony tomorrow.'

'Are you unwell? Has the sickness returned?' Rosalyn asked, a little puzzled by her manner.

'No, no, I am quite well. I believe it was as your doctor thought, Miss Eastleigh. My powders had gone stale…that is why they made me sick. Now that I have replaced them I think I shall be quite well again. Yes, I am perfectly certain the nausea will not return…now.'

Rosalyn sat down for a few minutes after Mrs Jenkins had left. Such a terrible thought had come to her that it made her feel unwell…but she was letting her imagination run wild. It was not possible. No, no, she was entirely wrong. Mrs Jenkins was right…the shooting had probably been an accident and not murder at all.

She stood up, lifting her head. She must speak to Freddie. He would be worrying about the wedding, and she did not want him to disturb Mrs Jenkins. No, that would never do…not until she had had time to rest and recover her composure.

Chapter Ten

It seemed ages until that evening. Rosalyn could not wait for Damian's return. She was on tenterhooks and longed for the chance to talk to him, to tell him what had happened.

'Damian, I need you so…' The words were only in her mind. 'I need you so…'

Perhaps he would meet her in the garden that evening? Her desire to be with him made her restless and impatient, very unlike her usual self. Even her quarrel with her brother paled into insignificance beside her need to see Damian, to be held in his arms. She did love him so very much!

Rosalyn saw Beatrice looking at her oddly throughout dinner that evening. She too was on edge and clearly suspected something was being kept from her. At Freddie's insistence, she had not been told about the death of her aunt's brother—nor the quarrel between her fiancé and his sister.

The interview in the library between brother and sister had been very formal. Freddie had thanked her for the news that the wedding was to go ahead, but he had not apologised for his behaviour and Rosalyn had made no move to heal the breach between them. Indeed, she was very angry with him. Had it not been for her very real affection for Beatrice, she would have left the house immediately afterwards, but, meeting the girl in the hall as she came from the unpleasant interview, had been forced to smile in answer to her greeting.

Fortunately for Rosalyn's peace of mind, Freddie took himself off after dinner. Although not intending to indulge in a pre-wedding fling, he was staying overnight with a friend so as not to see his bride before they met at the church the next morning. Because he was not there, Rosalyn was able to sit with her aunt, Beatrice and Maria in the parlour and make comfortable conversation, though Mrs Jenkins had remained in her room, refusing even the light repast Mrs Simmons had carried up to her.

They were all ready for an early night after the hectic celebrations of the previous few weeks, and of course Beatrice wanted to be fresh for the wedding itself. She embraced Rosalyn before they parted, thanking her for everything she had done to make things easier for her.

'I hope you know how fond I have become of you, dearest Rosalyn?' she said. 'I am so glad we are to be sisters—and I hope we shall often meet.'

Clearly, Freddie had made no mention of Rosalyn's plans to marry. Perhaps he hoped his sister would change her mind?

Rosalyn merely smiled and kissed her. Let Freddie tell her the truth after they were married, if he chose.

Alone in her own room, Rosalyn took the pins from her hair and brushed it, letting it hang loose on her shoulders. She packed a few possessions while she waited for time to pass; some of her clothes could perhaps be sent on later. Many of them would not be suitable for her new life. She had decided she would take only a few of her newest garments, and her personal treasures, things given her by her parents: her mother's jewellery and items she had kept for various reasons.

She went to the drawer where she had kept her father's pistols. One of them was missing. She stared at the empty aperture in the box—surely she had replaced the weapon after using it to drive off the men who had attacked Jared? Yes, she was sure it was missing—and the box containing the balls used as ammunition was almost empty. When she last used it, it had been half-full.

A cold chill ran down Rosalyn's spine. Where had the pistol gone? Someone had taken it—could it have been Freddie? Or someone else? Had the pistol been used to kill Bernard Harrington?

That thought made her feel slightly sick, and she could not wait to unburden her thoughts to the only person she could tell of her suspicions.

It must be time, surely? If Damian was coming, he would be here by now. Rosalyn picked up a branch of candles and looked out of her door to make sure she was unobserved. There was no reason why she should not meet Damian, yet even now she would do nothing to disoblige her brother if she could help it.

She went down to her parlour, unlocked the French windows and slipped out. The moon was bright, its silver light giving the garden an air of romance and mystery. Was Damian here? Was he back yet? Her heart beat faster in the hope of seeing him, but though she called softly and waited for nearly an hour, there was no sign of him.

'Oh, Damian, where are you? I need you. I need to talk to you, to hold you. I need you so very much…'

Rosalyn sighed her disappointment and went back inside. Perhaps he would come tomorrow.

The morning of the wedding was fine and warm. Beatrice looked as beautiful as everyone expected, her face alight with happiness as she walked down the aisle to stand beside Freddie and take her vows.

Rosalyn watched her. She surreptitiously wiped away a tear, smiling as she saw her aunt doing the same thing.

'I do hope she will be happy,' Aunt Susan whispered.

'Do you not think Sarah Jane looks very grown up, my dear?'

Rosalyn nodded. She suddenly found she could not speak, because as she turned to watch the newly-wed couple leaving the church, she saw that a man was standing at the very back. He had taken his place behind a pillar so as not to be seen too clearly, but Rosalyn knew him at once and her heart began to race wildly.

Damian was back! He was back. It took all her resolution not to go to him at once. As she followed her aunt and the other guests out into the sunshine and the peal of joyful bells, Rosalyn saw that Damian had moved away to a far corner of the churchyard and was watching her. She smiled and moved as if to go to him, but he shook his head and mouthed the word 'later' to her. She nodded, her spirits soaring. Damian was right. She had waited this long, she could wait a little longer.

Yet it was so difficult to keep a smile on her face, to listen to all the chatter and laughing jests made by the guests at her brother's expense, when she wanted to put all this behind her and go to her lover.

At last they were back at the house, and the reception was under way. The table in the dining room had been set out with all manner of delicious trifles. Monsieur Maurice had surpassed himself, Rosalyn thought as she moved amongst the guests, making polite conversation.

'And when shall we have the pleasure of your company in town again, Miss Eastleigh?'

'I do not know, Mr Carlton,' she replied. 'I have no plans to return for the moment.'

'That is a pity. I had hoped to see you there this season.'

Rosalyn smiled and shook her head, moving on to various guests. She was sure Damian would be waiting for her in the garden. Dare she slip away to meet him for a few minutes? Why not? She had done her duty. No one would miss her. There were plenty of others to entertain Freddie's guests.

She made her way unhurriedly through the crowded rooms, leaving by the French windows of her parlour. There was no sign of Damian. He would not risk being seen, of course, but as she hurried across the lawn to the shrubbery, he came out and caught her in his arms. Her heart leaped as he held her close, gazing down at her hungrily.

'You came,' he said, bending his head to kiss her on the mouth. 'I was not sure you would manage it until this evening—but I could not stay away. I have been longing for you, my darling.'

'And I for you,' she said, pressing herself against him, surrendering her mouth to his as the heady desire swept over her. 'I have everything ready. I can leave as soon as Freddie and Beatrice have gone—' She stopped as she saw the way his eyes were looking at something behind her. 'What…?' Swinging round, she saw her brother striding towards them, his face tight with anger.

'I thought I should find you with him,' Freddie said coldly. 'Are you so mad for him that you care nothing for your reputation, Ros? If what people say of you matters not to you, then at least have a thought for my wife's good name.'

'Freddie!' Rosalyn felt as if he had slapped her. This was so unfair. She had done all she could to make things easier for him—and now he had so unjustly accused her of thinking only of herself. 'No one has seen us. Besides, we shall be leaving soon. You are married now—what can it matter if someone does see us?'

'It matters to me if my sister is seen embracing a murderer.'

'Freddie!' she cried, dismayed. 'How can you say such things?'

'What is this?' Damian's eyes narrowed. 'You are not

speaking of the duel, Eastleigh? Damn it, you cannot believe I was responsible for Bernard Harrington's murder?'

'So you do not deny it was murder?' Freddie glared at him. 'I was prepared to accept the situation between you and my sister as things stood—a duel is not murder—but this changes everything.'

'I give you my word I had nothing to do with this,' Damian said, eyes cold, proud. He was very still, watchful. He glanced at Rosalyn. 'Do you believe me?'

'Yes, of course,' she said quickly. 'I know you did not do it, Damian.'

'You are being foolish,' Freddie said glaring at her. 'You have only his word that he did not shoot Harrington. How can you marry him, knowing he may be a murderer?'

'I would marry him whatever he had done,' Rosalyn said quietly. Her back was very straight, her manner calm and dignified. 'Damian loves me—that is something you have never done, Freddie. You are not my legal guardian. I can marry whom I choose.' She lifted her candid eyes to meet those of the man she loved. 'I am going to fetch my things now, Damian. Please wait for me. Everything I want is packed. It will take me only a few minutes to fetch them.'

'Are you sure?' he asked.

'Quite sure. Please be here when I return.'

'If you leave with him now, I've finished with you,' Freddie said, lips white with fury. 'You can never come back. I shall forbid Beatrice to speak to you ever again.'

Rosalyn lifted her head, her face pale. She was tense but determined. 'I shall not wish to return,' she said with painful dignity. 'This is no longer my home—and you are no longer my brother.'

She walked away, refusing to glance back even when her brother called to her. How dare he? How dare he say such things to her—to Damian? She would never, never forgive him.

As she disappeared into the house, Freddie turned on Damian in fury.

'Do you know what you've done?' he demanded. 'You've ruined her. You may think you can get away with murder, Wrexham—but people will talk, they will believe you killed Harrington. Some of them will think in private that you've done the world a service, but in public they will refuse to know you. You will be tainted—and so will Rosalyn. You have dragged her down to your level—I hope you are satisfied?'

Damian curled his fists at his sides, willing himself to control his temper. If he struck Rosalyn's brother in anger the breach would never be healed—and that would hurt her. She was angry with Freddie now, but perhaps in the future she would begin to miss him, to miss all her family. He must not do anything which might make it impossible for her to return to her home one day.

'If you were not her brother, I would call you out for that,' Damian said. 'If you ever do anything to hurt her in the future I shall take a horsewhip to you. Say what you like to me—but never hurt her like that again.'

'Damn you!' Freddie yelled. He lunged at Damian, throwing a wild punch and missing. As he came at him again, Damian's fist connected with his chin, sending him down. He sprang up again, angry and ashamed. 'You devil...I'll teach you.'

'You had best take yourself back to your bride before I make it impossible for you to play your part on your wedding night,' Damian said. 'Think yourself lucky I do not thrash you as you deserve. One day I have no doubt you will come to your senses, and you may wish to apologise to Rosalyn—'

'Never!' Freddie yelled, beside himself with anger. 'She has made her bed—and she can damned well lie on it.'

He turned and began to stride across the lawn, disappearing into the house without looking back.

Upstairs in her room, Rosalyn took a last glance around her, then picked up the two cloak bags she had packed herself. She had her father's pearls and a ring that had been her mother's, that was all she really wanted—and enough clothes to take her as far as France. She could buy anything she needed there; at least Freddie could not control her money, her father had seen to that.

She was about to leave when her aunt came in. Mrs Buckley saw her white face and the bags and took in the situation immediately.

'Freddie is in a terrible mood,' she said. 'Have you quarrelled with him again?'

'He forbade me to go with Damian—but I cannot obey him, Aunt. He says that he has finished with me, that he will forbid the family to acknowledge me—but I do not care. Nothing can stop me leaving. I must go with Damian. I love him.'

'Of course you do,' her aunt said. She moved to embrace Rosalyn. 'You have my blessing, my dear—and if you ever need a home I shall always be happy to receive you.'

'Thank you—' Rosalyn broke off as Maria came rushing into the room, her face white.

'You were not going without saying goodbye?'

'No, I was going to ask my aunt to tell you to meet me in the garden,' Rosalyn said and went to embrace her. Maria was crying. 'Forgive me. I cannot stay for your wedding, my dearest cousin—but I shall write to you as soon as we are settled.'

'You will visit sometimes?'

'Yes—if we can,' Rosalyn promised. She looked from Maria to her aunt. 'I am sorry, I must go. Damian is waiting.'

'Yes, of course,' Mrs Buckley said. 'Would you let me come with you, Rosalyn? I should like to meet him—to tell him that he has my blessing.'

'And mine,' Maria said. 'I do not care what Freddie

thinks. He has behaved very badly towards you, and I shall tell him so.'

'Yes, come with me,' Rosalyn said. 'I should like Damian to know that not all my family are against him.'

She went ahead of her friends, her emotions in turmoil. Would Damian be waiting? Surely he would not leave without her? Please God, let him not have taken Freddie's rudeness too much to heart!

She saw him standing where she had left him. Sarah Jane was with him, laughing at something he had said to her. The girl turned as they approached.

'I have been giving Mr Wrexham a message for Jared,' she said. 'I shall go in now, Rosalyn. Beatrice will be wondering where I am.' She came to kiss her on the cheek. 'I shall never forget how kind you have been to me—and I hope we shall meet again one day.'

'I am sure we shall,' Rosalyn said. She turned to Damian as the girl ran off. 'My aunt—Mrs Susan Buckley—wanted to meet you. And Maria would like to say goodbye.'

'I could not let you go without wishing you both good luck,' Maria said, a faint blush in her cheeks as Damian took her hand to kiss it. 'Please take good care of Rosalyn for us. We are very fond of her—but of course I know you will.'

'You will be welcome to visit us when we are settled,' Damian assured her. 'And perhaps one day we shall visit you.'

Their farewells over, Damian took Rosalyn's cloak-bags from her and slung them over his shoulder, a questioning look in his eyes.

'Ready?'

'Yes. Quite ready.'

'We must walk as far as the Hall. I was not expecting to leave quite this soon.'

'Nor I,' she admitted, giving him a smile that was perhaps a little too bright. 'Do not be concerned for me, Damian.

My brother has behaved badly, but we shall not allow him to upset us.'

Was she simply putting on a brave face for his sake? Damian was not sure. They had known each other such a short time, and this was a huge step for Rosalyn to take. What had happened had perhaps been inevitable from the start. Love had flared between them almost instantly, creating a need that could not be denied—but would love be enough to compensate for all she had given up?

He offered her his hand. 'Come,' he said, his strong fingers curling about hers. There could be no place for doubt or regret in their lives. 'We should go, my love. We have a long journey before us.'

It was dark long before they reached Dover. Rosalyn had slept for a part of the journey, her head against Damian's shoulder.

At first they had talked of the future, and the new life they had entered together. Damian told her about the house he had taken on the outskirts of Paris.

'It is just for a week or two,' he said. 'I think you will like it—it is away from the bustle and noise of the city, but near enough to enjoy all the benefits. We shall go shopping together, my darling. I want to buy you lots of beautiful things.'

'Why? I have the money from my trust. I can arrange for that to be paid into any account I choose. Freddie has no control over my income. You do not need to buy me things, Damian.'

'Will you deny me that pleasure?' His brows arched. 'For years I have done nothing but accumulate wealth. Now that I have someone on whom to spend the money, may I not do so?'

'Are you very rich?' Rosalyn was surprised. She had not considered it before, taking him to be a man of modest means.

'I fear so,' he replied, a naughty glint in his eye. 'My years in India were put to good use. Do you mind?'

She shook her head, the hint of a smile on her lips. 'It is not important either way. But if you wish to lavish your money on me, I must tell you I am extremely fond of good horses. It is a passion I have often wished to indulge—and I should warn you that you may find me extravagant where they are concerned.'

'Horses?' Damian laughed. 'Then we have more in common than I knew. You shall have the very best, Rosalyn—both for your carriage and for riding.'

She smiled but said nothing more on the subject.

'How long shall we be in Paris?'

'Long enough to be married,' he said, taking her hand in his. 'Jared has gone down to a secret location in the country and we shall join him there in a week or so—but I thought we could be married in Paris? We could of course marry before we leave England, but it would be a rushed, makeshift affair. In Paris I have friends. We could have a small reception—and you would have the chance to buy a pretty gown for the occasion.'

'Then we shall wait until you can arrange it all,' she said, looking at him curiously. 'I did not know you had friends in Paris, Damian.'

'It is only in England that I have been cast out by society,' he replied, a flicker of amusement in his eyes. 'Edward and Charlotte Forrester were with the British Company in India for seven years. We became close friends—and they have often asked me to visit them at their home in Paris.'

'Then I shall look forward to meeting them.'

'And I know they will be delighted to meet you. Charlotte has been nagging me to marry for years, but until now I had no wish to oblige her.'

Rosalyn laughed at the wicked look he gave her. The slight constraint, which had arisen over the suggestion that he wished to lavish her with gifts, vanished as though it had never been. She was not quite sure why she had objected; it was natural for a husband to spend money on his wife—but she did not wish to be bought. Her love had been given freely and she required only love in return.

It was her wretched independence again! Rosalyn scolded herself mentally. She would soon be married, and must get used to the idea of being a wife.

She had slept after a while, lulled by the comfort of the well-sprung carriage and her sense of being safe and cared for; she was vaguely aware that Damian's arm was about her, supporting her. When she woke it was dark and the carriage was pulling into the yard of a busy inn. She could hear the sounds of ostlers shouting to one another, the clatter of wheels on cobblestones, and the hissing of flaring lanterns in their scones on the walls; then their groom opened the door and the steps were let down.

'I had booked two rooms here for tomorrow evening,' Damian said as he gave her his hand to help her from the carriage. 'We must hope the host has accommodation for tonight. There are other inns, of course, but this is the best.'

'We shall find something.'

Rosalyn smiled as she took his arm. She was determined not to make a fuss whatever the case. Besides, this was the beginning of a great adventure. No matter what happened now, she was with the man she loved. There was no going back, no return to her old life, nor did she want there to be. Despite some natural apprehension, she felt alive in a way she never had until now.

It was clear that the inn was extremely busy. The yard was littered with bags and trunks, several carriages having arrived almost simultaneously. Inside, in the welcoming parlour with its oak panelled walls and comfortable settles, Damian was forced to wait his turn for attention, and was eventually told that there was only one room available that night.

He frowned as he turned to Rosalyn, who had found a

place to sit and was idly contemplating a magnificent painting of a stag. 'I am sorry, there is only one room. It seems we must try elsewhere.'

'Why? I believe one room will be sufficient for our needs.'

As he saw the glow in her eyes, his own lit with fire. 'You are sure?'

'Quite sure.'

Damian nodded, making no further objection. He booked the room, which the landlord assured him was one of their best, then led her into the crowded dining parlour, where they were fortunate to find a table by the window.

Rosalyn had eaten very little at her brother's wedding reception, and she enjoyed the poached salmon and asparagus spears in a light, creamy sauce that were served her. She drank two glasses of the delicious white wine Damian ordered; it went to her head a little, combining with excitement to bring a brilliant sparkle to her eyes.

She noticed that Damian ate sparingly, merely sipping his wine. He seemed a little reserved, a rather odd expression in his dark eyes. What could be troubling him? Rosalyn experienced a moment of unease. She did not really know this man to whom she had entrusted her life. The future would no doubt be a journey of discovery.

'Would you like to go up now?'

Rosalyn felt a tingling sensation at the nape of her neck. She looked across the table, seeing the question in his eyes. Her cheeks took fire and she was aware of butterflies fluttering inside her. Now that the moment had come, she could not help being a little nervous—as all brides must be on their wedding night, surely? For though she was not yet wearing Damian's ring, this was the first night of their marriage—the night when they would truly become one.

Rosalyn smiled and stood up. 'Yes, I am ready,' she said, and gave her hand into his keeping.

* * *

Alone in their room, which was clean and perfectly comfortable, Rosalyn untied the strings of her bonnet and laid it with her velvet pelisse on a small sofa by the window. She stood for a moment looking down at the inn yard, which was almost silent now, then reached up to draw the heavy curtains, shutting out the night. When she turned, she saw Damian watching her; again his expression was so strange that her heart caught with fright.

What could have brought that haunting sadness to his eyes?

'Is something wrong?'

'No…nothing is wrong.' He moved towards her, reaching out to touch her cheek with his fingertips. 'I was just thinking how lovely you are—and wondering what I had done to you.'

'What do you mean?' Rosalyn gazed up at him, her eyes dark with anxiety. 'Damian? Don't look at me so…it frightens me.'

'Forgive me, I meant not to make you anxious. Are you certain this is what you want? It is not too late to change your mind.'

'Do you wish to change yours?'

'No, of course not.'

'Then why should I? Do you doubt my love?' She frowned. 'Is this because of something my brother said?' She read her answer in his face and was angry. 'Freddie had no right to interfere—no right to say the things he did to you.'

'He accused me of murder…'

She pressed her fingers to his mouth. 'Hush, my love. I know you did not kill Bernard Harrington. No matter what Freddie or anyone else may say—I know you are innocent.'

'Have you so much faith in me?'

'I have no choice,' she replied. 'I love you—would love you, whatever you had done. Nothing else matters. Surely you must see that?'

'Then nothing can harm us,' he said and reached out to draw her into his arms. 'My lovely woman...my life.'

Rosalyn felt the heady desire move in her as he kissed her lips, her white throat and the sweetly shadowed hollow where her gown dipped to reveal a glimpse of her breasts. She turned, lifting her hair so that he could release the fastening of her gown, letting it slip down over her hips to the ground where it lay unheeded. Her chemise followed so that in a moment she stood before him in all her womanly beauty, the soft contours of her body arousing such a fierce need in him that he groaned and swept her up, carrying her to their bed.

Then he too was naked, his clothes cast away, his manly arousal so evident and needy that she gasped in wonder at the power of him. She yielded to him as he began his tender assault on her willing flesh, lavishing her with his tongue and lips to bring her swiftly to a quivering acceptance of his loving. So urgent was their mutual desire that Rosalyn knew only pleasure; the piercing of her maidenhead was a fleeting pain scarcely felt as she clung to him, her body arching, opening to accommodate him, to welcome him, deep inside her. Love consumed her in a golden flame, carrying her to a far distant place where she had never been.

When it was over, she nestled into him, her face buried against his chest. She loved the scent and taste of him, the tickle of masculine hair and the smooth hard contours of his shoulders as her hands roamed and explored him. To be held like this in the warm intimacy of love was beyond her expectations, opening up new possibilities, new realms of emotions and experiences. She had never been this close to anyone, never understood what love could mean—the pleasures it could bring.

Damian touched her cheeks and found them wet. He leaned over her, looking into her face, seeking the reason for her tears.

'Crying?'

'Tears of happiness.' she assured him. 'I did not know it could be this way—that I could feel such pleasure, such content.'

'You are a very special woman,' Damian said and kissed her lingeringly on the mouth. 'I was lucky no one else had snapped you up long ago.'

Rosalyn smiled but made no answer. What need for words when such glorious sensations were flooding through her whole body? She moaned with pleasure, giving herself up to his loving once more as his hands moved down to cup her buttocks, squeezing them gently, lifting her to ease himself inside her, gently, slowly, beginning to tease her until she whimpered and quivered with pure delight.

They had the rest of their lives to talk, time to tell him that she had never wanted any other man, that she had always believed her soulmate was waiting somewhere—that one day they would be drawn together by fate. She had refused to settle for less, to take a husband she did not love for the sake of comfort and her own home as so many women did—and now she understood why.

Chapter Eleven

'At last! You cannot imagine how often I have hoped for this day.' Charlotte Forrester enveloped Rosalyn in her warm, perfumed embrace. 'My dear girl! You are beautiful. I can see why you achieved what none of the young ladies I thrust endlessly under Damian's nose even came close to—though I must admit that some of them were exceedingly pretty.'

'I am not pretty,' Rosalyn protested with a laugh. She looked at herself in the large oval wall mirror, admiring the exquisite fit of her new evening gown. The colour was a wonderful sea-green, the material a fine silk that moulded itself to her figure in flattering swathes. 'But Madame Yvonne has done her best to make me stylish—and I believe she has succeeded.'

'She is an artiste,' agreed Charlotte, 'but she told me she has seldom had a better figure to dress. I only wish mine were half as good!' She pulled a face at herself in the mirror.

Fair-haired and possessing a perfect English-rose complexion, Charlotte was what her husband termed 'a luscious armful' in their private moments. Reaching only as far as his shoulder, she was a little too plump—at least in her own estimation. However, she had such an infectious smile and her manner was so engaging, that she was generally admired and spoken of as a beauty.

'You *are* pretty,' Rosalyn said warmly. 'And so kind to me. I was afraid you might think me shameless, for you must know Damian and I are lovers...' She faltered and blushed.

'That is not so very terrible. Especially after the way your brother behaved towards you, forcing you to leave your home so suddenly...' Charlotte pulled a face. 'Besides, you are to be married next week. As long as you are happy, my dear. Why should we quarrel over trifles?'

Although they had known each other only a few hours, Rosalyn realised it was typical of Charlotte to dismiss their unusual living arrangements as a trifle. It would, as she knew only too well, have shocked most women of her class, but once Rosalyn and Damian had made love at the inn, it would have been ridiculous to have insisted on separate rooms in their own house. Besides, she did not wish to sleep alone—why should she when she could be in his arms?

She had known more happiness in Damian's arms than she could ever have expected, and if, sometimes, she still sensed that inner sadness in him, she accepted it as a part of the man she loved. She did not pry, for if Damian had a secret he would tell her when the time was right. It was enough that she loved and was loved in return.

'Well, my love—shall we go?' Charlotte asked, taking her hand to lead her from the bedchamber. 'I am sure the gentlemen are becoming impatient. I must tell you that the play we are to see is a little naughty, but you will not mind that? Everyone says it is wickedly funny.'

'Oh, I have read Mr Sheridan's plays,' Rosalyn said. 'I like them.'

'But you have not seen them performed in quite this way,' Charlotte said with an enchanting lift of her fine brows. 'The French manage to make everything that much more risqué.'

Rosalyn laughed but said no more on the subject. Since

their arrival in the city some days earlier, Damian had already taken her to several of the Cafés Concerts, where the atmosphere was slightly decadent and the dancing girls so daring that she had felt her cheeks grow warm watching them. Yet she loved those nights, as she loved the days spent exploring the wonderful city of Paris on Damian's arm, strolling in the warm sunshine amongst the busy streets with their flower sellers, artists and the constant flow of life. It was all so colourful, part of the new experiences she was soaking up, and she found everything so exciting, so different from the quietness of her family home.

Life was so much fuller for her now. She had not had time to look back, or to regret—for what was there to regret? Perhaps the quarrel with her brother, but that was his fault, and she would not let it spoil her happiness.

They were driven to the theatre in the Forresters' carriage. Damian had not yet set up his own equipage. He was looking for the right horses, which were to be his special wedding gift to Rosalyn—though he had already given her so many gifts. Almost too many for her comfort.

Inside the foyer of the large and impressive theatre was a lush décor of crimson and gold with a grand, carpeted stairway leading to the private boxes. Ladies and gentlemen in evening dress were moving to and fro, meeting acquaintances or taking a glass of chilled champagne in the refreshment area. In the background, Rosalyn could hear the music of an orchestra.

'This is wonderful,' she whispered to Damian as she clung to his arm. 'I am so glad you chose this gown! I should have felt positively dowdy in my old one.'

'You could never look anything but lovely,' Damian replied. 'I think we should be finding our box. The play will be starting at any moment.'

'We must not miss the opening,' Rosalyn said. 'Charlotte told me it is very naughty.' Their friends were ahead of them, almost halfway up the stairs. 'I am looking forward to the performance.'

Damian smiled. She sensed that he was about to say something concerning the play, but instead he became very still, a little nerve twitching at the corner of his mouth. She followed the direction of his gaze, feeling a coldness seep through her as she saw Freddie and Beatrice moving their way.

It was quite obvious that Freddie had seen them. He was glaring furiously, as though outraged that they should have the audacity to come to the theatre at all. Rosalyn hesitated. How unfortunate that this should happen. If she had ever known, she had forgotten that her brother intended to bring his wife to Paris on their honeymoon.

What ought they to do? She glanced at Damian uncertainly. He looked angry, but seemed to be hesitating. Then Beatrice noticed them. She touched Freddie's arm, her manner indicating that she was urging him to go up to his sister. As Rosalyn watched, she saw Freddie say something sharp to his wife, then he took a firm grip on her arm and steered her away. Beatrice looked back, her expression one of both apology and acute distress as she was forced in the opposite direction.

Freddie had deliberately cut her! The hot colour washed into Rosalyn's cheeks and then faded, leaving her pale and sick to her stomach. How could her own brother behave so badly?

'I am sorry,' Damian said to her. He held her arm protectively, his eyes glittering with anger. 'That was a disgusting thing for him to do.'

'It doesn't matter,' Rosalyn replied, lifting her head proudly. 'I had thought Freddie might have got over his temper and regretted his hasty words—but it seems he has not.'

'He could at least have acknowledged you.' Damian was furious. He was tempted to go after Freddie and demand that he acknowledge his sister. 'He was abominably rude to you.'

'Let us forget him,' Rosalyn said, her hand tightening on his arm. The incident had shocked and distressed her, but she did not wish to make a fuss about it. 'Charlotte will be wondering where we are. It is not important, Damian. If my brother chooses not to know me, that is his affair.'

Damian said no more as they continued on up the stairs. Rosalyn was pretending not to mind, but he knew the incident had hurt her. He was so angry for her that it almost choked him. He would have liked to pursue Freddie, to force him to apologise, even if he had to thrash him—but that would have ended in a terrible scene and made things worse than they were already.

Damian hardly heard a word of the play. He sat watching Rosalyn as she went through the motions of enjoying herself, knowing that the evening had been spoiled for her, and his inner turmoil mounted. What had he done to the woman he loved? She had given up so much for him, and he had so little to give her in return.

During their first few hectic days in Paris, he had bought her more clothes than she could possibly wear. She had a magnificent diamond and emerald ring, which matched the necklace and earrings she was wearing that evening—other costly jewels lay in their boxes, as yet unseen by her eyes, waiting for the right moment to be presented. She always smiled and thanked him warmly for his gifts, yet he knew she did not need them: no jewels could match the beauty and grace of this special woman. It was he who needed to give, to make up for all she had lost by coming away with him—but what could make up for the hurt she had suffered that evening?

Rosalyn too was thinking deeply. She knew that Damian was angry. She was aware of him watching her as she struggled to control her seething emotions. Damn Freddie for spoiling things! It was so like him to go his own way with no thought for her. She had been hurt many times in the past by her brother's careless attitude, but never again. This was the very last time she would allow herself to care what Freddie said or did to her.

Rosalyn sat in her fine silk nightgown, brushing her hair. It fell like a shining curtain about her face, tumbling on to her shoulders and reaching almost to the small of her back. Hearing the door open, she turned to look as Damian came in. He had remained downstairs after their return from the theatre, and, as he came to her, she could smell the brandy on his breath. He did not often indulge in strong drink, and she knew she had her brother to thank for this: Damian's pride had naturally been hurt, and he was upset for her sake. Somehow she must make him forget the unpleasant incident.

She stood up and moved to meet Damian, holding out her arms; the scent of her perfume enveloped him, filling his senses and driving the anger to a corner of his mind.

'I was wondering where you were,' she said as he drew her close, his lips moving against her neck. 'Hold me, my darling. Love me. I want you, need you so very much.'

'Rosalyn…' He made a moaning sound in his throat, catching her to him in a desperate embrace. 'My lovely woman.'

'Make love to me,' she murmured huskily. 'Love me, Damian. Love me always. Never leave me.'

His answer was to carry her to the bed. Laying her down on cool, sweetly scented linen sheets, he lavished kisses on every tender, intimate place of her quivering body. His tongue teased and flicked at the deep rose of her gently swollen nipples, while his hand moved between her soft thighs, stroking and invading the centre of her femininity. The warm moistness of her invited his entry and, driven by his urgent need, he thrust himself inside her, deeper and deeper until she moved with him, gasping out her frantic pleasure as their passion intensified.

'Damian...ahhh! Damian...my love.'

She screamed his name, arching her back to meet him, her nails scoring his shoulder as she felt herself falling into space: falling...falling into a state of being where she knew nothing except the endless, aching pleasures of love, which seemed to go on and on until she lost all sense of time and place.

'You little witch,' Damian murmured huskily against her throat when they lay finally entwined, exhausted and at peace. 'My back feels as if I have lain with a tigress.'

'Have I hurt you?'

She attempted to rise and look at his shoulder, but he laughed and rolled her back into the pillows, holding her there as she half-heartedly struggled to free herself.

'Be still, witch,' he said. 'I was teasing you. I love it when you scratch me. I love it that you never hold back when we are together like this—you are a very giving, passionate woman.'

She gazed into his face, suddenly almost shy. 'Are you saying I'm wanton? Is that a good thing in a wife, Damian?'

'Very good.' He grinned at her wickedly. 'With you in my bed, I'm not like to look for a mistress. I wouldn't have the energy.'

'I am your mistress.'

The smile left his face as though it were a slate wiped clean. She saw anger spark in his eyes before he rolled away from her.

'Only because I could not arrange the ceremony sooner,' he said. 'It was your choice, Rosalyn. I would have waited.'

She knew that she had unwittingly touched a raw nerve. She lifted herself on one elbow, her hair hanging forward so that it brushed his face and chest as she looked down at him. What lay beyond that closed expression? Why torture himself so?

'I did not wish to wait,' she said softly. 'Do not be angry, my love. Wife or mistress, I love you—and I know you love me. Believe me, I do not feel used, nor have you taken advantage of my innocence. I came to you willingly, because I love you. All I want is to be yours, totally and forever.'

For a moment he stared at her, his expression hard, unchanged, then he reached up, tangling his fingers in her hair as he drew her face down to his and kissed her with a fierce hunger.

'I shall always love you,' he said as she slid down beside him, burying herself in the curve of his shoulder, melding her willing flesh with his. 'You may come to wish one day that you had thought twice about leaving your family but—'

'Never!' Rosalyn said, nipping at him with her sharp teeth. 'Do not be foolish, Damian. I love you…you are all I need, all I shall ever need. I want only you. You are my life.'

'I know. Forgive me.' He kissed her forehead, stroking her hair, letting it slip through his fingers as she pressed herself closer to his side. 'I was angry earlier, but not with you. Go to sleep, my darling. I am a strange, foolish creature, but I love you.'

Rosalyn muttered something against his shoulder. He smiled as he realised she was almost asleep: she possessed that enviable gift of being able to curl up like a kitten and sleep when she was comfortable. The fresh, clean scent of her hair filled his nostrils as she filled his senses. He could feel desire stirring deep within him again, but he quelled it with an iron control. She was always responsive to his needs, but he would not wake her. Let her sleep. He was too angry to let sleep claim his mind—angry with the man who had hurt her, and himself for being unable to prevent it.

When Rosalyn whimpered in her sleep, his anger deepened. She would never give him reason to think her unhappy, but he could not rid himself of his guilt. He had taken her from her home and family. She was content enough for the moment, but what of the future? Would she come to regret all she had lost? Would she begin to wish that she had never met him, never thrown her hat over the windmill for the sake of love?

Damian had known the pain of exile. Although he had finally won fortune and friends in India, he had never quite forgotten the hurt of being cast out by his family. Now, because of him, Rosalyn too was an outcast—at least as far as her brother was concerned.

What made Damian feel so frustrated was the charge of murder. This was the second time such a charge had been levelled at him, and it rankled deep in his soul. The first time he had believed in his heart that he was indeed guilty— guilty of killing the wrong man, and that had lain heavily on his conscience for many years. But this time he was innocent. Yet there was nothing he could do to refute the charge, no way he could clear his name—the name he was about to give to Rosalyn.

He had taken her from home and family, and all he could give her was a tainted name.

'Will you be all right by yourself?' Damian asked for perhaps the tenth time that morning. 'I hate to leave you, my dearest, but it is business. I have several calls to make, and you would be kept waiting for ages.'

'Of course I do not mind,' Rosalyn said. 'You do not need to be with me all the time. I am quite capable of amusing myself for a few hours. I shall write to Maria and Aunt Susan. I ought to have done so sooner, but we have hardly been in the house.'

'Give *poor* Maria my love,' he said with a twitch of his lips. 'Tell her we shall be leaving Paris after our wedding. We must go to Jared soon or he will think himself deserted.'

'I have enjoyed our stay here very much,' Rosalyn told him. 'But I shall not be sorry to be in the country again.'

Damian nodded and kissed her. After he had gone, Rosalyn sat down at the pretty little inlaid writing desk in the back parlour; it was set in the window embrasure and looked out at a garden with rose-beds and secret arbours. The top of the desk was littered with expensive trifles Damian and she had bought during their stay in Paris. She had just picked up a rather attractive gold and enamel pen to begin the first of her letters when she heard the front door-knocker.

Now who could that be? They had made several new acquaintances in Paris, but she did not expect any of them to call that morning, especially as she knew for certain that Charlotte had a previous engagement.

Hearing voices in the hall, Rosalyn got to her feet, her heart beginning to beat uncomfortably fast. Surely that was Freddie! Why had he come here? The maid entered to announce him. Rosalyn stood stiff and straight, the colour draining from her face as she saw the look on his. He was in one of his black moods, and clearly still angry with her.

'This is not a social call,' he said as the maid withdrew. 'There is a small business matter which needs attention. Father's will provided for the release of your capital on your marriage…' His eyes went to her left hand and his lip curled scornfully. 'I see that has not yet taken place…'

'It is arranged for next week,' Rosalyn said, her chin lifting with pride. 'Will you sit down, Freddie? Beatrice is not with you?'

He remained standing, his manner indicating that he was here only because it was necessary.

'You think I would bring my wife here—to this house?'

The note of contempt in his voice made Rosalyn flinch.

'That is enough!' she cried, a flash of anger in her eyes. She would not stand for this in her own home. 'I do not intend to let you insult either me or Damian again. Say what you have to say and leave.'

'Very well. I had hoped you might have come to your senses—but I see you have not. You were always headstrong and stubborn. I am sorry for it and hope you will not regret your choice.'

'You have no need to fear for my future, sir. I am happier than I could ever have hoped.'

He inclined his head. 'I shall leave you these papers, which are in accordance with Father's will. You may look through them and return them to my lawyers when you have signed them. This will mean there is no need for further communication between us.'

'As you wish.'

Rosalyn felt cold with anger. How selfish he was! How uncaring!

'I have forbidden Beatrice to write to you. I do not wish my wife to associate with the wife of a murderer.'

Oh, how could he? Rosalyn itched to slap him, but maintained her dignity. 'I am ashamed of you, Freddie,' she said, giving him a look filled with contempt. 'I would never have believed you could be so cruel—so unfeeling. You were always selfish, but I thought you loved me as a brother should. I see now it was not so.'

'You chose to cut yourself off from your family. You are the arbiter of your own fate.'

'Am I, Freddie?' Her candid gaze caused him to look away. 'You accused Damian of murder—but I think it was in your own heart at one time. Look into your heart, brother, and see if you can find a part of what was once there, for if you do not, I believe you will suffer for it.'

Freddie refused to look at her. 'I have said what I came to say. Mrs Forrester told me where you were living. I know her husband slightly. We both belong to White's Club. Should you need to contact me in the future, you may do so through my lawyer.' He gave her a brief nod, turned and walked from the room without another word.

Rosalyn remained standing as the door closed behind him. Then she gathered up the papers he had left and thrust them into her writing box. She could not face them now, or the letters to her family.

She would go out into the garden and walk in the sunshine.

'Oh, Damian, they are beautiful! Thank you so much. I could never have wished for anything better.'

Rosalyn stood at the head of the pair of magnificent carriage horses Damian had purchased for her. They were both black with a flash of white on their noses, as close to a perfect match as it was possible to find and both spirited, handsome creatures. She knew at once that he must have gone to a great deal of expense and trouble to find them for her.

'I am glad they please you,' he said, smiling at her evident pleasure. None of his other gifts had brought such a sparkle to her eyes. 'When we are settled, I shall buy more horses for you...' His brows arched in inquiry. 'I thought perhaps you might like to set up your own breeding stables...thoroughbreds you could ride yourself or race if you chose?'

'Could I really do that?' She looked at him in wonder, her face alight with excitement, eyes glowing. 'How did you know it was what I have always wanted?'

'I did not know,' he said, bending his head to brush his lips lightly over hers. 'I merely hoped the idea might appeal to you—give you something to fill your days, to amuse you.'

To make up for the loss of family and friends.

'It is what I should like of all things,' she assured him, laying her face against that of the horse she was fondling. 'Oh, you beauty!'

'They are called Blackberry and Midnight,' Damian said. 'But you may choose new names for them if you wish.'

'It would merely confuse them,' Rosalyn replied. 'If we are to breed horses, I shall have the naming of many horses in time.' She stood back as their new coachman led the horses away, slipping her arm through Damian's. 'Where on earth did you find them?'

As they went into the house, Damian spoke of the contacts he had made, confessing that he had seen more than a dozen matched pairs before making his final choice.

'I wanted them to be perfect,' he said, glancing at her face which still carried the glow of surprise and delight. 'So—what have you been doing, my love?'

'Sitting in the garden for most of the time,' she answered, avoiding his penetrating gaze. She did not wish to spoil his surprise by speaking of the visit from Freddie. 'I did write my letters eventually.'

Damian sensed she was not being quite open with him, yet he could not think what she could be keeping from him. Perhaps it was merely that the act of writing letters to her family had made her realise exactly what she had done—what she had lost?

'Did you finish all your business?' she asked as he was silent.

'Yes—everything.' Damian frowned. 'There were letters waiting for me at the Embassy—the news is not good as far as Jared is concerned, I am afraid.'

'Letters—from his father?'

Damian nodded, his mouth thinning. 'It seems he has decided to bow to the wishes of others. He has officially cast off Jared and made his second son his heir.'

'Oh, how unkind of him!' Rosalyn's concern was all for the youth who had been forced into permanent exile by this act. 'How could a father do that to his son?'

'I do not believe Ahmed had much choice at the end,' Damian said. 'He has acted properly as far as Jared's inheritance is concerned. Besides the jewels we brought with us, he has lodged a large sum of money with a bank in Paris for Jared—enough to make him a wealthy young man one day.'

'Can money ever replace a father's affections?'

'No, of course not—but I hope to do that in some small measure. I wrote to Ahmed some weeks ago and asked for his permission to stand as a father to his son—and he has granted me the right to give Jared my own name. This means that Jared will now be safe from further attack—and that was perhaps the main reason for Ahmed's decision.'

Rosalyn reached up to kiss his cheek, her eyes soft with love. 'I am glad Jared has you,' she said. 'I just hope that he will not be too hurt by what his father has done.'

'I shall tell him myself,' Damian said, 'which means that it will be best if we leave for the country immediately after our wedding.'

'Yes, of course,' Rosalyn agreed. 'I am ready to leave when you are.'

She recalled the papers Freddie had tossed down, which were still tucked into her writing case, unread. Her brother had expected her to return them to his lawyers within a few days, but it could make no difference either way. She did not need more than her allowance; the papers could wait until she was ready to look through them.

'You look lovely,' Charlotte said and kissed Rosalyn on the cheek. 'I am so happy Damian has found you, my dear. There was a time when I believed he would be haunted by his memories...that he would never forget her...' She pulled a wry face as she realised what she had said. 'What am I saying? And on your wedding day! My foolish tongue!'

'Who was it you thought he would never forget?' Rosalyn frowned. Was this what lay in Damian's past? Was it his memories of a woman he had loved and lost that brought such a bleak look to his eyes sometimes?

'Helen...surely he has told you? You must know why he fought that duel?' Charlotte looked puzzled, contrite. 'Forgive me, I believed you knew his story.'

'I knew about the duel...' Rosalyn turned away to pick

up her white gloves. 'I thought Helen was his friend's sister.'

'Yes, she was...' Charlotte was instantly remorseful. 'I should not have mentioned her. Especially today—but I meant only to say how pleased I am that Damian has finally put the past behind him and found happiness.'

Rosalyn smiled, her head slightly raised, hiding her confused emotions. Charlotte had not meant to hurt her, nor to raise doubts in her mind. She would not allow the knowledge of Damian's love for the girl who had taken her own life out of shame to spoil her special day. She ought to have realised sooner that he would not have fought a duel unless the girl meant a great deal to him—but she had never suspected that he had carried the memory of his lost love in his heart all these years.

Did it matter? Rosalyn told herself it did not; she had proof enough of Damian's love for her. It would be foolish to let herself be haunted by jealousy of a long-dead girl. No, no, she was far too sensible to let such a trifle distress her.

'Have I upset you with my foolish chatter?' Charlotte asked anxiously.

'No, of course not,' Rosalyn said, giving her a bright smile. 'I have known about Helen for a long time.' She pulled on her gloves. 'I think we should go now, Charlotte—or Damian will believe that I have changed my mind.'

The ceremony was quite brief, witnessed only by a handful of friends, the chief of whom were the Forresters. A brilliant sun hung in the sky as Rosalyn left the small church on Damian's arm to the sound of bells pealing and a shower of rose petals, which floated on the breeze.

The reception was held at a hotel, just a simple meal shared with friends who toasted them in the finest cham-

pagne and then waved them off in the splendid new carriage
Damian had purchased for his bride.

Once their journey was under way, Damian leaned across
to kiss his wife on the lips.

'Happy, my lady?'

'Yes. Very.'

Rosalyn laughed. Damian had used his title for the wedding ceremony, and she was now the Countess Marlowe,
something that she found amusing in the circumstances.

It occurred to her that if she were ever at a dinner party
where her brother was being entertained, she and Damian
would take precedence. Had she been of a spiteful nature
she might have gained satisfaction from the thought but,
possessing a certain kind of humour which saw the ridicu-
lousness of such conventions, she merely smiled to herself.

'Why are you smiling like that?'

'No particular reason,' Rosalyn replied. 'Except that it
seemed so odd to hear myself addressed as Lady Marlowe.'

'I wanted there to be no doubt about the legality of our
marriage,' he said, a wry expression in his eyes. 'The title
means nothing to me—but you are at liberty to use it if you
wish.'

Rosalyn shook her head. 'I am content to be your wife—
by what name I am known, I care not.'

The subject was dropped, and they turned to idle chatter
and to staring out of the window at the changing scenery:
fields, sloping hillsides covered with vines from which the
rich wines of France were created, sleepy little villages
drowsing in the evening sun—and then the cobbled yard of
the inn where they were to stay for the night.

That night Damian's love-making reached new heights,
as if by making her his wife he had reached firmer ground
and found peace of mind. Rosalyn slept in his arms, content

and happy. By the following evening, they would arrive at the house which was to be their home for the next few weeks, though eventually they would travel on to Andalucia and their future.

Chapter Twelve

'Here we are, my love,' Damian said as the carriage turned into a long drive. 'I hope you will like the house I have chosen. It is quite old, but adequate for our needs for the time being. We shall not stay here too long.'

Rosalyn looked out of the window as the house came in sight.

'It is lovely,' she said. 'A charming house.'

A groom opened the door of their carriage, and Damian got out first, turning to help his wife down.

'Ah, I see our arrival has been anticipated.'

Rosalyn looked and saw Jared walking towards them.

'I have been waiting for you,' he said, coming out to meet them. The evening shadows were just beginning to fall across the old courtyard, and the rays of a dying sun had turned the stone walls to rose. 'It is beautiful here, is it not? Can you smell the fragrance of the flowers? That's the jasmine, it always smells beautiful at night.' He stopped and looked at Rosalyn a little shyly. 'I do not know what to call you—should it be Lady Marlowe?'

'No, indeed it should not,' she said and leaned towards him, kissing his cheek. 'We are to be a family, Jared—and my family call me Rosalyn. I should be happy if you were to use my name.'

She saw her suggestion had found favour. He bowed to her, offering his arm, every inch the fashionable young gentleman he was fast becoming. She had noticed a distinct change in him, but perhaps it was just that he was growing up. He seemed to have shot up at least two inches in a few weeks, and she told him so. They went into the house together, laughing and talking as Rosalyn described Paris in lively detail, telling him of the places they had visited and the sights they had seen.

'I have bought several small tokens for you,' she told the youth. 'Just trifles I thought would amuse you. If we return to Paris before we leave France, you must come with us, Jared. I am sure you would enjoy the experience—though I know you love the freedom of the countryside…'

Rosalyn glanced about her, taking stock of her surroundings.

It was a large, old house which had obviously been important in its day, but was now fading into genteel decay. She supposed Damian had chosen it for its beautiful grounds, which he had told her led down to a private beach. There was plenty of room here for Jared to roam at will in safety…though there would be less need for security in the future. It was most unlikely that further attempts would be made on his life now that he was no longer his father's heir.

Rosalyn wondered how Jared would react to the news that his father had cast him off, and her concern made her redouble her efforts to amuse and please him.

She began to tell Jared about her plans to breed horses in Andalucia, and his enthusiasm for the project was such that they were on excellent terms as they went into one of the shabby but comfortable salons, where refreshments had been prepared for their coming.

Their lovemaking that night was perhaps more special, more passionate and deeply felt than it had ever been. Afterwards, Rosalyn lay entwined in her husband's arms, her face pressed against the moist warmth of his shoulder. He had been all hers while they were making love, but now she sensed a withdrawal in him.

'What is wrong, Damian?' she whispered. 'Is something the matter?'

'Nothing, my dearest,' he murmured and kissed her. 'Everything is perfect. Go to sleep now.'

Rosalyn said no more. She slept in his arms for a while, but woke when he left the bed. For a moment she lay with her eyes closed, then when she heard the door close softly behind Damian, she'd sat up, waiting for him to return. Something was bothering him, and she needed to know what.

Could it be that despite his feelings for her, he could not forget Helen? Did the terrible fate of his lost love still haunt him?

Rosalyn felt the pain twist inside her. Would Helen's ghost always be between them?

She waited for Damian to return for a long time, but he did not come and at last she slept. When she woke the next morning it was a new day, and she made up her mind to put the past behind her.

If Damian had his ghosts, he must be the one to speak of them. All she could do was to show him how much she loved him.

'Oh, you are too good for me!' Rosalyn laughed as Damian's ball knocked hers aside. They had been playing croquet on the lawn at the back of the house. Now she threw down her mallet and went to sit in one of the basket chairs overlooking the sea. 'It is too warm to play any more,' she said as he came to look at her inquiringly. 'Is that Jared down there on the shore?'

Damian looked down at the beach and frowned. 'Yes, I think so. He went off in a mood after I told him about his father's decision. As I feared, it upset him a great deal.'

'He isn't wearing a turban.' Rosalyn shaded her eyes as she looked up at Damian. 'Why has he taken it off? I thought it was a part of his religion?'

'Perhaps he has decided to cast off his past life entirely,' Damian suggested. 'We must leave him to find his own way, Rosalyn. He is torn between two worlds—and perhaps it will be easier for him if he makes a new world for himself. Indeed, he must, for he can never return to the old one. He would not be welcomed and his life might be in danger from those who feared his influence.'

'I think I shall go down to him,' Rosalyn said. 'This has been very hard for him, Damian. He needs to know that we care if he is to make this transition. Do not be concerned, I shall not try to persuade him either way, now or in the future.'

'I believe he has begun to see you as a stand-in for Anna,' Damian replied. 'He is beginning to love you, Rosalyn.'

'I want only that he should be happy,' she said, and reached up to kiss Damian's cheek. 'As happy as we are.'

'You are happy?'

'Of course. Why should I not be?'

'No reason.' He smiled wryly. 'Do you want to go to this party tonight? These people are friends of Charlotte's. We met Devere's younger brother and his wife in Paris, if you recall?'

'Yes, of course. I liked them,' Rosalyn replied. 'I remember Monsieur Devere speaking of the *comte* once or twice. It was courteous of him to invite us to his house when he discovered we were living near by. I think we should go, Damian—unless you do not wish to?'

'It does not matter to me one way or the other,' he said, reaching out to tuck a wisp of wayward hair behind her ear. 'I care only for your happiness. Go down to Jared, my love. I have some letters of business to write.'

She smiled and nodded. As he went into the house, she began to make her way leisurely down the gentle wooded slope to the beach below. Jared had been throwing sticks into the sea, but, hearing her voice calling to him, turned to greet her. She saw that his hair had been cut quite short, changing the appearance of his features so that he looked even more European than before.

'I have cut my hair,' he said, a defensive look in his eyes as she came up to him. 'Nessa was angry with me—and Rajib said nothing. He is angry, because he thinks I have betrayed him and all that he believes in, but I do not care. I have told them that they should return to India. I am no longer a child. I do not need a nurse.'

'Your hair suits you like that,' Rosalyn said truthfully. 'But you must not turn against those who love you, Jared. Especially your father. He did not want to disinherit you, he had no choice—what he did was for your own sake.'

'He put me aside to favour the son of his new wife,' Jared said bitterly. 'He has betrayed both me and the memory of my mother.'

'Yet you must try to forgive him if you can, dearest.' Rosalyn saw the tears glistening in his eyes. Despite his grown-up ways, he was still a child and he had been hurt. She understood how it felt to be cast off by the family one had loved and opened her arms to him invitingly. 'You are not alone—we love you. Damian and I think of you as our own,' she said. 'I know what has happened hurts but—'

She got no further. Jared rushed into her arms, sobbing out the grief he had held inside him for so long. Rosalyn's arms closed about him, holding him, rocking him as he sobbed. She kissed the top of his head, and stroked the rather roughly shorn hair, comforting him until he was still, his grief spent.

'It will get easier,' she promised him. 'In time you will come to understand that your father did what he thought was best for you. Try not to become bitter, my dear. Nothing will be gained by hating your father.'

Jared drew back from her as the storm of grief subsided.

His head lifted and there was pride in his face. 'You are very wise,' he said. 'I shall try to do as you say—but it is very hard.'

'Let us go back and have our tea,' she said, giving him her hand as they began the climb up to the house. 'Damian and I have been invited to a grand party this evening by the Comte Christophe Devere—tell me, should I wear my green gown or the crimson?'

'You always look beautiful,' Jared told her as she put an affectionate arm about his waist. 'But I think the crimson gown is very elegant. If there are to be important guests, you should wear that—with the diamonds Damian gave you yesterday.'

'I shall look very grand, shan't I?' Rosalyn was laughing as she entered the house, her arm still loosely about him. 'Yes, I think you are right, Jared. I shall wear the crimson gown...'

Damian came into the bedroom as Rosalyn was changing for the evening. She smiled at him, turning her back so that he could fasten the hooks at the neck of her gown.

'Jared thought I should wear this tonight,' she said. 'Do you like it?'

'You are always lovely, whatever you wear. Surely you know that?'

There was an odd note in his voice which made her look at him more intently. She remembered the night he had left her bed and not returned.

'Is something wrong, Damian?'

'Why should anything be wrong?' He took the diamond necklace she was trying to fasten and slipped the catch into place, then kissed the top of her shoulder. 'Why do you ask?'

Rosalyn turned to face him. There *was* something wrong, but he obviously did not want to talk about it. Perhaps it would be better to leave well alone for the moment? If he was still in this same mood when they came home from the party, she would ask him again then. She felt that he was shutting her out and it hurt, but she was determined not to let him see it.

'No reason, it does not matter. Are you ready to leave?' she asked. Her manner, though she did not know it, was a little reserved. Damian noticed it at once, but made no comment. He nodded, holding her velvet wrap to place it around her shoulders. 'I wonder what the *comte* will be like. Have you ever met him, Damian?'

'No.' He frowned, thinking how magnificent she looked in the crimson gown. She had always been beautiful, but of late there had been a new glow about her. She would draw all eyes—just as she had at the ball in London, when he had felt so jealous. 'No, I have not met the Comte Devere, but I have heard of him.'

'Oh…?'

She moved towards him, her perfume so intoxicating that he felt an urgent need to make love to her. He wished they need not go to this dinner party, yet perversely was pleased that they had been invited for her sake. She had every right to shine in society, and he was proud of his wife.

'He is as yet unmarried,' Damian answered her question with a wry twist of his lips. 'Rich, handsome and charming, so they say—but determined to remain single despite the best efforts of a legion of young ladies.'

'Ah…' Rosalyn laughed. 'I see. It will be interesting to meet this paragon, do you not think so, my love?'

'We shall see…' Damian smiled. 'Your carriage awaits, my lady.'

Rosalyn was surprised by the richness of the *comte*'s château, which was filled with treasures of every kind. Paintings by the old masters adorned the walls, and the furniture was as fine as that she had seen at Versailles and the Louvre in Paris, both of which she had visited with Damian. The *comte* was obviously very wealthy, and a connoisseur of beautiful things.

Rosalyn and Damian walked up the grand staircase to be greeted by their host in an even larger and more lavishly decorated salon than the one downstairs. Her first sight of Christophe Devere told Rosalyn that Damian had not exaggerated when telling her the stories about this man. He had raven black hair and eyes so blue they rivalled the Mediterranean on a summer's day. He was dressed with exquisite care, his cravat falling in folds of the finest lace and pinned with a diamond so large that it dazzled the eyes when caught by the light of the crystal chandeliers. However, it was his only extravagance and the elegance of his attire came from its simplicity.

His manners were perfect. He bowed over Rosalyn's hand, kissing it briefly but holding it a fraction of a second longer than necessary. His look told her that both she and her gown, which was cut quite daringly low over her breasts, had found favour in his eyes.

'Enchanting, *madame*,' he murmured huskily. 'Seldom have I seen such perfection…such poise.' His eyes mocked her slightly. 'They told me you were English—but surely not?'

'I am indeed English,' Rosalyn replied, amused despite feeling wary of this charming predator. She had met his kind before, and was well aware of the danger they posed for women foolish enough to be taken in. 'But I believe I do not have the English rose style.'

'A far more exotic bloom,' the *comte* replied. 'My lord, you are to be congratulated in your choice of a wife. She is exquisite.'

'Yes, so I have always thought,' Damian replied drily. 'I count myself very fortunate that she chose to marry me instead of one of several devoted admirers.'

His tone made Rosalyn glance at him in surprise. He sounded as though he were warning the other man off.

Surely he could not be jealous? He could not imagine that she would be in the least interested in any other man? He must know she loved him, and only him! Yet there was a dangerous glitter in Damian's eyes, which disturbed her. She gave him a little warning frown, but he had turned away.

The *comte* bowed but made no further comment. They passed on, mingling with the other guests milling around the huge reception chamber until dinner was announced. The long dining table was a work of art, set with fabulous silver-gilt epergnes and dishes, delicate glasses with fine air twist stems, and an array of flower displays which perfumed the air.

Rosalyn discovered that she had been placed at her host's right hand; Damian was much further down the table on the same side, which made it difficult to look at each other. She saw that there was an attractive lady on each side of him, and hoped that would be enough to make him content with the arrangement. She herself was very conscious of her attentive host, who made it the business of the evening to attend to her every need, pressing her to try each new delicacy offered.

'Tell me, Lady Marlowe,' the *comte* said, leaning close to whisper in her ear after they had been at table for some twenty or thirty minutes. 'Is your husband always so possessive of you? Not that one can blame him. Such a treasure must always be closely guarded.'

Rosalyn felt that he was mocking Damian and frowned reprovingly. 'My husband does not think of me in those terms,' she said. 'We are happily married, sir.'

'Then he is even more to be envied,' the *comte* replied, a hint of laughter in his mesmerising eyes. 'Wedded bliss is even rarer than the treasures I pay a fortune to acquire for my collection. May one inquire how long you have been married, *madame*?'

'A few weeks.'

'Ah…then the novelty has not yet worn off,' he murmured. 'It is a pity we should have met at this time. A beauty such as yours should not be wasted on one man…unless that man has the eye to appreciate it, which I take leave to doubt.'

The look in his eyes left her in no doubt of his meaning.

'No more of this, I beg you,' Rosalyn said, beginning to feel distinctly uncomfortable. She glanced at Damian, but he seemed engrossed in his conversation with the lady sitting beside him. 'I do not care for foolish compliments.'

'No? An unusual woman indeed.' A wolfish smile played over the *comte*'s mouth. He gave her a speculative look. 'What would appeal to you, *madame*? I wonder.'

Rosalyn shook her head but did not answer. It was clear the *comte* had decided to hunt her, probably because she had shown reluctance to be flattered. It was no doubt a game with him, a game he played to alleviate the tediousness of a life which contained no real purpose. Although he could be charming, she considered him a rather vain and foolish man, and wished he would not be so intense towards her.

Her wish was not to be granted. The *comte* continued to give her his undivided attention throughout the meal, as course after course of delicious food was brought to table.

At the end of the long meal, a huge sugar confection was carried in, accompanied by cries of delight and polite clapping. It depicted a scene from a Greek legend and included nymphs, satyrs and men fighting mythical beasts—a triumph of the chef's art that even Monsieur Maurice would have found difficult to surpass.

After this, the ladies were led to a separate salon by the *comte*'s sister, Madame Moreau, leaving the gentlemen to their brandy or port. Rosalyn found herself singled out for attention over the teacups by the *comte*'s sister, who seemed to imagine her a favourite of her brother.

'Christophe has never married,' she told Rosalyn. 'I fear he is spoiled, *madame*. He loves beautiful things but he has never found a woman to grace his home. I tell him he is too particular. It is time he married and provided an heir for the family.'

'Yes, of course. I suppose you must wish for your brother to be happily settled,' Rosalyn replied dutifully. She did not particularly care for the *comte* or his sister—neither of whom were as pleasant as their brother, whom she had met at Charlotte's house in Paris. She was beginning to find the evening tiring and wished the gentlemen would join them so that she could ask Damian to take her home. 'With such a treasure house as this, your brother must wish for an heir to follow him, I think. There are so many beautiful and rare things here, are there not?'

'What do you particularly admire, Lady Marlowe?'

'Oh, there is far too much to pick out any one thing,' Rosalyn replied. 'But I suppose the cabinet with the collection of gold and enamel curios is very interesting.'

'You have a good eye,' the older woman replied with a satisfied smile. 'My brother has collected pieces from Italy, Russia and the Orient. Yes, there are some very valuable things in that particular cabinet.'

Rosalyn smiled but made no further comment. She was uninterested in the value of the *comte*'s collection, and she had just seen Damian enter the drawing room. She sent him a look of appeal, which brought him immediately to her side.

'Can we go home?' she asked in a whisper. 'Are you ready?'

'They are about to set up the card tables,' he said. 'Do you wish to leave so early?'

She did wish it but could see he was not ready to leave. He was obviously in the mood to gamble, and as the card tables were being set up, she was herself obliged to join the *comte*'s sister in a four at whist.

Rosalyn played with mixed success, something that annoyed her partner, and for which she was quick to apologise.

'I fear I have never excelled at cards,' she explained. 'My

father and I were more inclined to play at chess in the evenings.'

After some hands, her place was taken by another lady,
and, seeing that Damian appeared to be enjoying himself,
Rosalyn got up and wandered over to the window. She was
staring out at the night, and a sky that was sprinkled with
stars, when she became aware of someone standing close
behind her. Turning her head to look, she saw it was the
comte: the look in his eyes was speculative and sent a shiver
down her spine.

'You do not care for cards, *madame*?'

'Not very much,' she admitted. 'I was taught chess by a
master and much prefer the challenge of pitting one mind
against another, instead of relying on the cards one is dealt.'

'Ah, I see…you like to take your destiny in your own
hands.' He nodded, seeming pleased with the interpretation.
'Then perhaps you would care to see one of my special
treasures? I have a rather splendid chess set in my own
private parlour. If you wish, we could go there now.'

Rosalyn hesitated, not wanting to offend him, yet determined not to be lured into an obvious trap. She glanced
towards Damian, who had just won the game he had been
playing. He had turned in his chair to look at her, his expression unreadable.

'You must forgive me, sir,' Rosalyn said to the *comte*. 'I
believe I shall ask my husband to take me home now. I
have a slight headache.'

'I am sorry to hear that.' The *comte* arched his brows.
'Perhaps another day you will favour me with a game of
chess? I have seldom found an opponent worthy of my
time—but perhaps you…?' He left the question open, inviting her comment.

Rosalyn merely smiled. Damian was rising as she walked
to join him.

'Do you want to go home?' he asked.

'Yes, please. If you are ready. I have a slight headache. I have explained to the *comte*.'

'You should have said something earlier.'

'I thought you wanted to play cards?'

'I felt obliged once asked,' he replied. 'But I do not care to continue. Gambling is something I can take or leave.'

Rosalyn said nothing. His father had been ruined at the tables. The fever might be in his blood for all she knew. That evening he had played for small stakes and risen a modest winner, but in other circumstances he might not have been so prudent. How could she know?

There was so much she did not know about him, and his recent moods had made her feel there was an invisible barrier between them.

Their carriage having been sent for, they took leave of their host and fellow guests. Damian helped her into the carriage and settled into the seat beside her, leaning his head back against the squabs and closing his eyes.

He did not speak once during their journey home. She sensed he was angry about something, but did not feel inclined to ask what was wrong. If he was jealous of the *comte* paying her attention, it was his own fault. She had done nothing to court that attention, but had been forced to respond politely to her host's civility. Besides, Damian had been in a mood even before they left the house.

He was perfectly civil as he wished her goodnight before she went up, but he did not kiss her and he made no attempt to follow Rosalyn to their bedroom. At the top of the stairs, she paused to look back and saw that he was staring after her, his face set in an expression that chilled her.

What on earth could be wrong with him? Damian had once said that she might regret marrying him—was he beginning to have regrets himself? Had he discovered he was still unable to forget Helen, despite his marriage? Was that the reason he left her bed while she slept, because he wished she was Helen?

It was a bitter thought and one that, despite all her efforts, refused to leave her.

Rosalyn slept alone that night. It was the first time since they had left her home in England that Damian had not come to her. In thinking about it, she realised with a shock that she had not seen her womanly flow since before that time.

Could she be carrying Damian's child? It was surely too soon? And yet she had always been so regular.

Rosalyn thought about the very real possibility. She was not sure whether she was pleased to have fallen so quickly or not. It might have been better if she and Damian had had more time alone, before all the complications that child-bearing must bring.

Would Damian be pleased? She was uncertain, not of his love for her—but of his needs and hopes for the future. He did love her, she believed that, of course she did. She must believe it or she was lost! Damian cared for her, but something was playing on his mind, giving him no peace. Or perhaps it was just a part of his nature to be restless?

Rosalyn decided to keep her suspicions about the child to herself for the moment. She could not be sure that he would welcome her news, and she might be wrong. No, no, better to be certain before speaking of her hopes to Damian.

Why had he not come to her that night? Why had he seemed angry? His mood had started before they left for the *comte*'s dinner party—after they had parted, Damian to write some letters and she to meet Jared on the beach.

What had annoyed him? Rosalyn could find no reason for it. They had been happy enough earlier, playing at croquet. Why had that haunted look come back to his eyes?

What was it that worried him so? The thoughts went round and round in her mind, tormenting her.

Damian went for a long, hard ride before Rosalyn was awake the next morning. He had stayed up late, drinking alone in his study, cursing himself for his foolishness in allowing his jealousy to show. Rosalyn's headache was surely a sign of her displeasure? She had always valued her independence, she would not take kindly to having her freedom questioned.

He had behaved like a heavy-handed husband, when he ought to have been amused by Devere's attempts to seduce her—attempts which had been given the dismissive treatment they deserved. He was well aware that Rosalyn had given the man no encouragement; he had nothing to blame her for…nothing to cause the foul mood which had come over him when he'd noticed her standing near the window with Devere and seen the predatory look in the other man's eyes.

It was not unexpected from such a man. Devere wanted her the way he desired one of his rare *objets d'art*. He was attracted by her beauty—and because she was out of reach. The *comte* had become accustomed to taking his pick of pretty women; they fell over themselves to please him—the girls looking for marriage to a wealthy man and the bored wives who were flattered to be invited into his bed.

Rosalyn was different; there was something exciting about her, something that made men want her. She had aroused the *comte*'s hunting instincts. Damian had sensed danger from the beginning. One part of him had wanted to carry her off immediately, back to the safety of their home: the other, saner side knew that she was quite safe as long as she did not allow Devere to lure her into a compromising situation.

Damian laughed at himself. What a fool he was to worry! Rosalyn's quietness of late meant nothing. He was wrong to think she was brooding, regretting the impulse which had made her throw away all that she held precious for his sake.

Rosalyn was not Helen. She would not fall victim to abduction or seduction as that innocent child had all those years ago; she would not take her own life because she was unhappy. He had no need to fear it. Yet he could not quite rid himself of the idea that she might be in danger, that he might lose her.

'Damned fool!' Damian cried aloud. Would he never rid himself of the past? Of his feelings of guilt…the nagging fear that he did not deserve to find happiness, that any attempt to do so would be punished by the fates who ruled man's destiny.

It was not Damian's fault that Helen had taken her own life, but he had never been able to forgive himself for not preventing the tragedy. Although he had learned to live with his failure, it had remained at the back of his mind—and the business of Bernard Harrington's murder had made all the old sores fester once more.

He knew that he had been given something infinitely precious. Rosalyn was all that he had ever desired in a woman and more, but he was haunted by the fear that it would not last: that she would grow tired of living in exile and long to return to her old life, a life that was now denied to her. He was afraid that she might already have begun to regret her hasty action in leaving England with him.

Damian had the previous afternoon, when looking through his wife's writing box for a stick of sealing wax, accidentally discovered the papers relating to Rosalyn's capital, which was released on her marriage under the terms of her father's will. They had not been signed by her, but the date stamped in the official wax seal told him that she must have seen her brother in Paris. Why had she not mentioned it to him?

It seemed to Damian that she had deliberately kept the meeting with Freddie a secret. Why? Had her brother agreed to see her, providing she met him alone? The thought rankled, bringing a bitter taste to his mouth. Rosalyn had a perfect right to see her brother if she wished—but he would have preferred it if she had mentioned it.

Now he was being stupid! Damian was angry with himself for allowing such a small thing to matter. This business of the Comte Devere was far more important. He must warn Rosalyn to be vigilant…and yet she had shown herself well able to handle the *comte*. Perhaps it was better to say nothing. They would in any case be leaving France for Spain in a few weeks…and yet he carried a nagging fear that would not let him be.

Chapter Thirteen

Rosalyn discovered the prettily wrapped package on her dressing table. Another gift! Damian gave her presents all the time, but she was growing used to it and had discovered that she enjoyed being spoiled. After all, why should she mind that the husband who loved her liked to buy her things?

She picked up the box, turning it over in her hands, speculating on the contents. Could it be yet another piece of jewellery? It felt a little too heavy. She smiled as she untied the ribbon and took off the outer wrapping, looking for a card and failing to find one. That was unusual. Damian normally wrote funny, tender messages of love, slipping them inside the paper, but this time there was none.

She frowned as she took the lid off the box and saw what was lying inside. It was a delicate object made of gold and some kind of pink crystal, which she thought might be quartz. The stem was of twisted gold wire and bore a cluster of flowers made from the pink stone; the centres were studded with rubies and the leaves were probably jade, she thought. It was an exquisite thing, and quite different to anything Damian had given her previously. She set it down on the dressing table as the door opened and he came in.

'Damian,' she said, holding out her hand to him. 'Thank you for your gift, my darling. It is exquisite—'

'Gift?' Damian saw the pretty trifle amongst the discarded wrappings on her dressing table and frowned. 'Where did that come from?'

'Did you not leave it for me?' She looked at him in surprise. 'It was on my dressing table when I woke. I thought you must have left it there.'

'That did not come from me,' he said, a little nerve flicking at the corner of his mouth. 'You must realise who sent it, Rosalyn. Did you not see other similar pieces last night?'

'Comte Devere sent it?' She stared at him in dismay. 'One of the maids must have brought it up while I was sleeping. I cannot accept such a gift from the *comte*. It is far too valuable. I shall have it packed and returned immediately.'

'You would certainly be well advised to do so,' he said. 'Unless you wish to encourage his pretensions?'

'Damian!' Rosalyn had risen at his entrance. She took a step back, shocked that he could even suggest such a thing. 'You must know that I do not? I am your wife.'

'Which would make it all the easier for you to have an affair with the *comte* if you wished, would it not?'

It was accepted that married women sometimes had affairs, whereas the same behaviour in single ladies was frowned upon—but the idea that Damian should think she might be willing was so distressing to her that she could only look at him in horror. Surely he could not mean that? How could he insult her so?

The pain whipped through her. Why was Damian being so harsh towards her? He could not imagine she wanted the *comte*'s gift?

'That is a wicked thing to say,' she said, eyes mirroring her hurt. She raised her head, looking at him proudly. 'I cannot believe that you have said such a terrible thing to me.'

Nor could Damian. The words had come out of his jealous confusion. He knew them to be both cruel and unworthy and regretted them the instant they left his tongue.

'Forgive me,' he said, his manner stiff and reserved. He wanted to apologise abjectly, but pride—or jealousy—held him back. 'You are right to be angry, Rosalyn. It was wrong of me to say that. I know you would not consider...but you must realise that the *comte* intends to make you his mistress if he can?'

'That is nonsense,' she retorted, angry in her turn. Did Damian imagine that because she had gone to him before marriage, she had no morals—that she would contemplate being another man's mistress? How could he! 'The *comte* was merely being a polite host last evening—and this gift is the thoughtless impulse of a generous man.'

Even as she spoke, Rosalyn knew she was being untruthful. The gift was bait to lure her into a gilded trap. She had no intention of accepting it, none at all.

'Then keep it,' Damian said coldly. 'It seems to please you more than anything I have given you.'

He turned on his heel and left the room. Rosalyn stared after him, feeling stunned and disbelieving. What was wrong? Damian had never been like this with her. It was their first serious quarrel and it hurt her, it hurt her so much that she felt as if he had struck her.

What had she done that he should be so distrustful of her? Rosalyn blinked back her tears. It was not her fault that the *comte* had decided to pursue her; she had given him no encouragement: indeed, she had done her best to make him see that she was not interested in him.

Hot tears stung her eyes, but she held them back. She would not give way to her emotions.

Rosalyn rang the bell, summoning a maid. She gave instructions for the box to be wrapped and returned to the *comte*—and that any further gifts from him should be sent back immediately.

The maid dismissed, she began to brush her hair. She was about to ring for her personal maid to help her dress when the door opened again and Damian came in. He hesitated in the doorway, giving her a look full of contrition.

'I am sorry,' he said in a husky voice. 'I am a jealous fool. It made me angry to see the way Devere looked at you last night. When you were pleased with his gift, I lost my temper. I have behaved stupidly—will you forgive me?'

'Of course. I sent his gift back. You could not think I meant to keep it?' She rushed to his arms as he shook his head, a surge of relief rising in her. She was not sure she could have borne it if their quarrel had continued. 'I love you, Damian. No one else. You must know that?'

'Yes. I did not truly doubt you.' He touched her cheek, a rueful look in his eyes. 'Forgive me. I cannot help my jealousy, Rosalyn. It is a demon I must try to control in future—but you will take care? Devere is not to be trusted. If anything were to happen to you…I should not be able to answer for my actions.'

She gazed up into his face. His expression frightened her. He looked almost desperate. It made her wonder what he might be capable of if the *comte* attempted to seduce her…would he kill for her sake?

Had he already done so?

She had been so certain he could not have shot Bernard Harrington, but now she had begun to wonder…

Rosalyn kept her thoughts to herself. Over the next two days, Damian was very attentive and concerned for her. He put himself out to please her, taking both her and Jared to an English fair that had come to the district.

It was a warm, sunny day, without a cloud in the sky. They wandered around the stalls, Rosalyn delighting in the various trinkets and games that were on offer. She watched Damian bowling in vain for a pig, laughing as all his efforts failed to win the prize—but when it came to the shooting range, it was a different matter.

Each shot struck its target in the exact centre. Jared was excited and applauded enthusiastically.

'Damian was the best marksman at my father's palace,' he told her. 'Everyone knew that he would always win if there was a competition. And when a tiger attacked the villages, he was always the one who was called upon to kill it. He was fearless, and he saved my life when the assassins tried to kill me. There were three of them, and he shot them all…'

Jared's tale sent shivers down Rosalyn's spine. What did she really know of the man she loved?

Damian was obviously skilled with guns of all kinds. Rosalyn smiled and accepted the china fairing he won for her, but she could not help wondering if he would kill a man as easily as he shot at a target.

He had killed Roderick Harrington because of what he had done to Helen, but it was truly Bernard who had shamed the innocent girl. Had Damian killed him because of that…had he taken his revenge coldly and without mercy?

Rosalyn had believed him innocent of the crime. She had been almost sure that she knew the identity of the real culprit, but now she was not sure. Damian's moods could come so suddenly, and while they lasted he was capable of anger.

If only she could understand what it was that haunted him. She longed to ask him, and yet she was afraid that she might not like the answer.

Their quarrel had been soon mended, but she sensed Damian's growing frustration and it made her afraid.

She woke one night from a dream…the dream she had had once before. She was running in a mist. Damian was there, just ahead of her, but she could not reach him. She cried his name aloud, but when she opened her eyes and turned, needing to touch him, to feel the reassurance of his arms about her, he was not there.

'Oh, Damian,' she whispered into the darkness. 'Do not leave me, my darling. Come back to me. I need you…I need you so much.'

She was afraid that they might drift apart, that she might lose him. And she could not bear it.

'Madame Moreau,' announced the parlour maid. 'And Comte Devere.'

Rosalyn glanced round as the new arrivals entered her sitting room where she was presiding over the teacups. Since the *comte*'s dinner party three days previously she had received a steady stream of callers, most of them ladies who were curious to discover more about the woman who had commanded so much attention from Comte Devere.

'*Madame—monsieur.*' Rosalyn rose to greet her guests. 'It is a pleasure to welcome you here.'

Madame Moreau was looking about her in a superior way, obviously thinking that the house did not compare to her brother's.

'Madame.' The *comte* bowed over Rosalyn's hand, a gleam of appreciation in his eyes. 'You grow more lovely each time we meet.'

Rosalyn had wondered if the prompt return of his gift might offend him, but judging from the way he was looking at her—like a hungry wolf stalking its prey—she sensed that it had merely intensified his interest in her. The *comte* clearly enjoyed the thrill of hunting his intended conquests.

She wished that Damian had been at home to support her that afternoon. However, he and Jared had gone to an isolated estate some distance away, to look at a stallion they had been told was particularly fine.

'If it is what we want I shall buy him,' Damian told her. 'We can take him with us when we leave for Spain.'

'When are we leaving?'

'Soon,' he promised. 'I am waiting for my lawyers in Paris to complete the papers necessary for Jared's adoption, then we shall go.' He had smiled and kissed her. 'I already have agents looking for the right place for us...somewhere with good grazing for the horses and plenty of water.'

Rosalyn had still said nothing to him of her suspicion that she might be with child; she was not yet certain, though her conviction grew with each passing day. She hoped they would be settled in their new home before her condition began to make things uncomfortable.

She had let Damian go with a smile and a kiss that morning, but now she felt suddenly alone and vulnerable. No, no, that was ridiculous! She had a house full of servants, and half a dozen guests to keep her company. There was not the slightest need to be uneasy.

Yet as her other guests began to say their farewells after the customary twenty minutes or so, her anxiety intensified. Why must the *comte* keep staring at her in that particular way? Why was she beginning to feel trapped?

Eventually only Madame Moreau and the *comte* remained. When the sister stood up, telling her brother that he must not leave on her account, Rosalyn knew a moment of panic.

'No, no, Christophe,' Madame Moreau said to him. 'I know you wish to talk privately to the countess so I shall leave you together. I am perfectly well able to find my way home.'

She gave him such an arch look that Rosalyn was angry as the Frenchwoman swept from the room. It seemed clear to her that Madame Moreau was a party to her brother's plans for seduction. She suspected the pair had played this game before.

Well, it would not work this time! She was no innocent to be deceived by a philanderer.

As soon as the *comte*'s sister had gone, Rosalyn got up and went to ring the bell for the maids to clear the tea things. She turned to look at the *comte*.

'You will forgive me if I ask you to leave now, *mon-*

sieur?' she said. 'I have a little headache and I wish to rest for a while.'

'Another headache?' The *comte* looked amused. He arched his brows. 'I am alarmed, *madame*. You are perhaps ill? Will you allow me the privilege of recommending my own physician?'

Rosalyn was prevented from answering by the arrival of the maids. As they began to clear the used tea things, she walked out to the open French windows and went out to the stone terraces. She walked down three steps to the lawns below. The *comte* followed her.

'Yes, you are very wise, *madame*. Fresh air will often cure a headache, I believe. Perhaps more so than lying down in an airless room. Unless of course one had company to ease the tedium...'

His meaning was so clear that she turned on him, eyes sparking with anger. 'Very well, sir, you force me to speak plainly. I do not wish to be alone with you. Your attentions are unwelcome to me.'

'You returned my gift,' he said, ignoring her outburst. 'Did it not please you? I was told you had a preference for such trinkets, but if you would prefer something else you have only to ask. Tell me, *madame*, what can I offer that would make you smile for me? Both my person and my fortune are yours to command.'

'Nothing. I want nothing you can give me.' Rosalyn glared at him. Was the man so thick skinned that he could not be told? 'Please leave now and do not bother me again.'

She walked away from him, across the lawn. The sun was hot and she had not lied when she'd said she had a headache. It was a dull, heavy feeling that had been pressing down on her for a while.

When she realised the *comte* was still following her, she swung round, temper flaring.

'Will nothing I say make you understand?'

He smiled his disbelief, so used to having his way that he could not believe her refusal to be final.

'You are magnificent when you are angry,' he said, his voice husky with desire. 'Such a woman as you would be worthy of my home. If I have given you the impression that I want only a brief affair, I must beg you to forgive me. If you were free I would marry you—as my mistress you would have a king's ransom at your command.'

'I have no wish to marry you or to become your mistress. Nor am I interested in your wealth, *monsieur*.'

She was beginning to feel very uncomfortable. The pressure in her head was becoming hard to bear.

'But you will be mine,' the *comte* muttered, angered by her apparent indifference. An ugly lust twisted his features as he made a grab at her. 'I shall taste the honey you deny me…if only briefly…'

Rosalyn was so shocked that he should physically assault her in broad daylight and in the very gardens of her home that she did not react fast enough. His arms closed about her, pulling her, resisting, against him. She beat at him with her fists as he bent his head to take possession of her mouth in a hateful, greedy kiss that filled her with disgust. Such was her horror that she summoned all her strength, wrenching away from him and wiping the back of her hand across her mouth to take away the taste of him.

'How dare you? How dare you insult me so?'

'That was only the beginning.' His eyes narrowed. Unused to being thwarted and denied his pleasures, her resistance had brought out the worst in him. He had heard rumours about this woman that had made him think she might be available and his disappointment at being rejected was all the stronger. 'I always get what I want in the end, believe me. You were Marlowe's mistress before he married you—why not leave him and come to me? I can give you far more—'

'Never!' she cried. 'Please—leave me alone.'

'Why not make this pleasant for us both? I can be a bad enemy if I choose. I want you—and I intend to have you, if I have to abduct you and kill your husband.'

He could not mean it! Rosalyn was too shocked and confused to think clearly. 'No...' she whispered, as his face began to go fuzzy before her eyes. She was feeling most unwell. This could not be happening: it was like a nightmare playing out in slow motion. She pressed a hand to her forehead as the garden began to spin around her. 'No...you must not say such...' Through the mists, which were closing in on her, she was aware of danger and she cried out to Damian. 'Please help me...help me...'

Everything was going black. She was falling...falling into a bottomless void...

When Rosalyn came to her senses some time later, she was lying on a sofa in the parlour. Nessa was bending over her, bathing her head with a cloth wrung out in cool water, and a maid was hovering in the background: there was no sign of the *comte*.

'What happened?' she asked, a faint moan escaped her. 'How did I get here?'

'The *mem-sahib* fainted,' Nessa said. 'You were kissing that man—and then you fell to the ground. Rajib was in the garden; he saw what happened and went to your assistance. It was he who carried you here.'

'I must thank him...' Rosalyn put a hand to her head as she tried to sit up. 'The *comte*...' The room still seemed to be moving and she lay back, sighing and closing her eyes. 'He...forced himself on me. I did not kiss him. He threatened to...' She recalled Devere's threat to kill Damian and a thrill of fear went through her. 'My husband must know nothing of this. If he knew what the *comte* said to me, he would—'

'What would I do?'

Rosalyn's throat caught as she looked up and saw Damian

coming towards her. His expression was so stern. When had he returned? What had he seen or heard that had made him look like that?

'Damian…' She faltered, feeling nervous. Was he angry with her again? 'I did not know you were home.'

'Did you not, my dear?' His tone was so cold, so angry. 'Perhaps it is fortunate that I did return a little sooner than planned. Otherwise I might not have discovered what has been going on.'

'Damian…' cried Rosalyn in distress. 'You cannot think…'

She pushed herself up against the pillows someone had placed behind her. Why was he looking at her in that way? She stared at him, the coldness spreading through her as she sensed his fury. He had already sent the maid scurrying from the room; now he jerked his head at Nessa, dismissing her.

'I said leave!' Damian glared at the old woman. 'I want to be alone with my wife.'

'Damian—there is no need to shout at her,' Rosalyn protested. 'She was helping me, because I had fainted.'

'And why did you faint, my love?' Damian asked as Nessa went from the room. 'Was it at the prospect of becoming the *comte*'s mistress—or your disappointment that you had not waited and married him?'

There was such bitterness in his face!

'How can you?' Rosalyn stared at him, tears she refused to shed stinging her eyes. What had happened to him? He was like a stranger. A hard, cold man she had never before seen. 'Comte Devere called with his sister. I was obliged to entertain them.'

'I met Madame Moreau's carriage as she was returning to her home,' Damian said, a hard glitter in his eyes. 'When I reached the house, I was told the *comte* was with you—but before I could come in search of you, Rajib told me you had fainted. I came at once…in time to hear you beg Nessa to help you conceal your indiscretion.'

'No, that is not true. You do not understand,' she cried. 'This is unfair, Damian. You accuse me without having heard my story. It was not what you think. You must believe me!'

'Then tell me. I shall be interested to hear what Devere said to you.'

Rosalyn got to her feet. She was still feeling unwell, but she could not allow this misunderstanding to continue.

'Listen to me,' she begged. 'Please listen, Damian.' There was no chance of concealment now. She must tell him the whole story and hope he would not lose his temper again. 'I did not wish you to know, because I feared you might force a duel on him and I do not wish…'

'You feared for his life? You would do well to do so.'

'Do not be ridiculous!' Anger helped her stand straight despite the fuzzy feeling in her head. 'I cannot believe you think so ill of me, Damian. Have you lost your senses? The *comte* insulted me. He told me he knew I had been your mistress—and promised me a king's ransom if I left you for him. When I naturally refused, he became resentful and seized me. He kissed me but I fought him off. Then he became abusive…he said he would have me if it meant abducting me and killing you. I was feeling most unwell and called for you to help me—and then I fainted.'

Damian was staring at her oddly; the fierce anger had died out of his face to be replaced by an expression of shame. He had been incensed when he heard her telling Nessa to keep the incident from him, but now he saw why she had done so: it was entirely for his sake, to protect him from the duel he was in honour bound to fight. He must certainly fight: he could not allow this insult to his wife to go un- challenged. Damian acknowledged the whole thing was his fault: by making her his mistress before they married, he had opened the way for an insult of this kind.

'Forgive me,' he said. 'I should not have said such terrible things to you. I most humbly beg your pardon, Rosalyn.

This is all my doing. All my fault. None of it was of your making.'

'No, it was not, nor should you have accused me so unkindly,' Rosalyn said. Her head was going round and round so fast that she could scarcely see his face. She felt very ill and did not know what she said, 'If you are going to be so jealous…so angry…every time a man looks at me, I do not think I shall be able to bear it.'

'Rosalyn…' She sounded so odd, so detached—as if his behaviour had so disgusted her that she had begun to regret their marriage. 'Forgive me…please?'

Damian was about to explain his reasons for being so overwrought when she made a little sighing sound and fainted again. He moved swiftly to catch her in his arms, fear coursing through him. Everything else faded into insignificance as he realised she must be ill. If Devere's despicable behaviour had caused her to faint once that would not have been surprising, but this was different.

Carrying her in his arms, he went swiftly from the parlour and up the stairs. He called loudly for assistance, sending a footman scurrying to fetch a physician from the village, and two maids to prepare the bed. As he laid her gently down, she moaned and fluttered her eyelids. He stroked the damp hair back from her forehead, cursing himself for quarrelling with her when she was ill. What a thoughtless brute he was! And all because he was afraid of losing her.

'Rosalyn dearest,' he whispered as he sat beside her, bathing her head with cool water. 'I am a wretch to upset you so, my love. I am so sorry…so very sorry.'

Her eyes opened at that, and she caught his hand. 'You won't call him out, will you? Please, Damian! You must not fight him because of what happened this afternoon. I was not really harmed…and he has sworn to kill you. I could not bear it if…'

So he had not quite killed her love! Damian felt the relief sweep through him. He had allowed his fears to drive a wedge between them, but it was not too late. She still loved him.

'I shall not be killed,' he reassured her. 'Rest, my darling. Nothing will happen to me. All that matters is that you should be well again. I have sent for the doctor. He will soon be here.'

Her head was beginning to clear at last. She smiled at him, sensing his anxiety, his guilt for having been angry with her. Her fingers entwined with his lovingly.

'I believe I may know what is wrong with me,' she told him softly. 'I think…it may be that I am carrying our child, Damian.'

'Carrying our child?' Damian stared at her, first in disbelief and then in dawning wonder. If this was true, it was so much more than he had hoped for! 'Do you mean it, Rosalyn—you are carrying our child?'

'Yes…I think I must be,' she said, a strangled laugh escaping her as she saw his joy. And she had wondered if he would be pleased by the news! 'I cannot be certain until I have consulted a physician, of course, which is why I did not say anything before this—but I do believe it to be so.'

'No wonder you fainted,' Damian said, a rueful look in his eyes. 'And I was so unkind to you—can you forgive me?'

'Yes, I can forgive you,' she said, clinging to his hand, 'but I do not understand your anger, Damian. You cannot for one moment think that I encouraged the *comte*'s advances?'

'No…' A little nerve flicked in his throat. 'No, Rosalyn. Despite what I said to you downstairs, I did not truly think it. Not in my heart—only with my jealous mind.'

'But why?' she asked. 'Why should you be jealous? You must know why I came with you? You must know that I love you?'

'Yes…' He stood up and walked away to the window, looking out into the garden. How to tell her when he did not truly understand himself? 'It makes no sense…I do not know how to explain it to you.'

'Won't you try, Damian?'

'I suppose I feel that I do not deserve you,' he said, and turned to face her. She saw that the bleak look was back in his eyes. 'That…if I allow myself to be happy, it will all go away.'

'But why? Why should you not deserve to be happy? Please tell me, my love.'

Damian was silent. She sensed that he was struggling with himself, trying to find the words to tell her what was in his heart, but before he could do so, one of the maids came rushing in to tell them the doctor was on his way upstairs.

'Another time, my love,' Damian said and bent to kiss her forehead. 'I shall wait downstairs while the doctor examines you.'

Rosalyn nodded, sensing that the moment for explanations had passed. She wanted to beg him not to leave her, but could not. He pressed her hand, turning as the doctor came in.

He was a fussy little man in a black frock-coat and striped trousers.

'Well, well, what have we here, *madame*?' he said, giving her an indulgent look. 'They tell me you have been fainting. Have you been sitting too much in the sun?'

Damian smiled and left her alone with the physician.

Why had he found it so difficult to put his thoughts into words? She deserved an explanation for behaviour she must think unreasonable. How could he tell her that he was haunted by his fear…that because he had failed Helen, he would lose the woman he loved?

It was not a rational fear. He had tried to tell himself so many times that it was not his fault Helen had taken her own life, and yet the guilt remained even after all these years.

If he had not left Helen there, sitting alone on that bench in the garden of her home, she might still be alive. She had begged him to go, told him that she felt much better, that she needed a little time alone—but he should not have listened. He should have taken her to her family, made sure that she was being cared for.

His own anger and disgust at what had been done to her was such that he had not been able to think sensibly; he had shown his feelings too clearly, and as a consequence of his neglect a girl had died. He had killed a man because of that—but it had not brought her back, nor had it eased his own guilt. Indeed, when he had discovered the wrong man had paid a cruel penalty, it had made his burden harder to bear.

But that was so many years ago! It was foolish to let the old memories haunt him still. No more! He would put them from his mind, crush the fears that lingered and take the happiness Rosalyn had brought him with both hands.

Damian waited alone in the parlour, to have a word with the physician when he came down after examining Rosalyn.

'Is she ill, sir?' he asked, torn with anxiety. 'Has she been doing too much?'

'Your wife seems to think she is with child,' the physician replied with a reassuring smile. 'Although too soon to be certain, I think she is possibly right in her diagnosis. It is not unusual for ladies to faint in this condition. However, you would do well to keep an eye on her—and she should rest for an hour or so in the afternoons.'

Damian thanked him, asked him to call again in a couple of days and then went back into the parlour. He sat down at the elegant rosewood desk he had bought for his wife in Paris. Rosalyn liked to sit at it when writing her letters, so that she could gaze out at the garden. What to do now? Rosalyn had begged him not to call the *comte* out, but Devere could not be allowed to insult her and get away with it.

Frowning, he looked down at the desk and saw there was a little pile of letters waiting for his wife. The franking showed that two of them had come from England, the third from Paris. He could smell Charlotte's perfume on that one, but who were the others from? He looked at the writing. One of the hands seemed familiar—he thought it had probably come from Maria—the other was unknown to him.

He rang the bell, summoning a servant. Letters from home were always welcome to his wife. Rosalyn would enjoy reading these while she was resting.

A maid had come in answer to his summons. He gave her the letters for Rosalyn, requesting her to take them up to her mistress immediately.

'Please tell my wife that I have had to go out,' he said. 'I may not be back in time for dinner. Tell her that I think she should stay in bed and rest. I shall see her in the morning.'

'Yes, sir.'

Damian left the parlour after the girl had departed. There was something he needed to fetch first, and then he would pay Comte Devere a little visit.

He went into the room he used as a study, taking a polished mahogany box from his desk and opening it. Inside lay a pair of perfectly matched pistols. It would be Devere's right to provide the pistols, or indeed to use swords if he so wished—but Damian thought it best to be prepared. He doubted the *comte* had killed a man in his life—and certainly not a maddened tiger at close range. It took a certain kind of man to hold his nerve under those circumstances. If Damian were any judge, the *comte* was not the type to wait until his opponent had fired.

Devere might be able to hit a practice target, but not many had the courage to put a ball in a man's heart. A grim expression drew Damian's mouth into a hard line. If he chose, Devere could die this night. No matter what the cost, this business must be settled for once and all.

Chapter Fourteen

Rosalyn took the letters from her maid without enthusiasm, scarcely glancing at them before laying them on the chest beside her bed. She had recognised Maria's hand but did not feel in the mood for reading her cousin's letter. Her head had cleared a little. She realised she was at last beginning to feel better, and would have liked to talk to Damian.

It was time they talked. Something had been bothering him for a while now. He had confessed that he did not truly believe she had betrayed him, even in her thoughts—so what was it that lay behind the moods that had come on him since they left England?

Was it possible that he had killed Bernard Harrington? Had he done so to protect her—and was it the act of murder which lay heavy on his conscience?

Rosalyn shook her head. No, for a while she had wondered, but she was able to think more clearly now and she would not believe any such thing! She had dismissed the idea as impossible from the beginning, even thinking that Freddie might have been the culprit for a while, and then something very different had occurred to her. Her doubts had been roused by Damian's haunted expression, but she believed there was a different explanation for his moods.

Damian was innocent of murder—but something was causing him to be uneasy.

Was it his memories of the woman he had loved and lost? Had he been unable to forget, despite his love for Rosalyn? She knew a moment of terrible jealousy but fought it. This was unworthy of her. She could not be jealous of a girl who had died of shame!

The maid had told Rosalyn that Damian would be out for the evening. He had requested that she should rest, have her supper sent up to her on a tray, but she did not feel like eating. Nor did she want to stay in bed now that the dizziness had passed.

Where had Damian gone? Had he decided to challenge the *comte* to a duel for insulting her? She was suddenly sure in her own mind that he had gone out for that very purpose.

Rosalyn felt cold all over. How foolish of him! Surely it was not necessary? She had been upset at the time, but no real harm had been done, and now she thought about it calmly, she did not believe the *comte* would have carried out his threats to abduct her and kill Damian. He had spoken in the heat of the moment and would surely reconsider his hasty words once he'd had time to reflect. He did not love her, he had merely wanted to add her to his collection—which was not worth the risk of fighting a duel.

Unable to rest, Rosalyn threw off the bedcovers and went over to her dressing table. She brushed her hair; the action was soothing, easing the headache that had plagued her since her fainting spell.

She felt restless. It was impossible to sit here in her room, not knowing where Damian was or what he was doing. She would go downstairs and wait for Damian. Surely he could not be gone all evening?

If her husband had gone to fight a duel, he might be killed.

The thought filled her with terror. She could not bear it

if he died. Oh, why must men be so foolish? It was such nonsense, to fight a duel for so small a thing!

Alone in her parlour, Rosalyn ran her fingers over the ivory keys of a pretty little spinet. She sighed, wishing that Damian would come back and take her in his arms. She was missing him, the more so because they had come close to quarrelling again, and that distressed her. Why was Damian behaving so oddly of late? Was it only jealousy?

She turned as she heard a sound behind her. Rajib was standing in the doorway, staring at her strangely.

She felt a sudden coldness at the nape of her neck.

'Yes, Rajib—what is it?'

'I wanted to speak to you, *mem-sahib*.' His dark eyes were intense as he looked at her. 'May I speak openly?'

'Yes, of course.' She rose to her feet, waiting for him to begin.

'I have decided to return to India, and Nessa is to come with me.'

'Oh…' Rosalyn hesitated. 'I do not quite understand. You should properly say this to my husband—or to Jared.'

'Jared knows of my decision. He has grown away from us. We are no longer needed.'

Rosalyn heard the resentment in his voice. 'I am sorry that you should feel rejected,' she said. 'I know you love Jared—both of you.'

'He is my master's son.' Rajib said. 'I did what my master bid me. Now I must go home.'

'But you are angry?'

Rajib's eyes met hers, then he inclined his head once. 'You are not to blame. Nessa blames you for taking Jared's love, but I do not. I came to tell you this—and one other thing.'

'Thank you for your confidence,' Rosalyn said. 'What else did you wish to tell me, Rajib?'

'The *sahib* has gone to fight a duel with the man who came here today. I thought you should know.'

'A duel…' Rosalyn stared at him in dismay at having her fears confirmed. 'How do you know this?'

'He took his pistols with him. Besides, it is a matter of honour. The man who came here today attacked you. The *sahib* must kill him. It is his destiny.'

'No!' Rosalyn cried, her heart standing still with fright. 'Please, do not say so. He must not fight the *comte*. He could be killed.'

'The *sahib* will not die,' Rajib said and bowed his head to her. 'I shall not see you again, *mem-sahib*. In the morning Nessa and I will be gone.' He was about to turn away when Rosalyn stopped him.

'I should like to thank you,' she said. 'For what you did earlier today.'

'You saved my life,' he said. 'I have only given back what was owed.'

Rosalyn felt the barrier in place between them. It had always been there, though once for a few moments it had lifted—but they were from different worlds.

'Goodbye,' she said softly. 'I wish you and Nessa good fortune, Rajib.'

He bowed his head, his dark eyes giving nothing away. Then he turned and left her standing there alone.

Rosalyn felt suddenly light-headed. She was so tired! She sat down on the elegant daybed, gathering the cushions so that they made a pillow for her head.

She was concerned for Damian, but knew there was nothing she could do, except pray for his safety. She must think of her child and rest—but she would stay here for a while before she went back to bed.

The sound of a chair being overturned woke Rosalyn. She sat up, startled and blinking in the semi-darkness. Was someone in the room?

She strained her eyes to see, then got to her feet as she heard a muffled curse. 'Who is it?' she said. 'Who is there?'

'Rosalyn?' Relief swept over her as she heard Damian's voice. 'Damnation! Stay where you are—let me light a candle. I thought you long abed and asleep. Why are you sitting in the dark?'

The candle flared to life. The effort to fetch it had almost been too much for Damian. He was wounded! She saw him slump down on a sofa, a grimace of pain on his lips. Blood was seeping through his breeches. She strangled the scream of fright that rose to her lips. Now was not the time to become hysterical. He needed her help.

Oh, the foolish, foolish man—to fight a duel over such a small thing!

'Damian!' She went to him at once, her heart racing. 'What have you done? Have you fought a duel with the *comte*? Have you killed him?' She bent over him, catching the smell of brandy on his breath. 'You have been drinking!'

'Yes…a glass or two,' he muttered, sounding a little slurred. 'It helped to dull the pain when the physician dug Devere's ball out of my leg. Damn him for being a poor shot!'

'If he had not been, he might have killed you!'

Damian gave a snort of laughter. He seemed vastly amused and she wondered if he were drunk.

'Not a chance in hell. He meant to fire into the ground but the pistol misfired, his arm jerked and he hit me by accident.'

'How do you know he did not mean to hit you?'

Damian pulled a wry face. 'It would not have mattered if he had, he could not have done it in his condition; he was three sheets to the wind and could barely stand straight. Damn it! We should never have come to a duel in the first place if he had been sober.'

'You did not force it on him?'

He shook his head. 'Devere insisted. I tried to reason with the fool, but there was no dissuading him. He was adamant we should settle it between us in a gentlemanly fashion—and that it should be immediately.'

Rosalyn was looking at his wound. It had obviously been bound up but the blood had started to seep through the bandages.

'You should be in bed,' she said. 'Your wound has opened again.'

'I had to ride home,' he replied. 'Couldn't stay there all night. Devere wanted to give me a bed for the night, but somehow it didn't seem quite the thing to do in the circumstances.'

She saw a gleam of laughter in his eyes and recognised it: this was the old Damian, the man she had fallen in love with so desperately. He had come back to her. Whatever had happened that night had somehow released him from the shadow of his past.

'No, I would not think so,' she said, a faint smile on her lips. 'You have not killed him, then?'

'If I went round killing every man who wanted you, I should wipe out half the male population of wherever we happened to be,' he said, a wicked look in his eyes. 'I never intended to kill him in the first place. I just wanted to let Devere know he was not at liberty to insult my wife.'

'But you took your pistols with you…didn't you? You meant to challenge him to a duel.'

'Who told you that?' Damian groaned as he tried to stand. 'Was it Nessa? She is forever spying on me. Damn her impudence! She will have to go, Rosalyn. Jared won't like it, but it cannot be helped.'

'Rajib has already decided to leave,' Rosalyn said. 'He told me this evening. He believes Jared has outgrown him and Nessa—and I think he is right.'

'I shall not be sorry to see them go,' Damian replied with a frown. 'Rajib has proved his worth, but they have both resented me from the beginning. It will be better for us all if they leave.'

Rosalyn agreed, though she did not say. Her concern at that moment was for his injury.

'If you were to lean on me, Damian, I might be able to get you upstairs. Then I could change the dressing on your leg.'

'You will do nothing of the kind,' he replied. 'Sit still and listen to me. In a few minutes you can summon a footman and he will take me up. You have been told to rest. Why are you not in bed?'

'I couldn't rest,' she said. 'I wanted to talk. We must talk, Damian. I do not know why you have been so restless of late, but...'

'Guilt,' he said frankly. 'Freddie was right, Rosalyn. I have taken you away from your home and family. I *have* laid you open to insult from men like Devere. I admit, it was in my mind to challenge him, but by the time I got there I realised it was ridiculous. Can't kill a man for wanting you. I meant to have it out with him. I demanded an apology—to you, not me—and would have knocked him down, but he was drunk. And then he insisted on the duel. I fired into the air, of course—and he meant to do the same. He apologised afterwards, both for wounding me and for insulting you. But the fact remains, I am at fault. I brought you to France. Had I not done so, this would not have happened. '

'I came because I wanted to,' she replied. 'Because I love you.'

'That does not make it right,' Damian said and winced. 'This damned leg is giving me hell. Would you pour me a glass of brandy, please?'

'Yes, of course.' She went over to the decanters on the sideboard and brought him back a glass half-filled with a pale golden liquid. 'You must let me look at your leg, Damian.'

'Later,' he said, gulping some of the brandy down. He gazed up at her as she stood over him, waiting to take the glass. 'Thank you, that was welcome. Have you seen your brother since we left England?'

The sudden change of subject made her stare.

'Yes. He brought me some papers to look over when we were in Paris. Charlotte told him where we were living— apparently he knows Edward. But why do you ask?'

'Why didn't you tell me he had called?'

'I did not think it was important.' She sighed. 'It was not a pleasant interview, Damian. He came only on business— and informed me that there would be no need for us to meet again.'

'Damn him! How dare he treat you so scurvily?' Damian was furious. 'That settles it. I was wrong to run away. I should have stayed and sorted things out. We must go back, Rosalyn—we must face up to the scandal. Only then shall we be free of it.'

'Go back...to England? Why?' The idea appalled her. 'Give up our dreams? What about Jared? How can we go back?'

'Jared will be safe enough now that he is no longer his father's heir. Besides, if we do not, the rumours will follow us,' he said. 'Don't you see, my love? We...I have to face those who would call me a murderer. And I intend that Freddie shall apologise to you.'

'I do not care what Freddie says or does.' Rosalyn was disturbed. He might be in serious trouble if they returned to England. He might even be accused of murder officially. 'No, I do not see why we should go back,' she said. 'We both know you did not kill Bernard Harrington, so...'

'Have you never thought it?' he asked, looking at her intently. 'Never for one moment?'

She could not lie when he looked at her like that.

'I have wondered once or twice,' she confessed. 'I be- lieved it would have been for my sake, because he threat- ened me...and yet in my heart I knew you would have challenged him to a duel. I have never truly thought you capable of murder, Damian. Besides…'

'You loved me enough to come with me whatever the truth,' Damian said softly. 'You put your faith in me, your life in my hands. And because of your trust, I must go back…please try to understand that, my darling. If I force you to share my exile, I can never live with my conscience. Once before I let a woman down and she died because of it. She died of shame. I could not bear it if that happened to you.'

'Oh, Damian,' she cried, kneeling at his feet and looking up at him. 'How can you think that I…' Tears sparkled on the ends of her lashes and he bent down to brush them away with his fingers. 'I love you. I would follow you anywhere and never regret it for a moment.'

'You asked me why I have been restless,' he said. 'I shall try to tell you, though I hardly know myself. It is all so confused and goes back so many years. I left Helen alone in the garden that day. She begged me to go and I went…because my feelings had been so lacerated by what had been done to her that I could hardly bear to look at her. I did not truly think of her pain. I was so angry, so overcome with disgust, that I did not realise she was contemplating taking her own life. It was my fault she killed herself, Rosalyn. I failed her—'

'No!' She pressed her fingers to his lips, her eyes bright with tears as she felt his pain—the pain he had carried too long alone. 'No, my darling. How could you think that? How could you believe it was your fault? It was Bernard Harrington who shamed her. It was his vile act that drove her to take her own life. Whatever you had done that day, you could not have saved her if she was determined to die.'

'Yet I did nothing to help her,' he said, that haunting sadness in his eyes. 'I left her alone and she took her own life…. I think because I had shown my horror and revulsion too plainly. I fought that duel to ease my conscience, Rosalyn—and an innocent man died.'

'Hardly innocent,' she said. 'Roderick enticed her into that coach. He must share his brother's blame.'

'Did he deserve to die?' Damian looked into her eyes and found his answer there. 'No, my darling, he did not.' He smiled wryly. 'Can you see now why I have felt so frightened of losing you? Why I do not deserve the happiness you have given me?'

'I see that you were badly hurt when your father called you a murderer and drove you into exile,' she said robustly. 'Roderick brought what happened on himself, Damian. Charlotte told me what happened that day. After his shot missed, you would have let him live. You were walking away when he fired at your back. You killed in self-defence. If there is blame, it is entirely his own.'

'I killed in anger,' he replied, determined that she should have the truth from him. 'The laws of duelling cleared me of murder—but my own conscience will not. I should have thrashed him for what he did, or put a ball in his shoulder—but I took my time and fired deliberately. I meant him to die, because of what he had done to that child—and she was a child, Rosalyn. Roderick deserved his punishment—though later I would have done anything to change what had occurred. I wantonly took a man's life, and it has haunted me all these years.'

'You wrong yourself,' Rosalyn cried. 'You are too hard on yourself.'

She saw what it was: his father had called him a murderer and alone, exiled from everyone he knew, he had come to believe it—but it was not so. Fate had played a cruel trick on him and he had suffered enough.

'Have you not paid for your mistake long since?' she asked. 'Damian, my dearest love. Is it not time to forgive yourself? To put the past behind you and think only of the future—of us?'

'Perhaps…but to do that, I must go back,' he said. 'I must face up to it—to whatever accounting may be demanded of me. Please try to understand, Rosalyn.'

'Yes,' she said. 'I see it now.' There was no denying him. Unless he followed his conscience, he would never be free of this guilt. 'Yes, you must go back, and I shall come with you. And now you must rest.'

'Then ring the bell for the footman and let us go to bed,' Damian said. 'This damned leg of mine is giving me hell!'

'But why should we go back to England?' Jared asked, looking at her angrily as they sat talking in the parlour the next morning. He jumped up, walking away from her, before turning to look at her once more. 'Damian promised we were going to Spain—and you promised we would breed horses.'

'We can still do that in England,' Rosalyn said. 'I am sorry you are disappointed, Jared. I am too—but Damian has to do this, for his own sake.' She could see he was still unconvinced, perhaps because he feared his freedom would be curtailed as it had been before. 'It may only be for a short time…'

'Damian broke his word,' Jared said. 'I'm going to find him—to have this out with him.' He walked off, his back stiff with pride.

'Jared…' Rosalyn was about to go after him when she heard a commotion in the hall. As she hesitated, a maid came in. She was carrying a huge basket of wonderful, exotic blooms: huge lilies, roses, camellias and several strange, new flowers Rosalyn had never seen before. 'This came for you, *madame*—and there are visitors asking to see you.'

'Thank you, Isabel,' Rosalyn said. 'You may leave the flowers. Please show the visitors in.'

She saw a card attached to the flowers and bent to pick it up. The flowers had come from the *comte* and she was still frowning over the message his card bore, when she became aware that two people had entered the room. Glancing up, she was shocked to see her brother and Beatrice standing there, looking hesitant and uncertain of their welcome.

'Beatrice!' she cried, getting to her feet gladly. Then she hesitated, looking at her brother uncertainly. 'Freddie…I do not understand, why have you come?'

'You did not get my letter?' Beatrice gave a little cry of distress. 'I sent it some days ago. It was to tell you that we should be calling today. I hope you do not mind that we have come, Rosalyn? My letter would have explained everything.'

'Of course I do not mind. It is a surprise—but I am pleased to see you, Beatrice. Of course I am,' Rosalyn said. She stood up and Beatrice came rushing to embrace her. She was so emotional that Rosalyn was surprised. 'Is something wrong, my dear? You are not ill?'

'No, not all,' Beatrice said, tears trickling down her cheeks. 'It is just that I have been so upset over this quarrel between you and Freddie. It was so unkind of him to deliberately cut you that night in Paris. I promise you, I have given him no peace over it.'

Rosalyn glanced at her brother. He looked ashamed of himself and was finding it hard to meet her gaze.

'Freddie?'

'It's deuced awkward you haven't had the letter,' he said. 'I suppose you still imagine I killed Harrington?'

'No,' Rosalyn said. 'It seemed to me once that you might have done it, Freddie—but I never believed you capable of such a thing, not truly.'

'You accused me of it!' he cried, indignantly. 'I can tell you, Ros, I was furious. Bea says I should apologise to you for…being so short with you, but I think you have something to apologise for, too.'

'If I accused you of murder, I do so unreservedly,' Rosalyn said, looking into his eyes. 'However, you accused

Damian of the same crime. It was you who said you did not wish to be associated with the wife of a murderer. *You* who told me you had no wish to see me again.'

'Oh, Rosalyn!' cried Beatrice, gazing at her in distress. 'It was wicked of Freddie to speak to you like that—and I told him so, even before—' She broke off and looked straight at her husband. 'Tell her, Freddie. Tell your sister what has happened. We know the truth now, Rosalyn. We know who killed Bernard...'

'How can you?' Rosalyn stared at her, an icy chill moving slowly down her spine. 'Unless...did she tell you herself?'

'You know!' Beatrice was astonished. Her eyes opened wide with distress. 'How can you know if you did not read my letter? We only discovered the truth after she died.'

'Mrs Jenkins is dead? Oh, I am so sorry,' Rosalyn said. 'Was it her illness? She seemed so much better before I left, that I quite thought she would soon be well again.'

'She...she took her own life,' Beatrice said, and began to cry into her handkerchief. 'It has been so awful. When we heard of her death, we had to leave Paris, to go home—and then to discover what she had done!' She ended on a sob.

Rosalyn went to her, putting an arm about her shoulders, leading her to the sofa. She pressed the sobbing girl to sit down. Beatrice turned to her, burying her face against her shoulder. Rosalyn comforted her, looking to Freddie for further clarification.

Freddie cleared his throat. 'Mrs Jenkins took something, laudanum, I think...foolish woman. If she had confided in us, I dare say we could have sorted things out between us. It need not have come to law. A man like that deserved all he got. She left a letter telling us the whole story.'

Rosalyn nodded. 'Yes, I imagine it played on her conscience. She discovered that it was Bernard who raped Helen Renshaw, didn't she? Roderick enticed Helen into his coach, but it was his brother who shamed her so deeply that she was driven to suicide. Damian did not know the whole story at that time. He went after Roderick and killed him in a duel…but it ought to have been Bernard Harrington who died that day, not his younger brother. The truth has haunted Damian for years. His father somehow discovered it, but it seems not to have been generally known.'

'It appears you know the whole story,' Freddie said, somewhat disgruntled at finding she had guessed the whole.

'I should have realised it at the time. Indeed, I did wonder. I know what must have happened. Mrs Jenkins heard me accuse Bernard Harrington of being his brother's true murderer,' Rosalyn said. 'When he attacked me in the garden, she was standing at the window on the landing and she heard everything.'

'Yes, that's about the size of it,' Freddie said, 'but not quite everything. You see, Bernard had been putting something in her powders to make her ill. He was hoping to inherit some of her money…and was prepared to hasten her death to get his hands on it.'

'He was poisoning her?' Rosalyn stared at him in shock. 'And she knew it. Of course, she knew he had been tampering with her powders after the doctor took them away…so when she heard the truth about her younger brother…'

'Who was the only person she ever really loved,' Beatrice said and sat up to dry her eyes on a lace kerchief. 'She took one of your father's pistols, Rosalyn, and she went after him. She killed him…intentionally. It was not an accident. She meant him to die. Her letter made that perfectly clear.'

'Oh, the poor woman,' Rosalyn cried. She had sensed that something was wrong that afternoon, after Bernard had assaulted her, when she'd knocked at Mrs Jenkins's door. It had crossed her mind that Mrs Jenkins might have witnessed the incident—but how could she have guessed what would happen later? 'How distraught she must have been to do such a terrible thing.'

'She said in her letter that she had nothing left to live for now that I was married,' Beatrice said. 'She has left every-thing to me—except a diamond brooch for you and also a letter confessing her crime, which she says you may do with as you wish. It was to bring you the letter and brooch that we came here today.'

'And to apologise,' Freddie said. 'Damn it, Ros! If you knew all along who had killed Harrington, why did you not say?'

'Because I could not be certain,' she replied. 'Besides, it did not matter so very much…or so I thought at the time. No one could prove anything one way or the other. We were leaving England for good and…I did not want to make more trouble for anyone. Besides—'

'Rosalyn loved me enough not to care what people might think of her,' Damian spoke from the doorway. 'It was only my foolish conscience that made me imagine a little scandal might matter to her. I know now that I was wrong. My wife is made of finer material than the rest of us, Freddie.'

Freddie's neck had gone bright red. He made an embar-rassed noise in his throat, his gaze directed at somewhere beyond Damian's head as he apologised.

'I have been a damned idiot,' he said. 'I was furious be-cause Rosalyn seemed to accuse me…and I *did* think it might have been you. If I had met Harrington when Bea first told me what he had tried to do to her, I might have thrashed him. I might even have killed him, if I could man-age it, though it would have been with my bare hands, not a pistol. I have an aversion to guns. Nasty things, have a habit of making loud noises.'

'Oh, Freddie…' Beatrice got up and went over to him. She reached up to kiss his cheek, then looked at Damian. 'I hope you will forgive him, Lord Marlowe, because I do miss Rosalyn so very much. I could not bear it if we were never to be friends again.'

'Then I should be a brute to bear a grudge, should I not, Beatrice?' he said and smiled at her. 'Rosalyn, of course, has already forgiven you both, and I could do no less.' He limped across to where his wife was sitting, lowering himself a little awkwardly to lodge beside her.

'Should you be up?' Rosalyn asked, looking at him in concern. 'Your leg is obviously still painful.'

'A mere scratch,' he murmured, a wicked glint in his eyes. Her heart caught as she saw his smile. Damian had come back to her, all the dark clouds were gone. 'And quite my own fault. As any other woman would have pointed out long before this.'

'Had an accident, did you?' Freddie asked.

'Yes, you could say that,' Damian murmured with a glance at Rosalyn. He had noticed the huge basket of flowers. His mouth twisted in a wry smile. 'From an admirer?'

'An ex-admirer,' she replied. 'To apologise…'

'Ah…I see.' He nodded. 'I thought as much.'

'Damian?' Rosalyn looked at him, but the haunted look of the past few days had gone. She could see he was amused by the *comte*'s gift. Relief flooded through her: this was the man she loved, wanted to spend her life with. 'I think I shall keep them.'

'Yes, indeed. Why not?' He looked at Freddie, who was still hovering. 'Won't you sit down, Freddie? Care for some tea—or perhaps you might like to try a rather nice burgundy I have discovered? I bought several cases. You may take a couple back with you if you wish.' He stood up. 'Shall we leave the ladies to talk for a while…settle a few matters between us in my study?'

'Settle…' Freddie looked slightly alarmed, then recalled the papers he had left with his sister. 'Oh, business, I suppose? I gave Ros some papers, but I dare say she hasn't bothered to sign them. Never could get her to take an interest in things like that.'

Rosalyn watched as Damian limped off with her brother, then turned to Beatrice, who had come to sit beside her on the sofa once more.

'It is lovely to see you again,' Beatrice said and kissed her cheek. 'I was so cross with Freddie that night at the theatre, Rosalyn. We quarrelled over it and he went off in a temper the next day.'

'He came to see me—and he was in a terrible mood. I did not realise he had quarrelled with you.'

'Was he awful to you?'

'He was thoughtless, as he sometimes is,' Rosalyn replied carefully. 'I dare say you have not noticed, but…'

'Oh, I am well aware of Freddie's faults,' Beatrice said, a spark in her eyes. 'Do not imagine he can do no wrong in my eyes. He is used to having his own way. I think he has been spoiled, Rosalyn, but he must learn that he cannot always do just as he pleases. He must take more note of other people's feelings.'

Rosalyn smiled inwardly. There were hidden depths to her sister-in-law! She did not think Freddie would be getting quite so much of his own way in the future.

'I am sorry you quarrelled over me,' Rosalyn said. 'But I am glad that you persuaded him to visit us. It is much preferable that we should all be on friendly terms.'

'He did not need so very much persuading once he had read my aunt's letter,' Beatrice said. 'That was very sad. If I had only guessed what was in her mind, I might have been able to do something…to prevent her taking her own life. I know she could be unpleasant when she chose, but I believe she had led a very unhappy life.'

'Yes, I think perhaps she had—and I dare say she had come to regret what she had done,' Rosalyn said. 'She was hurt and angry when she took Papa's pistol. Bernard said some cruel things that afternoon, things that must have driven her past the point of bearing. What she did was wrong, of course, but understandable in the circumstances.'

'I do not think it was so very wrong,' Beatrice said, a flush in her cheeks. 'He was a horrible man, Rosalyn. He frightened me and I am glad I shall not have to meet him ever again.'

Rosalyn kept her silence, as she had since it had first occurred to her that the most likely person to have killed Bernard Harrington was his own sister. It had been such a terrible thought that she had told herself she must be wrong.

'Well,' she said now. 'It has all been most unpleasant, but I think we should try to forget it and look to the future. Tell me, Beatrice—what did you think of Paris?'

Rosalyn was sitting, brushing her hair in front of her dressing table that night when Damian came in. She put down the brush and stood up, turning to greet him as he came towards her.

'Are you tired?' he asked. 'It has been quite a day for you, my love. And you ought to be resting.'

'I am perfectly well,' she said, opening her arms to him. 'I know I fainted yesterday, but…'

'Twice,' he reminded her. 'You must take care in your condition, Rosalyn. I do not want to risk your health, or that of our child.'

'Do not scold me,' she said, lifting her face for his kiss. 'It was very warm yesterday and I was feeling the heat. It has been much cooler today. Besides, I have been sitting with Beatrice most of the day.'

Damian kissed her, then released her, retreating to the bed to perch on the edge and watch as she finished brushing her hair. She was so beautiful, so serene. He could still not quite believe he had been lucky enough to find her…to marry her. Fortune had smiled on him at last. He must not let his memories destroy their happiness. It was time to let the past go.

'It was a surprise finding Freddie and Bea here,' he said. 'You had not realised they were coming, had you? I sent up some letters for you last evening—did you not read them?'

'I did not feel like it,' she said, 'and then I forgot.'

'It is not surprising, considering what happened later.' Damian frowned.

'It was quite an eventful evening,' she replied, laughing at him. 'First Rajib's announcement that he and Nessa were returning to India—and then you stumbling in with blood all over you.'

'I should not have disturbed you, had I known you were there.'

'But I am glad you did, my love.' She looked at him anxiously. 'Is your leg truly better?'

'Much. It is merely a scratch, Rosalyn.' Damian said, looking at her thoughtfully. 'I have been thinking. Do you want to be with your own people? Now that Mrs Jenkins has confessed to murdering her brother, we could go home without fear of scandal. We might not be universally welcomed, but I dare say we should soon make a few friends— enough so that you would not feel ostracised.'

'I have no doubt that we should be invited to the houses of all but a few narrow-minded people,' Rosalyn said. She put down her brush and moved towards him, the scent of her stirring his senses, making him aware of a sharp desire. 'And I should not care for them—but I have never cared particularly for mixing in polite society. It was not just the *comte*'s attentions that made me want to leave early the other evening, Damian. To be honest with you, I was bored.'

'As was I,' he admitted with a wry smile. 'I was ready to go when you first asked me, but I thought you were doing it for my sake—so I was determined we would not leave. Perverse of me, I dare say.'

'You do not care for gambling, then?'

'It ruined my father,' he said, his mouth hard. 'Playing for small sums, for amusement's sake, is one thing—but reckless plays can be so destructive. Men who become addicted ruin themselves and their families. I worked hard for what I have, I see no point in throwing it away on the gaming tables. I can find better uses for it.'

Rosalyn stood before him as he sat on the edge of the bed. He put his hands about her hips, looking up at her.

'Do you still need to go back to England?' she asked. 'Jared was very upset about it—but if you want to go…'

'I do not need to go now that I have nothing to prove,' he said, pulling her down so that she was across his lap and gazing into her eyes. 'It is your choice, my love—we can go back to England or we can go to Spain as we planned…'

'We'll think about that tomorrow,' she whispered, pressing her lips to his neck, her tongue nibbling at his earlobe, teasing him so that he felt desire leap inside him. 'Does your leg hurt very much, Damian?'

He chuckled deep in his throat as he caught her meaning, then laid her back on the bed and bent over her, beginning to kiss and caress her with such tenderness that her body melted with delight.

'Not so much that I cannot make love to my wife,' he murmured throatily. 'You are so lovely…all that I have ever wanted…'

Rosalyn gave herself up to his loving, which was even more tender and sweet than it had ever been. Their bodies fit together perfectly, moving with a slow rhythm which brought them both gradually to a satisfying climax.

Long afterwards, Rosalyn lay with her head against his shoulder, dreaming of the future. She was not yet sure where it would take them, but she knew it would be wonderful.

*   *   *   *   *

Lady Knightley's Secret
by
Anne Ashley

Anne Ashley was born and educated in Leicester. She lived for a time in Scotland, but now lives in the West Country with two cats, her two sons and a husband, who has a wonderful and very necessary sense of humour. When not pounding away at her keyboard, she likes to relax in her garden, which she has opened to the public on more that one occasion in aid of the village church funds.

Chapter One

1815

Sir Richard Knightley woke with a violent start. He was sweating profusely and his every muscle seemed suddenly to have grown taut. What in the world had woken him? he wondered. Cannon fire? No, it couldn't have been. Just a bad dream—that was all: nothing more than vivid memory; a deep-seated fear. It was over... Surely it must be over? He just couldn't go through it again, not that carnage! He detected the distant rumble once more and released his breath in a deep sigh of relief. Thunder...only thunder.

Trying to ignore the throbbing ache in his shoulder, and the sudden darting pain in his left leg, he eased himself into a sitting position. His night-shirt, damp with perspiration, clung to him like a second skin. Ye gods, wasn't it oppressive tonight! he thought, pulling the offending garment over his head and tossing it aside in disgust.

Perhaps this storm might clear the air. Mary had warned him earlier that there was one brewing. He could quite easily discern those claps of thunder getting steadily louder, even if he was oblivious to the flashes of lightning.

Instinctively he raised a hand to touch the bandage over his eyes. The sabre gash in his right shoulder had been excruciating, and so too had the lead ball which had torn through the flesh in his thigh, but it had been the damage to his eyes when that pistol had been discharged which had caused him most concern. To be deprived of one's sight didn't bear dwelling on. To be led about by the hand for the rest of one's life…

A further clap of thunder, which seemed to shake the house to its very foundations, broke into his depressing thoughts and brought him back to the present by reminding him of how oppressive it was in the room. Had Mary inadvertently closed the window when she had paid that last visit before retiring for the night? He turned his head in the direction in which he knew the window to be, and after a moment's indecision decided to make the attempt.

Wincing slightly as he moved his injured leg, he swung his feet to the floor, and then reached out a hand to the wall. Mary had not delayed in encouraging him to exercise his muscles by taking a gentle turn about the bedchamber twice a day. He quickly discovered, however, that it was one thing having that blessed girl to guide him, and quite another trying to feel his way about a room he had never yet seen, a room where every object was a potential danger to a man who had been as good as blind for the past month.

"Oh, confound it!" he muttered as his elbow made contact with something, sending it crashing to the floor. What the devil had he broken? he wondered before his toes came into contact with a wet patch on the floor. It must have been the pitcher.

"Don't you be taking another step, sir!" came a gently warning voice, spiced with an unmistakable West Country accent, "otherwise you'll be a-stepping on broken porcelain."

"Oh, I'm sorry, Mary. I hope it wasn't valuable."

He discerned the slight click as she closed the door, and then heard that soft footfall of hers as she came across the chamber towards him.

"As you know, sir, this don't be our 'ouse, so whether it be valuable or no I can't rightly say, but it's of no matter, anyhow. What be you a-doing out of bed? 'Ave you need of the chamber-pot?"

He couldn't prevent a smile at this rather base enquiry. But then, he reminded himself, anyone less matter-of-fact, less practical would hardly have coped so admirably in nursing the six British casualties brought into this house.

Not that he retained any memory whatsoever of the journey back to Brussels in that lumbering cart filled with the dead and wounded. It had been Sergeant Hawker who had informed him that it had been Mary herself who had agreed to the army surgeon's request to offer sanctuary to the injured men, and it had been she who had insisted that three of those six must be men from the lower ranks. There would be no discrimination under her roof, no preferential treatment to those higher born.

Richard couldn't recall being carried up to this room, nor had he any memory of those first few days after the surgeon had tended the deep gash in his shoulder and had removed the piece of lead shot from his thigh. The last thing he could remember was hav-

ing his mount shot from under him and seeing a blind-
ing flash whilst he lay, momentarily stunned, on the
scorched, bloodstained ground; though who had discharged the firearm, a fellow soldier or the enemy, he
had no notion. Then, as he had made to rise, his vision
blurred, his eyes smarting, he had been felled again
by a French cavalryman wielding a sabre. The next
thing he remembered was someone gently raising his
head and coaxing him to take a little water.

That, of course, had been Mary, several days after
he had been carried into this house. Since then she
had administered to his every bodily need, had nursed
him back to health and had forced him to come to
terms with his brother's tragic death.

"No, my darling girl, I don't have need of that
particular receptacle at the moment. But I do require
the window opened before I expire from the heat."

"It is open, but I'll open it a little more, once I've
got you safely back into bed."

He felt the warm touch of gentle fingers on his
wrist before a slender arm encircled his back. He was
instantly aware of soft curves pressed against his side,
and was both astounded and faintly embarrassed by
his body's immediate reaction. He recalled that it had
been some weeks since he had assuaged his needs in
that particular direction, and was aware in those moments before returning to his bed that he was far
stronger than he had realised.

Praying she hadn't noticed his arousal, he didn't
waste a second in pulling the covers up to his chest.
He heard the grating of the sash window as it was
raised higher, and then felt a blessed waft of fresh air.
"That's better!" he remarked with genuine relief be-

fore he detected a faint chink as Mary busied herself with picking up the fragments of porcelain.

"I suppose it never occurred to you to throw the bedcovers off?" she chided, placing the broken pieces in the bowl. "There! That's cleared that up. Now, let's have no more middle-of-the-night wanderings!"

He couldn't forbear a smile at the scolding tone; he had grown quite accustomed to it by now. He heard her light tread once more and arrested her progress to the door by asking her to stay for a while.

He felt the bed go down slightly under her light weight, and instinctively sought one of those infinitely capable hands. "I'm a selfish devil, because you must be tired, but just sit with me for a while."

He couldn't see the smile which played around the exquisitely formed lips, but couldn't mistake the gentle understanding as she said, "I know you must be concerned about tomorrow, Richard, but everything will be all right...I know it will."

He brushed his thumb back and forth over the soft skin, easily detecting the small bones beneath. How often during these past weeks had he held these tapering fingers for comfort and support? He would know these caring hands anywhere. He had not infrequently marvelled at the fact that such a slender creature could be so strong, manoeuvring his six-foot frame in those first early days when he had been too helpless to do anything for himself. He had learned from Sergeant Hawker, the old rogue, that she was a very pretty young woman; knew too, from Mary herself, that her long hair was the colour of sun-ripened corn and that her eyes were blue. Such a delicious combination! But he had never looked upon what

Hawker considered the sweetest smile in Christendom… Would he ever be privileged to see it?

"I wish I had your confidence, Mary."

Her soft laughter had a teasing quality. "You will see," she assured him again. "Call it the gypsy in me that knows."

He was still far from certain, but knew he was probably being too pessimistic; behaving like a spoilt child, as Mary had told him in no uncertain terms on more than one occasion during these past weeks. Darling little scold! His sight hadn't been permanently damaged—the doctor had assured him of that. His eyes had been inflamed, certainly, and everything had been just a blur, but the condition was only temporary. His eyes had needed only resting and nature would effect its own cure. Tomorrow, when the bandages were removed, he would see again. He must believe that! Surely life wouldn't heap the torment of blindness upon him on top of everything else?

He found himself experiencing that same gnawing ache of grief, infinitely more painful than any one of the several wounds he had sustained during his years in the army. It had been just over two weeks since Mary had read that letter informing him of his brother's tragic death. He still found it difficult to accept that, when he did eventually return to England, Charles wouldn't be standing outside the ancestral home waiting to greet him, as he had done so many times in the past; that dear Margaret wouldn't be there either, nor little Jonathan. A racing curricle, driven at breakneck speed, had forced his brother's carriage off the road and it had tumbled down a ravine. Because of some mindless fop's attempts to win a wager,

Charles and his wife, and their nine-year-old son, now lay six feet beneath the earth.

Learning about the tragedy so soon after seeing so many comrades fall at Waterloo had been almost too much for him to bear. He had come perilously close to losing the will to live; might well have not survived his injuries; might never have attempted to come to terms with his tragic loss if it hadn't been for Mary.

Mostly gently coaxing, but occasionally rounding on him like a spitting virago, Mary had somehow managed to transfuse a small part of that indomitable spirit of hers into him, lifting him from the nadir of despair, and instilling in him a determination to face up to the responsibilities which had been placed upon him by his brother's untimely death. It would take a long time before he got over his loss; perhaps he never would, fully; but, for the sake of the baby niece he had never yet seen, he must face the future.

Charles and Margaret had considered their baby daughter too young to make that long journey to Derbyshire to stay with their friends, and had left her in the care of a close relative residing in London. Thankfully, Juliet was too young to understand the tragedy which had struck. Now it was up to him to ensure that her life was as carefree and happy as possible by taking the place of the father she would never remember.

He automatically reached out for his sweet preserver with his other hand and, pulling her down against his chest, ran his fingers through that long mane of silky hair which always smelt so deliciously of lavender-and-rose water. ''What would I have done without you, you darling girl!''

Without conscious thought he removed his hand

from her hair to run an exploratory trail down her cheek, brushing gently against the outline of her jaw before taking a hold of the softly rounded chin and raising her face. He lowered his head and his mouth retraced the path his fingers had taken before coming to rest on soft lips, invitingly parted.

He had intended nothing more than a brief display of his genuine affection for this wonderfully caring young woman, but as he felt those soft lips tremble deliciously beneath his own, as he became acutely aware of the firm young breasts pressed against his chest, his need returned with an urgency, reigniting that fire of desire in his loins. Before he realised what he was doing, he had eased her into the bed beside him and was peeling away that last flimsy barrier of her clothing with hands that now shook slightly in their urgency to touch every last inch of her.

It must have been this loss of sight which had finely tuned his other senses, he decided, for never before could he recall touching skin so satiny-smooth, so beautifully unblemished. She was perfect. Her breasts reacted instantly to his caressing touch, hardening and inviting his lips. Her soft moans of pleasure as he ran his fingers down to the softly swelling hips was music to his ears, a delightful encouragement for further intimate caresses.

Not for an instant did it cross his mind to wonder why the hands which began to explore the triangular mat of dark hair covering his chest were trembling slightly; nor did he consider the very real possibility that the body which reacted so deliciously to his gentle caresses might not be that of an experienced woman, but that of a hitherto untouched female who was responding quite naturally to a knowledgeable man's tender lovemaking. It was only when he eased himself on top and inside her and heard that betraying tiny cry of pain that the truth dawned on him. But it was all too late now: his need too urgent for him to stop.

"Why didn't you tell me, Mary?" he asked gently when at last he lay beside her once more, and cradled her head on his chest. "Did I hurt you very much, my darling? Had I known, I—"

"Had you known, Richard," she interrupted, "I suspect you wouldn't have made love to me at all."

He wasn't so certain. He wasn't a man accustomed to curbing his natural desires. A string of mistresses over the years had satisfied his needs, but he had never before tampered with innocence. Maybe if it had once occurred to him that she might be untouched he wouldn't have reached a point where he was incapable of stopping, but it was rather too late to question the wisdom of his actions now. There was only one course open to a man who possessed any degree of honour.

He brushed his lips lightly over her forehead. "We'll be married just as soon as I can arrange matters." He felt her stiffen. "What's wrong, Mary? Don't you want to marry me?"

"More than anything in the world, Richard!" It was like a desperate cry from a loving heart. "But—but you know next to nothing about me."

"I know that you're one of the sweetest scolds I've ever met," he told her laughingly. "I also know that your hair is blonde and your eyes are blue."

"Ah, yes," she murmured, a distinct catch in her voice, as though she were finding it difficult to speak.

"That's always been your favourite combination, hasn't it, my Richard?"

"How do you know that? Has Sergeant Hawker been gossiping again?"

She didn't respond to this, but asked instead with that bluntness which so characterised her, "Do you truly want to marry me?"

"Of course!" he answered without a moment's hesitation and only hoped his voice hadn't betrayed his grave misgivings. "Besides, now that I've come into the title it's essential I produce an heir. And I've come to know you well enough in these past weeks to be certain you'd make a wonderful wife and mother. So, we'll take it as settled."

There was no response.

When Richard woke again it was to discover himself alone and that portion of bed beside him quite cold. By the tramping of feet in the passageway outside his room—which sounded like a regiment of infantrymen parading up and down—he knew it must be morning, a morning he had been longing for and dreading by turns; a morning that, no matter whether he would see again or not, would change his life forever.

Raising his arms, he rested his head in his hands and gave vent to a heartfelt sigh. He was honest enough to admit that for a newly betrothed man he certainly wasn't experiencing untold joy; honest enough to admit, too, that Mary wouldn't have been his ideal choice for a wife. He liked her very well, probably more than any other woman he had ever known. She was both kind-hearted and amusing, and for all that she spoke with a pronounced West Country accent she was far from uneducated.

It had been she who had penned the letter to his London solicitors in response to the one they had sent informing him of his brother's tragic demise. He had also learned from Sergeant Hawker that she had spent many hours with him improving his reading and writing skills. But this, he was only too well aware, was hardly sufficient reason to suppose that she would make a suitable wife for a baronet. The truth of the matter was, of course, that she was totally unsuitable. She could have no notion of what was expected of her. Those vicious society tabbies would have a field day at her expense when they discovered her former station in life.

''But you know next to nothing about me.'' He frowned suddenly as Mary's words echoed in his mind. It was true: he knew absolutely nothing about her life. She had received a good education. He knew this from the numerous conversations they had had when she had spoken intelligently on a wide range of topics. She might well be the daughter of some country parson or practitioner. If this did turn out to be the case then the outlook was not all doom and gloom. She could be moulded and taught the ways of his social class. Added to which, she must surely come from a family with sufficient means to have been able to afford to hire this house for several weeks. Was she the daughter of a wealthy merchant, perhaps? But it was pointless speculating, he told himself. He would discover all he wanted to know, and perhaps a great deal that he didn't, when she visited him next.

The door opening interrupted his thoughts. "Mary?"

"No, sir. It's me."

He recognised his sergeant's rough voice instantly and smiled. "What brings you here so early, you old rogue? And what the devil's that confounded din?"

"The servants be moving some trunks, sir. Captain Munroe be leaving us this morning. We be the last two 'ere now."

"Where's Mary?"

There was a tiny pause, then, "She be a bit—er—busy at the moment, sir, so she asked me to see to you. High time I took up me dooties again. I can get about well enough, even though the old knee's still a bit stiff. Now, sir, I'll just pop this towel round you and give you a bit of a shave."

No sooner had this task been completed than the doctor arrived, and Richard, for once not having Mary there offering comfort and support, found himself grasping the bedclothes. Not once during any one of those many cavalry charges in which he had taken part could he recall being in the grip of such intense fear as he was in those moments when the bandages were removed and he opened his eyes for the first time since that never-to-be-forgotten last battle.

At first all he could detect were dark, blurred shapes. It was like trying to peer through a thick London fog, but then, blessedly, the mists slowly began to clear and the concerned face of his sergeant staring down at him gradually came into focus.

"I never thought I'd experience pleasure at seeing that ugly phiz of yours, Hawker. And I have to say it hasn't improved any since last I saw it!"

The sergeant, far from offended, laughed heartily

as he moved across to the window so as not to impede the doctor's further examination. He looked down into the street below, his amusement vanishing as he gave an almost imperceptible nod of his head, and then watched as the carriage pulled away from the house.

"Where is Mary?" Richard asked again, making his eagerness to see her very evident.

Giving a guilty start, Hawker looked back across at the bed. "She's—er—just this minute stepped out for a bit of air, sir."

"Well, when she returns to the house tell her I'd like to see her." Richard smiled at the choice of words. "Tell her I'm longing to see her."

The sergeant didn't respond, but he knew it would be only a matter of time before this gallant commanding officer realised there was something amiss.

The moment he had been dreading came early that evening when he brought Richard his dinner.

"Where is she, Hawker? Why hasn't she been to see me today?"

He saw little point in trying to conceal the truth any longer. "She be gone, sir."

"Gone? Gone where?"

"She be journeying back to England. She left in the carriage as soon as she knew you were back to normal, as yer might say." He couldn't bring himself to add that it had been he who had signalled to her from the window.

Richard experienced such a maelstrom of conflicting emotions that it was several moments before he could think clearly. "Did she say why she had to leave so suddenly?"

"Her old lady were right poorly, sir. Never once left 'er room in all the time we've been 'ere. Miss Mary must 'ave wanted to get her back 'ome before she weakened any more, I suppose. Don't think Miss Mary would 'ave stayed this long if she hadn't been nursing us lot." Reaching into his pocket, he drew out a letter. "Before she left, she asked me to give you this, sir."

Richard almost snatched it from the outstretched hand and, ignoring his sergeant's reminder that he wasn't supposed to strain his eyes by reading for at least a week, broke the seal.

Dearest Richard, he read. *This is to say goodbye— a cowardly way of doing so, I know, but it is for the best. Had I seen you again I might have weakened and agreed to be your wife, which would have been a grave mistake for both of us. I know you felt honour bound to ask for my hand after what had taken place between us, but I cannot allow you to make that sacrifice. I gave myself willingly, and do not regret what happened, nor shall I ever. But how can a marriage be a happy one, my darling, when the love is all on one side? One day you will meet someone and fall in love, and bless me for my actions of this day. God keep you safe. Mary.*

Richard swallowed the hard lump which had lodged itself in his throat, and cast his eyes again over those words written in a beautifully flowing hand, a hand which for some obscure reason seemed oddly familiar. His Mary had released him from his obligations, but did he want to be freed? He wasn't certain, but knew that he couldn't leave things this way. He owed that young woman so much. He simply couldn't allow her to walk out of his life like this. It was his duty to find her.

"She hasn't written down her direction." He looked up at the rather concerned face of his sergeant. "Did she leave a forwarding address, do you know?"

"That I don't, sir. Miss Mary left with all 'er servants. There's only the Froggies 'ere now."

"They're Belgians."

"All the same to me, sir. Do you want I should fetch the 'ousekeeper?"

Richard nodded, but she wasn't able to help him. Mademoiselle had never mentioned her address. The only thing the housekeeper could suggest was that he wait until her master returned from Italy at the end of the month, and ask him if he knew where Mary resided in England.

But Richard was not forced to await the owner's return. Tragically, a little over a week later, he was to read a report in a newspaper of the passenger vessel *The Albatross*, bound for Southampton, capsizing in mid-Channel. Amongst those listed as missing, believed drowned, were a Mrs and Miss Mary Smith.

Chapter Two

With all the exuberance of an excitable child, Lady Dartwood uttered a shriek of delight as she watched the carriage pull up outside the front entrance and saw a young woman in a very fashionable fur-trimmed travelling outfit step gracefully down the steps.

"She's here, Brin! She's arrived at last!"

"Will you stop jumping up and down that way!" her husband admonished with a passable attempt at sounding severe. "For heaven's sake remember your condition!"

"I can hardly forget it, now can I?" Glancing down at the rather large, figure-damaging protuberance at the front of her gown, the Viscountess's expression managed to betray dismay as well as a deal of motherly love for her unborn child. "And Elizabeth's so beautiful, too. I know you'll fall instantly in love with her!"

The Viscount rose from the comfort of his armchair and took his young wife gently in his arms. "I promise I shall like her for your sake, Verity. I know how very fond you are of your old school friend. But you're the only girl for me. How many times do I need to assure you of that?''

She rewarded him for his sound good sense, but quickly extricated herself from his embrace as the door opened and a young woman in her early twenties swept into the room and came tripping lightly towards them, looking so gracefully ethereal that the Viscountess couldn't help but feel a tiny stab of resentment, but hid it quite beautifully as she gave her friend an affectionate hug.

''I swear, Elizabeth, you get lovelier each time I see you. And slimmer, too!''

''And you are blooming, my dear Verity. The very picture of health!'' Elizabeth then turned and held out one hand to the Viscount. ''How do you do, my lord. Your wife mentions you so often in her letters that I feel I have known you for years.''

''And I must reciprocate, Miss Beresford,'' he responded, executing an elegant bow before releasing his brief hold of the slender, tapering fingers. ''My wife has spoken of nothing else since she received your letter accepting her invitation to be our guest.''

''How odiously stuffy!'' Verity's expression of staunch disapproval drew spontaneous chuckles from both her husband and her friend. ''Now you must know that in my delicate condition it isn't very sensible to vex me. So let's have no more of this unnecessary formality!''

''In the circumstances it might be wise to indulge her, sir,'' Elizabeth suggested. ''But only on condition,'' she added, casting the most winning smile up at him, ''that you refrain from addressing me in any one of those repulsive abbreviations so widely used where my name is concerned. I cannot abide Lizzie or Eliza. And I'm not enamoured of Beth, either.''

The Viscount readily agreed, thinking what a graciously charming young woman Verity's friend was, her manners open and wonderfully unaffected, and by the time she had left them a short while later to dress for dinner, he had decided, without any further coaxing from his wife, that he liked Elizabeth Beresford very well.

''Why in heaven's name isn't that charming young woman married? She's not only extremely pretty, but intelligent too.''

Not in the least surprised that he had been captivated so easily by Elizabeth's engaging manner, Verity smiled with satisfaction. ''I honestly don't know, Brin.'' The smile faded. ''I wouldn't be at all surprised, though, if it didn't have something to do with her upbringing. She had quite a miserable childhood. From odd things she has let fall from time to time, I gather her parents' marriage wasn't a happy one. I believe Elizabeth was quite close to her father, but didn't deal at all well with her mother. And as for that sister of hers…!''

''Mmm.'' He glanced thoughtfully at the logs burning brightly on the hearth. ''I hope you've forewarned her that it isn't unusual for Lady Chiltham to pay us impromptu visits?''

Verity's sudden scowl betrayed her feelings quite beautifully. She disliked Elizabeth's sister intensely and considered Lord Chiltham a pompous nincompoop. The Chilthams, however, resided less than three miles distant and for the sake of neighbourly harmony she had managed to conceal her dislike whenever they had happened to meet.

"She was so spiteful to Elizabeth when they were children. Elizabeth never returned to school after a vacation without having acquired at least one livid bruise from that sister of hers."

"It isn't uncommon for brothers and sisters to quarrel, my dear," his lordship countered fair-mindedly.

"I realise that. But Evadne's seven years Elizabeth's senior. It was nothing short of malicious bullying." A sudden gurgle of laughter escaped her. "I'd like to see her try it now," she went on, the wicked glint in her eyes betraying how she would relish the prospect of an unfriendly encounter between the sisters. "Elizabeth has changed out of all recognition since she went to live with her grandmother. I think darling Evadne's in for a rather severe shock when she does see her again."

"Well, Elizabeth certainly didn't strike me as a shrinking violet. She certainly is nothing like her sister, though, not even in looks."

"Very true," Verity concurred. "She was painfully shy at school, but thankfully that's no longer the case. She appears to be remarkably resilient too, now. Which is a blessing considering her recent loss. I must say she seems to have got over her grandmother's demise very well."

In this, however, Viscountess Dartwood couldn't have been more wrong, as Elizabeth's personal maid and lifelong devotee could have enlightened her if asked.

None knew better than Agatha Stigwell, who had been employed as nursemaid in the Beresford household, what a miserable existence her young mistress had endured in her formative years. She had wit-

nessed, first hand, the petty cruelties the pampered
Evadne had inflicted on her sister and had been appalled by the sheer indifference Mrs Beresford had
always shown when dealing with her younger daughter. The only displays of affection and kindness
Elizabeth had ever received had come from her maternal grandmother when she had stayed with her in
Bristol, and from her father, but as his visits to the
family home had been infrequent and of short duration, Elizabeth's periods of childhood happiness had
been few and far between.

Agatha had never regretted the decision she had
taken, after her master had died, in aiding Elizabeth
in running away to her maternal grandmother.
Elizabeth had seemed to blossom overnight under that
wonderful old lady's constant loving care. Although,
even then, weakened by years of ill-health, Mrs
Smithson had been more than a match for Elizabeth's
mother when she had come hotfoot to Bristol, demanding her daughter's return.

Agatha herself hadn't been privileged to overhear
what had passed between Mrs Smithson and her
daughter that day, but whatever the old lady had said,
it had been sufficient to send Mrs Beresford on her
way again rather abruptly. Agatha was honest enough
to admit that she hadn't been sorry to see the last of
her old mistress; honest enough to admit, too, that she
had been completely unmoved when she had learned
of Mrs Beresford's death two years later. What Miss
Elizabeth had felt was difficult to judge. She certainly
hadn't shed any tears over her mother's unexpected
demise; but the poor girl had wept bitterly when her
dear grandmother had passed away the previous autumn. She just hadn't been the same person since; but

then, Agatha reminded herself, her young mistress hadn't been the same since their return from Brussels last summer.

"Why are you staring at me with that peculiar look in your eyes, Aggie?"

Unable to hold her young mistress's gaze, she went across the bedchamber to collect a shawl. "You're imagining things, miss. I was merely thinking how sensible it was of you to accept Viscountess Dartwood's kind invitation. You've locked yourself away from the world for far too long. You know your dear grandmother didn't want that."

"No, I know she didn't. She even begged me not to deck myself out in mourning." A sigh escaped her. "I kept that promise at least. I've never once even donned black gloves."

Rising to her feet, Elizabeth remained only for the time it took to have the shawl arranged about her shoulders, and then went back down to the salon, where she had left her host and hostess earlier, to find them looking the picture of marital bliss, seated side by side on the sofa.

The Viscount rose at once and went over to the table on which several decanters stood. "I believe Verity omitted to inform you that we're expecting another guest, a friend of mine from my army days, but I'm not quite certain just when he'll be arriving—it could be today, or tomorrow."

He watched Elizabeth seat herself in one graceful, sweeping movement before handing her the glass of Madeira. "You were in Brussels last year, on hand, as one might say, to celebrate that famous victory. And I understand from Verity that you stayed to nurse some of our brave soldiers back to health."

"Yes, I was there," she admitted in a colourless tone, "but I saw little worth celebrating. The sight of that endless procession of carts, filled with the dead and dying, pouring into the city after the battle was over is an experience I shall never forget." She shook her head at the all-too-vivid recollection. "Where is the glory, sir, in all that waste of life...that suffering?"

Verity noticed a look of respect flit over her husband's features before he raised his head, his acute hearing picking up a sound from the hall.

"What is it, Brin? Has your friend arrived, do you think?"

"Yes, I believe so. I'll go and see."

Verity waited until he had left the room before turning to Elizabeth with a rather impish smile. "I never realised until a few moments ago how similar your shade of hair is to Brin's." She studied her friend's beautifully arranged locks once again. "Except, perhaps, yours contains a little more red. Why, you might be brother and sister!"

"I should have very much enjoyed having him as a brother. You're a lucky girl, Verity. He's a charming man." She cast her grey-green eyes over the Viscountess in a swift appraisal, deciding that marriage and the prospect of imminent motherhood suited her very well. She looked glowing and so utterly contented with her lot. "When is the baby due? Any time now, I shouldn't wonder."

"Great heavens, no! Not for several weeks, unfortunately." Verity noted the slight frown. "I know I'm huge already. And to think I've still another month to go!"

Her pained expression vanished as the door opened

and she watched her husband return with a tall and ruggedly handsome gentleman in tow. She had never met this particular friend of Brin's before and was instantly aware of his aura of powerful masculinity. So captivated was she by Sir Richard Knightley's spontaneous and most engaging smile, as her husband made the introductions, that she failed completely to notice the effect the very personable gentleman's presence was having on her friend.

With a hand which trembled slightly Elizabeth took the very sensible precaution of placing her glass down on the conveniently positioned occasional table beside her chair, before she foolishly disgraced herself by spilling the contents down the folds of her rich green velvet gown. No one's unexpected appearance could possibly have unsettled her more, but with a supreme effort at self-control she contrived to appear as composed as ever.

"There is absolutely no reason to introduce Sir Richard to me, Brin," she interrupted when he turned, about to do just that. "I knew him quite well when I was a child."

Looking a trifle pale, but maintaining quite beautifully that self-assured air, she rose to her feet and even managed a semblance of a smile at the three rather startled expressions bent in her direction. "It has been several years since you last set eyes on me, sir, so I'm not in the least offended by your all-too-evident bewilderment." She held out her hand, which thankfully no longer trembled. "Elizabeth…Elizabeth Beresford."

He didn't utter "Good Gad!" but the expletive hung in the air, none the less, drawing forth a gurgle of wicked amusement from the irrepressible Viscountess.

"I'm not in the least surprised, either, that you appear dumbfounded, sir, especially if you haven't seen her for some time. When I met up with Elizabeth again last year I could hardly believe that it was my old school friend sitting in that famous Bond Street modiste's."

"Indeed, you are vastly altered, Miss Beresford," he agreed in that attractive deep voice that she remembered so well, "but I ought to have recognised you." His dark eyes rested for a moment on the charmingly arranged rich red-brown hair before returning to the delicately featured face turned so enchantingly up to his. "Unlike your sister, you always did bear a marked resemblance to your father. With your unusual colouring you are unmistakably a Beresford."

"I cannot express strongly enough how relieved I am to hear you say so, sir," she responded with feeling, before turning and bestowing such a dazzling smile upon the Viscount that Sir Richard experienced a most unexpected and rather unwholesome spasm of jealousy gnaw at his insides.

"Your darling wife, Brin, has recently remarked that we might well be mistaken for brother and sister. You must be aware that she has never been known to put a guard on that unruly tongue of hers. Before you know it, rumours will begin to spread and we shall find ourselves on the receiving end of some rather strange looks!"

He laughed heartily at this before offering her his arm and escorting her across the hall and into the dining-room. Verity, following with Sir Richard, experienced a deal of wicked satisfaction when she noticed that her husband's very personable friend seemed incapable of preventing his gaze from wandering in Miss Beresford's direction.

Elizabeth became increasingly aware of this fact too as the evening wore on but, unlike Verity, found nothing satisfying in those all-too-frequent dark-eyed glances. Never in her wildest imaginings had she considered the possibility that the Dartwoods' other guest would turn out to be none other than the man she had secretly, and quite foolishly, loved since she was a girl.

Calling upon that all-important inner reserve of self-control, she managed to conceal this all-too-painful truth. However, trying to behave towards him as she might have done any other acquaintance of long standing, with a kind of polite, friendly interest, inevitably took its toll. So, when Verity announced her intention of retiring early, Elizabeth wasn't slow in making her own excuses to leave the gentlemen to their own devices.

Managing, still, to retain that serene look that suggested she hadn't a care in the world, Elizabeth accompanied her friend up the staircase. She accepted with alacrity the Viscountess's invitation to come to her suite of rooms later so that they could enjoy a comfortable coze before finally retiring for the night, but the instant she entered the sanctuary of her own bedchamber her expression changed dramatically.

"Ha! I knew it. In a right fix you are, and no mistake!"

Elizabeth flashed her maid a glance of impatience. "I might have guessed that you'd have got wind of his arrival. And don't stand there gloating! Come help me off with this gown!''

Completely undaunted by the brusque tone, Agatha helped her young mistress get ready for bed. ''What are you intending to do, miss? You mark my words, he'll find out.''

Elizabeth pulled a brush through her silky russet-coloured hair with impatient strokes as she stared at her maid through the dressing-table mirror. ''How can he possibly do that? Only you and I know. And if you ever reveal my secret, Aggie, I'll never forgive you!''

''Wild horses could never drag it from me, miss. You know that. But he's no fool. You might let something slip.'' Her expression betrayed her concern. ''It might be best if you make some excuse to leave,'' she suggested, but Elizabeth shook her head.

''I cannot deny that that solution is very tempting, but it won't answer. It would look most odd if I suddenly upped and left.'' She gazed sightlessly at her own reflection in the mirror, her mind deep in thought. ''No, that course of action would certainly give rise to conjecture. And besides, I'm quite adept at keeping a guard on my tongue, and concealing my feelings. I've had years of practice, after all.''

She saw sadness replace the concern in her maid's dark eyes and gave her arm an affectionate squeeze before rising from the stool to collect her robe. ''I must confess, though, that I'm more than a little annoyed with the Viscountess. I think for friendship's sake she might have taken the trouble to forewarn me that this friend of her husband's was none other than Richard. But—'' she shrugged ''—annoyed though I am, I couldn't with a clear conscience desert her now.'' A worried frown suddenly marred the perfect symmetry of her own brow. ''Have you by any chance caught sight of her ladyship since we arrived, Aggie?''

''I have that, miss. Spied her crossing the hall when you all went into the dining-room earlier.''

''In your expert opinion, when do you consider the baby will be born?''

''Any day now, I shouldn't wonder.''

''Just what I've been thinking!'' The frown of disquiet grew more pronounced. ''The Lord only knows what kind of practitioner has been in attendance upon her ladyship. Some antiquated old fossil who hasn't picked up a medical volume in years, I shouldn't wonder. I can perfectly understand why Tom works himself into such a passion over the old-fashioned notions of many of his colleagues. It's a thousand pities he isn't here now!''

She moved across to the door, but turned back to enquire, ''I don't suppose you happen to know precisely where her ladyship's bedchamber is situated, by any chance?''

''Turn left at the end of the passageway and it's the second door on the right.''

Elizabeth, marvelling at her maid's quite remarkable ability for acquainting herself with the layout of strange houses within a relatively short space of time, went along to her ladyship's apartments and discovered the Viscountess sitting up in bed, supported by a mound of frothy lace-edged pillows. She received a warm smile and was invited to sit on the edge of the huge four-poster bed, but she remained standing, her eyes betraying her very understandable resentment at her friend's rather heartless disregard for her feelings.

Verity was not slow in perceiving the look. "What is it, Elizabeth? What's wrong?"

"Why didn't you inform me that you had invited Richard here, too?"

The enquiry was uttered lightly enough, but Verity couldn't mistake the note of censure in the soft voice and was frankly puzzled by it. "I didn't realise until a few days ago that he would be coming. Brin met up with him in London the other week and invited him to stay. Why, you don't object to his being here, surely? You seem to get along quite well."

Elizabeth cast her a look of comical dismay. "Sir Richard, my dear Verity, is the gentleman my parents wished me to marry. At least," she amended with a rueful smile, "my father certainly desired the match. Don't you recall my telling you that when we met in London last spring?"

In truth, she did not, although she vaguely recalled Elizabeth mentioning that there was someone she had refused to marry because she had been convinced they wouldn't suit.

"Oh, I am sorry! Does it make you feel so very uncomfortable…his being here, I mean?"

There could be no mistaking the genuine distress, the undoubted concern her friend was experiencing on her behalf, and Elizabeth found those slight feelings of hurt and annoyance ebbing away.

Accepting the invitation at last, she seated herself on the edge of the bed and gave her friend's hand a reassuring squeeze. "I should be a liar if I said no. But you mustn't concern yourself on my account." A wistful little smile hovered around her very attractive mouth. "Richard, I should imagine, was as relieved as I not to be forced into the union."

Verity subjected her friend to a rather long and thoughtful look, her husband's bluntly voiced amazement at Elizabeth's unmarried state echoing in her ears.

Yes, now that she came to consider the matter, it was most odd that Elizabeth had chosen to remain a spinster. The reason might well be what she herself had suspected: that Elizabeth recoiled at the mere thought of contracting a marriage so desperately unhappy as her parents' union had been. Or the answer might simply be that she had never as yet met a gentleman with whom she wished to spend the rest of her life. A sudden vision of Sir Richard—tall, muscular and perfectly proportioned—appeared before her mind's eye, drawing a rather puzzled frown to crease her forehead. If, in truth, Elizabeth had never married because she had yet to meet a man to her taste, then she must be very hard to please, for how many gentlemen were there as handsome and personable as Sir Richard?

She found herself unable to quell her rampant curiosity, and after a moment found herself asking outright what her friend had glimpsed in his character to give her a dislike of him.

"Oh, I don't dislike him, Verity," she responded without the least hesitation. "Far from it, in fact. As you might have gathered earlier, I like him very well. I cannot see how any female could take such a well-mannered and intelligent gentleman in dislike."

Just what I've been thinking myself, Verity thought, and said with that bluntness which was so much a part of her charm, "Then, why in heaven's name did you refuse to marry him?"

Elizabeth, far from discomposed, smiled rather serenely. "Because, my dear, I couldn't bear the mortification of going through life knowing that in the eyes of my husband I would always figure as second best."

Verity's jaw dropped perceptively. "Do you mean that he was in love with someone else at the time?"

"I wouldn't go as far as to say that, exactly," Elizabeth responded after giving the question due consideration. "But you must remember that it was our respective fathers who desired the match. They had been close friends since boyhood, and that friendship continued until Sir Percival Knightley's death. Richard was, in fact, my father's godson, and although my father's sojourns at our home were rare, he did occasionally bring Richard for a visit."

She paused for a moment to stare blindly at one ornately carved bedpost. "From a very early age I knew Richard preferred the company of my sister. Hardly surprising when one considers how very pretty Evadne was in her youth, whereas I... Added to which, they were of a similar age, Evadne being only a year his junior."

"Are you trying to say that he wished to marry her?" The Viscountess not only looked astounded, but sounded it too, and Elizabeth couldn't prevent a gurgle of laughter escaping.

"Most young men who met my sister swiftly became infatuated. And Richard was no exception. I came upon them together in the shrubbery one day, and overheard Richard saying that he wished she were the one his father had wished him to marry... Then he kissed her.'' Her amusement faded and the grey in her eyes seemed to intensify. ''I think that must rate as one of the lowest points in my life. But I made up my mind, then, that I would never marry unless I was certain of my future husband's regard for me.''

Verity shook her head in disbelief. ''And here I was thinking that Richard was a man of sound good sense. How could any gentleman of discernment prefer Evadne to you?''

''Why, thank you, my dear! You do my ego the world of good!'' Elizabeth exclaimed, genuinely gratified by the compliment, but then became serious once more. ''You must remember, though, that this happened years ago. Richard himself wouldn't have been much above twenty at the time. And there could be no denying that Evadne was quite captivatingly lovely.''

The Viscountess lay quietly mulling over what she had learned, then her ever-lively and rather wicked sense of humour came to the fore and she suddenly gurgled with laughter, a delightful tinkling sound which echoed round the room.

''No wonder Richard looked so dumbfounded earlier, but he should have remembered that plain little cygnets grow into quite regal creatures. I think he'll consider it most fortuitous that he never married your sister. What a blunder that would have been!''

''My dear, there was never any question of that. Evadne might have liked him very well, but she was ambitious, and had set her sights high. She wouldn't have settled for less than a title, and Richard, you must remember, was a younger son… Which reminds me. I must offer my condolences. His brother's death was—must have come as a bitter blow. They were very close.''

She rose from the bed. ''And now I really must leave you, otherwise that very doting husband of yours will quite rightly take me roundly to task for keeping you from your sleep,'' and, without giving her friend the chance to argue, whisked herself from the room.

Completely satisfied now that there had been no ulterior motive in Richard's invitation to this house, Elizabeth smiled to herself as she moved almost soundlessly along the red-carpeted passageway in the direction of her own room. She ought to have known that the darling Viscountess would never do anything so underhanded, nor indeed anything which might cause her old school-friend embarrassment. But this didn't alter the fact, Elizabeth reminded herself, that she must remain on her mettle throughout the time Richard was here, for just one unguarded look, just one ill-chosen word, might alert the far-from-obtuse Viscountess to the true state of her friend's rather foolish heart.

Rounding the corner, she stopped dead in her tracks and only just managed to prevent a gasp escaping as her eyes focused on the tall figure standing in the shadows only yards ahead. Her robe had fallen open and she didn't realise that, with the candles behind her, the nightgown which modestly covered almost every inch of her became virtually transparent. But Richard was instantly aware of the fact.

The gentlemanly thing to do, of course, was to bid a swift good night and retire to his bedchamber. He swiftly discovered, however, that he was first and foremost a man, and couldn't prevent his eyes from wandering over one of the most perfectly proportioned figures he had ever been privileged to see, dwelling with intense pleasure on the softly rounded curves and, oh, so tantalising shadows before forcing his eyes up to a sweetly curved mouth just begging to be kissed.

Only iron self-control kept him firmly rooted to the spot, but he was powerless to prevent that telltale husky note of desire from creeping into his voice as he said, "Miss Beresford, I thought you'd retired long since. I'm sorry if I startled you."

"Not at all, sir. It's entirely my own fault for wandering about the place at this time of night." He watched a tentative little smile briefly curl up the corners of that delectable mouth as she glided towards the door leading to the bedchamber almost directly opposite his own. "I shall bid you good night, Sir Richard. I dare say we'll see each other again in the morning."

"Oh, yes, Miss Beresford," he murmured as she disappeared into the room without another word, "you can be very sure of that...very, very sure."

Chapter Three

Casting a far from appreciative eye round his allotted bedchamber, Richard rose wearily from the bed and went across to the bell-pull. He felt decidedly unrefreshed, but was only too well aware that he couldn't blame his singular lack of sleep on unfamiliar surroundings, or on the four-poster bed which had proved both comfortable and roomy. Oh, no, the sole culprit for his insomnia lay not in this elegantly appointed room, but in the bedchamber almost directly opposite. And wasn't that damnably frustrating in itself?

Unable to suppress a crooked half-smile, he seated himself at the dressing-table. Even now, he still found it difficult to accept that the elegantly poised young woman who had introduced herself the evening before, with all the calm self-assurance of some Grand Duchess, was the same Elizabeth Beresford he had known years ago.

Mother Nature, he mused, had wrought nothing short of a miracle there. In the space of a few short years *she* had transformed an unappealing nonentity into something quite out of the common way. To say that Elizabeth was the most beautiful woman he had ever clapped eyes on would be a gross exaggeration, he knew, but there was no denying that she was quite captivatingly lovely, both face and figure a delightful vista to any gentleman of superior tastes.

He experienced yet again the stirring of desire as his mind's eye, for perhaps the hundredth time, visualised her as she had rounded the corner of the passageway the night before, seeming to float, not walk, towards him, like some enchanted, ethereal creature well above his touch. But this ought not to be the case, he reminded himself. By rights he ought to be able to touch that young woman whenever he desired; by rights she ought at this point in time to belong to him, body and soul; and he experienced a sense of acute disappointment, not to say resentment, that this was not the case.

Running slightly impatient fingers through his sleep-tousled dark brown hair, he cast his mind back over the years, trying to remember the last time he had set eyes on the young girl whom both his father and godfather had wished him to marry. His memory was hazy, but he vaguely recalled having glimpsed her at Henry Beresford's funeral, a forlorn and solitary little figure standing quite apart from her mother and vivacious elder sister.

It must have been a year or, maybe, two later, when he had been out in the Peninsula fighting for his country, that he had received that one and only letter from her. She had considered that they were no longer obliged to comply with the wishes of their deceased fathers, and had released him completely from any obligation he might still have been harbouring to marry her.

Honesty prompted him to admit that he had experienced immense relief after reading that missive. After all, what man in his right mind was wishful to tie himself for life to a rather drab and plump female who had seemed incapable of stringing more than half a dozen words together at any one time? Of course he had felt duty-bound to write back suggesting that they wait a year or two before finally coming to a decision. He had received no further communication from her and, truth to tell, he hadn't given Elizabeth Beresford a single thought during the intervening years... No, not one, until he had unexpectedly come face to face with her again the previous evening.

The bedchamber door opened and his valet entered, breaking into his far from satisfying reflections, and Richard managed with a modicum of success to put thoughts of Elizabeth aside. This relative peace of mind was destined not to last very long, however, for the first person he set eyes on when entering the breakfast parlour a short while later was none other than the sweet torment who had deprived him of so much sleep throughout the night.

As he seated himself at the table he experienced a rather irrational stab of irritation. He wasn't quite certain whether this stemmed from the fact that Elizabeth, bright-eyed and cheerful, betrayed all too clearly that she hadn't suffered from lack of sleep, or that she appeared on remarkably friendly terms with their host, who was still looking highly amused at something she had just said.

"I trust you slept well?" Brin enquired after a servant had supplied Richard's needs.

"Very," he lied. "You have a remarkably comfortable home here. It was a pleasure to sleep in a bedchamber where the fire didn't billow out smoke every five minutes. I really must attend to the chimneys at Knightley Hall. Several of the fireplaces there are quite shocking.''

''I recall a similar problem at my parents' home,'' Elizabeth remarked, ''especially when there was an east wind. Thankfully, I'm not plagued by such a nuisance at my home near Bristol.''

Richard frowned slightly at this. He had assumed, quite wrongly it seemed, that she still resided in her childhood home in Wiltshire, although he vaguely recalled learning of her mother's demise a few years ago.

''I wasn't aware that you no longer resided in Wiltshire, Miss Beresford. Do you live with a relative?''

''I did reside with my maternal grandmother. Sadly, she died last autumn.'' A veil of unhappiness clouded her eyes as she looked directly across the table at him. ''And may I offer you my belated condolences. Some time ago I learned of your brother's death. Such a terrible tragedy!''

Offering him no time in which to respond, Elizabeth rose to her feet and transferred her attention to their host, that spontaneous, sweet smile which had won his regard so quickly touching her lips. ''I shall pay a visit to Verity's room first. So, shall we meet in the stable yard—say, in half an hour's time?''

Watching her leave the room, Brin experienced, yet again, amazement at her continued unmarried state, and shook his head in complete bewilderment. ''I still find it difficult to understand why that lovely creature isn't married.''

The hand raising the fork to Richard's mouth

checked for a moment. Yes, he ruminated, she most certainly ought to be. And if it wasn't for the fact that the contrary little madam had suddenly taken it into her head to go against her deceased father's expressed wishes, she would now be married to me!

Suddenly finding his appetite had deserted him, he pushed his plate aside and turned to his host as a thought suddenly occurred to him. "Am I right in thinking that Miss Beresford's sister resides not too far from here?"

"Yes, about three miles away."

In that case, why hadn't Elizabeth chosen to stay with her? Richard wondered. She could quite easily have visited her friend the Viscountess whenever she wished. Evadne must surely feel affronted knowing that her sister had preferred to stay here. Why, it was tantamount to a direct snub!

"I hope Verity has remembered to warn Elizabeth that Lady Chiltham is not an infrequent visitor," Brin continued, and failed to notice his friend's rather puzzled expression. "Apparently the sisters don't get along too well. But, then, you'd know all about that, I dare say, your being a friend of the family."

"No, I didn't know," Richard freely admitted, and was rather intrigued by this snippet of information. "Up until yesterday evening I hadn't set eyes on either of them since the day of their father's funeral."

"Well, no doubt you'll be given ample opportunity to renew your acquaintanceship with Lady Chiltham during your stay with us. As I've already mentioned, she's not an infrequent caller," Brin responded, his tone betraying clearly enough that he could wish it were quite otherwise.

Not offering his friend the opportunity to enquire

further into the reason behind the sisters' antipathy, Brin rose to his feet. "I'm an appalling host, deserting you like this on your first morning here, but if I don't hurry and change, Elizabeth will be kept waiting." He made to leave, then checked as a most obvious solution occurred to him. "Why not join us? I'm taking Elizabeth on a tour round the estate."

Richard needed no second prompting. Grand though it undoubtedly was, the estate was of precious little interest to him; Elizabeth Beresford, on the other hand, most definitely was. So he wasted no time in returning to his room to change into his riding gear, and accompanied Brin outside to the stables a short while later to discover Elizabeth, becomingly attired in a bottle-green habit, which seemed to emphasise those gorgeous red tones in her hair, already mounted on her ladyship's chestnut filly.

"You are a rare female, indeed," her host remarked approvingly. "One of the few I've ever known who can be on time!" He glanced briefly in Richard's direction, watched him mount the handsome bay, and then turned back to Elizabeth with a conspiratorial wink. "You do realise that we're going to be made to look a pair of veritable whipsters in the company of the man who was reputed to be the finest horseman in Wellington's army."

Elizabeth couldn't prevent a chuckle at Richard's pained expression. "I am well aware of his prowess, sir. My father was not infrequently heard to remark that his godson could ride before he could walk."

"A gross exaggeration!" Richard put in before either of them could utter any further absurdities at his expense. "This is a fine animal you have here, Brin," he went on, quickly changing the subject and giving the bay's neck a fond pat.

"I acquired him a couple of months ago. Yes, I'm rather pleased with him myself," he admitted as they all trotted out of the stable yard. "Do you still possess that brute you had with you in Spain?"

"Sultan…? Sadly, no. The poor old fellow was shot from beneath me at Waterloo." Richard saw Elizabeth pale visibly, and cursed himself for an insensitive clod. "I'm so sorry, Miss Beresford. We seasoned campaigners tend to reminisce at the drop of a hat and frequently forget we're in mixed company."

"My fault entirely," Brin interposed, feeling extremely guilty for raising the subject in the first place. "Dashed thoughtless thing for me to have said, considering your own experiences in Brussels last year."

"You do me too much honour, sir," Elizabeth countered with a dismissive wave of her hand. "Like so many other faint-hearted souls, my one and only desire after hearing that first distant rumble of cannon fire was to make a bolt for the nearest port."

Brin didn't know which shocked him more: Elizabeth's frivolous, and far from truthful, response, or Richard's openly contemptuous smirk in reaction to it. He was about to set his friend straight on the matter when his thoughts suddenly turned in an entirely different direction as he spotted his steward, in the company of one of his tenants, approaching them.

"It looks as if my presence is required elsewhere." He cast them an apologetic smile. "Would you be good enough to accompany Elizabeth, Richard? Hopefully, I shouldn't be too long and shall catch up with you both later."

Although he was far from content to remain for long in the company of a female whom, with a complete turnabout of his former opinion, he now suspected of being quite light-minded, he politely agreed, but Elizabeth swiftly began to rise in his estimation again when she proved herself to be a very competent horsewoman. She handled the far-from-docile filly with praiseworthy ease, her light hands, deceptively, in full control.

"I cannot recall ever seeing you ride before, Miss Beresford," he remarked as they headed towards the western boundary of the estate.

At this, her lips curled into the strangest little smile. "No, I don't suppose for a moment that you can, sir. But, then, I doubt there's very much you do remember about me."

Although she had spoken lightly enough, without so much as a hint of pique in her soft and very pleasant voice, he seriously suspected that he had just received a reprimand and didn't know whether to feel amused or annoyed by it.

After a moment's deliberation he chose to be diverted. "Ungallant though it is of me to confess to it but, no, I don't recall very much about you, ma'am. But, then, in my defence, I had little contact with you when you were a child, and it has been several years since we last met."

"Seven, to be exact."

Little baggage! Was she deliberately trying to set him at a disadvantage? Or was it simply that she refused to indulge in the gentle art of dissimulation? Again he found himself more amused than annoyed, and not just a little intrigued as well.

"Yes, of course, it was." He risked a sidelong

glance in her direction, registered with a feeling of irritation that she was looking perfectly composed and experienced the most overwhelming desire to penetrate that shroud of cool dignity which seemed to be wrapped around her and glimpse the real essence of the woman beneath. "It was on the very sad occasion of your father's funeral. If my memory serves me correctly, that was the last time I saw your sister too." He gazed intently at her delightful profile. "I hope she is in good health?"

"Very, as far as I know." She turned her head to look at him then, and couldn't prevent a smile at the quizzical lift of one dark brow. "Ours could never be described as a close family, sir. I became estranged from both my mother and sister when I chose to live with my maternal grandmother. Evadne did take the trouble to inform me of my mother's demise, and I wrote to her last autumn informing her of our grandmother's passing, but apart from those two instances, there has been no communication between us, verbal or otherwise, for several years."

Because he had been so close to his own brother, he felt rather saddened to learn this, and not just a little appalled at Elizabeth's seeming indifference to the state of affairs which existed between her and her sister. He decided, however, that it would be wrong of him to make a snap judgement on a situation about which he knew next to nothing, and changed the subject by enquiring if she now had a companion living with her to bear her company.

"No, I live quite alone, except for the servants, that is. Oh, and Aggie, of course! But I don't consider her a servant, even though she is my personal maid," she explained when he looked a trifle bewildered. "You perhaps wouldn't remember her, but she was employed in my father's household. She has known me since the day I was born, and is quite touchingly devoted.'' He found the rather wistful little smile which accompanied the admission most engaging. ''I must say, Sir Richard, it is rather wonderful having someone around who is so concerned for my well-being, but she does tend to fuss over me like a mother hen.''

He tactfully refrained from voicing his staunch disapproval of a young lady of quality living alone and, as they made their way along the high ridge which formed the western boundary of his lordship's land, encouraged her to talk about those years she had lived with her grandmother.

It didn't take him long to discover that she had been touchingly devoted to her grandparent. She could not speak highly enough of the lady who had, through sheer determination and hard work, built up a thriving company, owning several sailing ships which had travelled to distant points on the globe, and who had died one of the richest women in Bristol.

As he listened he vaguely recalled his father once remarking on the fact that a substantial dowry was the only thing that had made Elizabeth's mother acceptable to the younger son of an earl. Many of the top Ten Thousand still looked down on those who had any connection with trade, and he found himself admiring Elizabeth's total lack of snobbery or embarrassment over her maternal grandparent's humble origins. It was quite evident that she felt nothing but admiration for her grandmother's businesslike acumen, and didn't shy away from the fact that she owed her comfortable existence, now, to that woman's hard-working life.

"I wish I had had the pleasure of making her acquaintance," he remarked with total sincerity when she fell silent. "You make her sound a very interesting character."

"Oh, she was! There's no denying she was a hardheaded businesswoman, as shrewd as they come, but there was a softer side to her nature too. She fell in love with my grandfather when she had just turned eighteen. Their marriage lasted such a tragically short length of time, less than six years, but she never married again, even though she received numerous offers throughout her life. She told me once that we were alike in that...that we were destined to love only once."

For a brief moment he glimpsed a faraway look in her eyes, then she seemed to collect herself and looked at him with that completely unforced smile of hers, which never failed to reach her eyes, igniting a sparkle in those lovely grey-green depths.

"My apologies, Sir Richard. You must think my tongue runs on wheels. I've done nothing but chatter about myself since we began our ride."

Drawing her filly to a halt, she gazed at the rippling stream gurgling its way along the shallow valley below. "How beautiful it is here! Brin and Verity seem very contented in their new home, but they must find the landscape vastly different from their native Yorkshire."

Richard, too, cast his eyes over the hilly terrain. "The more I travel about this glorious land of ours, the more I come to realise that each county possesses its own individual charm and beauty."

"Mmm." Elizabeth frowned suddenly. "I ought to travel more. It's a dreadful thing to confess, but I've never ventured further north than Gloucester. I've always wanted to visit Scotland, and I could take in other places on the way—the Peaks, and the Lake District, to name but two. Late spring or early summer would be the ideal time to travel, don't you agree?''

''Emphatically no, Miss Beresford!'' he astounded her by responding in forthright tones. ''Your father was my godfather, so I suppose I'm the closest you've ever had to a brother. Therefore, I do not scruple to tell you that it would not only be extremely foolhardy, but grossly improper for you to embark on such a venture without the support and guidance of some male relative.''

He could easily discern a look of combined annoyance and astonishment in her eyes, and was not just a little surprised himself that he had tried to interfere in something which was, after all, none of his concern. He was surprised, too, and not just a little bewildered by the totally unexpected and overwhelming desire he was experiencing to protect this young woman who was quite evidently battling against the very understandable compulsion to tell him to mind his own business.

''I think, sir,'' Elizabeth said with careful restraint, ''that it might be wise if we made our way back now. It doesn't look as if Brin will be joining us, and I think if we are left alone together for very much longer we shall be in the gravest danger of coming to cuffs.''

His response was to throw his head back and roar with laughter, which only succeeded in annoying her further, but by the time they had arrived back at the Dartwoods' charming country residence genial relations had once again been restored.

As she walked with Richard towards the house, Elizabeth was vaguely aware that there was a carriage standing in the courtyard, but gave not a single thought to the possible identity of the person who had called, until she entered her bedchamber and saw the disgruntled look on her maid's face.

"And what has put you out of temper this morning, Aggie? Had a difference of opinion with one of her ladyship's servants, have we?"

"To hear you talk, Miss Elizabeth, anyone would think I was the kind of odiously bossy female who always tried to rule the roost."

"And so you are!" Elizabeth returned, never having put a guard on her tongue where Agatha was concerned. "Well, out with it, then!" she encouraged when her maid regarded her in tight-lipped indignation. "If it wasn't one of the servants then who, or what, has sent you into a fit of the sullens?"

"Her ladyship has a visitor," Agatha unlocked her mouth to announce in tones of dire foreboding.

"Ha! I begin to see daylight." Peeling off her habit, Elizabeth regarded the maid with an understanding smile. "So, darling Evadne is here, is she? Well, we knew it would be only a matter of time." A hint of mischief sparkled in her eyes. "Do you know, Aggie, Wellington could have done with your services during the Peninsular Campaign. You would have made an excellent spy. You possess the most uncanny knack of discovering things with quite remarkable speed," but Agatha refused to be diverted and looked at her mistress in some concern.

"Be careful, my lamb," she urged. "She were a nasty, malicious child. I know people can change over the years, but it's been my experience that they never do to that extent, unless forced to mend their ways.''

''Pray, don't concern yourself on my account.'' Elizabeth was completely undaunted at the prospect of coming face to face again with the female who had bullied her quite mercilessly years before. ''You above anyone else should know that Evadne would never show herself in a poor light when in public. She will be all charm and social graces.''

A hard look, rarely glimpsed in her, suddenly took possession of Elizabeth's fine features. ''One viper in a family is more than enough. But if she is foolish enough to cross swords with me again, then she might be surprised at the venom I possess. My grandmother taught me well. I'm more than a match, now, for my beloved sister.''

Although Agatha said nothing further while she helped her mistress change her attire, she was still experiencing a deal of concern; but she was, as she had been told, fretting quite needlessly. When Elizabeth left the bedchamber and descended the ornately carved staircase she was complete mistress of herself.

In point of fact, her self-confidence had reached a new high. She had, after all, coped superbly with Richard's unexpected and rather unnerving presence in this house, not once betraying her true feelings for him. But it wouldn't do at all to become overconfident, she reminded herself, recalling vividly that moment earlier when he had dared to presume that he could dictate how she should go on. Such impudence! She had come perilously close to losing her temper, but that, she knew, would have been a grave mistake. If she allowed anger to surface, what other emotions might she foolishly betray to the man whom she had adored since her girlhood?

A young footman opened the salon door for her and she couldn't prevent a smile at the anxious glance the Viscountess shot in her husband's direction before he rose to his feet. Richard rose also, and she thought she could detect a flicker of unease in his eyes before she transferred her gaze to the elegantly attired woman seated beside a total stranger on the couch.

If Lady Chiltham was experiencing shock over her sister's drastically altered appearance she certainly betrayed no sign of it as she went rushing forward to embrace her warmly. Elizabeth, however, was far too experienced in the ways of her elder sister to be fooled by the false display of affection and, refusing to return the embrace, merely said, "You are looking well, Evadne. Marriage and motherhood evidently agree with you." The large cornflower-blue eyes were as brightly sparkling as she remembered, but her sister was betraying clear signs that she was rapidly approaching her thirtieth year. Tiny lines were beginning to mar what had once been a flawless complexion, and there was a definite hard, pinched look about the mouth that had once been so softly inviting to members of the opposite sex. "I trust your husband and children are keeping well?"

"Clara and little Edwin go on very nicely, unlike their poor papa who does tend to suffer from the gout from time to time."

An image of the obese Baron when last she had seen him sprang before Elizabeth's mind's eye. He was not renowned for depriving himself of his creature comforts and she wouldn't be in the least surprised to discover that his girth had increased over the years.

"Do the children resemble their father, Evadne?"

"Edwin does, certainly, but most say that Clara is the image of her mama." Lady Chiltham then prudently changed the subject, before her sister could remark on the fact that she had never set eyes on either her niece or nephew, by introducing her to Mrs Westbridge who was at present staying with them and who, it transpired, was Sir Richard's nearest neighbour.

"Before you entered I was on the point of inviting Sir Richard to dine with us on Friday, and sincerely trust that you will accompany him."

"I shall be honoured to act as your sister's escort, Lady Chiltham," Richard responded, thereby offering Elizabeth no opportunity to accept or otherwise.

Evadne appeared genuinely pleased and smiled delightedly as she transferred her gaze to the occupants of the red upholstered couch on the opposite side of the room. "I fully understand why your ladyship is disinclined to accept invitations at the present time," she remarked, "so shall not press you, ma'am. I'm certain, though, that you'd have no objection to my depriving you of my charming sister's company for just one evening."

"Of course not," Verity responded, having little choice, and could only hope that Elizabeth wasn't too disturbed at the prospect of dining at the Chilthams' home, but gained some comfort from the knowledge that Richard would be there too.

Conversation then became general, but Lady Chiltham, never having failed to adhere to the strict rules governing polite behaviour, rose to her feet a few minutes later as the socially acceptable time al-

lotted for paying morning visits drew to a close.
"Would you be kind enough to escort me out to my
carriage, Elizabeth?"

A wickedly mischievous look added an extra sparkle to a pair of grey-green eyes. "Believe me,
Evadne, nothing could afford me greater pleasure!"

The *double entendre* might have escaped Lady
Chiltham, but Richard was very well aware of precisely what the younger sister had meant and cast a
frowning glance at her slender retreating back as the
three ladies left the room.

"Phew!" The Viscount put his fingers to his neckcloth as though it had suddenly grown uncomfortably
tight. "Well, that went rather better than we had dared
to hope."

Verity smiled. "I must confess I was on tenterhooks, but I should have realised that Elizabeth would
rise to the occasion."

"You'll forgive me for saying so," Richard remarked, delving into his pocket to draw out his snuff-
box, "but aren't you making rather too much of it? I
understand the coolness between the sisters is of several years' standing, but I'm certain that, now they
have been reunited, the breach will soon be healed.
Lady Chiltham, at least, seems eager to make up their
differences."

Verity regarded him in open-mouthed astonishment
for a moment. "It's quite obvious to me, sir, that you
know nothing about the matter. Elizabeth warned me
before we even moved down here that her sister possessed two faces—one she keeps for public show, and
a very different one for private. And Elizabeth doesn't
lie."

"I'm not so certain of that," her husband responded unexpectedly, and she looked up at him sharply.

"What on earth do you mean, Brin?"

"It was something she said to me earlier," he explained, looking decidedly puzzled. "I recall clearly your telling me that Elizabeth's only reason for going to Brussels last year was to take care of her grandmother who was concerned for the welfare of her godson. Thankfully, he was amongst the lucky ones and came through the battle unscathed. We also both know for a fact that Elizabeth remained in Brussels for far longer than had been originally planned in order to nurse several wounded British soldiers. She mentioned that in the letter she wrote to you from Brussels last summer, remember? So why, when I brought the subject up, did she try to give the impression that it had been quite otherwise—that she had fled the capital shortly after the battle had begun?"

Richard transferred his gaze from the Viscount's rather puzzled expression to study the delicately painted box in his hand. Yes, he silently agreed, that was most odd. Perhaps, though, she was by nature very modest and didn't want her highly commendable acts of kindness to become generally known. Or, maybe, there was some other reason? She must have realised, surely, that Brin knew the truth already? So there could have been only one other whom she had been trying to mislead. His eyes narrowed. How very intriguing!

Before returning to his estates in Hampshire, he decided, clamping his jaws together in hard determination, he intended to get to know the delightful Miss Beresford a good deal better!

Chapter Four

Settling himself more comfortably in the corner of his well-sprung travelling carriage, Richard looked across at his intriguing companion with narrowed, assessing eyes. Although they had resided under the same roof for several days, he knew little more about Elizabeth Beresford now than he had after that first exploratory ride across Viscount Dartwood's estate.

It would be grossly unjust to suggest that she had deliberately gone out of her way to avoid him, because she most certainly had not. He'd spent many pleasurable hours in her company, either exploring the Devonshire countryside on horseback, or enjoying a hand or two of piquet in the evenings after dinner; but since that first ride across the estate, they had never once found themselves alone together.

Of course this went some way to explain why he'd been unable to discover anything further about the life she had been leading since leaving the protection of her family home; nor, indeed, what had induced her to seek sanctuary with her maternal grandmother in the first place. He could hardly question her in any great detail when in the company of either their host or hostess. To do so would give rise to the wildest suppositions, especially on the part of the sportive Viscountess, who was quite obviously as touchingly fond of Elizabeth as was that dragon-faced maid who always accompanied her whenever she took a stroll in the gardens.

Not that he believed this was done with the deliberate intention of thwarting his attempts to be alone with her, nor through any reasons of propriety, either. If that were the case, why hadn't Miss Beresford insisted on her maid accompanying her out this evening? After all, it was hardly considered correct behaviour for a young, unmarried female to ride in a closed carriage with a gentleman who wasn't a close relative without the support of some female companion.

"Something appears to be troubling you, Sir Richard," Elizabeth remarked, turning her head suddenly and catching the frowning scrutiny. "If it is the prospect of dining with the Chilthams which has brought on a bout of ill-humour, then let me remind you that it was you who accepted the invitation, not I."

"On the contrary, I am looking forward to it." He didn't add that it might offer the opportunity to discover why—and this was pure supposition on his part—she seemed disinclined to make up her differences with her sister. "I'm rather surprised, though, that you chose to leave your maid behind."

He had long since come to the conclusion that she was far from slow-witted and wasn't in the least surprised, therefore, to see a spark of mischief suddenly brighten her eyes. "Sir Richard, let me assure you that you're in no danger of being compromised. Nor do I consider my reputation is likely to suffer by taking a short carriage ride with you. Besides which, I deemed it far more important for Aggie to remain at the house.''

She wasn't slow to recognise the unspoken question in his eyes, either. "It's my belief that the Viscountess is nearer her time than she supposes.''

His brow rose. "I didn't realise, Miss Beresford, that amongst your many other accomplishments you were such an expert on childbearing.''

"Certainly not in childbearing, sir. But I have some experience of childbirth.''

Again his brow rose and he regarded her with amused interest. "May I be permitted to know how you acquired this knowledge?''

"Unlike many young females of my class, I have not frittered away my time in sewing or painting water-colour pictures. During the past few years I have not infrequently accompanied Tom out when he has made calls.''

"Tom?'' he echoed, totally bemused.

"Dr Thomas Carrington, a licentiate of the London College of Physicians.'' Her lips curled into a warm smile, betraying clearly enough her regard for the doctor. "His father was an apothecary and a close friend of my grandmother's. He died when Tom was little more than ten years old, and my grandmother virtually brought Tom up. She took him into her home, paid for his education and provided him with funds when he went to train in London. When he returned to Bristol he continued to live in my grandmother's house up until her death.''

Her sudden scowl revealed quite beautifully her feelings of intense annoyance, even before she added,

"He then considered that it would be grossly improper for him to remain there with me, and now resides in the far from comfortable rooms above his father's old shop." She raised her hand in an impatient gesture. "I've come to the conclusion that your sex can be quite foolishly stubborn at times!"

He decided that, as she seemed in an informative frame of mind, it might be wise to refrain from agreeing wholeheartedly with the actions the doctor had taken on her behalf, but could not resist remarking, "And I suppose the experience you gained by accompanying Dr Carrington on those visits to his various patients over the years came in very useful when you were in Brussels last summer?"

Her expression betrayed her immediate understanding. "I see! So you've been gossiping about me behind my back."

"It was remarked upon that you nursed some British soldiers, certainly," he admitted.

"And so did many others, sir," she responded with yet another dismissive wave of her hand. "My grandmother and I were in no way unique. Many opened their doors to the injured." She looked at him steadily. "I understand that you, too, were wounded and offered sanctuary. I trust you were not badly hurt?"

"As you see, ma'am, I survived." Richard turned his head to stare out of the window at the rapidly fading light as he experienced again that all-too-frequent gnawing spasm of grief. Would thoughts of Mary Smith, and her untimely death, always remain a painful torment?

He forced himself to look back at Elizabeth again, saw that she was regarding him rather thoughtfully

and decided it might be to his advantage to change
the subject before she turned the tables on him and
began to enquire too deeply into certain aspects of his
past that he would far rather be allowed to forget.

Consequently, they continued the journey with him
only raising topics as impersonal as the weather,
which had in the past twenty-four hours grown mark-
edly colder. Evidently, Elizabeth was feeling the drop
in temperature, for he noticed her shiver and glance
up at the dark early evening sky as she stepped down
from the carriage, after it had drawn to a halt outside
the front entrance of the Chilthams' imposing but
rather gloomy greystone mansion.

The high-ceilinged, draughty hall was anything but
inviting, but no fault could be found with the warmth
of the welcome bestowed upon them by their hostess
as they entered the drawing-room. Lord Chiltham,
too, was urbanity itself, praising his sister-in-law on
her charming appearance before introducing her to his
youngest brother, Edward, who was at present residing with them and who, Elizabeth noted with a wry
smile, was in the gravest danger of continuing the
family tradition by doubling the size of his girth by
middle age.

Several people had been invited to dine and the
sumptuous meal, which included numerous courses
and a wide variety of richly prepared dishes, as Lord
Chiltham was not famed for his abstinence, was most
enjoyable. Afterwards the ladies returned to the drawing-room and Elizabeth found herself seated beside
the lady who had accompanied Evadne on her visit
to Dartwood Manor two days before.

Apart from the fact that Caroline Westbridge resided in Hampshire, and happened to be Sir Richard's

nearest neighbour, Elizabeth knew absolutely nothing about her. She had seemed rather ill at ease when she had made that visit with Evadne, barely uttering a word, while at the same time watchful.

This evening, however, she appeared far more relaxed and chatted away on a variety of topics before announcing quite unexpectedly, ''You are nothing like your sister, Miss Beresford.''

Elizabeth had heard this remarked upon too many times in the past to experience the least pang of jealousy. Although she held her sister in scant regard, she had to own that Evadne, even though not in her first flush of youth, was still an extremely pretty woman.

She glanced across the room to where her sister stood conversing with the Rector's wife and eldest daughter. Considering Evadne had borne two children, her figure was good, and although perhaps her complexion could no longer withstand close inspection, her blonde hair still retained its guinea-gold lustre.

''No, I bear no resemblance to my sister whatsoever. There's no denying that Evadne was the beauty in the family, and I must confess she has retained her looks remarkably well.''

''She certainly has,'' Mrs Westbridge agreed. ''But I was thinking more of the difference between you in temperament.''

Although she had spoken levelly enough, there was something in the tone which puzzled Elizabeth. She had assumed that Mrs Westbridge was an old friend of Evadne's, but she experienced the oddest feeling, now, that this was far from the case.

''Have you been acquainted with my sister long, ma'am?''

"My husband was Lord Chiltham's cousin. We became acquainted through our husbands."

"Was?" Elizabeth echoed.

"I've been a widow for five years."

"I'm so sorry. I didn't know."

"One grows accustomed, Miss Beresford. My son is my life now. He'll be going to university in the autumn, and I must confess I miss him dreadfully when he's away from home."

"I see you two are getting along famously."

Evadne's sudden interruption brought the little tête-à-tête to an abrupt end. It seemed to bring a cessation to Caroline Westbridge's friendly and easygoing manner too. Although she added one or two snippets to the ensuing conversation, she appeared to have grown tense quite suddenly, with that watchful, almost wary look returning to her eyes.

Elizabeth was not granted the opportunity to dwell on this rather puzzling circumstance, for a few minutes later the door opened and the gentlemen rejoined them. Evadne was in her element, and it rather amused Elizabeth to discover just how much pleasure her sister derived from playing the hostess.

There was no denying that she was extremely adept at the role, dismissing such mundane entertainments as cards or charades as commonplace, and encouraging most of her guests to join in one of her, now, famous treasure hunts. Only Lord Chiltham, the Rector and his wife refused to be tempted. Names were written on pieces of paper and placed in a bowl, and Richard, his being the first name to be drawn out, found himself partnered with Caroline Westbridge, which seemed not to displease either of them. The Rector's daughter was teamed up with the very handsome son of the local squire, which left Edward Chiltham to make up the last pairing with Elizabeth.

She was not too disappointed at this. Edward was an amiable enough young man, if a trifle light-minded, but the bright glint in his eyes, which suggested that he had been imbibing rather too freely of his brother's port, did cause her a moment's disquiet.

Handing each pair a folded sheet of paper on which was written their first clue, Evadne started each couple off at ten-minute intervals. Elizabeth and Edward were the last to begin and it didn't take Elizabeth very long to realise that she would be doing most of the searching and solving of clues on her own, as Edward appeared far more interested in reducing the levels in the decanters placed in the various rooms.

By the time she had discovered the whereabouts of the fifth clue, taped to the back of the mantel-clock in the Yellow Salon, Edward had succumbed to his excesses and had fallen sound asleep on the sofa; whereas Richard and Caroline, having satisfactorily completed the hunt in record time, were making their way back along the gallery towards the head of the stairs.

"Evadne is quite famous for her treasure hunts, and I must say it does make a pleasant change from sitting down and playing cards."

"Yes, most enjoyable," Richard concurred. "But I think someone should drop Lady Chiltham a hint to play her games only during the summer months. Some of these rooms are confoundedly draughty!"

Caroline laughingly agreed. "I must say my bed-chamber is not the most comfortable of rooms. Fortunately my visit this time is only a brief one," she confided, smiling up at his handsome face.

She had been a close neighbour of the Knightleys for almost sixteen years. Richard had been little more than a boy when she had first gone to live in Hampshire with her husband. She had liked his brother very much, and Richard's sister-in-law had been a particular friend. Their deaths had upset her deeply; but she had never doubted Richard's ability to take his brother's place as head of the family. He had inherited the Knightley temperament, steadfast and reliable, and had already won the respect of his tenants and estate workers during the few short months he had been back in England.

"How long do you intend to remain in Devon?" His sudden scowl surprised her. "I'm sorry, Richard. I didn't mean to pry."

"No, no. I wasn't thinking that," he hurriedly assured her, his attractive smile erasing the lines in his forehead. "I really haven't given it much thought... Another week, maybe two."

"Lord and Lady Dartwood seem a charming couple," she remarked after a moment's silence.

"Yes, they are. I've known the Viscount for some time, of course. Before he came into the title he was in the army. We spent several years together out in the Peninsula. But this is the first time I've met his wife."

"Am I right in thinking that she and Miss Beresford were at school together?"

"Yes, yes, they were. The Viscountess thinks a great deal of her."

Caroline paused for a moment before descending the stairs. "I had the pleasure of speaking to her earlier and thought her a most charming and likeable young woman."

She chanced to glance up at him as he opened the drawing-room door for her and caught a look in his eyes, a strange mixture of tenderness and what appeared suspiciously like exasperation, and couldn't help but wonder whether the Dartwoods' hospitality was the reason he seemed disinclined to leave Devonshire, or something else entirely.

"How quick you have been!" Evadne exclaimed as they entered the room. "I can see I'm going to have to make the clues more difficult in future."

She then invited them to play a game or two of whist while they awaited the others. The Rector's daughter and her partner were the next to return; but half an hour later there was still no sign of Elizabeth and Edward.

Richard glanced up at the clock. It was getting quite late and he didn't wish to delay his departure too long. His coachman, no longer a young man, was not as dependable as he had once been, and might well lose his way on the unfamiliar roads. "I think I'd better go in search of Miss Beresford," he announced, rising to his feet. "It's time we were taking our leave."

Evadne, betraying a moment's alarm, rose also and drew him to one side. "I haven't as yet been given the opportunity, but I was hoping to persuade Elizabeth to remain here with me tonight." She couldn't mistake the surprised look in his eyes and smiled dazzlingly up at him. "Yes, I'm sure, Richard, you have gathered by now that relations between my sister and me have not been—well, very good. And I wish to rectify this."

She paused as though expecting a response, but when he remained silent, staring down at her almost quizzically, she added, "Like most family disagreements, ours grew out of all proportion. My mother was deeply upset when Elizabeth suddenly took it into her head to live with our grandmother and, naturally, I took Mama's part. But I never intended the estrangement between Elizabeth and myself to continue all these years. So very unnecessary! So foolish!"

His expression changed instantly to one of approval. "Far be it from me to throw a rub in your way, but I think it only right and proper that I go in search of her and inform her that I intend to leave."

"Oh, no, don't do that!" Placing a restraining hand on his arm, she stared into his dark eyes with a look of entreaty in her own. "She'll very likely wish to go with you, and I shall be denied the opportunity to speak to her alone. I cannot abandon my other guests, and was hoping to have a long talk after the others have gone. I cannot expect to heal the breach in five minutes and if, after she has heard me out, she is still determined to leave, then I shall return her safely to Dartwood Manor in my own carriage."

In the face of these assurances Richard couldn't find it within himself to thwart her plans. He saw no earthly reason why he should remain, though, and after saying he would order his own carriage brought round from the stables, he made his farewells and went out into the hall.

As a young footman helped him on with his coat, Richard heard the sound of a door closing and turned in time to glimpse a flash of Elizabeth's dark blue velvet cloak before she disappeared down a narrow passageway. Where on earth was she going? he wondered. Evidently she had gone hopelessly wrong somewhere in the hunt, for all the clues and answers were to be found on the upper floor.

"Where does that lead?"

The footman turned his head in the direction of Sir Richard's pointing finger. "The kitchen area, sir, and the cellar."

"Good heavens! She has got herself hopelessly lost!"

"I beg your pardon, sir?"

"Nothing. Don't bother to order my carriage just yet," he called over his shoulder as he set off across the hall. "I'll arrange for it to be brought round later."

The passageway was dimly lit and, like the rest of the house, prone to draughts. Picking up a candle off an old wooden table placed against the wall, he turned the corner, and was about to open the door on his left, when he saw a faint glimmer of light through an open doorway at the very end of the passage. Shielding the candle flame with his cupped hand, he approached the door and, seeing a series of stone steps, realised it must lead to the cellar.

"Miss Beresford," he called. There was no response, so he descended the steps to the cold stone floor below. "Miss Beresford, are you down here?"

"Sir Richard?" Her head appeared from behind one of the huge wooden wine racks. "I see you had the sense to put on your coat, too. This house is abominably draughty. And it's absolutely freezing down here!"

"Very true. But what quite amazes me, my dear girl," he responded as he moved towards her, "is what you're doing down here in the first place."

"The same as you, I should imagine. I'm looking

for clues. I sincerely hope this is the last one. I'm rather tired of this game. It seems to have gone on for—''

Elizabeth caught herself up abruptly as the sound of the door being slammed shut echoed loudly round the cold stone walls. There followed the unmistakable grating of a key being turned in a lock, and Elizabeth looked up at Richard, the all-too-obvious question in her eyes.

''It would certainly seem so.'' He removed a fleck of dust from his sleeve. ''How exceedingly tiresome!''

Elizabeth ran back up the steps and her groan as she tried to turn the doorknob was confirmation enough. ''What are we to do?''

''Wait until someone comes searching for us.''

He sat himself on the edge of a large wooden table. It creaked slightly beneath his weight, but he had every confidence that it would support him and began to swing one well-muscled leg to and fro, for all the world as though he hadn't a care.

''Aren't you coming up here to help me attract someone's attention?'' Elizabeth paused in her pounding of the door to ask.

''No. But far be it from me to stop you making yourself hoarse and bruising your hands if you've a mind to do so.'' The look she cast down at him left him in no doubt that she would have derived great pleasure from pounding her fists against him. ''I think I should warn you, though, before you become completely exhausted, that there isn't an earthly chance of someone hearing you unless he happens to be in that passageway. And it's quite obvious to me, at least, that the culprit has long since departed, or is profoundly deaf.''

''Yes, I suppose you're right.'' After descending the steps again, she moved towards the table, a sudden frown creasing her brow. ''If you didn't come down here searching for clues, why did you come?''

''To bid you farewell. I was on the point of departure when I happened to catch sight of you disappearing down the passageway.''

''You were leaving?'' Initially she experienced surprise, but then felt quite aggrieved. ''What...*without* me?''

He couldn't prevent a slight smile at this. ''Your sister hopes to persuade you to stay the night. She's wishful to make up your differences.''

''Is she, indeed.'' Elizabeth was decidedly sceptical. She would never trust her sister an inch, but at the same time would have granted her the opportunity to say her piece. ''I shall certainly listen to what she has to say, but I've no intention of remaining here all night.''

''Let us hope we're permitted a choice, my dear,'' he responded drily and, easing himself off the table, held his candle aloft. ''In the meantime, we may as well make ourselves as comfortable as possible. There's no saying how long we'll be forced to wait before we're released from our temporary confinement.''

He discovered a pile of sacks in a crate and began to carry them across to the table. ''Spread these out. At least we'll have something soft to sit on. And, thankfully, we're not short of something to quench our thirsts, either.''

He began to inspect the wine racks while Elizabeth

placed the sacks neatly over the table. "If I know anything of butlers, there's sure to be an opener here somewhere. Ha! Here it is, ready for his secret tipple, but no glasses, I'm afraid. Still," he shrugged, "one cannot expect every creature comfort."

He rejoined her at the table and, after helping her to climb upon it, settled himself down on the sacks beside her. The opening of the bottle was accomplished easily enough, and he offered her the first taste, smiling at her grimace as she foolishly took rather a large swallow of the excellent old brandy.

Her eyes watered and it was a moment or two before her throat had cooled sufficiently for her to speak. "How long do you think we've been down here?"

"Ten…fifteen minutes, maybe."

"It shouldn't be too long then, surely, before we're missed?"

"I wouldn't have thought so, no." He cast her a glance of approval. How thankful he was that she was quite calm and matter of fact about it all. He might well have found himself trapped here with some hysterical female, prone to fits of the vapours! "It's very likely that your partner has already set up the alarm."

"Edward?" She couldn't help chuckling at this. "I doubt it. I left him sleeping off his excesses on the couch in the Yellow Salon."

"Yellow Salon?" he echoed. "What the deuce were you doing in there? In fact, I still don't understand why you came down here. All the answers to the clues were to be found on the upper floor."

"How very odd!" She looked nonplussed for a moment, then shrugged. "Well, unless we were hopelessly out with the solution to the first clue, I can only assume there must have been two sets. All our answers were found in the rooms on the ground floor. We never ventured upstairs at all. Where are you off to now?''

Richard had eased himself down from the table and began searching abut the cellar once more. ''I'm looking for more candles. Yes, here they are. I thought I recalled seeing some. We may as well try to keep as warm as we can.''

Elizabeth watched in some amusement as he began to light the candles and place them on the floor around the table. ''I feel like a sacrificial lamb placed on the altar,'' she quipped, looking down at the semicircle of light.

There wasn't so much as a ghost of a smile round Richard's mouth, however, and the look in his eyes as he raised his head was faintly disturbing. ''That, my dear girl, is precisely what you shall be if we're not rescued soon.''

Chapter Five

Richard cast a jaundiced eye up at the faint morning light filtering through the metal grating at the grimy window. The novelty of enforced confinement having long since worn off, he could only chafe over the amount of time they had already spent in this freezing prison and broodingly ponder over how much longer they would be forced to remain. Surely the servants must be up and about by now? He flexed the fingers of his right hand. He could hardly feel them, or his toes. The candles had long since guttered, but he was loath to move to find replacements.

Transferring his gaze to the tousled mass of hair cascading over his shoulder, he managed a smile. At least Elizabeth had kept his left side warm. Unused to strong liquor, she had eventually succumbed to the effects of the brandy and had been sleeping soundly for the past two or three hours. He could have wished for more comfortable surroundings for their first night together; would have expected a more intimate contact. The next time they lay together it would be in the soft comfort of a large bed, he decided, experiencing immense pleasure at the delightful prospect.

Raising his eyes once more, he gazed about the depressing, dank cellar. Forced confinement was hardly the most conventional way to acquire a wife, but he didn't doubt that they would deal extremely well. It felt so right, somehow, having this young woman lying beside him.

She murmured suddenly, and after a few moments moved her head against his shoulder and opened her eyes. It was quite obvious that she was still half asleep, for she gazed up at him in a kind of half-dazed bewilderment and frowned as though she couldn't quite bring his features into focus. Then she sat up abruptly, virulent colour suffusing her cheeks.

"Richard! What in the world…? Oh, yes, of course, I remember… Oh, my head!"

"If you have a hangover you've only yourself to blame," he told her with a merciless lack of feeling. "If you will consume half a bottle of brandy, what do you expect?"

"Was it as much as that? Dear me!" She tried to appear shamefaced, but failed quite miserably. "Oh, well, at least it kept me warm."

Swinging her feet to the floor, she swayed slightly, but regained her balance almost at once when Richard's long-fingered hands gripped her shoulders, steadying her. She was about to reassure him that she was perfectly all right when she detected a distinct noise in the passageway. Richard heard it too and, jumping off the table, was halfway up the cellar steps before she had a chance to move.

Pounding his fist on the door, he called out, but only silence answered him. He tried again, louder this time, and his efforts were rewarded.

"W-who be that?" a frightened voice enquired from the other side of the door.

"Sir Richard Knightley. Lady Chiltham's sister is here too. Let us out at once!"

A long silence, then, "I can't sir. I ain't got no key. Only Mr Quimper 'as a key to the wine cellar, sir."

He looked down at Elizabeth with raised brows. "Who the deuce is Quimper?"

"The butler, I should imagine. I expect he's that seedy little man with the shifty eyes who admitted us to the house yesterday evening."

"Sounds delightful!" Richard murmured, failing completely to bring an image of the servant to mind. He turned back to the door. "Are you still there, girl? Good! Go and find this Quimper and tell him to let us out at once."

"Has she gone?" Elizabeth asked eagerly.

"Yes, but whether she does as bidden is not so certain. Sounded half-witted to me."

But here he did the young servant girl an injustice, for a few minutes later they both heard the key being placed in the lock, and then the door, blessedly, swung open.

A sea of astonished faces greeted them as they emerged from their temporary prison, but Elizabeth was far too relieved to be freed at last to concern herself with gaping expressions; and Richard, raising his quizzing-glass, cast his eyes over what he suspected was the entire staff, his keen gaze seeking the one who fitted Elizabeth's rather unflattering description. He spotted him at last, half-hidden by the cellar door.

"Ah! Quimper, I presume?"

"Y-yes, sir." He seemed more stunned than all the rest of the servants put together. "I cannot imagine how this happened...how you came to be locked—"

"Yes, yes! We'll no doubt sort that out later," Richard cut in impatiently. "What Miss Beresford and I need is to sit before a fire and thaw out. Escort us to the nearest one at once!"

"But that's in the kitchen, sir!" he informed him in patent disapproval, but Richard was in no mood to pander to the outraged feelings of a high-ranking servant.

"I don't care if it's in the wash-house. I just want warmth, Quimper. And now!"

By the time Richard had seated himself on a hard wooden bench placed in front of the kitchen range, and had consumed half the contents of a cup of piping-hot coffee, he was feeling more himself. Really, he was becoming quite soft, he reflected. Quite spoilt, in fact! During these past months back in England he had quickly grown accustomed to every comfort and luxury. The disagreeable night spent in that cellar was as nothing when compared to the privations he had been forced to endure during his years in the army, and yet here he was thinking himself quite ill-used.

He cast a quick glance at Elizabeth, seated on the bench beside him, and experienced a tiny stab of irritation. Apart from the fact that most of her hair had escaped its confining pins, no one observing her would suppose for a moment that she had just spent possibly the most uncomfortable night of her life. Here she was chatting away merrily to the cook, complimenting her on the excellent dinner served the night before, just as though she hadn't a care in the world! Did nothing ever daunt that young woman?

The patter of footsteps drew his attention and he looked up to see Lady Chiltham peering over the metal handrail. The face beneath the fetching lace cap was quite pale with mortification, but there was something rather more than stunned disbelief glinting in the depths of those cornflower-blue eyes as she hurried down the last few steps towards them.

"I just couldn't believe it when Quimper informed me." She rounded on the hapless butler who was trying to make himself as inconspicuous as possible. "How came you to lock them in the cellar, you fool?"

"It's hardly fair to place the blame on any of the servants, Evadne," Elizabeth put in before her sister had a chance to berate the major-domo further.

"At least, not all the blame, certainly," a voice from above corrected, and Elizabeth raised her eyes to see Caroline Westbridge staring down at them with a very thoughtful expression on her kindly face. "After all, Evadne, it was you who assumed that Richard had left with your sister. Might it not have been wise to make sure?"

Lady Chiltham looked decidedly ill at ease, but regained her composure almost at once. "Yes, of course it would. But when I was informed that Elizabeth's cloak was missing I quite naturally supposed that she'd left with Richard. What defeats me completely," she continued, transferring her gaze to the pair on the bench, "is what you were doing in the cellar in the first place."

"From what I can make out," Richard said before Elizabeth had a chance to open her mouth, "Miss Beresford seemed to have been engaged in a completely different hunt from the rest of us."

Once again all eyes turned in Lady Chiltham's direction. "Well, I don't see... Oh, dear! I must have inadvertently given you the wrong first clue. We had a treasure hunt here at Michaelmas, and that did include a venture down to the cellar. I asked the servants to leave all the clues in place, as I fully intend to use them again at Easter when we're expecting quite a large party of guests." No one could have appeared more contrite. "What an ordeal for you both!" She paused for a moment before adding, "Where, by the way, is Edward? Don't tell me he's still down there!"

"He never was there." Elizabeth's eyes twinkled with amusement. "What a comedy of errors! I left Edward asleep on the couch in the Yellow Salon. For all I know he's still there."

"Go and see, Quimper," Evadne ordered before turning back to her sister. "I cannot apologise enough. What an uncomfortable time you must have spent. What I cannot understand, though, Sir Richard, is why your coachman didn't apprise us of your continued presence here."

"Perhaps if you were to take a look out of the window, Evadne," Mrs Westbridge remarked, having by this time joined the group by the fire, "the reason might become very clear. There must be four inches of snow covering the landscape. I remarked upon it last night, after the Rector and his family had departed. Don't you remember? I'm sure Richard's coachman must have assumed that his master had decided to spend the night here in view of the deterioration in the weather."

"You're possibly quite right, Caroline," he agreed, rising to his feet. "But I don't intend spending another night here. My apologies for my incivility, Lady Chiltham, but what I need, and possibly your sister too, is a bed, breakfast and a bath, but not necessarily in that order. So if you would be kind enough to order my carriage brought round from the stables, we'll not trespass on your hospitality further.''

"Of course, it shall be attended to at once." She reached out to place a reassuring hand on his arm. "The sooner things get back to normal, the sooner this whole unfortunate episode can be forgotten."

Elizabeth was very well aware of just what her sister had been so delicately trying to impart: in a roundabout way Evadne had been assuring Richard that he must not feel himself under any obligations whatsoever to do the honourable thing. And, of course, she was absolutely right!

Elizabeth was not insensitive to the very unfortunate position in which they now found themselves. Richard had behaved like a perfect gentleman, which was no more than she would have expected of him; and she had treated him just as she might some elder brother, successfully, as always, keeping her feelings firmly under control, although if the truth be known it had caused her a moment's disquiet when she had woken to discover herself in his arms.

It would be foolish to imagine that the happenings of the previous night would not be spread abroad. Although her sister, Elizabeth didn't doubt for a moment, would be discretion itself, there was nothing servants enjoyed more than a juicy snippet of belowstairs gossip. No doubt it would be the talking point of the neighbourhood for some considerable time to come, but she was more than able to put up with that for the duration of her stay in Devonshire. What she

could never reconcile herself to was the knowledge
that a gentleman had been compromised into offering
her the protection of his name. She would never contemplate an offer of marriage on such grounds, least
of all one from Richard.

Just what he thought about the whole unfortunate
episode was difficult to judge, but as he never alluded
to it once throughout the entire journey back to
Dartwood Manor, she assumed with a deep sense of
relief that he, like herself, considered the sooner the
unfortunate episode was forgotten the better.

Trying to catch up on lost sleep and writing several
letters kept her in her bedchamber for most of the day,
so it wasn't until early in the evening when she went
down to the salon where her host and hostess always
sat before dinner that she realised that she had been
rather naïve to suppose that Sir Richard would conveniently forget the whole unfortunate affair.

The instant she entered the room the conversation
ceased abruptly and Brin, after a quick glance in his
friend's direction, looked faintly embarrassed; but his
wife, never having been one not to speak her mind,
said, "Richard has just been telling us what befell you
last night. Brin and I naturally assumed you'd decided
to stay over because of the weather. If only we'd
known!"

Resolute, but slightly disappointed that Richard had
chosen not to keep his own counsel, Elizabeth joined
the little group by the fire. "Yes, one could almost
believe it was a conspiracy," she remarked, little realising that she would come to regret her joking response, "with my sister, her servants and Sir

Richard's head groom all involved in a devilish plot to keep us prisoners in a freezing cellar.''

Richard looked far from amused. ''I would certainly never suspect my coachman of such a thing. Obadiah Hodge has been with my family for more than forty years.'' His frown grew more pronounced. ''And that's just the trouble. He's getting too old now to tool a carriage for any great distance. He's extremely forgetful and frequently takes the wrong road. But how do you tell a devoted servant, who sat you on your first pony, that he's not up to his work any longer without hurting his feelings?''

''Yes, old retainers can be a problem,'' Verity agreed, and Elizabeth almost sighed with relief at the change in conversation, but she was sensible enough to realise that this respite would not last very long.

Throughout dinner she was conscious of the furtive glances her host and hostess, and occasionally Richard, cast in her direction. She felt like a rare specimen in a jar being examined and assessed. She knew it was going to be only a matter of time before the conversation returned to the happenings, and possible repercussions, of the previous night, and was determined to formulate some well-rehearsed speech to put an end to the matter when it was raised again.

Her thoughts, however, took an entirely different and unexpected turn when she and Verity returned to the salon, leaving the gentlemen to their port. No sooner had the tea things been brought to the room than Verity suddenly gave a tiny cry, and placed a hand to her side.

''Oh, dear,'' she murmured when the pain began to subside. ''The little one seems rather lively this evening,'' and Elizabeth was instantly alert.

Coaxing Verity to return to her room, she helped her back up the staircase. No sooner had they entered the bedchamber than Verity uttered a further gasp, and then looked faintly embarrassed when she suddenly found herself standing in a pool of water.

"Oh, no, it cannot be!" she cried in distress. "It's too soon!"

"Your baby evidently doesn't think so," Elizabeth countered and went across to the bell-pull.

Meg, her ladyship's very efficient young maid, was not slow in answering the summons, but it was Elizabeth, calm and collected as ever, who issued instructions. Directing the maid to inform his lordship that his child was on the way and that it might be wise to summon the doctor, she then requested the abigail to go in search of Aggie.

Within minutes Agatha had arrived and aided her mistress in helping the Viscountess into her nightgown and making her as comfortable as possible in the large bed.

"I forgot you once mentioned you had experience in such things," Verity said as her friend examined her. "How very comforting it is having you here!"

Elizabeth's spontaneous smile would have reassured anyone, but Agatha was instantly aware that all was not as it should be when her young mistress turned away from the bed a moment later, an unmistakable frown of concern erasing the smile. Agatha had had a deal of experience in looking after newly born infants, but nowhere near as much as her mistress in delivering them, and drew her to one side.

"What is it, Miss Elizabeth?" she whispered. "What's troubling you?"

"The baby isn't quite in the correct position for

birth, Aggie. I do hope the doctor doesn't delay too long in getting here.''

Meg returned to inform them that a footman had been despatched for the doctor but, unfortunately, also disclosed that the weather had deteriorated again and that it was snowing quite heavily. Within the space of an hour the wind had picked up strongly, gusting round the stone walls of the mansion with increasing ferocity. It certainly didn't improve Elizabeth's peace of mind to learn that the footman had returned without the doctor. He had apparently been out on another call, but his housekeeper had assured the servant that she would inform Dr Phelps of the happenings at Dartwood Manor as soon as he came home.

It became quite evident as time went on that the doctor was disinclined, or perhaps unable, to venture out again on such a wild night. It also became quite obvious that her ladyship was becoming increasingly distressed by the very real possibility that her husband would foolishly go himself for Dr Phelps.

Beads of perspiration were glistening on Verity's forehead, and her hand felt clammy as she held her friend's wrist in a viselike grip. ''Elizabeth, you must stop him! He wouldn't dream of sending a servant out again on a night like this, but he'd go himself...I know he would! You can deliver the baby...I have every faith in you. Promise me you'll prevent Brin from going himself for the doctor!''

Elizabeth looked down into her friend's wildly anxious eyes for an endless moment, then nodded. ''You have my word, Verity, that your husband shall not leave the house this night.'' She turned to her maid. ''Aggie, look after her ladyship until I return.''

Delaying only for the time it took to pay a brief visit to her own room in order to collect a small bottle from the medicine chest which she always carried with her whenever she travelled, she went back down to the salon. Richard and his lordship rose at once, their expressions betraying their all-too-evident anxiety.

"How is my wife? When's that damned doctor going to get here!" the Viscount snapped, forgetting to put a guard on his tongue in his distress. "If he doesn't arrive soon, I'm going for him myself."

"I'll accompany you," Richard didn't hesitate to assure him, but Elizabeth had been prepared for that and merely smiled to herself as she moved over to the decanters.

"Yes, I was hoping you would. But why not fortify yourselves for the journey by partaking in a glass of brandy first?"

Without waiting for a response she poured out two large measures and, concealing her actions, poured half the contents of the small bottle into one of the glasses. "Drink up, gentlemen," she encouraged after handing them the glasses. "You'll need something warm inside you on a night like this."

To her immense satisfaction both tossed the brandy back without a second prompting. Brin was halfway to the door when he suddenly swayed slightly and placed a hand to his head.

"Quickly, Richard, help me get him over to the sofa!"

He was at her side in an instant and together they managed to get Brin on the couch before he succumbed completely to the effects of the drug.

For a few moments Richard looked down at his

friend, unable to account for this rapid slide into unconsciousness, then realisation dawned and he reached for the empty glass his lordship had placed on a table. "What the deuce are you about, Elizabeth!" he demanded after detecting the faint sweetly smelling odour.

"I'm doing my level best to make the ordeal ahead as easy as I possibly can for the Viscountess. She has enough to concern her without the added burden of worrying over her husband's safety."

Completely unmoved by the continued expression of staunch disapproval on Richard's face, she gently positioned the Viscount's head on a cushion and covered him with a blanket. "Neither you nor Brin would send a dog out on a night like this, and yet you were both foolish enough to contemplate venturing forth yourselves." She turned towards him again, giving him back look for look. "Have you seen just how bad it is out there? It's impossible to distinguish the roads from the verges. Even if you did, by some miracle, manage to reach the doctor's house without having an accident, there's no guarantee that you'd find him at home, or that you could persuade him to return here with you."

He knew she was right: it was madness to attempt that four-mile journey in what was nothing less than a howling blizzard. "What else can we—I do?"

"You can ensure that Brin doesn't attempt to leave. I've given him as much of the drug as I dare, but he's a man with a strong constitution. There's no saying just how long he'll remain asleep. Should he wake, I rely on you, Richard, to keep him here."

He looked at her closely for the first time and saw

the unmistakable signs of strain in her young face.
"What is it? What's wrong?"

She hesitated for a moment, uncertain whether to
confess her fears or not, but then decided that she
desperately needed this man's support and said, "The
baby isn't lying in the correct position for birth. I
might be able to move it. I've watched Tom perform
this feat often enough; have even successfully made
the attempt once myself. But if I can't..."

"If you can't?" he prompted, and he watched a
moment's fear flicker in her eyes.

"The baby isn't small. If I'm unable to turn it, and
Verity becomes exhausted, then I shall be forced to
bring it into the world by other means... I've witnessed that, too, on more than one occasion."

In two giant strides he had bridged the gap between
them, and took such a firm grip of her upper arms
that she winced. "Elizabeth, you can't! The mothers
always die."

"That isn't strictly true," she countered, calling
upon her superior knowledge in this particular subject. "The first recorded Caesarean operation successfully performed in this country occurred during
the last decade of the previous century. And I've witnessed Tom perform it successfully once." She
thought it prudent not to add that she had also been
present on two occasions when the mothers had died,
but something in her expression must have given her
away.

"It's too risky, Elizabeth, and you know it."

"What choice do I have?" The anguish in her
voice was heartrending. "If I leave it too long we
might lose them both." With a supreme effort she
managed to break free from his hold. "If I'm forced

to use the knife, and my friend dies, then I shall find myself in very serious trouble, but I would far sooner face the consequences of my actions than do nothing—'' she cast her eyes down at the sleeping Viscount ''—and have to face that man again.''

Richard watched her leave, mingled anxiety and frustration gnawing at his insides. For the first time in his life he felt totally inept. He was incapable of doing anything positive to aid that brave young woman who would possibly be putting her own life at risk this night. All he could do was that very small thing she had asked of him and ensure Brin remained in the house. But at first light he would go for the doctor himself and bring him back, by force if necessary. He glanced at the clock. It was a fair few hours until dawn, though, and all he could do in the meantime was wait and pray.

Placing two more logs on the fire, he sat himself in the armchair and watched the logs hiss and crackle and burn away to almost nothing before replacing them with two more. Time dragged interminably, each minute seeming like an hour. There were moments when he almost wished Brin would wake and revile him. At least it would relieve the tension of waiting alone; might ease that raw pain of torment that continued to gnaw at his insides with ever-increasing fierceness.

The howling wind slowly lessened in strength and the silence was broken by an occasional murmur from his lordship, but Elizabeth had performed her task too well. The Viscount didn't begin to stir until after the mantel-clock had chimed six, and it was a further hour before he became fully conscious.

''Dear God! What on earth were we drinking last night?''

Richard watched him swing his feet to the floor and cradle his head in his hands. The actions reminded him vividly of Elizabeth's the previous morning when she had done much the same thing. A rather rueful smile curled his lips. He was beginning to think that he would never be allowed much rest while he remained in this part of the country. He hadn't enjoyed a decent night's sleep since he arrived!

Brin raised his head from his hands to stare at the logs on the hearth, and Richard knew by the sudden widening of his friend's eyes that memory had returned.

The Viscount rose rather too abruptly and was forced to grip the back of the sofa for support. ''My God...Verity! I must go to her!'' But Richard had other ideas, and easily arrested his friend's progress to the door.

Any husband with a modicum of feeling would betray deep anxiety at such a time, and Brin's distress over his wife's well-being was only natural, but Richard's concerns were for quite a different person. If the Viscount burst into the bedchamber at the wrong moment, he would do far more harm than good. He had to be stopped!

''I sincerely trust you are not proposing to indulge in a bout of fisticuffs, gentlemen.''

Richard, lowering the fist which had been aimed at the Viscount's powerful jaw, swung round to see Elizabeth framed in the doorway. She had removed her apron and looked as neat as wax, without so much as a single strand of hair out of place.

The Viscount, taking advantage of his friend's

loosened grip, easily broke free and took an urgent step towards her. "Verity…? Has the doctor arrived?"

"No…but your son has."

"My…?" He swallowed in an attempt to move the sudden obstruction lodged in his throat. "Is he…?"

"He's a fine, healthy young fellow, sound in wind and limb," she assured him, knowing the question he couldn't bring himself to ask.

"And Verity?"

"Tired, but that's only to be expected. See her by all means, but please do not remain too long. She needs to rest."

"And so do you, my darling girl," Richard said gently when Brin, almost running from the room in his eagerness to see his wife and new-born child, had left them.

Taking her arm, he guided her to the chair he himself had sat in for that interminable length of time. "What a night you must have had! Did you need to…?"

"No, thankfully. The baby decided, with a little coaxing from me, that he would aid his mother by getting into the correct position. After that, it was a simple matter of waiting."

He couldn't prevent a smile at the matter-of-fact tone. Anyone listening to her might be forgiven for thinking that she had done nothing more arduous than turn the pages of a novel for the past eight hours, but he had long since come to the conclusion that she possessed a masterly knack of always appearing outwardly calm.

Thrusting his hands deep into his breeches' pockets, he stood before the fire and stared down at the rapidly dying embers. The outcome of the night had been a joyous one, but it could so easily have been vastly different, so very tragic for all concerned. But he would never have allowed her to take the consequences on her own. Strangely enough, he felt responsible for her; just as any husband would for his wife. And his wife was precisely what she must become in the not-too-distant future, he decided firmly. So the sooner that stubborn, adorable little witch was brought to realise this fact the better!

He turned, about to broach the subject which had occupied his thoughts almost to the exclusion of everything else for the past twenty-four hours, only to discover that the future Lady Knightley, having succumbed to the tense pressures of the night, had fallen sound asleep.

Smiling tenderly, his eyes devoured the lovely contours of her face. Well, perhaps it might be wise to declare himself at a more appropriate time, he mused and, without disturbing her, very gently picked her up in his arms.

He was halfway to the door when he checked, his smile fading as he detected the distinct fragrance of lavender-and-rose water in her hair. The delicate perfume was achingly familiar... But where and when had he detected that sweetly smelling fragrance before?

Chapter Six

Viscountess Dartwood turned her head in the direction of the window where her friend stood holding the Honourable Arthur Gerald Charles Carter. Her baby seemed quite content to be cradled in those infinitely capable and comforting arms and to listen to that soft singsong voice talking absolute nonsense, telling him that he was born during one of the worst blizzards Devonshire had ever known, with him howling louder than the wind itself after he had taken his first breath.

How completely natural Elizabeth looked holding a baby, she mused. She really ought to have children of her own. She would make the most wonderful mother... But first, of course, she must become a wife!

A tiny crease of consternation furrowed her brow as she pondered over the few days since the birth of her son. Elizabeth had spent much of her time in this room. Verity couldn't deny that she had been pleased to have her company, but she couldn't rid herself of the disturbing suspicion that Elizabeth's attentiveness hadn't stemmed from a wish to prevent her friend from becoming bored, but from a desire to avoid a certain someone's company as much as possible. The reason for her doing so, of course, was abundantly obvious: she was avoiding the declaration that she knew he would make.

She had broached the subject of a possible union between Elizabeth and Richard when her husband had paid her a visit late the previous evening, but Brin had said that nothing had been decided upon as far as he knew. Elizabeth, of course, could do no wrong now in his eyes, and he had strictly forbidden Verity to become involved in something which had absolutely nothing to do with them. As far as he was concerned Elizabeth was an intelligent young woman who ought to be allowed to make her own decisions without pressure or interference from anyone else.

And he was absolutely right, of course. But why did Elizabeth seem disinclined to accept an offer of marriage from a gentleman whom she obviously liked very much? Surely love would grow from the mutual respect they had for each other?

The door opened and Agatha, looking as grim-faced and purposeful as ever, came striding into the room to collect her charge.

"I thought it wouldn't be too long before you came to reclaim him," Elizabeth remarked, reluctantly handing over the precious bundle. "You just cannot bear to be parted from him, can you?"

"I'll have to get used to it, won't I," was the terse response. "The new nurserymaid arrives tomorrow, and I've no intention of interfering." She sniffed loudly. "I wouldn't have any reason to be jealous, though, if someone else was to furnish me with a babe or two to look after."

Verity suddenly found the nails on her left hand of immense interest, but couldn't resist saying when Agatha had left them, "Not that she isn't perfectly right, of course. You would make a wonderful mother!"

Only too well aware where this conversation would eventually lead, Elizabeth came slowly towards the bed. Her expression was as serene as ever, but there was an unmistakable thread of steel in her voice as she said, "Let me make it perfectly clear here and now that I haven't the slightest intention of accepting an offer of marriage from a gentleman who feels himself in honour-bound to offer the protection of his name because of an unfortunate episode over which he had no control and, I might add, during which he couldn't have behaved with more propriety."

Verity agreed fully with her friend's sentiments, but refused to leave matters at that. "Richard certainly doesn't appear to be averse to a union between you. Quite the opposite, in fact!"

"Really?" There was a decidedly sceptical arch to Elizabeth's left brow. "Although I have been acquainted with Richard for a number of years, I would be the first to admit that I do not know him very well. Nevertheless, I wouldn't have suspected him of being the garrulous sort who doesn't balk at discussing his most private concerns with all and sundry."

The Viscountess had the grace to blush at this. "You know full well that he hasn't spoken a word to me on the subject. I've set eyes on him only once since the baby's birth. I don't believe he's broached the subject with Brin, either," she admitted. "It was the impression I gained on the last evening we all dined together when he disclosed what had befallen you both at your sister's house. And if,'' she went on, not giving her friend a chance to respond to this, ''you weren't afraid that he would make you an offer, why have you been doing your level best to keep out of his way as much as possible?''

Elizabeth couldn't help but smile. There was absolutely nothing amiss with her friend's understanding, but it was rather a pity that she spoke in such a no-nonsense fashion, thereby giving the recipient of her staunchly voiced opinions little room for manoeuvre. She decided, therefore, that it wasn't in her own best interests to seek sanctuary with her friend this time, and went over to the door.

''Perhaps because I believed that, given time, Richard would come to realise that there's absolutely no need for him to make such a sacrifice on my account,'' and with that she left the room, but not before she had heard the far-from-ladylike derisive snort in response.

Not that Verity wasn't perfectly correct, of course, Elizabeth mused, making her way back along the passageway to her own room. She had been avoiding Richard's society as much as she could. If the truth be known, though, the reason wasn't that she feared he would make her an offer: unfortunately, that was all too inevitable; but she did fear that she might foolishly give way to the deepest yearnings of her heart and accept him.

She reached the door of her bedchamber, then paused, her hand on the doorknob. But this was no answer, she told herself roundly. Unless she intended skulking in her room for the remainder of her stay, like some frightened rabbit, then she must start behaving normally. It was ridiculous to suppose that she could avoid him indefinitely. Sooner or later he would get her on her own, and from somewhere she must find the strength to refuse him. She'd done so before, she reminded herself. So she was quite capable of doing so again!

Determination added an extra spring to her step as she continued along the passageway. As she descended the stairs she saw the butler crossing the hall, and after learning that both his master and Sir Richard had gone out for a ride, she went into the library to pass the time until their return by reading a book. She had just made her selection from the wide and varied choice when the butler entered to inform her that Mrs Westbridge had called.

Elizabeth thought it rather strange that he should choose to apprise her of this fact, unless, of course, he was uncertain whether his mistress would be willing to receive visitors so soon after her confinement. Elizabeth, however, experienced no such doubts. "It's quite in order for your mistress to receive visitors," she assured him. "I'm certain her ladyship will be delighted to see her."

"You misunderstand, Miss Beresford. Mrs Westbridge is wishful to see you."

How very odd, she thought, but didn't hesitate to request him to show the lady in, and moments later Mrs Westbridge, dressed in a very becoming carriage outfit of dull yellow, and appearing much younger than her thirty-six years, swept into the room.

"Forgive this intrusion, Miss Beresford," she began, after Elizabeth had politely asked her to sit down, "but I'm leaving Devonshire today and felt I had to see you before commencing my journey home."

More intrigued than ever now, Elizabeth gave the

unexpected caller her full attention, wondering why this lady, with whom she was barely acquainted, should be so wishful to see her. She wasn't left in ignorance for long.

"I gather from things Evadne has from time to time let fall that you and she are not upon the best of terms." She paused for a moment, but when Elizabeth continued to regard her in silence, she smiled before adding, "That, of course, is your own affair and has nothing whatsoever to do with me, but I considered it only fair to warn you—although that is perhaps too strong a word…make you aware of something rather puzzling."

"Warn me about what, ma'am?" Elizabeth prompted, when her unexpected visitor fell silent.

Mrs Westbridge didn't respond for a moment, and for the first time since entering the room appeared slightly ill at ease. "About your sister, Miss Beresford."

"Evadne? Why? What has she done?"

"It isn't so much what she has done as what, I strongly suspect, she intended to do."

Although Elizabeth felt loath to discuss a member of her family with a woman who was a virtual stranger, something in her visitor's tone caused a feeling of disquiet and she was prepared to listen to what she had to say.

"I think I had better begin by recounting certain curious events which took place on the evening of the dinner-party. It was quite some time after Richard had left, or so we had believed, that your sister made enquiries about your continued absence. It did occur to me at the time that it was rather strange that she didn't merely ring for a servant and request a search for you. She went out of the drawing-room herself and returned a short time later to inform us that you had left with Richard.''

She regarded Elizabeth steadily, her eyes never wavering for an instant. ''Now, this I did find most odd. I had been favourably impressed by your polite, open manner, Miss Beresford, and thought it rather strange that you hadn't taken the trouble to bid us all farewell before your departure, but it wasn't until the following morning, after I had discovered that you and Richard had been locked in the cellar, that I began to piece together the rather curious happenings of the previous evening, and swiftly came to the conclusion that your enforced confinement had been far from the innocent mistake I had believed it to be.''

She paused for a moment to untie the strings of her reticule. ''No one could have doubted your sister's genuine distress when she discovered you both seated in her kitchen. However, not long after you and Richard eventually departed, I happened to be passing Evadne's bedchamber and overheard her berating the butler again. 'You fool, Quimper! You ought to have made certain,' I distinctly heard her say. This in itself was not suspicious, but her next words most definitely were—'Your bungling has ruined all my plans.'''

''Unfortunately that was all I managed to hear, as a maid emerged from one of the other rooms, but it was enough. Something made me go back downstairs to the drawing-room. The servants hadn't had a chance to tidy up in there. Which was most fortuitous, for in the wastepaper-basket, where your sister had deposited them the night before, I found these.''

After delving into her reticule, she reached forward and deposited several small pieces of slightly crumpled paper into her interested listener's lap. Elizabeth frowned as she examined each one in turn. "But they're all blank, Mrs Westbridge."

"And yet on those our names were supposed to have been written."

The implication was all too obvious. "So we didn't find ourselves partnered that way by mere chance, but by design," Elizabeth remarked after a moment's intense thought. "To be precise…my sister's design."

"Exactly! And I do not now believe, although I have no proof, that it was a mere accident that you were given a different set of clues to solve, one of which would eventually take you down to the cellar."

"Where someone was keeping watch, waiting to lock the door once I was safely inside," Elizabeth murmured, gazing at an imaginary spot on the wall behind her very informative visitor. "And, unless I much mistake the matter, the person who should have been locked in the cellar with me was none other than Edward Chiltham."

"That is what I believe, Miss Beresford. No one would think to question Edward's continued absence on the night of the dinner-party. It is not unusual for him to succumb to his excesses and retire early. The mistake Evadne made was to suppose her brother-in-law might curb his usual overindulgence because she had other guests present."

Drawing together the strings of her reticule, Mrs Westbridge rose to her feet. "No doubt you find all I've told you rather difficult to accept. What prompted her to lock you in the cellar in the hope of forcing a union between you and her brother-in-law, I can only wonder at."

"Her actions do seem rather difficult to understand.'' Elizabeth's voice was soft and as smooth as silk. ''No doubt, though, she had her reasons.''

Mrs Westbridge looked as though she were about to say something further, then seemed to think better of it and moved across to the door, but turned back to add, ''I would deem it a great favour if what we have discussed in this room goes no further. My visit to this house, of course, would not be considered unusual in the light of the recent happy event. Might I also request that you pass on my sincere congratulations on the birth of their son to Lord and Lady Dartwood.''

Elizabeth thought the request for secrecy rather odd, but didn't hesitate to agree, and after Mrs Westbridge had left, she remained in the house only for the time it took to toss the evidence of her sister's perfidy into the fire and to make a brief visit to her room in order to collect her cloak.

This was the first time she had ventured out of doors since the morning of darling little Arthur's birth. The early March sun was doing its best to rid the landscape of those last stubborn pockets of white, the only lingering evidence of the unseasonably late snowstorm which had swept the county three days before.

After taking a leisurely stroll round the perimeter of the Dartwoods' fine country residence, she wandered along the path that traversed the formal gardens at the back of the mansion, and then decided to walk a little farther to explore the shrubbery. Here, she discovered definite signs that spring was not too far away, but it was rather too early for any of the shrubs to be in flower. She swiftly found her interest in her surroundings fading and her mind returned to that rather informative and most unexpected visit of Mrs Westbridge's.

She shook her head, not in disbelief, but in wonder at her sister's continued acts of malice. One might be forgiven for supposing that a woman rapidly approaching her thirtieth birthday would have long since outgrown acts of childish spite; but Evadne was a law unto herself. Perhaps if she hadn't had ample experience of this darker side to her sister's character she might have been inclined to dismiss Mrs Westbridge's suspicions as ludicrous, but sadly she knew her sister's nature too well.

A tiny chuckle escaped her as she absently kicked at a pile of rotting leaves on the path. No wonder Evadne had looked so ludicrously crestfallen when she had seen Richard, and not Edward, sitting before the kitchen range. But it truly was the most foolish and ill-conceived attempt to force two people into wedlock. And why should she have wished to compromise Edward in the first place? Certainly not through any consideration for her sister's future well-being. That much was certain! Elizabeth mused, before she forced herself to consider seriously just what might have prompted her sister's underhanded scheming.

Evadne's marriage had taken place a few months before their father's death. She had by that time attained her majority, and had received from the age of sixteen numerous offers for her hand, all of which she had refused. Many a brow had risen when she had quite surprisingly become betrothed to Lord Chiltham, a man almost twenty years her senior. He would hardly have been considered by any romantically inclined young woman as an ideal partner: he was portly and not remotely good looking; but he was an amiable enough soul who possessed both title and wealth; and social position, of course, had always featured very strongly in Evadne's evaluation of a suitable mate.

Perhaps during the ensuing years, though, she had come to repent her choice; had come to regret putting the pursuit of social standing above the attainment of those more tender emotions. Maybe her twisted mind had nurtured the hope that the sister whom she had always despised would suffer the same fate: a loveless union with a great lump of a man who was not precisely witless, but who was certainly not academically over-furnished. And who better to fill that role than the young man who was yearly turning into a mirror image of her unprepossessing husband?

The sound of footsteps on gravel drew her out of her not unamusing reflections and she turned, the wry smile curling her lips swiftly fading. Curbing the childish inclination to dive into the shrubbery in the slim hope that he hadn't spotted her, she studied Richard's elegant, long-striding gait as he approached. The sight of him in riding garb, which seemed to emphasise the breadth of shoulder and the strength of his well-muscled legs, was enough to send the most hardened female's heart a-fluttering. It certainly did little to restore her composure recalling being told that he had carried her, sound asleep, up to her room on that eventful morning not so long ago, and it took a monumental effort to raise her eyes to his when at last he stood before her.

"I'm pleased to see that you have risked a venture out of doors at long last for a breath of fresh air."

He was probably being rather sarcastic, but she decided to give him the benefit of the doubt. "It was too fine a morning to waste,'' she responded, thankful that her voice betrayed none of her inner turmoil. "Did you have an enjoyable ride?"

"Yes, but I would have found it more pleasurable if you had accompanied us.'' He couldn't prevent a smile at the becoming little blush which added extra colour to the perfect complexion. "Perhaps if the weather continues fine you'll grant me the pleasure of escorting you out tomorrow?"

As her brain for some inexplicable reason seemed unable to function sufficiently quickly for her to think up a reasonable excuse to refuse, she had little choice but to acquiesce to the invitation.

"You cannot imagine how relieved I am to hear you say that, Miss Beresford! I was beginning to dwell on the rather lowering possibility that you found me a bore. And with good reason!'' He slanted a mocking glance. "You have, after all, made it abundantly obvious that you've been doing your level best to avoid my company."

Mortified that her actions had been so obvious, but more determined than ever, now, to put an end to the rather embarrassing predicament in which they now found themselves, she said, "Sir Richard, I cannot deny that I have done my level best to keep you at a distance these past days. In view of the unfortunate happenings which took place at my sister's house, sooner or later the question of a marriage between us would need to be broached, and it was rather foolish of me to try to avoid the inevitable. I now feel that the matter ought to be brought out into the open and settled without delay so that we can continue our sojourn here without awkwardness or recriminations."

"What a very sensible young woman you are, Miss

Beresford! I applaud your sentiments.'' Arresting her further progress along the path by placing a restraining hand on her arm, he turned her round to face him squarely before taking a firm and yet surprisingly gentle hold of her hands. ''I shall not insult your intelligence by feigning ignorance of the present delicate situation. Nor shall I risk causing further offence by requesting a little time to consider the very generous offer you have just made and, therefore, have no hesitation in telling you that I shall be extremely honoured to become your husband.''

''W-what?'' She gaped up at him in astonished incredulity, her thoughts in complete turmoil. ''Sir, you misunderstand. I wasn't…I never meant…I wasn't suggesting for a moment that we…''

She was so deliciously confused that he had to curb the almost overwhelming desire to take her in his arms and add to her discomfiture by ruthlessly kissing her. Then he felt the fingers in his tremble slightly, and the desire to tease her further instantly vanished.

''My dear young woman, I am very well aware of what you were trying to say.'' Releasing one of her hands, he reached for her chin and forced her to look up into his face. ''Not many hours after first meeting you again, I had begun to realise ,that at last I had found a woman with whom I could quite happily spend the rest of my life. The more I was in your company the more I grew to like and to admire you, Miss Beresford.''

Elizabeth gazed up at him in wonder, not daring to believe what she was hearing, and yet what she saw mirrored in those wonderfully sincere dark eyes of his almost made her heart turn a somersault.

''In the normal course of events I would have

wished to give you more time to come to know me a little better. For my part, I have no doubts, and refuse to be thwarted in my desire to achieve what I truly believe would turn out to be an admirable match because of a rather foolish occurrence over which neither of us had any control.

"Therefore, Miss Beresford…Elizabeth, would you do me the very great honour of becoming my wife?"

Chapter Seven

To be married to a man who was both thoughtful and generous, as well as being well blessed in both face and figure, was surely every young woman's dream, Elizabeth reflected, tossing her book aside and leaning back against the mound of frothy white pillows.

Her marriage had taken place the week before by special licence. There had been absolutely no reason at all for such unseemly haste, except that Richard, surprisingly insistent, had seen no reason why they should wait and had brushed aside all those small arguments put forward for delaying the ceremony until late spring. She couldn't prevent a wry little smile as memory flooded back. Almost from that deliriously happy moment in the grounds at Dartwood Manor, when she had accepted that rather touching proposal, it seemed that her life had been taken over by a will far stronger than her own.

Within days she had been whisked back to Bristol, where Richard had left her while he journeyed to London to obtain a special licence. His return to her home the following week had sent her poor servants into a whirl of activity, for he had insisted on departing for Hampshire without delay. She had then been deposited for propriety's sake in Caroline Westbridge's home, where she had spent the night, and the following day the ceremony had taken place in the tiny church nestling in the picturesque village just beyond Knightley Hall's boundary wall.

Everything had happened so fast that she still felt somewhat bemused by it all, frequently wondering if she would wake to find the whole thing had been nothing more than a delightful dream. But no, it was real enough, she assured herself, smiling tenderly down at the ring on her finger. That simple gold band was wonderful proof that she was now Lady Knightley, married, surely, to one of the most charming men in the land. Her smile slowly faded. Yes, she was married right enough…but as yet no wife.

Fleetingly her eyes moved in the direction of that connecting door. Not once since her belongings had been placed in this room had that door been opened. Richard had delicately touched upon the fact that, considering the speed with which their marriage had taken place, he was prepared to give her time to accustom herself to her new role in life. He had been all kindness and consideration, attentive to her every need. Since the day of their marriage they had spent almost every daylight hour in each other's company, riding across the estate, receiving the occasional visitor and eating their meals in relaxed comfort; but their nights had been spent apart.

She was very conscious of the iron control he was exerting over himself. She had glimpsed on more than one occasion a look in his eyes that betrayed rather more than warm regard. She was far from the naïve little innocent Richard evidently supposed her to be. During her years in Bristol, when she had eagerly gone about helping Dr Thomas Carrington in his work, she had acquired a deal of experience in human behaviour. She had been offered numerous opportunities to witness the results of happy marriages. Sadly, she had glimpsed the tragic results of failed ones, too, where discontented husbands had sought their pleasures elsewhere, many venturing into the more noisome parts of the city, where they risked far more than just their health by associating with women of a certain calling to satisfy their carnal desires.

She wasn't foolish enough to suppose that Richard hadn't satisfied his needs over the years with a string of experienced mistresses, but there was no reason for him to continue to do so now. She was more than willing to take on all the duties of a wife, and knew quite well just what was expected of her in the marriage bed. But how in the world could she assure him of her willingness to comply without appearing vulgarly immodest to a man who would, perhaps, expect her to find the whole act of procreation quite repugnant, at least at the beginning?

Seeing no immediate solution to her present predicament, and not being a young woman to worry unnecessarily over a problem that would no doubt resolve itself given time, Elizabeth decided, as she wasn't in the least tired, to write a letter to Viscountess Dartwood. She had promised faithfully to do so on the morning she had left Devon, but somehow her days had been so busy that she just hadn't found time to put pen to paper.

Tossing the bed covers aside, she padded across the thickly piled carpet to the wardrobe and took out her robe. As she went to place her arms in the sleeves she rather clumsily caught one of the scent bottles on the dressing-table in the robe's silken folds, sending the tiny glass container tumbling to the floor.

With a cry of dismay she bent to retrieve it before the entire contents had seeped into the carpet. It was a lovely, delicate fragrance when used sparingly, but half a bottle wafting through the air was quite another matter. She was about to go across to the window to let in some much-needed fresh air when the connecting door was unexpectedly thrown wide and her husband came striding into the room.

"Are you all right, Elizabeth? I heard you cry out. You're not feeling unwell, I trust?"

She was touched by the evident concern for her welfare, but couldn't resist saying, "No, but I shall very soon become asphyxiated if I don't get some air."

He was puzzled for a moment, then the powerful odour hit him too. "Phew! Yes, I see what you mean!" He obliged her by throwing both windows wide. "It smells like an opera dancer's boudoir in here." The rather unfortunate comparison was out before he realised just what he was saying. "I'm so sorry, my dear," he apologised, slanting a look of comical dismay. "I shouldn't have remarked on such a thing in the presence of a lady."

"You have experience of such places, sir?" she enquired, one finely arched brow raised in hauteur.

He realised he would probably be digging himself into a deeper hole, but was about to apologise further when he detected an unmistakable glint in her eyes. "Elizabeth, you little baggage!" Reaching for her shoulders, he gave her a playful shake. "You weren't offended in the least."

She dissolved into laughter, a delightful, infectious gurgling sound, and he found himself laughing too. Then, without quite knowing how it happened, he found he had his arms about her. It was one thing keeping a tight rein on his passion when she remained at a discreet distance, but quite another when every contour of that lovely slenderness was pressed so enticingly against him. Iron resolve crumpled beneath an uncontrollable surge of desire and he lowered his head to capture her lips with a hunger that left little doubt of his urgent need of her.

Elizabeth was hardly aware of being led towards the bed. The removal of her clothes was executed with such consummate skill that before she knew what had happened she was lying naked beside him, bathed in a pool of candlelight. Eyes, darkened by desire, swept over her in a slow, intimate appraisal, from cascading russet curls to slender white thighs, before hands and lips explored the silky smoothness of her skin with infinitely gentle and well-remembered caresses. No words of love had ever passed his lips, but no man could be so tender and be totally devoid of that sweet emotion.

The conviction swept aside that last barrier of restraint. She began to caress him in return, a little tentatively at first, but then with an increased confidence. His throaty moans of pleasure acted like a stimulant, fuelling her own passion, so that when, finally, he eased himself on top and inside her she instinctively moved her body to meet his in perfect harmony, one entity spiralling ever upwards to the heady delights of blissful fulfilment.

Supreme contentment which follows a perfect union left Elizabeth floating on a cloud of euphoria, but her rapid return to earth was as unexpected as it was painful. She sensed a change in him, even before she opened her eyes to see him staring down at her with an almost frozen expression on his face.

"What is it, Richard?" She touched his cheek with gentle fingers. "What's wrong?"

Thrusting her hand away, he scrambled up from the bed, as though her nearness, now, was abhorrent to him. Snatching up the robe which earlier he had let slip to the floor, he shrugged himself into the strikingly patterned crimson brocade. "Not that a strumpet like you, madam, would blench at the sight of a man's naked torso, but one of us at least should strive for a modicum of decency in this sordid union of ours."

The totally undeserved name he had called her smote her like a physical blow, and his contemptuous look made her feel even more vulnerable, and ashamed of her own nakedness. She reached for the covers which he had carelessly tossed aside, only to have her wrist captured in a bone-crushing grip.

"It's a little late for a display of maidenly modesty now! You should have considered that stratagem earlier at the crucial moment, instead of behaving like a wanton." His lips curled into a cruel sneer as he watched a surge of colour rise from the base of her throat. "My God, you're good! I'll give you that. How long did it take you to perfect that little trick?"

Elizabeth could only stare up in disbelief at eyes hardened by anger and loathing. He looked like a madman. In fact, he must be insane, she thought. Why else would a man turn from gentle lover to cruel tyrant in a matter of minutes?

"Richard, what's wrong?" She was desperately striving to remain calm, but that wasn't easy when in the presence of someone who looked as though he might unleash his wrath in a display of physical violence at any moment. "What have I done? I don't understand."

"But I do...and only too well. Where is the evidence of your lost virginity?" His cold, accusing glance swept the crumpled sheets. "I certainly didn't take it, so who did? And how many tumbles have you enjoyed since? A dozen...two...a hundred?"

Suddenly she understood what had wrought this drastic change in him. He believed her a woman of easy virtue, and his anger was not unreasonable. It was foolish to have remained silent on certain important happenings in the past for so long, but she'd hardly been granted the opportunity to explain during these last two hectic weeks and, truth to tell, she simply hadn't given the matter a thought since leaving Devon.

"Richard, I'm so sorry." At last he released the cruel hold on her wrist, and she didn't hesitate to reach for the covers. "I should have told you before the wedding, but—"

"But you were sensible enough to realise," he interrupted in a voice as cold as steel, "that if I'd had the smallest inkling that you were far from chaste, then there never would have been a question of a marriage between us."

"That isn't true! If you'd only allow me to explain," she pleaded. "It happened once, Richard."

But he was in no mood to listen, his cruelly mirthless shout of laughter proof enough of that, even before he said, "My dear, you take me for a fool. You didn't acquire your experience from one coupling. No!'' he rasped, holding up his hand in an arresting gesture when she tried to reason with him further. ''Don't nauseate me with more lies.''

Completely lacking his usual grace, he swung away and began to pace the room like a prowling beast just waiting to strike. ''I can see it all now.'' His voice was even, but edged with venom. ''I've been a damnable fool, but you played your part well, madam wife. I'll give you that. Right from that first night in Devon you had your strategy well planned, offering a tantalising glimpse of rose-tipped breasts and slender shapely thighs. What red-blooded male would not have been bewitched!''

Had he taken a moment to glance at her he couldn't have failed to notice the look of total bewilderment on her face, but he was too wrapped up in his own hurt and anger to care what effect his accusations were having on her, and kept his eyes firmly glued to the floor.

''Ye gods! And to think it never once crossed my mind to suspect that the evening spent at your sister's home had been carefully planned, planned down to the finest detail by you and that sister of yours.''

He did take the trouble to glance across the room at her then and saw a look of horror in her eyes, like that of a terrified animal caught in a trap with no possible means of escape; but he was far from finished with tormenting her yet.

''I recall clearly that there was a time years ago when you couldn't bring yourself to accept me as a husband, but no doubt my coming into the title made me an entirely different proposition.'' The cynical twist to his mouth was a further cruel taunt. ''Well, madam wife, you have achieved your objective... But you have yet to know the man who comes with the title.''

Some detached part of her brain registered that on this point, at least, he was right—the man with that hard, intractable look in his eyes was a stranger; nothing like the friendly, carefree youth she had known years before; nothing like the charming man who had spoken such endearing words in a Devonshire garden not so very long ago. This man was as cruelly unjust as the accusations he had levelled at her and, she suspected, just as false.

''Why did you ask me to become your wife, Richard?'' she forced herself to ask in a voice that sounded nothing remotely like her own.

The softly spoken enquiry seemed momentarily to surprise him, but the hateful smirk remained. ''Why does any man in my position marry? I require an heir. I believed that in you I would be getting a virtuous woman, admirably suitable for the wife of a baronet. A ludicrous error of judgement on my part, but I shan't be foolish enough to make any more.''

He came slowly back towards the bed, but Elizabeth, numbed by merciless reality, was now oblivious to the darkly threatening expression, and the continued hard-edged tone of his voice as he added, ''There can be no happiness now in this union of ours, but wedded we'll stay. When I can bring myself to touch you again you will fulfil your duties as my wife. But first I shall demand proof that you're carrying no other man's spawn. It would be unfortunate, therefore, if our activities between the sheets this night bore—er—fruit, for I should never believe the child was mine.''

He paused for a moment to study her closely. She was not staring at him but at some distant spot, with such a look of complete desolation in her eyes that he experienced uncertainty and a surge of pity, but quickly had the momentary weaknesses under control and hardened his heart.

"In the meantime, however, I have no intention of depriving myself of my own bodily needs, and shall seek my pleasures elsewhere. I shall leave for London in the morning, but you will remain here." Once again he regarded her for a moment in silence, then stalked over to the door. "During my absence you will behave with propriety... Woe betide you, madam wife, if news reaches me to the contrary!"

Elizabeth was only vaguely aware that he had left the room. For endless moments her eyes remained glued on that imaginary spot, her happiness, all hopes for the future, now ashes at her feet. Then she lay back against the pillows, but sleep, which might have brought a temporary respite from the ice-cold desolation gripping her heart, never came.

The candles in their sconces had guttered one by one, and then the first light of a new day filtered between the gap in the curtains. She wasn't certain whether the man in the next room had slept or not, but she was suddenly aware of the sounds of footsteps, of doors opening and closing and of a low murmur of voices. It seemed no time at all before something heavy was being dragged along the passageway. Then her bedroom door was thrown wide and the numbness which seemed to have taken possession of her with an ever-increasing intensity slowly began to subside and a degree of feeling, of nightmarish reality, returned.

"Has he gone, Aggie?"

Nodding, the maid closed the door quietly and came over to the bed. Her rather harsh-featured face seemed, for once, less severe and those dark all-seeing eyes betrayed more than just a modicum of disquiet.

"It's finished, Aggie…it's ruined." A solitary tear hovered for a moment on the dark lashes before running down one pale cheek. "I thought he loved me. What a fool I've been! If he had cared for me at all he would never have said—believed such things," she managed to confide before great racking sobs shook her body and she found herself cradled in a pair of loving arms.

Agatha didn't attempt to check the flow, for the hurt, she knew, was better out than in, but it was a hurt that could—should have been avoided. She guessed what must have taken place the instant she had learned that Sir Richard had given orders for his trunk to be packed, and she couldn't help but feel that her young mistress had only herself to blame for the despair she was now feeling.

"You should have told him the truth from the beginning, but you would have your way. And look where it's brought you." Absently she began to stroke the silken red-brown hair. "He were bound to realise, my lamb. A man of experience wouldn't be easily fooled." She felt the slender body stiffen. "You think your Aggie didn't know. Oh, my lamb, I've known since that night," she admitted, softly. "I heard you get up and go to him, and you didn't return to your bed until almost dawn. You shouldn't have left

Brussels without telling him the truth—that it was you who had nursed him so tenderly all those weeks.''

Easing herself away a little, Elizabeth looked into her maid's worried eyes. ''You know why I couldn't tell him. I didn't want his gratitude, Aggie. I knew he didn't love me, just as I'd known years ago when I wrote to him... But I believed he had come to care for me during our stay in Devon.''

''He does love you, my lamb. Anyone can see—''

''No!'' Elizabeth cut in, virulent anger suddenly thrusting aside the searing pain of hurt. ''He doesn't love me...he never has. He admitted as much. He married me for the sole purpose of producing an heir, and for no other reason.''

In silent dismay Agatha watched her young mistress walk over to the window and stare out at the park for what seemed an interminable length of time. She appeared to have regained her composure, but when, eventually, she did turn her head to glance across the room, the look of undisguised hatred in the depths of her eyes made Agatha's blood run cold.

''He wouldn't even grant me the opportunity to try to explain everything to him. He was determined to think the worst of me—even accused me of being a wanton, a woman of experience.'' Her shout of laughter was mirthless. ''I could almost wish that that were true, Aggie, for it has brought me nothing but sorrow being his, and his alone. Well, let him think what he likes, for he shall never learn the truth from me, now! Let him take his pleasures where he may—the longer the better—for he shall never touch me again...that I swear!'' The green in her eyes seemed to intensify. ''He said that I had yet to know the man I had married... Well, he has yet to know the woman he took to wife.''

Chapter Eight

If one or two eyebrows were raised at Sir Richard Knightley's unexpected arrival in the capital, no more than a casual remark here and there was passed about a newly married man deserting his bride so soon after the nuptials had taken place. Perhaps it was nothing more than urgent business which had brought him to town, or maybe he was arranging his honeymoon abroad, something that he had had precious little time to organise considering the speed with which the marriage had taken place.

Those who initially gave the unconventional behaviour any thought at all expected him to be gone within days. When, however, he betrayed no signs of a speedy return to Hampshire and, furthermore, began to accept invitations for events taking place rather later in the Season speculation quickly grew, and the rumour that Sir Richard had already come to repent his rather hurried marriage began to circulate.

Lady Knightley herself, being something of an enigma, only added to the rife conjecture. No one seemed to know very much about the new bride, not even Sir Richard's close friends, a circumstance the tattle-mongers considered most odd. She was well connected, of course—the Earl of Eastbury's niece, and according to him a very pleasant ''gel'', although rumour had it that he hadn't set eyes on her himself for several years.

Her sister, of course, was none other than Lady Chiltham. What a pity the Chilthams had decided not to come up to town this Season! Dear Evadne was always so forthcoming; and hadn't it been remarked upon by her very good friend Lady Hartley that Evadne was not precisely jubilant over her sister's marriage to the Baronet?

Naturally, Sir Richard's tight-lipped attitude only fuelled the gossip-mongering. He was as uncommunicative with his close friends, most of whom had served with him in the army, as he was with any society hostess who tried to coax a little information out of him. It didn't help to quash rumours when he began to indulge in flirtatious behaviour with several highborn ladies; and, when he was seen on several occasions entering a certain house owned by a lady who was not averse to more intimate, if discreetly conducted, relationships, most of Society began to assume that Sir Richard's marriage, if not one of convenience, had speedily proved to be an unmitigated disaster.

As the weeks passed Sir Richard continued to keep his own counsel. In public he behaved with that easy charm of manner which had always endeared him to those leading ladies of society; but, when in the privacy of his own home, he became quite a different person: moody, withdrawn and having recourse to the brandy decanter rather more frequently than was good for him.

It was only to be expected that his own servants found the present situation rather hard to understand: their new mistress in the country; their master in town, and behaving in a way that did him little credit. Medway, who had been placed in charge of the town residence by Sir Richard's brother several years before, and who hoped one day to take Mr Finch's place in Hampshire when the ageing butler eventually retired, quickly quashed the below-stairs tittle-tattle. He was both diligent and loyal and would never dream of gossiping about Sir Richard's private affairs, but that didn't prevent him from wondering himself just what had brought about this drastic change in his master.

He was emerging from the library, after having refilled the brandy decanter yet again that day, when a sharp rap of the door-knocker echoed loudly round the hall. He knew well enough that his master didn't wish to be disturbed that evening and, therefore, had no hesitation in informing the distinguished visitor, whom he recognised instantly, that Sir Richard was not receiving.

''He'll damned well receive me!'' was Lord Dartwood's forthright response to this intelligence and, brushing past the startled servant, stepped into the hall. ''There's no need for you to announce me,'' he went on, handing over his hat and gloves. ''Where is he? In the library?''

''I thought I told you I didn't wish to be disturbed, Medway,'' he heard his master say before the library door was firmly closed.

''You might not wish to be,'' his visitor countered, ''but you're most certainly going to be.''

''Brin?'' Peering round the wing of his chair, Richard blinked several times in a vain attempt to reduce the effects of his overindulgence and clear his vision a little. ''What the deuce brings you to town?''

''You took the words right out of my mouth,'' the Viscount responded, glancing fleetingly at his friend's half-finished brandy before going over to the decanters and helping himself to a glass. ''Business is what brings me to town.'' Without bothering to wait for an invitation, he sat himself down. ''But from what I've been hearing since my arrival, it certainly isn't business keeping you here.''

He cast a critical eye over his friend's dishevelled appearance. His cravat was crumpled, there were one or two stains down the front of his shirt and he looked in urgent need of a shave. ''It's perhaps just as well that Elizabeth is in Hampshire if half the reports about you are true.''

Richard kissed the tips of his fingers in an exaggerated gesture. ''The ample charms of the delicious widow are enough to induce any red-blooded male to stay.''

The Viscount's lip curled. ''So it is true. My God, and you haven't been married five minutes!''

''But minutes were all it took for me to discover I'd been tricked—deceived by my, oh, so very lovely but not-so-virtuous wife.''

''What the deuce are you talking about?''

It was Richard's turn to sneer now. ''Isn't it obvious? Elizabeth didn't come to the marriage bed— how shall I put it?—*virgo intacta*.'' Even in his far-from-sober state, he could see his friend was stunned.

"How would you have felt if you'd discovered you were not the first man to enjoy your wife's charms? Elizabeth swears it happened only once." The unpleasant sneer grew more pronounced. "But how can I believe her? How can I believe anything she says after the way she deceived me, after the way she, with the help of that sister of hers, tricked me into marriage?"

The injustice of the last remark drew Brin's head up. "If you truly believe that then your wits must be addled. She told Verity that she would never accept a proposal of marriage from a man who believed himself to have been compromised."

"Then why did she accept me?"

Brin didn't even take a moment to consider the answer. "I suspect, Richard, it was because the poor deluded girl believed you loved her. You certainly gave Verity and myself that impression before you whisked Elizabeth away from Devon in such romantic style."

Finishing off his brandy, he placed the empty glass on the table before rising to his feet and staring down at his friend in some concern. It had been a mistake to come here; he realised that now. In Richard's present condition it wasn't likely that he could be made to see sense, and Brin feared that, if he remained, he might end by raising his fist to a half-drunken man, but he couldn't resist one final attempt to make him see sense.

"Perhaps if I'd discovered Verity wasn't chaste, I would have felt as bitterly resentful as you do now. But remaining here will solve nothing, Richard. It's my belief that Elizabeth loves you deeply, but if you should discover that you cannot find it within yourself to forgive and forget her past indiscretion, then it would be better for you both to terminate the marriage before more misery is caused.''

Richard didn't attempt to respond, nor did he attempt to show his friend out. He merely stared blindly down at the empty hearth, his tortured mind once again plagued by painful memories and bitter regrets. He wasn't so inebriated that he couldn't appreciate Brin's sage advice. After all, it was no more than he had been telling himself since his arrival in town.

A heavy sigh escaped him. Had he really been so unjust? Had hurt and bitter disappointment clouded his judgement? He closed his eyes, trying desperately to blot out the heart-rending image of his wife's lovely face when last he had seen her; of the look of sheer desolation in those beautiful grey-green eyes of hers. No matter how well he had succeeded in hood-winking Society as a whole, he had found precious little enjoyment, precious little solace here in London. Even those times spent in the voluptuous widow's bed had not succeeded in erasing Elizabeth from his mind, and during the past week he had experienced no desire to visit Lady Torrington at all. Their brief liaison was over. It was to his shame that it had begun in the first place.

Yes, Brin was right: remaining in London was achieving nothing. If, as his friend suspected, Elizabeth had agreed to become his wife because she loved him, then all was far from lost. It might take him a long time to come to terms with her deception, but he still cared enough to try.

Rising rather unsteadily from the chair, he gave the bell-pull by the marble grate three hard tugs, and almost at once the door opened. "Make the necessary arrangements, Medway. I leave for Hampshire in the morning."

Richard arrived back at Knightley Hall the following afternoon. At first everything seemed quite normal, as lovely and tranquil as ever. The lawn at the front of the house had been recently cut, there wasn't a weed to be seen in any one of the numerous flower beds, nor on the paths, and the early May sunshine seemed to enhance the golden warmth of the mansion's deep yellow stone, making the whole place feel so wonderfully welcoming.

As he approached the front entrance the door was thrown wide and he knew at once that all was not as it should be by his butler's grave expression as he came out to meet him.

"Thank goodness you've returned, sir! I wanted to send word to you, but was informed that you weren't to be told."

"Told what, Finch?"

"About the mistress, sir. Very poorly she is."

Richard looked at the ageing retainer sharply. "What's wrong with her?"

"Typhus," Finch responded in a whisper, as though to speak the dreaded word aloud were to sign his lovely young mistress's death warrant.

Sublimely disregarding Finch's warning to keep well clear of the sickroom, Richard bounded up the staircase and, after a perfunctory scratch on the door, entered his wife's room to see the faithful Agatha seated beside the bed with some sewing resting in her lap. Betraying a moment's surprise at his unexpected appearance, she rose at once and he could see instantly that she was looking tired and drawn through lack of sleep.

"How long has she been ill, Aggie?" he asked, having fallen into the habit before leaving Devonshire of using his wife's pet name when addressing the maid.

"Almost a week, sir."

Without another word Richard strode across to the bed and placed a gentle hand on his wife's forehead. She was burning hot, her cheeks a feverish scarlet against the whiteness of the pillow. She murmured something and moved her left hand as though wanting to brush his away. It was such a pathetically weak and helpless gesture that he experienced a surge of compassion, swiftly followed by a veritable torrent of self-disgust as his eyes focused on the solitary ring on her third finger.

It was he who had slid that plain gold band into position and the reason he had done so was quite simply that he had desperately wanted her as his wife. There had been no question in his own mind of a forced union between them because of what had occurred that night at the Chilthams' house, and he had felt fairly certain that she had felt the same, no matter how many times he had tried to convince himself to the contrary during his stay in London.

She was without question a lovely, desirable young woman who possessed many fine qualities, but, even so, he would never have sought her hand in marriage if it hadn't been for the undeniable fact that for the first time in his life he had fallen deeply in love.

Perhaps this depth of feeling went some way to explain his cruel and unreasonable attitude on the night before he had left for London. Any man would feel deeply hurt and resentful at discovering the woman he loved so much had played him false, but this was a poor excuse for his behaviour. He had allowed battered feelings to override common sense. She had wished to explain, but his confounded pride would not even grant her that small courtesy. Pray God he was allowed to make amends for his cruelly insensitive attitude!

"Why didn't you send for me at once, Aggie?" His voice, edged with censure, sounded rather harsher than he had intended, but she held his reproachful gaze steadily, and he knew the answer even before she said,

"She wouldn't hear of it, sir. Said it wasn't necessary to disturb you." Her young mistress's sentiments had lost a little something in the retelling, but Agatha couldn't bring herself to repeat, "Don't you dare to send for that black-hearted demon, Aggie! Let him rot in London with his filthy whores!"

Sir Richard regarded her rather quizzically for a moment, but thankfully didn't probe further, and after a moment asked how his wife had managed to contract the dreaded scourge.

Once again Agatha found herself in something of a quandary. She had no intention of being disloyal by disclosing that her mistress had been behaving quite out of character, almost like a thing possessed, galloping about the countryside alone on her husband's most spirited mount, not caring what happened to her.

"She was wont to explore the surrounding countryside, sir. One day about three weeks back she came upon a village some five miles distant, and learned of a family in trouble. Poor folk they were, sir, with no money for doctors and the like. Lady Knightley has never been one to turn the other way when she sees folk in trouble. She purchased medicines and visited every day. The widowed mother and youngest child were very poorly, sir. The little girl died, but the mother was on the mend when my lamb goes and takes the sickness.''

Her lip trembled, but she managed to keep her emotions firmly under control. ''She knew the danger she were in, sir, but refused to put anyone else at risk. She went nowhere near your little niece, and kept clear of the servants, having her meals brought up here on a tray, but she couldn't stop me tending her. I've kept my distance from the others too, sir, since my mistress took sick.''

He regarded her with the utmost respect. ''Well, you cannot continue to nurse her on your own. You're worn out, Aggie. From now on we'll take it in turns to sit with her. Go and get some sleep. We'll talk again later.''

She seemed to debate within herself for a moment, then went slowly to the door, but turned back to add, ''I did take it upon myself to send for Tom, sir. Sent an express to Bristol three days ago.''

''Tom?'' he echoed, not realising for a moment to whom she referred.

''Dr Thomas Carrington. A fine young physician he be. He'll come, sir. I know he will. If anyone can pull my little lamb through, he can!''

Richard wished he had her faith, and during the next few hours there were occasions when he began to think that nothing short of a miracle would save his wife. In his most despondent moments he would tell himself that he had precious little experience of sickrooms, and that her condition probably looked far more serious to him than, in fact, it was. When she moved her head, in vain attempts to find a cooler spot on the pillow, all he could do was bathe her face with water scented with lavender, which brought vividly to mind his own convalescence in Brussels the year before and with it bittersweet memories of Mary. He had lost that wonderful young woman through no fault of his own, but that had not stopped him suffering the most searing pangs of guilt during the past months. How much deeper would the pain of guilt eat into him if he were to lose Elizabeth too? Had stupid pride not induced him to desert her, she wouldn't be in this condition now.

An unexpected knock on the door pierced his mood of black gloom, and Finch entered to inform him that a gentleman by the name of Carrington had called.

"Furthermore, a gentleman who refuses to be kept waiting in the hall," a deep, authoritative voice announced from somewhere behind the butler, and a moment later a tall, powerfully built young man with overlong, waving light-brown hair and a pair of piercing clear grey eyes came striding purposefully into the room, almost thrusting Finch aside as he did so.

Richard rose from the chair and found his outstretched hand taken for a moment in a firm clasp. "Thank you for coming so swiftly, Dr Carrington. Did you journey in a hired carriage?" At the brief nod of confirmation, Richard turned to his butler. "Have Dr Carrington's baggage brought in and pay the post boys, and then arrange for one of the maids to wake Miss Stigwell. Also inform Cook that there will be a guest for dinner, and have a bedchamber made ready."

"As close to this one as possible," the doctor

added before going across and seating himself on the bed.

Richard watched the butler leave the room and then turned his attention to the young man who had already begun to examine Lady Knightley.

Thomas Carrington was unlike any other doctor Richard had ever seen before. He was young, twenty-seven—eight, at most—with a tall, lean and athletic figure, kept finely honed by moderate eating and hard work, no doubt. The waving hair reached the collar of a coat that was both unfashionable and slightly worn in places. His rather shabby appearance gave one to suppose that his practice in Bristol was not precisely lucrative, but if this were the case, then it certainly wasn't through a lack of medical expertise, for he carried out a brief examination with faultless efficiency.

With a sound of impatience Dr Carrington glanced at the bandages on Elizabeth's arms, evidence of the bloodletting performed by the local physician the day before. Then he placed his hand on her forehead and gently raised each eyelid in turn.

"Elizabeth. Elizabeth, come, wake up," he commanded in a voice that was both gently coaxing and imperious. "Come, my little love. Open your eyes. It's Tom…your Tom."

Richard stood as though turned to stone. Anyone listening to the doctor might be forgiven for thinking that the young woman lying in the bed was his wife, such was the unmistakable note of tenderness in the deep attractive voice. The most dreadful suspicion began to take root, and it certainly didn't help restore his peace of mind to see Elizabeth's eyes flutter open and to see a hand weakly raised to the doctor's cheek.

It was perhaps just as well that Agatha chose that auspicious moment to re-enter, for Richard was battling with the almost overwhelming desire to grasp that worn collar firmly, haul Dr Carrington from the room and kick him down the stairs.

"Ah, Aggie, well timed!" A boyish smile erased the serious lines in the young doctor's face. "Come over here and lend a hand. And while you're about it you can tell me what this young madam has been doing to herself."

"Perhaps, when you've finished examining my wife, you would care to join me in the library?" Without giving Dr Carrington time to respond to the curtly spoken suggestion, Richard swung round on his heels and left the room.

Trying desperately to control the rising anger, and marshal his wildly conflicting thoughts, he went down to his library and poured himself a stiff drink. The conviction that there was something rather more than mere friendship between Elizabeth and the young physician refused to be quashed, but by the time the doctor had joined him he had at least managed to regain a modicum of control over his temper.

"It's typhus right enough," Dr Carrington confirmed without preamble as he accepted the glass held out to him and sat himself in a chair. "The good news is that it's a milder form of this scourge. Her head aches continually and she's more feverish at nights, but that's only to be expected."

This brought some comfort, but anxiety still remained. "But one of the people my wife took it upon herself to nurse died," Richard pointed out.

"Yes, so Aggie informed me. A little girl, I understand." One of the doctor's broad shoulders rose, but the shrug didn't seem one of indifference, more that of inevitability. "Bad diets and lack of hygiene make the poor much more vulnerable to disease. Thankfully, Elizabeth is not of that class."

He paused for a moment to savour his wine, but his clear grey eyes never wavered from Sir Richard's face. "I should like to remain for a few days. I don't envisage any complications arising, but one can never be one-hundred-percent certain. However, it would be most unethical for me to treat your wife without you informing your own practitioner that you have sought a second opinion, sir."

Richard didn't even take a moment to consider. No matter what suspicions he might still be harbouring he felt, like Aggie, that one could put complete trust in this young man's abilities. "I shall inform him of my intention today."

"Very well. I shall, you understand, be able to remain only three days, four at the most. I cannot desert my other patients for long. Aggie, of course, is extremely capable, but Elizabeth can twist her round her little finger." A sudden frown creased the high, intelligent forehead. "Whilst I remain the little wretch will do as she's bidden. She'd not dare to do otherwise! But when I'm gone, Sir Richard, I rely on you to ensure that she takes the medicines I've prescribed. She isn't going to recover from this overnight."

"You may rely on me, Doctor."

"I was certain I could." Tut-tutting, Thomas Carrington stared broodingly down into the contents of his glass. "Of course, I was expecting something of the sort to happen sooner or later, and I blame Mary for it."

"Mary?" Richard experienced that all-too-frequent

spasm of pain. Would the mere mention of that particular name always affect him so deeply?

"Elizabeth's grandmother, Mrs Mary Smithson. Didn't you ever meet her?"

"No, I was denied that pleasure," Richard responded, suddenly recalling those moments in church when they had exchanged their vows. "Elizabeth's second name is Mary. She must have been named after her grandmother, I suppose."

"Very likely," Dr Carrington responded without much interest. "As I was about to explain, the old lady spoilt Elizabeth quite shockingly during the six years they lived together. Mary worshipped the ground her granddaughter walked on. There wasn't anything she wouldn't do for the girl; refused her absolutely nothing. Still..." he shrugged one broad shoulder again "...there's some excuse, I suppose, when you consider the life the poor girl endured before she lived with Mary."

Richard was instantly alert. "Yes, I've heard mention of that... Didn't get on too well with her sister, so I understand."

"You don't know the half of it, sir." He muttered something unrepeatable under his breath. "I hope to God I never come face to face with that sister of hers!"

Richard regarded him keenly. It was evident to anyone of the meanest intelligence that the doctor was touchingly fond of Elizabeth, and yet there was naught of the lover in his manner when he spoke of her. "You're very fond of my wife, aren't you?"

The doctor's rare and rather charming smile flashed out. "Yes, very," he freely admitted. "She's the nearest I've ever had to a sister." He then fell into a reminiscent mood, recalling the many times he had been forced to take her out on his visits, simply because she would only have followed him had he not done so. He spoke of their years together at Mary Smithson's house with gentle affection, his voice tender for the most part, but occasionally spiced with disapproval at what he considered Elizabeth's frequently headstrong behaviour.

As Richard listened intently to the softly spoken reminiscences, he became increasingly convinced that there had never been anything deeper than a loving brother-sister relationship between his wife and the young practitioner; and by the time he retired to his bed that night he was not only beginning to like Dr Carrington very well, but admire him too.

During the following days Richard was more than happy to leave his wife's well-being in the doctor's capable hands; although Dr Carrington spent a great deal of time in the sickroom, Richard was offered numerous opportunities to enjoy his company. His admiration and liking for the serious young man rapidly grew, and he became increasingly convinced that such a dedicated and gifted person ought to be offered every assistance to better himself. But climb the professional ladder Dr Carrington could not if he remained in his present situation.

During the many hours they spent together, Richard discovered that Mrs Smithson had left Thomas a sum of money in her will, but by his rather shabby appearance it was quite obvious that he hadn't spent a penny of this bequest on even modest luxuries. His dedication to the poor of Bristol was commendable, but the poor couldn't afford doctors' bills, and Richard suspected that Thomas had been tapping into this inheritance just to survive. Although the bequest had been substantial, it wouldn't last forever, and Richard couldn't help but feel that the money could be put to better use. The doctor was a young man with radical opinions, but his views would never achieve recognition if he didn't gain the respect of his peers, and the only way to achieve this end was to become accepted and respected by people of Sir Richard's own social standing.

On the day of Thomas's departure, Richard suggested that they go out for a ride. Thomas had ridden out with his host on several occasions and, as he was a great believer in fresh air and regular exercise, readily agreed. It was only when he found himself a short while later, seated astride his borrowed mount before a charming red-brick house, located in the centre of the thriving market town some three miles distance from Knightley Hall, that he began to think there was rather more to this excursion than a final enjoyable ride out together.

He cast his companion a penetrating glance, wondering why on earth he should have wished to come here, before dismounting and tying the reins to the metal railing. "Yes, a very attractive property in an ideal position, I should say, Richard," he remarked, having dropped all formality during their first evening together. He followed his silent host up the short path to the front entrance. "Who owns it? A thriving lawyer, perhaps?"

"No, I do," Richard responded, drawing a key from his pocket and unlocking the door. "My father had it built for one of his aunts. Great-aunt Matilda was a dear soul, and much loved. Being extremely kind-hearted, my father was prepared to take an interest in her well-being, but was not prepared to endure her incessant prattling up at the Hall. Consequently, this house was erected at a discreet distance. She outlived him by some ten years, as it happens. For some reason my brother couldn't bring himself to sell the place and, since Great-aunt Matilda's demise, the property has been rented out from time to time. As you can see, at present it awaits a new tenant...and I sincerely hope that you will take up that position.''

Offering his rather astonished companion no opportunity to respond, Richard commenced a guided tour of the excellently maintained property, which offered all the creature comforts, while at the same time explaining the reasoning behind his unexpected suggestion.

Without interruption Tom listened intently to all the arguments put forward for his removal from Bristol and his setting up of a new country practice, and when Richard led the way back down the stairs to the large front parlour, he said in his usual no-nonsense and practical way,

''I'd find little time for entertaining morning callers, and this room would make an excellent apothecary's shop. It could be fitted out quite easily. It would have the added benefit, of course, of inducing people who might not otherwise make the attempt to come to the doctor's house, where the physician might be on hand to diagnose precisely what ailed them.'' He sighed. ''It's tempting, Richard, I can't deny it, but I have patients in Bristol who are in desperate need of my services. There's no one else to whom they can turn.''

''Tom, there are poor everywhere, even here,'' he

countered. "Are the needs of poor country folk less than those in the towns? Had there been a practitioner with a ha'p'orth of fellow feeling in him in this area, Elizabeth would not be suffering now."

The truth of this hitting him quite forcibly, Tom went over to stand by the window. The street was busy with many townsfolk going about their daily business. He quickly caught sight of a child who had obviously contracted rickets in infancy. A moment later a man of about his own age went by, dragging his left leg which, Tom suspected, had been broken at some time, and badly set. Yes, Richard was only too right: the poor were everywhere.

"Would you give me a week or two to think it over?" he said at length. "I'm not unappreciative of the opportunity you've given me to set up a practice here and move into this house at a ridiculously low rent, but I have many considerations to take into account."

"Take all the time you need," Richard assured him, but Tom shook his head.

"No, I'm accustomed to coming to decisions quickly. A week will suffice, two at the most." He regarded his companion with a deal of respect. "I wondered why Elizabeth, who shares a deal of my views, should have suddenly upped and married a peer of the realm... But I rather think, now, that I'm beginning to understand."

But I am not at all certain why she did, Richard thought, turning abruptly to lead the way out of the house. *But I mean to find out!*

Chapter Nine

Releasing her breath in a heavy sigh of discontentment, Elizabeth, decidedly lacking her usual grace, slumped down on the *chaise-longue* in her bedchamber. By the quite painless act of lowering her eyelids it was a simple matter to blot out her elegant surroundings. Would that she could erase so easily the painful truth of her present situation!

During those weeks of her illness Richard couldn't possibly have shown more consideration for her wellbeing. Since the day of Tom's departure he had made a habit of visiting this room several times a day. At first she had felt highly resentful, deeming his presence nothing more than an unwanted intrusion, and she had certainly made her feelings quite plain by frequent bouts of ill-humour; but as the days had passed she had grown accustomed to his visits, even if she had been unable to bring herself to greet his arrivals with any degree of enthusiasm.

There was no denying that she hadn't made an easy patient, she mused, managing a semblance of a smile. The illness, naturally, had brought with it a lowness of spirits, but the disease could not be held entirely responsible for those frequent swings in mood: one moment accepting her lot with a kind of resigned, placid indifference; the next, bitterly resentful, when nothing anyone said or did seemed to please her. Poor Aggie had had a deal to contend with, and Richard, too, for that matter, for he had not infrequently been on the receiving end of some barbed remark, and had even had the occasional object hurled in his direction.

But she had absolutely no excuse now for behaving like some overindulged, unruly child. She was, perhaps, a little thinner than she had been before her illness, but getting stronger with each passing day. There really was no reason now for remaining in her rooms. She was no danger to others any longer, and so she really ought, she supposed, to think about resuming her duties once again as mistress of this house... But how many of Lady Knightley's duties was she willing to resume?

She couldn't deny that she still felt a deal of resentment towards her husband. His cruel, unjust accusations remained firmly embedded in her memory, just as surely as if each bitter word had been branded there with a red-hot iron. The hatred that had consumed her on the morning of his departure to London had long since ebbed away, leaving discontent and mistrust at every thing he said and did in its wake. She had times without number tried to convince herself that she no longer cared for him in the least, that he had completely destroyed the deep love she had once borne him, but if that were the case, why then had she felt such searing pangs of jealousy when she had learned from one of their not-so-pleasant neighbours about the light-skirt his name was being linked with in London? And why had she felt so bitterly resentful yesterday when he had unexpectedly announced his intention of returning to the city that morning?

The bedchamber door opened and she turned her head to see Agatha, carrying Juliet in her arms, enter the room. This was the first time for several weeks that she had seen the little girl and her bright smile of recognition and squeal of delight did Elizabeth more good than a dozen bottles of the very best tonic could possibly have done.

''There! I said she wouldn't have forgotten you,'' Agatha announced, plumping the two-year-old infant down on her mistress's lap.

Instantly Juliet reached up a hand to Elizabeth's hair, which was loosely dressed and cascading about her shoulders. ''Ouch! I see your manners haven't improved any, young lady,'' she admonished gently, trying to free the silken strands from the podgy clenched fingers. ''And you're certainly heavier. We'll need to put you on a diet at this rate.''

''The master spoils her. And you, too, for that matter,'' Agatha proclaimed with a loud sniff of disapproval. ''The poor man has the patience of a saint, so he has!''

Elizabeth, knowing only too well what lay at the root of the disapprobation, raised her eyes from Juliet's cherubic face and fixed them on her maid's displeased countenance. ''I do realise, Aggie, that for some time I haven't been quite myself; if, during my recent illness, I've been less than fair in my dealings with you then I can only apologise and thank you for your forbearance in putting up with my megrims.''

Now, this was much more like her darling Elizabeth of old, so considerate to others' feelings! A smile pulled at her nutcracker mouth, but Agatha easily suppressed it and continued in the same censorious tone as she said, "It isn't me you should be apologising to. You didn't hurl that soup bowl or that glass of lemonade in my direction. Any other man would have taken a birch-rod to you, ill as you were!"

Elizabeth wasn't so successful at suppressing a smile, wicked though it was. The glass of lemonade she had hurled had narrowly missed his head, but the soup bowl, depending on whose viewpoint you happened to take, met with more success, its contents ending up down the front of her husband's immaculately cut blue superfine jacket.

"He shouldn't have been forever badgering me about eating my meals," she offered in a feeble attempt to justify her appalling behaviour. "For heaven's sake, Aggie, he was enough to try the patience of someone with the most placid of temperaments! He never entered this room without demanding to know whether I'd eaten my food or taken my medicine."

"Well, of course he did!" Agatha countered in defence of her absent master for whom she had acquired a deal of respect during the weeks since his return from London. "He was desperately concerned about you. Any fool could see that!"

Elizabeth didn't need reminding of this but, unlike Aggie, who evidently looked upon him as some kind of paragon of all the virtues, she was suspicious of his motives. After all, his reputation had certainly been liberally stained during his weeks away from Knightley Hall. How much more might his character have been blackened had he remained in London to enjoy the widow's charms whilst his wife had been in Hampshire, and so desperately ill?

She came out of her musings to discover her maid regarding her rather quizzically. "I am hardly in a position to apologise to your master, now am I, Aggie?" she pointed out with a touch of asperity. "He returned to the metropolis yesterday, or had you forgotten?"

"He's back now," was the surprising response. "Arrived about half an hour ago." She turned and went out of the room, thereby hiding the wickedly satisfied smile that this time she was unable to suppress.

Reports of Sir Richard's amorous activities during his spring sojourn in the capital had also come to Agatha's ears. One of the parlourmaids, whose sister happened to be in the service of that acid-tongued Lady Pentecost—whose home, unfortunately, was not four miles distant from Knightley Hall—had been indiscreet enough to spread rumours of her master's rather disreputable behaviour. Agatha had known by the sudden change in Elizabeth's behaviour that she also had got wind of her husband's unfortunate liaison with the sophisticated widow and, during those two weeks before she had taken the sickness, she had betrayed more than just angry discontent. No matter how often Lady Knightley had tried to convince herself that she no longer cared for her husband, Agatha knew better, for where there was no love there could be no jealousy and her poor young mistress had been—and still was, for that matter—suffering from a surfeit of that particular emotion.

Not that Agatha considered there was any need to be remotely jealous this time. After all, Sir Richard had stayed away only one night. She doubted very much that he had taken the trouble to visit his light o' love, but even if he had, it stood to reason that the widow's charms had offered insufficient inducement to remain in the capital.

Elizabeth, too, had swiftly come to the same conclusion, but she was not permitted to dwell on this rather puzzling circumstance. Juliet, having slipped to the floor, was making a beeline for those fascinating little bottles on her aunt's dressing-table, and Elizabeth was too occupied in trying to keep the little girl out of mischief to dwell in any great depth on her husband's behaviour.

They were engaged in a game of peek-a-boo when the bedchamber door opened again. Thinking that it was Agatha returning in order to collect Juliet for her afternoon nap, Elizabeth didn't look to see who, in fact, had entered until Juliet, suddenly uttering a squeal of delight, padded across to the door, and she peered round the end of the *chaise-longue* to see the little girl being held in a pair of strong, muscular arms.

It was difficult in the extreme trying to convey the impression that one had returned to the elegantly poised and sensible young woman of yore when one was on one's hands and knees, peering round an item of furniture as though one had been caught red-handed in some slight misdemeanour. It certainly did little to restore a modicum of self-possession to see a pair of dark brown eyes regarding her with a kind of amused interest, either. Fortunately help arrived in the form of Agatha who entered to collect Juliet, and the brief interruption offered Elizabeth the opportunity to

rise to her feet and put to rights her slightly dishevelled appearance.

"I didn't expect you back so soon," she remarked
lightly in an attempt to break the uncomfortable silence when Agatha had left them. No response, however, was forthcoming and the amused gleam in his
eyes seemed more than ever pronounced. "I thought
you would remain away for several days."

"My business was accomplished quickly, so there
was no reason for me to remain in town." He detected
the scornful look which for just one unguarded moment glinted in the depths of her eyes, and decided it
might be wise to change the subject. "During my
brief time away you seem to have improved vastly."

This was the first occasion he had seen her dressed
in anything other than one of her night-gowns for
what seemed a considerable time. She looked utterly
charming in the simple sprigged-muslin gown, and
appeared much younger, too, with her lovely russet-
coloured locks cascading loosely about her shoulders.
"As you deem yourself strong enough to indulge in
playful games with our niece, perhaps you might consider resuming your other duties?"

Ever watchful for any slight change in her mood,
he was instantly aware of the sudden tension in her,
even before she took a hasty step behind the couch,
for all the world like a frightened child who expected
to be severely reprimanded. He was well aware of
what lay behind the sudden panic, and didn't hesitate
to reassure her.

"I don't expect you to resume all your duties immediately, of course, only those you feel—er—able
to undertake." The wary look remained in her eyes
and he couldn't forbear a smile as he went over to

the door. "Perhaps you would care to accompany me down to the library? I called at the receiving office on my way home and there are one or two letters for you."

This was the first time that Elizabeth had ventured out of her bedchamber since she had become ill. She felt suddenly very vulnerable as she led the way down the stairs, and it took a monumental effort not to run back to the sanctuary of her bedchamber, but by the time she had seated herself at her husband's desk in the pleasant book-lined room, and was halfway through reading a letter from her dear friend Viscountess Dartwood, she began to feel more relaxed in the house which she had loved from that moment when she had first stepped into the hall. Nevertheless, she seemed unable to stop herself from casting the odd furtive glance in her husband's direction just to check what he was doing.

Richard unexpectedly rose from his chair, startling her, and without asking poured her a glass of wine. "Here, drink this," he ordered. "It might help to calm you."

"I'm perfectly all right," she assured him, but accepted the filled glass, all the same.

"In that case stop staring at me as though I were a serpent about to strike. What does your friend Verity have to say?" he asked, deciding that channelling her thoughts in a different direction might be beneficial. "I trust they are all well down there in Devonshire?"

"Very. Little Arthur, apparently, is growing rapidly." She kept half an eye on him as he moved round the desk, suddenly conscious of how tall and strong he was. Even the powerful masculinity he exuded, which had in the past attracted her, now seemed a threat in itself.

She gave herself a mental shake, determined to appear outwardly calm in his presence, at least. "Evidently you wrote apprising them of my illness."

"Yes, I did. Verity was all for coming here to see you, but I managed to dissuade her. Perhaps a little later in the year we can invite them to stay?" He watched the slender, tapering fingers raise the glass to her lips. She was still a little thinner than he would have liked, but apart from that, and this sudden and totally unnecessary diffidence in his company, she appeared to have got over her recent illness remarkably well.

"Perhaps in the autumn you would care to accompany me to the capital? We need stay only a week or two, but it would grant me the opportunity to introduce you to a number of people who are wishful to make your acquaintance."

She didn't respond, but always vigilant for any slight change in her, he didn't miss the sudden veil of contempt that passed over her strikingly pretty features. He didn't doubt that his associating with a certain widow had come to her ears, but now was not the time to offer an explanation about an affair which ought never to have taken place, and which, although she was not to know it, had ended weeks before.

"The subject of a future sojourn in the town house," he continued in a conversational way, "brings me to another matter I wish to discuss with you. It concerns Finch's replacement."

This drew her eyes to his. "Is he leaving us, then?"

"My dear, he has turned seventy. You must have noticed how badly he suffers from rheumatism. It's high time he was pensioned off. The servants are your department, and I don't wish to interfere, but if you would prefer that I broached the subject with him then, of course, I shall.''

"Yes, yes, I would prefer that you spoke to him." It was a cowardly way out, perhaps, but she didn't feel up to such a distasteful task just yet. She was very fond of the ageing retainer who had from the day she had become mistress of this lovely house always shown her the utmost respect. But Richard was right—it was pitiful to see the poor man coping with the stairs so many times during a day.

"He has been with your family for so many years that I think the suggestion of his retirement would be better coming from you. I'd hate him to think that I have found him wanting in any way. But at the same time, like yourself, I consider the position would be better served by a younger man.''

"Very well, I shall deal with it. I think Medway, who is in charge of the town house, would be the ideal replacement. I'll send for him. I should like you to see him first before I offer him the position here. If for any reason you take him in dislike, or think him unsuitable, then we can always look elsewhere for a new butler.''

"I'm sure I shall find him perfectly satisfactory, but send for him by all means," she agreed, thinking how natural it seemed discussing such topics with him. She felt the tension in her ebbing away, but sadly the rapport between them was not destined to last for very much longer.

"I could wish that my other rather unenviable task might prove to be as easy. Hodge," he explained when she cast him a questioning glance. "It's high time he retired, too. I should have replaced him soon after I returned here last year.''

"Then why didn't you, Richard?''

"Oh, I don't know,'' he responded, running impatient fingers through his hair. ''I suppose I didn't want him to think that I held him in any way responsible for my brother's death. He happened to be tooling the carriage at the time of the accident. Thankfully, he managed to jump clear before it tumbled down the ravine.''

"Do you think the accident might have been avoided if a younger man had been in charge of the equipage?'' she asked gently, and instantly he shook his head.

"No, I don't. I visited the spot where it happened, a narrow stretch of road, twisting and turning with a steep drop on either side. Hodge reacted instinctively. But that doesn't alter the fact that he's not up to the job any longer. He's so damnably forgetful. Why, look at what happened when we dined that night with your sister. Any servant worth his salt would have taken the trouble to enquire whether or not we had decided to remain for the night, instead of dropping off to sleep inside the carriage and forgetting all about us.''

She was instantly on her guard, with every nerve end in her body suddenly growing taut. ''That, perhaps, was a little remiss of him. But you can hardly hold him to blame for the unfortunate repercussions of that night.''

He looked across the desk at her searchingly. It had never been his intention to allude to that particular incident at all, or what had been the outcome, but now the subject had been raised he decided it would be

rather foolish to try to pretend that what had happened
between them had never taken place. Surely it would
be better to thrash their differences out now so that a
new beginning could be embarked upon without recriminations on either side?

"I don't blame Hodge for what happened between
us shortly after our marriage had taken place,
Elizabeth."

"No," she responded levelly. "You blame me."

"Not entirely, no," he countered, holding her suddenly hard-eyed scrutiny. "Neither of us is entirely
blameless. Do you think my anger so unreasonable
after what I had discovered about you?"

For a moment he thought she would stubbornly refuse to answer, but then she said in a voice that was
all the more disheartening because it betrayed no
emotion whatsoever, "Perhaps there was some slight
justification for your behaviour. But we cannot
change the past, even if we should wish to."

Rising to her feet, she went slowly to the door, but
turned back to add rather unexpectedly, "You were
certainly right about one thing, Richard. My sister did
intend that I should spend that night in her cellar. It's
my honest belief that she hoped to force me into marriage… But you were most certainly not her choice
for the groom."

Richard was too stunned by the admission to think
clearly for a few moments, and by the time the full
import of what she had disclosed had permeated his
brain she had already left the room.

Going across to the decanters once again, he felt
that it was he, now, in need of some urgent fortifi-
cation. Carrying the glass of Madeira back over to the
window, he stared sightlessly across his many acres

of delightful rolling park land while his mind went over the events during their stay in Devonshire.

So, Elizabeth had at last admitted that the night they had spent in the Chilthams' cellar had been planned; contrived, seemingly, not by herself, but by her sister. And there was little doubt in his own mind that Lord Chiltham's brother ought to have been the one to bear Elizabeth company during those hours of confinement, and not he. His eyes narrowed, but not against the sun's bright afternoon rays. When, precisely, had Elizabeth uncovered her sister's despicable plot? She hadn't suspected initially; of that he felt certain. But, assuredly, at some point during their stay in Devon she had discovered her sister's perfidy.

He doubted very much that Evadne had admitted to it herself. She hadn't once taken the trouble to pay a visit to the Dartwoods after the night of the dinner-party, not even to congratulate them on the birth of their son. Might she have written Elizabeth a letter confessing her sins? Somehow he doubted it. From what he had learned from Verity and Brin, and more recently from Thomas Carrington, he now had a pretty shrewd notion of Lady Chiltham's true character. She was a deviously cunning woman who would never admit to any misdemeanour in a letter, where it might be used against her at some later date. No, he doubted that Elizabeth had learned the truth of the matter from her sister... So who on earth had the informant been?

He was destined not to discover anything further that day nor, which added to his frustrations, during the following few days. Although Elizabeth resumed her duties as mistress of Knightley Hall with praise-worthy efficiency, she retained that air of reticence whenever she found herself alone with him, but at all other times her behaviour was exemplary.

When they dined together she was always politely conversational and when they made or received visits from neighbours her manners were faultless. He couldn't fail to notice, however, that whenever he assisted her in and out of the carriage her hand would rest in his only for the briefest of moments before it was withdrawn rather abruptly, and she would never remain alone with him for longer than was absolutely necessary.

It would, he knew, be highly detrimental to hint that he was wishful for more intimate relations between them to begin again, even though with every passing day he was finding it more and more of a strain to keep his desire for her firmly under control. It was patently obvious that she mistrusted him now; clear, too, that she had every intention of remaining aloof and keeping him at a distance. Any fool could see that she was nowhere near ready for a resumption of all her wifely duties, and until he had once more managed to rekindle her respect and regard, he must remain understanding and, most of all, patient.

But as the days turned into a week, and then a second, he looked for any slight change in her attitude towards him in vain. Despondency took a firm hold, and he began to think that they would never again live together as man and wife; that she would never completely forgive him for his outburst on that never-to-be-forgotten night, nor for his wanton disregard for her feelings in trying foolishly to find solace for a short while in another woman's arms. Having her so close and yet not daring to risk more than a fleeting contact was more than flesh and blood could withstand, and he was rapidly reaching the point where he despaired of ever rekindling her love when help came from an unlooked-for and most unexpected quarter.

He had not forgotten the need to attend to several of the chimneys at the Hall. The long, warm summer days continued, and it was the ideal time to put this problem to rights. On the morning the sweep and his apprentice arrived Richard rode out early to visit a tenant. Finch, who was quite surprisingly looking forward to his retirement, knew precisely which chimneys were causing concern and directed the sweep to the various rooms.

It was getting close to lunch time when the house echoed with several terrified, pitiful squeals. Elizabeth, writing a letter to Viscountess Dartwood, was seated in the small parlour at the back of the house, which she had turned into her own private study. Clearly hearing the commotion, she went out into the hall to investigate and saw several of the servants huddled round the door leading to the large salon, all peering into the room with apparent rapt interest.

"What on earth is going on, Finch?" she demanded after a further bout of squealing emanated from the salon.

"It's the climbing-boy, my lady. He's disinclined to clean another chimney and the sweep is being rather forceful."

"Stand aside!" Elizabeth ordered in a hard-edged voice none of the servants had ever heard their kind-hearted mistress use before, and instantly a path was cleared for her to march resolutely into the room in time to see the sweep raise a clenched fist to deliver a further stinging blow to his pathetically sobbing apprentice.

"Don't you dare to hit that unfortunate child again!" Her voice now was icy cold, brooking no argument.

The sweep automatically lowered his fist and stared across the room for a few seconds at the elegantly poised young woman with the commanding voice and the look of revulsion on her pretty face. Then he smacked his thick wet lips together before twisting them into an insolent smirk.

"Now, ma'am, don't you be a-fretting yourself over this young varmint. Jem 'ere needs a cuff or two to make 'im do 'is work."

Walking slowly towards the overweight, obnoxious individual whose watery eyes betrayed his evident fondness for spirits, even before she was close enough to smell the strong odour of gin about his person, Elizabeth glanced briefly at the cringing child still held firmly in the massive hand. "Unhand that child at once!"

"Now, ma'am, don't you be a-fretting—"

"There's no need to repeat yourself!" she cut in sharply. "I heard you clearly enough the first time."

The grasp loosened sufficiently for the boy to break free and he didn't hesitate to scurry away like a whipped pup, cowering and trembling with fright. Elizabeth looked him over from head to foot. He was a skinny waif of humanity. His clothes were little better than rags, ill-fitting and torn, and beneath the liberal coating of soot and grime she could clearly detect the many bruises and weeping cuts on his painfully thin limbs.

"Come here, child," she said, softly coaxing and,

after a wary moment when he continued to knuckle his eyes, he took several tentative steps towards her.

Gently raising his shirt, she saw to her horror the clear evidence of ill-treatment: evil red criss-cross welts covering his back. ''Did you do this?''

''Ee be a lazy good-for-nothin','' the sweep growled, casting the child a look which boded ill for him once they had finished their work, and were away from this house and this lady who, despite her youthful appearance, looked as though she might cause a deal of trouble for hardworking folk with her soft-hearted, pernickety views. ''I do right by the lad. Ee's got no cause to complain. When ee do work, ee do get fed proper.''

''Fed? Why, the child's half-starved!'' She glanced down briefly at the boy's rather unlovely snub-nosed face. ''How old is he?''

''Ee be ten now, I reckon, or thereabouts. Got 'im from the orphanage two year ago.''

''My God! It's a wonder the poor boy's survived all this time in your tender care!'' Elizabeth took her eyes away from the sweep's bloated countenance to glance briefly at the hearth, where several pieces of wood had been placed. ''Why has kindling been put there?''

''Just a little persuasion, like. Do 'elp 'im do 'is work a mite quicker, as yer might say.''

Elizabeth had heard reports of such wicked practices, but up until that moment she couldn't bring herself to believe that a member of the human race could be so mercilessly cruel. Her contemptuous glance swept the man from head to foot, bringing a deeper hue to his normally ruddy complexion.

''He shall not climb another chimney this day, nor

ever again!'' she announced, determination hardening her pleasant voice. ''Pick up your belongings and leave this house! The boy shall remain here.''

Jem looked up at Elizabeth in a kind of wonderstruck reverence, not quite able to believe that anyone could stand up to his brutal master, least of all a woman, and not daring to hope that in this fine house, of all the unlikely places, he had found a guardian angel who was willing to rescue him from his hitherto miserable existence. His master, on the other hand, saw matters in a far different light, and the belligerent look Jem had seen all too often sprang into the sweep's soulless black eyes.

''I'll leave when I've bin paid for me work, and not until,'' he ground out, waving his massive fist threateningly. ''And I'll leave wi' 'im an' all. Ee be my apprentice, and I got me rights.''

''And what rights might those be?'' a deep voice queried from the doorway, and Elizabeth, experiencing untold relief, turned to see her husband sauntering in his graceful way towards them.

One glance at the trio standing in front of the large marble grate would have been enough to give Richard a fairly shrewd idea of what had been taking place in his absence, even if he hadn't happened to overhear the latter exchanges between his wife and the sweep. Elizabeth, with the child frantically clutching one of her slender white hands, was regarding him with a look of combined pleading and defiance; and the sweep, who found himself now having to deal with a far more formidable opponent in the form of the master of the house, had evidently decided that it might be wise to adopt a different tack, and had begun to wring his hands together in a subservient and quite nauseating way.

''Your good lady wife, m'lord, being a mite overnice in 'er notions, as yer might say, and not 'aving much experience o' the 'ard life us poor folks be forced to lead, seems to think the boy 'ere be 'ard done by. Which I tell you plainly ee ain't. So, if you just lets us carry on wi' our work, m'lord, we'll be on—''

''What is your name, my good man?'' Richard interrupted in a faintly bored tone while removing a speck of fluff from his sleeve.

''Archibald Barton, Master Sweep, at your service, sir,'' he responded with the most inelegant attempt at a bow Richard had ever had the misfortune to observe.

''Well, Master Barton, loath though I am to disabuse you, but my wife has had a deal of experience of the life endured by the unfortunate poor, and knows the difference between doing a hard day's work for one's keep and being forced to endure malicious cruelty which borders on slavery.''

Swiftly realising that Sir Richard was not going to prove to be the sympathetic ally for which he had hoped, the sweep dropped the obsequious pose. ''Ee be my apprentice and I gots me rights! I can deal wi' 'im as I like.''

''Not so very long ago a certain person engaged in the same profession as yourself was swiftly disabused of that erroneous belief. He was imprisoned for causing his apprentice's death. The chief magistrate presiding at the trial felt that apprentices had their rights, too, and, being a Christian soul, could not find it within himself to condone such wanton acts of cruelty as lighting fires in hearths to encourage climbing-boys to do their work.''

Richard glanced briefly at the kindling in the hearth before returning his gaze to the sweep whose mien was suddenly chary. ''Our local magistrate is a gentleman with similar views. Do you happen to be acquainted with Sir William Carmichael?'' His lips twitched as the sweep visibly blanched. ''Ah, yes! I suspected that your paths might have crossed at some time or other. I think it behoves me to have a word or two with my good friend Sir William on this poor unfortunate child's behalf, but until that time I shall relieve you of your apprentice's companionship.''

He waited a moment or two to allow the sweep to digest this threat fully before adding, ''Now, pick up your belongings and leave. My butler will provide payment for any work already carried out.''

Elizabeth waited until the sweep, muttering a string of oaths under his breath, had left the room before turning to her husband with a look of dawning respect in her eyes. She had known, almost from the day of her arrival at the Hall, that those working in the house and on the estate held their master in high esteem. His concern for his workers' well-being was unimpeachable, but she had not been quite certain in those first few moments after he had entered the room whether he would be willing to display the same altruism towards a being who, in all fairness, had no right to expect it.

''Oh, Richard, how very glad I am that you arrived when you did!'' she exclaimed with real gratitude. ''I was experiencing the most lively dread that that hateful man would take this poor unfortunate child away by force.''

"Most would agree that he would have been well within his rights to do so, my dear," he responded with a wry smile before turning his attention with scant enthusiasm on to the scrap of humanity he had been instrumental in saving from a life of purgatory, short though that may well have turned out to be.

"What's your name, boy?"

"Jeremiah. But erryone calls me Jem, m'lord."

"When you address me you call me sir, not my lord. And why do you keep scratching that way?"

Jem, who was still retaining a firm hold on Elizabeth's fingers, was putting his other hand to necessary use, alternating beneath his shirt and in his hair. "I got crawlers, sir. Al'ays 'ad crawlers."

This rather alarming intelligence sent Elizabeth into whoops of laughter, and her husband, with a look of acute dismay, striding purposefully over to the bell-pull. Finch appeared in answer to the summons and was quickly despatched for the dependable Miss Stigwell.

"You observe this child, Aggie," Sir Richard said when she entered a few minutes later. "He's no doubt hungry and would appreciate some food. But first he's in the most urgent need of a bath. He has a deal of unwanted livestock about his person."

"Oh, my gawd!"

"Precisely what I thought myself, Aggie," he responded, casting his still highly amused wife a dour look. "When in your estimable opinion you consider him fit to mix with the human race, find him something suitable to wear. There are trunks full of old clothes in the attic. Then take him down to the kitchen and feed him."

"Will you be able to find him work on the estate?"

Elizabeth asked when Jem, though rather reluctantly, had left the room with Agatha.

''I expect so, but just precisely what eludes me for the moment.''

Smiling with gentle warmth, Elizabeth bridged the distance between them and, without the least hesitation, placed her hand on her husband's sleeve. ''It was very kind of you, Richard, to help the child that way. When he's older I'm sure he'll appreciate what you have done for him, just as I do now.''

He placed his hand over hers, and for the first time in what seemed a very long time she made not the least attempt to draw hers away.

Chapter Ten

Elizabeth paused in the act of placing another flower in the vase and glanced about her husband's library. Except for that one and only time, she had always felt extremely comfortable in this room. Which was most strange when she came to consider the matter, she decided, for this room, above any other, seemed to retain its master's powerful aura long after he had left it.

Not that she considered her husband's masculine strength a threat any longer. It was now a little over three weeks since he had suggested that she resume her duties, and she had accompanied him down to this room. She couldn't deny that for a time she had feared he might use that superior strength of his in an attempt to force her into acceding to all that was expected of her as his wife. After all, he had cruelly admitted that the only reason he had married her was to beget an heir.

That, above all those other terrible things he had said to her that night, remained a constant torment, for she had truly believed, when he had made his proposal in Devonshire, that he had loved her. She

shook her head, uncertain what to believe any more.
Perhaps, though, Aggie was right and he did love her.
If that was the case, then she could well understand
why he had become so bitterly angry when he had
believed she had played him false. Added to which,
his considerate behaviour towards her during these
past weeks gave her every reason to hope that his
feelings for her went rather deeper than mere regard,
but he had never put his feelings into words, and until
she was absolutely certain in her own mind of the
state of his heart, she could not bring herself to lie
with him again, at least not willingly.

As though by a natural progression of thought, she
began wondering why, in fact, he hadn't demanded
his rights as her husband? Her health was no longer
a bar to a resumption of intimate relations, and there
was no denying that Richard was a virile man, not
accustomed, she suspected, to curbing his natural desires. Surely he didn't still suspect her of carrying
another man's child? If that were the case then it
would be a simple matter, surely, to consult Aggie,
with whom he had become wondrous close, and she
would swiftly disabuse him. It was possible, of
course, that he was satisfying his bodily needs elsewhere. His affair with the vivacious Lady Torrington
had, she truly believed, ended, for he had never made
a further return visit to the capital. There was always
the distinct possibility, though, that he had a paramour
living nearby, but somehow she doubted this, though
of course she couldn't be completely certain.

She couldn't deny that she remained bitterly resentful over his affair with Lady Torrington, but was
honest enough to admit, now, that she must shoulder
her share of the blame for his seeking solace in an-

other woman's arms. If she had been totally honest
with him from the start, this rather unfortunate beginning to their marriage might have been avoided. So
many foolishly kept secrets! So many things which
ought to have been explained, not only concerning
herself but others, too. Granted the right opportunity,
she would willingly tell him everything... But it was,
now, a case of the right opportunity arising.

The sound of voices in the hall pierced through her
sombre reflections, and moments later the library door
swung open and her favourite neighbour swept into
the room.

Since her arrival in Hampshire she and Caroline
Westbridge had become firm friends. Caroline was
the only one, apart from the Rector and his good lady
wife, who had paid regular visits during the early part
of Elizabeth's illness. Richard had not permitted anyone to visit the sickroom itself until he had been certain that all risk of contamination had passed, but that
didn't alter the fact that Caroline had put her own
health at risk by merely entering the house.

"I must say, Elizabeth, you look positively blooming this morning! The colour is back in your cheeks,
so you've absolutely no excuse whatsoever not to attend my summer ball on Saturday evening."

"I have every intention of being there," she assured her. "From what I've learned from Richard the
event has long since become one of the county's most
celebrated, and not to be missed."

"A slight exaggeration, but I believe it is enjoyed
by many. My poor dear Giles did so love the summer—the hotter the better! Came from spending so
much of his early life in India, I suppose. Since his
death I've continued the tradition of holding a ball in

high summer, though I must confess there have been some years when the heat has been quite oppressive.''

She glanced across at the large oak desk, where Elizabeth had positioned the beautifully arranged vase of flowers. ''Where is Richard hiding himself this morning?''

''He went out quite some time ago. Very secretive he was about where he was going, too. But he did say he would be back in good time for our morning ride. We've taken to riding out together daily,'' she explained. ''Which, I suppose must have something to do with my improved appearance.''

Caroline was highly delighted to learn that they were spending so much time together. It was the only way, surely, to put right whatever it was that had caused that sad and most unexpected rift between them.

When news had reached her of Richard's rather surprising departure for London all those weeks ago she, like so many others, had thought it rather strange that he should pay a visit to the metropolis so soon after his wedding had taken place, leaving his lovely young wife behind; but hadn't really given his actions any more thought until rumours began to circulate of his association with Lady Torrington. Even now she still cringed inwardly at the memory. She had been here, sat in this very room, when that malicious Lady Pentecost, whose reputation as a spiteful tabby had been well earned, had called and had announced, with quite malicious intent, that Sir Richard's name was being linked, and not without good reason, to that of a certain attractive widow.

Caroline had always been very fond of Richard, but he had certainly plummeted in her estimation that day. During these past weeks he had retrieved his position somewhat. His devotion to Elizabeth's well-being throughout her illness had been quite touching to witness; but she still found it hard to understand why any man who was blessed with such a charming and lovely young wife should seek his pleasures in the arms of a notorious houri who was certainly not in her first flush of youth.

She had gained a slight insight into what might have brought about the rather unexpected rift between them during one of her visits a few weeks before. Elizabeth had still been keeping to her room at the time and in a mood of despondency had let fall that Richard had believed that she, together with her sister, had planned his incarceration in the Chilthams' cellar. Caroline had urged her to tell him the truth, and took the opportunity, now, of asking if her advice had been taken.

"Yes, I did broach the subject once, but whether he believed me or not is quite another matter."

"But surely you mentioned that it was I who had discovered the truth?"

"No, I didn't," Elizabeth freely admitted, casting her friend a fond smile. "You particularly asked me not to repeat our conversation of that day. Don't you remember?"

Caroline dismissed this with an impatient wave of her hand. "Richard's believing the truth is far more important than my rather ridiculous request. Tell him that you discovered your sister's underhandedness from me." She was silent for a moment before adding, "And talking of darling Evadne…have you heard from her recently?"

"My dear Caroline, I've mentioned on more than

one occasion that we are not close. I have had no contact, written or otherwise, since I left her house on the morning after that very eventful dinner-party.''

Caroline didn't attempt to hide her surprise at this intelligence. ''But...surely you informed her of your intention to marry?''

''No, I did not, but Richard did. And I believe he wrote informing her of my recent illness; she didn't bother to write back enquiring how I was going on... But then, I never expected her to.''

''Well, I've heard from her. She wrote to me last week, informing me that she has invited herself to my ball. She'll be arriving sometime this week, but just when, I'm not perfectly sure.''

It was abundantly obvious from the distinct lack of enthusiasm in her voice that Caroline was not precisely overjoyed at the prospect of having Lady Chiltham as a guest, so why on earth hadn't she simply written back putting her off? This was not the first time that Caroline had betrayed her lack of esteem for Lady Chiltham. Almost from the first time they had met Elizabeth had gained the impression that Caroline disliked Evadne excessively, and yet she continued to visit Devonshire two or three times a year, and never attempted to prevent the Chilthams from visiting her.

''Although you are far too well-bred to pull my darling sister's character to shreds in my company, Caroline, I do realise that you have as much regard for her as I do myself. Precious little! So I cannot help wondering why you make a point of seeing her so frequently.''

The shrug in response was not so much one of indifference as resignation. ''There are reasons, my dear,'' she admitted, and looked for a moment as if she might say something further, but then suddenly appeared to think better of it and hurriedly rose to her feet.

"Heavens above! Is that the time? I really must be going. I want to pay a visit to Melcham. I've heard that a young doctor has set up a practice there. I think I'll pay him a visit. If I like the look of him I shall certainly call upon his services in the future when it becomes necessary. Like yourself, I consider Dr Fieldhouse a pompous nincompoop."

This piece of good news, for they were in desperate need of a second doctor in the area, diverted Elizabeth's thoughts from the previous topic of conversation. "I might pay him a visit myself within the next few days," she remarked, accompanying her favourite neighbour outside to the waiting carriage. "I'd like him to take a look at Jem. Not that I think there's much wrong with the boy that a good and plentiful diet won't soon put to rights. But after the hard life the poor child has been forced to endure, one cannot be absolutely certain."

Caroline knew all about the plight of the unfortunate climbing-boy, and the reasons why he had been rescued by the Knightleys. "You haven't come to regret your act of charity yet, I see."

"Oh, no! Well, at least I haven't," she amended with an impish smile, "but I'm not quite so certain that Richard feels as I do. It was only to be expected that, after years of nothing short of slavish hardship and privation, young Jem would display a deal of exuberance now that his shackles have been removed. But I'm afraid his natural high spirits didn't meet with Cook's approval, so he has been relegated to the stables. It was rather fortunate that Hodge, the head groom, took such a marked shine to the boy. He's become a kind of surrogate grandfather, and has Jem sleeping in his room above the stables.''

''Let me know how he's progressing when you come to the ball. I doubt I shall find the time to visit again before then. There are several guests staying for the weekend, so I'm afraid I am going to be rather busy.''

Smiling fondly, Caroline climbed into the carriage, but Elizabeth's smile in response faded the instant the vehicle moved off. For a few moments she followed its progress along the sweep of the drive and then returned indoors and went directly up to her room to change into her habit.

Without waiting for Richard's return she collected a suitable mount from the stables and set off in the direction of one of her favourite spots on the estate. There were no signs of an immediate break in the weather, which had remained hot and dry for over a week, and by the time she had arrived at the small copse, where a stream gurgled its way beneath the shading canopy of branches, she was already feeling the effects of the mid-July sun's intensely warm rays.

Leaving her mount to champ contentedly on the sweet grass in the shade, she made use of one of the trees blown down in the severe gales which had swept the county the previous January. For a while she sat silently drinking in the peaceful beauty of the spot, where it was not uncommon to see the odd wild creature emerge from the undergrowth to refresh itself in the stream's clear, sparkling water, but it wasn't long before her mind began to dwell on the visit earlier of that person who had become quite dear to her.

Caroline was without doubt one of the most warm-hearted, even-tempered people one could ever have the pleasure of meeting. She seemed to get along with most people very well. There was little doubt in her mind now, though, that Caroline disliked Lady Chiltham intensely. Elizabeth didn't find this in the least difficult to comprehend, for Caroline was far too astute not to have realised long ago that Evadne's sweet smiles and friendly overtures were merely a façade.

''People can change over the years, but it's been my experience that they never do to that extent…''

Aggie's word came back so clearly, bringing with them vivid and highly unpleasant recollections from the distant past. As a child Evadne had attained the utmost pleasure in allowing others to take the blame for her misdemeanours. Elizabeth recalled numerous instances when she had been punished by her mother for what had, in fact, been her sister's malicious acts. Evadne had enjoyed nothing more than wielding power: having a hold on some poor unfortunate, whereby he or she was forced to do precisely as she asked or risk a secret being revealed. Could this be the case with Caroline? Was Evadne privy to something that Caroline would prefer not to become generally known…? But what?

The most obvious explanation, of course, was that some time during her marriage Caroline had foolishly indulged in a fling with another man, but somehow that possibility didn't ring true. From things Elizabeth had learned since living in Hampshire, it seemed that the Westbridges had been the most devoted couple. Caroline had been devastated by her husband's most unexpected and tragic demise, and it had been only her loving devotion to their sole offspring's well-

being which had instilled in her the strength and determination to carry on with life during those early
months after her husband's accidental death.
Supposing, though, that exposure as an adulteress was
the Sword of Damocles Evadne held above Caroline's
head—why after several years of widowhood did it
still matter so much? She frowned, perplexed. No,
that wasn't the explanation; she felt certain of it.
There was something, though…but what?

The sound of hoofbeats broke into her disturbing
thoughts, and she turned her head to see her husband,
astride the handsome grey that had taken the place of
the mount shot from beneath him at Waterloo, can-
tering up the slight rise towards her.

"Why didn't you wait for my return?" he asked,
not attempting to hide his disappointment because she
had chosen not to do so. "I haven't said or done
anything to upset you, have I?"

"Of course not!" She waited for him to sit down
beside her, and didn't attempt to move when she felt
one strong muscular thigh brush against the folds of
her habit: "To be honest with you, I had something
on my mind and left the house without thinking."

"Oh?" He was instantly alert. "Anything I can
help you with?"

"You might be able to, yes." She was staring
straight ahead, and didn't notice the sudden look that
softened his eyes as they studied her profile. "How
well did you know Giles Westbridge? What kind of
man was he?"

The unexpected enquiry surprised him slightly, but
he didn't hesitate to satisfy her curiosity. "He was a
good deal older than myself. My brother Charles
knew him rather better than I did, but I always got

on very well with him. He was a large, amiable sort. He acquired his wealth out in India where he lived for some years. When he came back to England he met Caroline and purchased Heathfield House within a few years of their marriage. He was a bit of a gambler by all accounts. Evidently Lady Luck favoured him, for he always seemed very plump in the pocket. He invested a considerable amount in a friend's venture in South Africa which has paid dividends. Caroline will never need to worry her head over financial matters.''

She digested this in silence for a moment, then said, ''He was discovered slumped over his desk in the library, so I understand. The bullet had entered his heart, so I assume death was instantaneous.''

''I was in Portugal when it happened, but from what Charles told me later, Westbridge had been cleaning his pistol at the time. Everyone assumed that he had been rather careless and hadn't realised the thing was loaded.''

''And no one suspected foul play or suicide?''

''Giles Westbridge hadn't an enemy in the world. There were no signs of a forced entry. And as far as suicide is concerned—'' Richard shook his head ''—what reason could there have been? If my memory serves me correctly, Lord and Lady Chiltham were staying at the house at the time. They both spoke to the magistrate. The verdict was accidental death.''

''So, my sister was there, was she? How very interesting.''

Richard studied her closely and saw a decidedly calculating look in her eyes. ''Why do you find that circumstance so intriguing, Elizabeth?''

''Because I very much fear that darling Evadne has

some kind of hold over Caroline—something she uses to make our very amiable neighbour do precisely as she wishes. But at the moment I'm still groping in the dark trying to unearth something unsavoury about a person who appears to have led a totally unblemished existence.''

''From what I've learned of your sister from various sources in recent months, her character leaves much to be desired, but is she so loathsome as to stoop to blackmail?''

Elizabeth didn't even take a moment to consider the question. ''Oh yes. Short of cold-blooded murder, I think her capable of anything.'' Her smile was a trifle rueful. ''Never take anything she says or does at face value. Just look at what she did to us when we were in Devon!''

Again he studied her closely, and she held his gaze levelly, without so much as a single blink. ''When did you discover that she had planned your incarceration in the cellar? You certainly didn't suspect anything at the time—I do realise that, now.''

''No, foolishly it never occurred to me that it was anything more than an innocent mistake. But I should have realised, knowing Evadne's character so well. My only excuse for being so foolishly obtuse is that I assumed she had outgrown her childish acts of malicious spite.''

Now that she had begun to confide in him, he wasn't prepared to let this golden opportunity to discover as much as he could slip away. ''How and when did you discover the truth?''

''From Caroline on the morning she left for Hampshire.''

Had he foolishly retained any lingering doubts

about Elizabeth's possible involvement they would have been irrevocably quashed by this intelligence. "But how on earth did Caroline uncover the truth?"

"After we had left the Chilthams' house that morning, she overheard Evadne berating the butler again. Something my sister said made Caroline suspicious. She went down to the drawing-room and retrieved those pieces of paper on which our names were supposed to have been written. We all saw Evadne go over to the table and pick up the quill...but the slips of paper were blank, Richard."

He shook his head. "It quite amazes me how anyone can be so despicably underhanded."

Elizabeth smiled rather enigmatically. "It must be something in the blood."

"If that is so, you've certainly escaped the malicious taint."

"Very true. Thankfully, I am not similarly afflicted."

She hovered for a moment, debating whether to tell him something rather astonishing about Evadne, but then decided against it. She fully intended to confide in him eventually, but now was certainly not the time. What she knew about her sister was so astounding that there was the very real possibility that she might not be believed without that all-too-important written proof. So, for the time being, at least, it must wait.

"I'm tired of talking of my sister. I shall see all I wish of her and more, I expect, on Saturday night at the ball." She rose to her feet and moved towards their mounts. "Whilst we're returning to the Hall you may tell me what you have been doing with yourself this morning."

After helping her back into the saddle, Richard

smiled up at her with all the indulgence of some doting uncle. "Had you done me the courtesy of awaiting my return, you would have been able to put the rather pretty dapple-grey mare I acquired for you earlier through her paces."

"You've purchased a mare for me?"

"Don't sound so surprised, my dear. You are my wife, after all, and I believe it's expected of a husband to bestow pledges of affection on his spouse from time to time."

He saw at once by the sudden guarded look which took possession of her features that she was suspicious of his motives; that his gesture had been misconstrued. Their relationship had improved immeasurably during the past couple of weeks, but she still wasn't ready to place herself entirely in his hands. What would it take to win her back completely?

The following afternoon Elizabeth journeyed to Melcham in the carriage. The equipage was being tooled by one of the estate workers because Hodge was busy moving his belongings out of the room above the stables and into a cottage on the edge of the estate, where it was to be hoped that young Jem might quickly grow accustomed to his new-found freedom and not prove quite so disruptive.

When she and Richard had returned to the Hall the previous morning to view the new mare, Jem, armed with a substantial shovel, had foolishly chosen that precise moment to declare war on a large rat which had found its way into the long stable. His frantic battle cries as he had given chase had startled the mare, who had been interestedly inspecting her new surroundings, and several of the other horses, too, and

Richard had decided there and then that Jem just could not be allowed to roam free near such highly prized and sensitive creatures. If Hodge wished to continue caring for the boy then he must move into one of the estate cottages. Elizabeth had not remained to hear what else Richard had had to say, but he had informed her later that Hodge had been quite happy to take full responsibility for Jem and, furthermore, had been quite content to retire once a replacement head groom had been found.

She smiled to herself as she glanced absently out of the carriage window. Yes, she mused, yesterday had certainly been a day full of incident. Firstly, there had been Caroline's rather revealing visit, and then later that relaxed conversation with Richard, followed by his rather unexpected gift of a dapple-grey mare. It had been a very kind gesture on his part to purchase a mount for her alone to ride. She couldn't deny, though, that it had briefly crossed her mind to wonder whether he would expect something in return, but she had wronged him—he had not attempted to come to her room last night. She wasn't perfectly certain whether this fact pleased her or not, and a heavy sigh escaped her as the carriage pulled up outside the haberdasher's in the main street. Her mind might advise a continuation of aloof caution, but her body was beginning to demand something else entirely.

After making several necessary purchases in the various shops and depositing them inside the carriage, she asked the rector's wife, who happened to be passing by, the whereabouts of the new doctor's house. Mrs Archer was a pleasant, kindly soul, an ideal wife for a man of the cloth, but her tongue did tend to run on wheels, so it was quite some time before Elizabeth finally discovered what she wanted to know.

Very well aware that Richard owned the smart red-brick house in the centre of Melcham, Elizabeth was rather surprised that he hadn't taken the trouble to inform her that his new tenant was none other than the new and much-needed doctor, especially as she had mentioned that very morning that she had every intention of making the physician's acquaintance and asking him to take a look at Jem.

A young boy was busily polishing the new brass plaque on the front wall, thereby obscuring the name engraved in the shining metal, as Elizabeth walked up the short path to the front door. So it wasn't until her summons was answered and she looked down in delighted surprise at the small, plump woman with kindly grey eyes, whom she knew so well, that she had her first intimation of who the new doctor might be.

''Middie!'' she exclaimed, using the pet name she had always used when addressing her grandmother's housekeeper. ''What in the world... Tom? Is the new doctor Tom?''

''Well, of course it is! Surely that handsome husband of yours told you that,'' Mrs Middleton responded after giving her old mistress's granddaughter a fond hug, and then leading the way down the narrow passageway where two workmen were busily engaged in fitting a second front door.

Still somewhat bemused, Elizabeth followed the housekeeper, whom she had firmly believed had every intention of retiring once the house in Bristol had been sold, into the small, cosy back parlour, where she wasted no time in echoing her thoughts aloud.

''And so I did, Miss Elizabeth…I mean, my lady. The new owner is taking up residence at the end of the month, and I had every intention of going to live with my sister, but then I got to thinking. I've a few good years left in me yet, and I didn't like the idea of sitting around all day with nothing to do. So when Master Tom came round to see me a few weeks ago, and told me that he was leaving Bristol and coming here to work, and that he would be needing a cook-housekeeper…well, I didn't take a moment to consider.''

''I did offer you the opportunity of coming with me to the Hall,'' Elizabeth reminded her.

''And very kind it was of you, too. But I don't think I would have fitted in there, Miss Elizabeth, not with all those gentry folk and their fancy ways. Not that I don't consider Sir Richard a charming gentleman, because he most certainly is. But I'm a plain-spoken woman, miss, as you well know, and I'm better suited in a situation like this. Besides—'' she gave a loud sniff of disapproval ''—Master Tom needs someone to look after him. He's lost a deal of weight since leaving your dear grandmother's house last autumn. He needs me around to make sure he eats proper!''

Elizabeth couldn't prevent a smile at this. Mrs Middleton wasn't above scolding Tom for rushing out and leaving his meals, just as though he were some unruly schoolboy, instead of a full-grown and very intelligent man. He would accept such reprimands from her, whereas he wouldn't, perhaps, from anyone else.

''I'm very glad that he has you to look after him, Middie. But what quite astonishes me is that he left

Bristol at all! I thought nothing would ever induce him to try to better himself.''

''I can't deny I was surprised myself. I rather think your husband might have had something to do with it,'' she disclosed, amazing her listener even more. ''Doctor Carrington thinks very highly of Sir Richard.''

''Oh, those dratted workmen!'' she exclaimed as a further bout of hammering reverberated down the passageway. ''It's been like this since we arrived. What with the large front parlour being fitted out and turned into an apothecary's shop, and now this second front door… Still, I suppose I oughtn't to complain, really. This new door is for my benefit. The first entrance will be for those wanting to purchase things in the shop, and will be left open during the day, so I'll only need to concern myself with those people wishing to see the doctor.''

''Is Tom here now?'' Elizabeth put in as the housekeeper looked as though she was about to stigmatise the workmen further.

''Yes, but he has someone with him… No, it sounds as though the patient's leaving,'' she added, hearing Tom's deep voice in the hall. ''I'll inform him you're here.''

''But please don't tell him who I am…just say there's a lady wishful to see him.''

Mrs Middleton had known Elizabeth for too many years not to have a pretty shrewd notion by the extra sparkle in her lovely eyes that her former mistress's granddaughter was about to play some mischievous prank. And she wasn't wrong. Although Elizabeth was overjoyed to have Tom living so close by, she was feeling slightly nettled because he hadn't taken the trouble to write to her informing her of his pending move.

After being told that her surrogate brother would see her now, Elizabeth whisked herself silently into the first room on the left of the passageway and quietly closed the door. Tom was seated behind his desk and glanced briefly up from the notes he was writing, but Elizabeth was fairly confident that he hadn't a clue to her identity. The large poke on her very fashionable bonnet hid much of her face when her head was lowered, and the handkerchief she had had the forethought to press to her lips hid the rest.

"Please take a seat, madam. What seems to be the trouble?"

"It's my nerves, doctor," Elizabeth managed in a high-pitched, beautifully disguised voice which shook slightly, but certainly not from any nervous disorder. She was very well aware that if there was one category of persons for whom Tom had scant regard, it was those females whom he irreverently called "twittie" women.

"Such palpitations!" She dared not peer across the desk at him, but instinctively knew by the sudden low growling sound in his throat that his heavy scowl had descended. "Such fluttering in my bosom!"

"And when, precisely, do you suffer from these attacks, madam?"

"W-whenever in the c-company of men."

"Are you married?"

"Y-yes." She could almost hear him saying, "I pity the poor fellow". "But my husband is quite old. It is only young, handsome men who seem to affect me so, you see."

A long silence, then, "Tell me, ma'am, would that be all young men or, perhaps, just one in particular?"

The oozing sarcasm was just too much for her, and she gave way to uncontrollable mirth.

"Elizabeth, you little baggage! I'll give you palpitations if you try any more of these tricks!"

After dabbing at her streaming eyes, she looked across the desk at him properly for the fist time, and knew that he wasn't really angry, just pretending to be. "Well, you deserved it, Tom. It was downright shabby not to let me know you were moving into the district!"

His brows rose. "Didn't Richard tell you? It was he who put the notion into my head in the first place. I wrote to him several weeks ago, accepting his kind offer."

"No, he never mentioned it at all," Elizabeth admitted, wondering why not.

"Ha! A man of sound good sense, then. Probably knew the first thing you'd do would be to try to badger me into letting you come with me on my calls, just as you did when we lived in Bristol."

"You make me sound like some stray pup that was forever following you about. I used to accompany you out occasionally."

"Well, you'll not do so again!" he informed her in his brusque, no-nonsense manner. "You're a married lady and have a position to uphold."

"I have no intention of offering you my help," she countered, looking and sounding decidedly miffed. "I have better things to do with my time than bear you company, Dr Thomas Carrington! And if it wasn't for the fact that I require your professional services, I tell you plainly I wouldn't be sitting here bandying words with you now!"

Smiling at her all-too-evident pique, he rose to his feet and moved round the desk. "Here, let me take a look at you."

"It isn't I who require your services," she informed him when he placed his hands on her neck, and was told in no uncertain terms to sit still and do as she was told.

"Yes, you've fully recovered," he announced after completing his brief examination. "So, who is it you want me to see?"

Elizabeth dropped her affronted pose and told him all about the climbing-boy she and Richard had rescued from a life of sheer misery. "I don't think there is anything seriously wrong with him that a continued substantial diet won't put right, but I'd just like to be certain."

"Any sign of a persistent cough?"

"No, not that I've heard."

"I'll check him over, none the less. I'll call on you tomorrow morning and you can take me over to the cottage. It will give us the opportunity to catch up on each other's news."

Friendly relations having been restored, she allowed him to accompany her outside as far as the gate. "You needn't walk with me to the carriage. It's only a short step away." She smiled glowingly up at him, all the deep sisterly affection she bore him mirrored in her eyes. "It is good having you close by, Tom," she admitted at last. "I missed you, you know."

"Strangely enough, I missed you, too, you infuriating little minx," and then, as he had done so many times in the past, he placed his arms about her and gave her a smacking kiss on one cheek, before holding her away, a rather rueful expression taking possession of his features. "Dear me, I must stop doing that. Here you are, a respectable married lady and flirting shamelessly with the doctor. What will people think!"

The lady who had just passed by in a very elegant travelling carriage was certainly doing plenty of thinking after witnessing the affectionate little scene. A rather calculating gleam sprang into her cornflower-blue eyes as she leaned back against the plush velvet squabs. "Well, well, well! And what goes on here? I was in two minds whether to make this trip or not. Now, I'm very glad I did. Unless I'm very much mistaken it will offer me some very good sport... Who would have thought it? And so soon after her marriage, too! My sweet little goody-goody sister really is full of surprises."

The inside of the carriage echoed with a trill of feminine laughter. "First thing tomorrow, Quimper, you are to return to this misbegotten place and discover precisely who lives in that red-brick house we've just passed."

Chapter Eleven

As Richard turned his head to stare through the carriage window at the passing countryside bathed in the pleasant glow of fading evening light, Elizabeth took the opportunity to study him closely, wondering yet again what manner of man she had married.

That erstwhile nonpareil of her childhood imaginings had been remoulded through the passage of time into something a little more human; but even on the day they had married she had, perhaps, credited him with rather more than his rightful share of the gentlemanly virtues. His expeditious descent into the stinking pit of debauched humanity had turned out, surprisingly, to be only a temporary fall from grace. Even in those early weeks of her illness, some detached part of her fevered brain had registered that he was far from the hardened roué her battered heart had proclaimed him. Now, she looked upon him as neither saint nor monster, merely as a man, a man who, for the most part, was touchingly thoughtful to the needs of others…but a man who continued to remain, frustratingly, something of an enigma.

Having looked his fill of the familiar countryside,

Richard turned to catch a pair of puzzled eyes studying his physiognomy with apparent rapt interest. "By your far-from-smiling countenance, I can only deduce that either you're not looking forward with any degree of enthusiasm to the evening ahead, or my appearance doesn't meet with your approval."

"You're wrong on both counts," she didn't hesitate to assure him, with a sudden lightening of her brow. "Although, if I'm truthful, I rather think riding gear is more flattering to a man of your excellent stature and rugged good looks."

The latter remark came so easily to her lips that it was out before she realised what she was saying. Heavens above! Whatever had come over her? She was flirting—yes, unashamedly flirting with him! Was it normal for wives to flirt with their husbands? By his spontaneous smile it was quite evident that he appreciated it, at any rate.

"I was considering you, though, Richard," she admitted, spurred on by his appreciative reaction to her honesty, "but not your attire. Amongst other things, I was wondering why you should have chosen not to inform me of Tom's arrival in the district. I cannot perceive what motive there could have been for keeping such a thing secret from me." If the admission surprised him he certainly betrayed no outward sign of its having done so.

"When I first put the idea to him you were still most unwell. Later, when he had made up his mind, I fully expected him to write to you personally, seeing how the two of you are so very close." He remarked upon this fact without experiencing the least pang of annoyance or jealousy. "When he didn't, I naturally thought that he wanted to surprise you, as his being in Melcham evidently did.''

He didn't add that he had feared at one time she might well suspect him of trying to curry favour by making it possible for the man she looked upon as a brother to live nearby.

It was quite evident, though, by her warm smile that she suspected him of nothing so base, even before she said, ''You are to be congratulated, Richard. I doubt there are many who could influence Tom in such a way. I certainly have never been able to do so. I tried to persuade him to accept Caroline's invitation to her party tonight, when he called to take a look at Jem the other day, but as usual the stubborn wretch flatly refused to commit himself.''

''It certainly wouldn't do his practice any harm to attend,'' he responded, somehow managing to suppress a smile at her obvious lack of patience with the young doctor. ''There are very few occasions when most of the gentry hereabouts are gathered together in one place. It's an ideal opportunity for him to make himself known.''

''Ha! I doubt even that consideration would prove sufficient inducement for him to bestir himself and socialise for an evening.''

But in this Elizabeth had wronged him, as she discovered not many moments after she had entered Caroline's large ground-floor salon, charmingly decorated for the special occasion with numerous vases of beautifully arranged summer flowers and several cool green potted-palms.

Tom, amidst a group of gentlemen, was standing at the far end of the room. Catching sight of Elizabeth within moments of her entering the room, he raised his glass in silent greeting. Her immediate response was a glowing smile of approval at his attendance, which was noted by several persons present, including Lady Chiltham who had been keeping half an eye on the doorway since the arrival of the man who, only days before, had been so warmly embracing Lady Knightley in the front garden of that smart red-brick house in the local town.

Whenever attending an occasion such as this, where most people present were completely unknown to her, Lady Chiltham could always somehow manage, within a very short space of time, to attach herself to some garrulous person who was not averse to indulging in a little malicious gossip. The lady seated beside her, dressed in a fussily adorned gown of purple silk and a rather ugly turban of the same hue, didn't disappoint her.

"It would seem that your sister is already on remarkably friendly terms with our new practitioner," Lady Pentecost remarked, levelling her lorgnette in the doctor's direction. "An excellent young man, I do not doubt, but I prefer a physician a little more advanced in years. Any young matron seeking his services with any degree of frequency will simply be begging the gossip-mongers' tongues to start a-wagging."

Evadne did not even attempt to respond to this. After excusing herself, she merely rose to her feet and made her way across the crowded room in the direction of the door. Lady Pentecost, without that affected use of the lorgnette, studied the younger woman's progress. Like her sister's, Lady Chiltham's carriage was undoubtedly graceful, the white spider gauze alternately swishing about and clinging to the wonderfully proportioned slender figure as she moved. Lady Pentecost approved wholeheartedly of the warm embrace Evadne bestowed upon her sister, but the sentiment most certainly wasn't experienced by the recipient, nor by the man who stood close by, watching the performance with a cynicism engendered by recently acquired knowledge.

Although he had tactfully refrained from alluding with any degree of frequency to his wife's early life, Richard had by this time gained a fair understanding of what Elizabeth had endured at her sister's hands during childhood. His lip curled at the nauseatingly false display of affection, and it took a monumental effort on his part to remain silent at Evadne's spurious expressions of relief and gratitude at seeing her sister looking so well. Caroline, however, for once was unable to exert such firm control.

"If the letters both Richard and I wrote were insufficient to assure you of Elizabeth's continued progress after her illness, you could quite easily have journeyed here and discovered the truth of the matter for yourself."

"I wished to do just that," Evadne responded, but the promptly spoken assurance fooled no one. "You must remember, though, that I had my family to consider. Deeply concerned though I was, I couldn't risk taking the infection myself and passing it on to my husband or children."

"Very understandable, Evadne," Caroline agreed fair-mindedly, "but it would have been a simple matter to assure yourself of your sister's progress by writing a letter. I wrote to you on more than one occasion, but I certainly never received a reply throughout your sister's illness."

The sweetly serene smile remained, but there was a menacingly calculating look in Evadne's blue eyes as she turned them in their hostess's direction. "You should know by now, my dear Caroline, that I've never been much of a scribbler. Besides, one needs to be so very careful when putting pen to paper. Letters can occasionally go astray, or even fall into the wrong hands entirely, can they not?"

Just for one moment, before she turned to greet some new arrivals, Caroline's complexion seemed to grow ashen. Evidently Evadne's observations had not been so innocent as they had sounded, but Elizabeth wasn't given the opportunity to dwell on the possible sinister connotations, for the eldest son of one of their close neighbours approached to claim her for a partner in the next set of country dances.

During her years in Bristol she had attended numerous parties where country dances were preferred to the waltz, a dance which was her particular favourite, but which many members of the older generation continued to view with disfavour. It took very little effort on her part, therefore, to perform the intricate steps while keeping an eye on certain other persons present. Richard, she noticed, had wasted no time in excusing himself, and was now conversing with Tom and several other gentlemen. Evadne had returned to her seat beside Lady Pentecost, who was following the set with apparent rapt interest, no doubt hoping to catch some poor unfortunate miss a step, and Caroline, still stationed by the door, was looking quite animated as she greeted yet more guests. Elizabeth couldn't help wondering, though, how much of that light-hearted manner was merely for show.

The set came to an end, and the musicians hired for the occasion immediately struck up a waltz, Caroline not being amongst those who disapproved of the dance. Elizabeth would have been quite content to leave the floor and refresh herself with a glass of champagne, but the gentleman swiftly approaching to claim her hand was someone she could never find it within her heart to refuse.

"My, my! You are turning over a new leaf," she teased as a shapely, long-fingered hand was placed lightly on her waist. "Indulging in such frivolous pastimes as dancing, Dr Carrington? Whatever next! And looking as fine as fivepence, too? Who loaned you the evening garb, by the way? Was it Richard?"

"No, it wasn't, you impertinent little baggage!" he returned good-humouredly. "Anyone listening to you might suppose I didn't have a decent shirt to my name."

She refrained from responding that she suspected he hadn't that many and asked, instead, what had prompted him to accept Caroline's invitation.

"Oh, I just thought I'd cast an eye over the local populace to see what ailments I'm likely to be called upon to treat. Not surprisingly, many here suffer from too much, rather than too little. Besides, I rather like Mrs Westbridge. Struck me as a kind-hearted, sensible sort. Which is more than can be said for that dragon-faced harridan seated beside your sister."

"Ah! So you've been introduced to the formidable Lady Pentecost and the oh, so charming Lady Chiltham, have you?"

"Yes. And didn't care for either of them," he responded in his usual forthright fashion. "A right pair of vicious tabbies, if I'm any judge."

"Remind me to loan you a book on etiquette, some time." She twinkled up at him. "I see that you still lack a number of the social graces, Dr Carrington. Might I remind you that it is my sister of whom you speak."

"Don't hide my teeth when I'm with you, Elizabeth. You should know that."

"No, and I'm very glad you do not. But it might be wise to choose your words carefully when conversing with Lady Pentecost," she warned him.

"It would be wiser for her to consider carefully anything she says to me," he countered, that all too familiar hard-edged note of determination in his deep voice. "I cannot abide people of that ilk, Elizabeth, as you very well know, and have no intention of kowtowing to them."

Although still in his twenties, Tom was already quite set in his ways, with definite and immovable views on certain subjects. Elizabeth knew him well enough to be sure that nothing she said would induce him to tread warily with certain members of the gentry hereabouts and, truth to tell, she had no wish to change him, even if she could. He wouldn't be her darling irascible Thomas if he were to become a grovelling toad-eater in order to make his way in the world. So, she prudently changed the subject and, when the dance was over, remained at his side to drink a glass of ice-cool champagne.

It was while Tom was speaking to the local squire and his wife, who also came across to refresh themselves, that Elizabeth happened to turn her head and noticed Caroline slip out through one of the long French windows, which had been left wide open to allow some much-needed fresh air into the crowded salon. At first she gave little thought to their hostess's sudden departure and continued to watch the dancers, all decked out in their finery, swirling about the room, but after some minutes, when Caroline hadn't returned, she began to feel a little uneasy and decided to investigate her new friend's continued absence.

There were several couples enjoying the cooler air on the terrace, but, surprisingly, Caroline was not amongst them. Several lanterns adorned those trees closest to the fine Tudor manor house, and Elizabeth had little difficulty in picking her way along one of the many paths which criss-crossed that part of the garden closest to the building. After walking some little distance, without catching sight of their hostess, she was about to retrace her steps, when she noticed a shadowy movement near one of the ornamental trees.

"Ah! So there you are!" Uninvited, she seated herself on the wooden seat beside her friend. "I was beginning to think I would need to return for reinforcements in order to track you down."

"Oh, dear! Have I been missed already?" She sounded genuinely perturbed, as though she had been found lacking in her duties as hostess. "I didn't realise I'd been out here for so long."

"Rest easy, you haven't," Elizabeth assured her, but added, having by this time detected the telltale signs of an unsuccessfully suppressed bout of weeping, "You haven't remained out here nearly long enough for your eyes to recover from tears recently wept."

Caroline made a half-hearted attempt at denial, but then abandoned the rather pointless exercise. "Yes, very foolish after nearly six years of widowhood, but it's at times like these when I miss Giles dreadfully.''

Elizabeth didn't doubt the sincerity of this, but felt certain that this fact alone wasn't wholly responsible for her friend's present distress. She had no wish to pry, but at the same time couldn't sit idly by while someone she cared for very much was suffering deeply when she might be in a position to help.

"Very understandable," she responded softly, staring sightlessly across the darkened garden, "but that doesn't account for your moment's disquiet earlier this evening. Has my sister said or done something to upset you since her arrival here?" There was no response, but, undaunted, Elizabeth added, "Or has she, perhaps, some hold over you?"

Caroline's audible gasp of dismay was confirmation enough. "You know, don't you!" It sounded more accusation than question. "She's told you, hasn't she?"

"No one has told me anything…yet." Elizabeth turned her head and gazed at her neighbour's distraught features steadily, knowing that if she was to get to the truth, she mustn't be reticent herself. "You hold my sister in scant regard. You've admitted as much. The darker side of my sister's nature is not unknown to me, so it didn't take a great deal of intelligence to puzzle out the possible reason for your strange behaviour.

"I shall not attempt to intercede on your behalf unless you wish me to do so, Caroline," she went on gently, "but if you do wish me to help, then I must know precisely why you find yourself in my sister's coils."

"Oh, if only you could help me!" Tears barely

held in check began to well again. "I have carried this burden of guilt for such a long time, and yet I don't deserve such torment, but for my son's sake I've been forced to endure your sister's malice, pander to her every whim. You see, Elizabeth, my husband's death was not an accident…it was suicide."

If she had hoped the pronouncement would be met with astonished disbelief, she was destined to experience disappointment. "You don't appear in the least surprised, and yet you couldn't possibly have known."

"No, I didn't know, but I cannot deny that that distinct possibility hadn't occurred to me," Elizabeth acknowledged with brutal candour. "And this is the hold my sister has over you, is it?"

"Not entirely, no," Caroline admitted without the least hesitation. Now that she had begun to unburden herself she experienced no reluctance in revealing the whole truth to this young woman whom she instinctively knew could be trusted implicitly.

"Giles was a wonderful husband and father," she began, a distinct catch in her voice, "but he wasn't without his faults. I'm sorry to say that his ruling passion was gambling. I never attempted to curb this weakness in him, and am honest enough to admit that I believe I would have been unsuccessful if I had tried. Lady Luck had been kind to him over the years, but I suppose it was only to be expected that *she* would transfer her loyalties eventually.

"Some months before he died he invested a deal of money in a friend's venture in South Africa. He ought, of course, to have compensated for this by exercising economy." She sighed. "Sadly, though, that wasn't Giles's way. He continued to gamble and lost heavily at the tables. I didn't know it at the time, but we were seriously in debt. Giles, then, committed the unforgivable sin of cheating at cards. Faced with ruin, the young man whose fortune Giles had stolen—and it can be termed nothing less than that—took his own life soon afterwards. The final irony was that Giles's investment in South Africa then began to show a return, but he couldn't live with what he had done.

"I discovered the terrible truth only after Giles had died," Caroline divulged, having taken a moment to regain her composure. "He left a letter for me confessing all. The Chilthams happened to be staying with us at the time. Foolishly, I left that damning letter lying about in my room, and your sister apprised herself of its contents, and has retained it to this day."

Elizabeth reached out a hand to grasp trembling fingers. "It was hard, I know, for you to tell me all this, but you shan't regret it."

"Could you succeed where I have failed and persuade her to return Giles's letter?" Hope sprang into Caroline's dark eyes. "Could you appeal to her better nature?"

"I wasn't aware that my sister possessed a better side to her nature," Elizabeth returned with gentle irony. "Oh, no. I must adopt methods of persuasion that Evadne would certainly not appreciate, but couldn't fail to understand. Fight fire with fire, as one might say."

She smiled at Caroline's look of bewilderment. "How long does Evadne intend remaining here with you?"

"I'm not sure. A few days, certainly."

"That's good, because there is something I must do before I confront her." The smile she bestowed could not have been more reassuring. "You had better return to the house now, otherwise your absence will be noted. It would not serve our cause if Evadne suspected that you had confided in me. Continue as best you can to behave quite naturally whenever in her presence. But be assured you shall not long remain in her clutches."

Mindful of the warning, Caroline took the precaution of returning to the salon with two of her female guests who had been amongst those enjoying a breath of fresh air on the terrace. As she resumed her role as hostess she found the smile coming quite effortlessly to her lips, a genuine smile of combined relief and renewed hope for the future.

Confiding in someone at long last had considerably lessened the heavy burden of guilt which she had been carrying round with her during these past years. Elizabeth, blessed girl, had betrayed not the least feeling of condemnation or disgust after learning the appalling events leading up to Giles's tragic death, and although Caroline still retained grave doubts about ever regaining her husband's damning letter, she was now determined never again to submit to what had been nothing short of emotional blackmail.

Darling Elizabeth's reactions had given her every reason to hope that other friends would behave with the same kind-hearted generosity when they learned the truth. But first, she must confide in her son. He had been twelve years old when his father had died. Now, he was no longer a boy, but almost eighteen: old enough to be told the sad truth. As soon as he returned from Scotland with his friends, she would confide all, but in the meantime she would do as Elizabeth had asked, she decided, fixing her gaze momentarily on the woman who had caused her untold anxiety during the past five years.

"Caroline looks sublimely pleased with herself," Evadne remarked, catching their hostess's swift scrutiny. "I wonder what has occurred to lift her spirits?"

"The success of this evening, I shouldn't wonder," Richard responded without much interest.

He had long since become faintly bored with his sister-in-law's company. While Elizabeth had been dancing with Tom, Evadne had positioned herself at his side, and he had considered many of the remarks she had passed highly provocative and faintly distasteful. She had almost insisted that he dance with her, and although it would have afforded him immense pleasure to refuse, he had decided that as relations between his wife and her sister were, to say the least, precarious, it would be wrong of him to place a further wedge between them.

Successfully suppressing a sigh of relief as the dance came to an end, Richard was on the point of returning his partner to the vacant chair beside Lady Pentecost, when Evadne thwarted his intentions of being rid of her by requesting him to accompany her outside for a breath of air. He managed to check the blunt refusal that rose in his throat at his lips, as he tried in vain to catch a glimpse of Elizabeth in the crowded room, but when Evadne made her way down the terrace steps into the garden, he momentarily hindered her progress by announcing quite bluntly, "I cannot remain with you for long. My wife has promised me the supper dance, which will be taking place very shortly."

"How very unfashionable to dance with one's wife!" she exclaimed, possessively entwining her arm through his and steering him ever further away from those people on the terrace. "Still, I suppose it's expected of a recently married couple to make, at least, a pretence of a joyful union."

Disengaging his arm with ruthless efficiency, Richard came to an abrupt halt just beyond the wooden seat where his wife and Caroline had been sitting a little earlier, and looked down at Evadne with a disdainful curl to his lips.

"Be assured, madam, there is no pretence on my part."

For a moment Evadne was taken aback by the vehemence of the assertion, but then she smiled, a sickly sweet smile which he found nauseating.

"Come now, Richard. There is no need for these blatantly false protestations. I am fully aware of the reason why you married my sister, and I did try to tell you that there was absolutely no need for such a sacrifice on your part."

He stared down at her in silence, his features as coolly expressionless now as those of a marble statue; but she refused to admit defeat on this romantic night when the balmy air was heavy with the fragrance of roses and sweetly scented stocks. He didn't care for Elizabeth. She was firmly convinced that a marriage between them would never have taken place if it hadn't been for her butler's stupid blunder on the night of the dinner-party. He had always preferred her; had wished to marry her once, she reminded herself with a deep feeling of satisfaction. And she was still a very desirable woman.

"Remain stubbornly silent if you will," she husked, running her hands up the muscular arms to entwine them at the nape of his neck, "but I know the truth. Reports of your amorous exploits in London during the early part of the Season even reached us in Devonshire. You quickly grew tired of my sister, but you won't so easily tire of me.''

Without waiting for a response this time, she pulled his head down and placed her invitingly parted lips on his, but the reaction to her advances could hardly be described by even the most optimistic as encouraging. His mouth remained firmly closed and coldly unresponsive during those few brief moments before he raised his hands and placed them round her wrists in a bone-crushing grip that almost brought tears to her eyes.

Retaining his far-from-gentle grasp, he held her at arm's length, that disdainful smirk she had seen earlier returning to twist one corner of his unreceptive mouth.

"If you are in need of further confirmation of my feelings for your sister then I shall tell you this. I married Elizabeth because I had fallen in love with her. She is the only woman I have ever truly loved. She is the only woman I shall ever love, and as long as I have her I shall neither require nor covet the charms of any other female.''

It was like being dealt a punishing slap in the face. Evadne could only stare up at him in astonished disbelief, unable to draw her eyes from the humiliating depths of disdain in his own.

"I trust I do not intrude?" a soft voice unexpectedly enquired. "But I think you should know, Richard, that the supper dance is about to begin.''

Releasing his hold abruptly, he swung round to find Elizabeth, with an unreadable expression on her lovely face, standing a little way down the path. In three giant strides he was beside her and, without knowing or caring whether his sister-in-law followed, escorted his wife back towards the house.

Evadne remained perfectly still, disbelief having been replaced by ice-cold anger at the humiliating rejection she had just received. Even after all Richard's assurances, there was still some doubt in her mind that her sister had won the heart of the man whom she herself would quite happily have married years ago if his position on the social ladder had been higher. She had never made any secret of the fact that wealth and status had always been of paramount importance to her and marriage to George Chiltham had given her both, even if it had provided her with precious little else. She had always found the physical side of their union abhorrent, and even though she had indulged in the occasional, if discreetly conducted, extramarital affair, intense satisfaction had come from the slavish adoration she had evoked in her various lovers rather than from any activities between the sheets. An interlude with Richard might have been different, might have proved more physically satisfying, for there was no denying he was an intensely attractive member of the male sex, but she was destined, now, never to find out. Richard, she felt certain, would never add his name to her list of devoted admirers.

Having her amorous overtures so blatantly spurned was a new and vastly unpleasant experience which had left her with an insatiable desire for revenge. She would make him pay dearly for his insulting behaviour, she vowed silently, vengeful determination adding an extra sparkle to her eyes. And if she could also manage to bring about her precious sister's downfall,

all well and good. But she must plan carefully, for Richard was no fool, and neither was Elizabeth. How that girl had changed during these past years, and not just physically, either! Her revenge on them both must be sweetly merciless, and that, she was very well aware, would take considerable thought and very careful planning.

Chapter Twelve

Debauched! An abhorrent scrap of humanity too loathsome to be touched was how Elizabeth must surely view him now, even if she hadn't before that sickening interlude with her sister had taken place earlier, Richard decided, his spirits plummeting to an all-time low. And who could blame her? How would he himself have felt if he had come upon his wife in a starlit garden, wrapped in another man's arms? The mere thought was enough to engulf him in a positive tidal wave of rage, so he could hardly upbraid Elizabeth for having jumped to the totally wrong conclusion when she had witnessed such a nauseating spectacle with her own eyes.

Suddenly ceasing his brooding pacing, he stared sightlessly across the bedchamber. The trouble was, though, she had given him no positive indication of just how she felt. There had been no tearful recriminations, no words of reproach. Had she turned on him, and lashed out with sharpened claws, he would have understood, but her impeccable behaviour throughout the remainder of the evening had been faintly unnerving.

When they had danced that one and only dance together she had disarmed him by indulging in polite small-talk. When they had gone in to supper later to join Tom and several others at one of the large tables, she had been both witty and animated, entertaining all with her amusing conversation. Only in the carriage during the journey home had he been given an inkling of how she had been feeling. Disinclined to talk, she had sat staring through the window into the darkness, deeply immersed in her own private thoughts.

Dear Lord! And what darkly depressing thoughts those must have been! He ran impatient fingers through his hair, sending his recently combed locks into disorder. Catching her husband in a compromising situation with her sister of all people! Why, it smacked of little short of incest!

It was so damnably unfair, too! Slumping down on the chair before his dressing-table, he suddenly felt bitterly resentful. No one could have tried harder than he had to prove how deeply he cared. He had been patient and understanding, which was nothing less than Elizabeth deserved after the heartlessly cruel way he had behaved towards her; but all his good intentions, all those weeks of trying to rebuild their relationship, had been destroyed in a few short minutes, simply because he had felt obliged to be polite to someone he didn't even like. And therein, he decided, his temper returning with a vengeance, was the reason he found himself in this unfortunate predicament now.

He didn't resent one single act of kind consideration which he had bestowed on Elizabeth during the weeks since her illness, but he was forced to admit that his behaviour could hardly be described as natural. The fault might have been his in foolishly accompanying Evadne into the garden, but he had certainly not instigated or desired what had taken place between them. So why the devil should he be held responsible for that scheming harridan's unwelcome attentions?

Patience and understanding had proved excellent weapons in the past, but they would not serve his purpose now. No, only a direct approach would serve. Much better to thrash things out tonight than allow her to continue to suppose that he was some monstrous cad who harboured unwholesome designs on her sister.

Some detached part of his brain had registered that Aggie had left the adjoining room some minutes ago. The chances were that Elizabeth would now be tucked up in bed, but it was unlikely that she would have succumbed to sleep so quickly, he decided, striding purposefully across to the connecting door and throwing it open so forcefully that it banged against the chest of drawers, startling Elizabeth who was not, in fact, in bed, but sitting at the gilt-legged table in the corner of the room, busily composing a letter.

''Elizabeth, we must talk! And it will not wait until morning.''

She found his moderately domineering tone as deeply attractive as the man himself. Dressed, she suspected, with nothing beneath the crimson brocade robe and with his bare feet planted slightly apart in the thick pile of the patterned carpet, he reminded her of some proud eastern potentate considering the fate of an erring subject.

''It just so happens that I wished to speak to you, Richard,'' she momentarily startled him by announcing. "This letter I'm composing is to my late grand-mother's man of business. He retains in his safekeeping a small chest containing several personal letters and important documents. I need it brought here urgently, and was wondering if you'd allow me to despatch Jenkins, the footman, to collect it first thing in the morning?"

"Yes. Yes, of course," he responded, taken aback slightly by the unexpected request and the impassive, enquiring way she was regarding him. How on earth could she remain so calmly self-possessed after what she had witnessed tonight? The dreadful fear that she might not actually care whether or not he was contemplating an affair with her sister momentarily crossed his mind, but he swiftly suppressed the soul-destroying notion. She wasn't so coldly indifferent to him. No, he was firmly convinced she was not.

"I—er—wanted to talk about tonight," he began cautiously, not quite knowing now how to broach the somewhat delicate subject.

"Oh, yes. A lovely party, wasn't it?"

"Yes. Yes, it was." He cleared his throat noisily. "But I was—er—referring specifically to that unfortunate interlude involving your sister." She unnerved him further by remaining silent, one finely arched brow raised in half-mocking enquiry. "I don't know what you must have thought—what you believed was going on between—"

"Oh, I know what was going on, right enough, Richard," she interrupted, turning her attention once again to the half-finished letter. "You were making love to Evadne."

"No, I was not!" he countered staunchly, and in

his rapidly growing irritation didn't notice the wickedly teasing smile playing about her mouth.

"Very well," she compromised. "You were merely kissing her, then."

"That's precisely it—I wasn't. She was kissing me!"

"Is there a difference?"

"Of course there is, damn it!" he snapped, forgetting to put a guard on his tongue in his determination to win back at least a modicum of her regard. "I didn't know the confounded woman was planning a seduction scene when she asked me to escort her outside for a breath of air."

"You must have offered some encouragement, Richard," she suggested, sounding so matter of fact about the whole business that he experienced the strong urge to take her by the shoulders and shake her until her teeth rattled. "I cannot imagine that even Evadne would demean herself by offering her charms to a man she knew to be completely indifferent to her."

"I don't give a damn what that designing harpy would or would not do," he responded sharply, fast coming to the end of his tether. "I have never ever given her any reason to suppose that I have designs on her person."

"Now that, Richard," Elizabeth countered, turning her head and waving her quill at him like some irate school-ma'm, "is a downright untruth. And well you know it! I recall quite clearly hearing you say that you wished Evadne was the one your father had wished you to marry... And you kissed her then, too!"

He couldn't have been more stunned if she had

announced that she was secretly married to Bonaparte himself. "What nonsense is this?" he demanded, making it abundantly obvious that he retained no recollection of the incident whatsoever. "I've never said any such thing!"

"Oh, but you did, Richard," she argued, certain of her facts. "You would have been about nineteen, twenty at most. You were taking a stroll with Evadne in my parents' garden at the time, in the shrubbery to be precise, and I overheard you. And that," she added before he could give voice to further denials, "is precisely why I sought refuge with my grandmother within a year of my father's demise."

Ignoring his astounded expression, she began to brush the feathers of the quill back and forth across her chin. "Although my father desired the match, I do not believe he would have forced it upon me in view of the fact that you preferred my sister to me. But my mother most certainly would have done so. It is quite a lowering experience discovering that the man one has been groomed to marry infinitely prefers someone else. And that, of course, is in essence the reason why I wrote to you when you were out in the Peninsula. I didn't refuse to marry you because you had no title then, as you seemed to suppose. I merely refused to marry someone who infinitely preferred my sister to me."

It was wicked of her, she knew, but she simply couldn't help feeling a deal of satisfaction from his bewildered discomfiture. He gaped across the room at her as though she had just sprouted a second head, and then clapped a hand over his eyes as if to dispel the hideous vision.

"I don't believe I'm hearing this," he muttered,

removing the hand from his face. He took a hesitant step towards her, about to reiterate that Evadne meant less than nothing to him, when he stepped on something sharp and ended by uttering a loud and rather rude expletive.

"What on earth have you done?" Elizabeth flew across to the bed where he had seated himself in order to examine his injured foot. "Here, let me. My nails are longer than yours."

"You can thank your niece for this," she told him after extracting the small, sharp object from the flesh. "She was in here this afternoon and had scattered my box of bits and pieces over the carpet before I could stop her. She is getting quite naughty, Richard. You really must take a firmer hand with her."

"She isn't the only one," he muttered, and this time he didn't miss the wickedly provocative smile before she went across the room to collect a towel.

Kneeling in front of him, Elizabeth began to dab the small cut, which was bleeding slightly, with the towel. Richard gazed down at her bent head, thinking as he always did how lovely she looked with those glossy russet locks cascading about her shoulders, while at the same time trying desperately to ignore the gentle touch of warm fingers on his ankle.

"You truly don't believe I care tuppence for your sister, do you?" he asked, his voice suddenly husky and throbbing with emotion.

"Not now, I don't."

"I never went out into the garden with her in the hope of seducing her. Believe me, that would never enter my head."

"No, I know it wouldn't."

"You do?" His triumphant smile was instantly

erased by a suspicious frown. "How long were you out there before you made your presence known?"

"I had been in the garden for a little while. I saw you and Evadne walking down the path, and hid in the shadows," she admitted at last. "There was a reason why I didn't want Evadne to know I had been outside. You stopped only a few yards away from where I was standing, and I overheard everything that was said. One should, I suppose, consider eavesdropping a reprehensible habit, but I'm not in the least sorry that for once I gave way to temptation."

She raised her head and what he saw mirrored in her eyes made his spirits soar to record heights. "If I hadn't remained to listen to your conversation I would have missed hearing something that I've been longing to hear for such a very long time."

"And what was that, Elizabeth?" he asked, his voice a gentle caress.

"That you loved me."

The towel slipped from her fingers as he took a hold of her upper arms and drew her unresistingly against him. "But you knew that…surely you must have known? I have been in love with you, Elizabeth, almost from the moment I walked into that small parlour at Dartwood Manor and saw you sitting there."

She didn't reply, couldn't reply, for Richard's lips had fastened over hers with a possessive hunger, and her immediate response was wonderful confirmation, had he needed any, that the breach between them had finally been healed.

He did sense a moment's restraint, a fleeting disquiet, after he had laid her gently into the bed and had peeled away her clothing, but his exploring fingers soon had the reserve melting away and he extricated those soft moans of pleasure he had waited so long to hear again. His many weeks of self-imposed abstinence was not without its penalty, however, and the exquisite pleasure was over all too quickly, but he consoled himself with the knowledge that next time it would be more rewarding for them both, and that the next time would not be long in taking place.

For her part Elizabeth was blissfully happy, but then she would have been so even if he had not come to her room and the inevitable outcome of two people very much in love hadn't taken place. His lovemaking had been a wonderful confirmation of those precious words he had spoken in the garden earlier, adding a further layer to the cloak of blessed contentment which had shrouded her during these past few hours.

History, however, had an unfortunate habit of repeating itself as she discovered moments later when he didn't attempt to gather her into his arms. Suddenly thrusting the bed covers aside, he swung his feet to the floor, and unpleasant memories returned with a vengeance and began to strip away the layers of exultation, threatening to leave her naked and vulnerable as she had been on that never-to-be-forgotten occasion before.

"What is it, Richard?" she forced herself to ask while at the same time dreading the answer. "What's wrong?"

His flashing smile acted like an emollient, instantly soothing away all distraught thoughts. Without bothering to retrieve his discarded dressing-gown he padded, naked, across to the connecting door, offering her the unfettered view of his wonderfully proportioned muscular frame before he disappeared for a few moments into his room.

"I am taking the very necessary precautions of ensuring that we shall not be disturbed," he answered on his return, repeating the procedure of moments before by locking her bedchamber door and then blowing out the various candles, leaving just the one on the bedside table alight. "I give you fair warning now, madam wife, that it is unlikely I shall allow you to rise early in the morning, if I permit you to rise at all."

By the contented smile she cast him as he slipped into bed beside her again, and propped himself up on one elbow, it was quite evident that she had no fault to find with these arrangements. "But first we must talk, Elizabeth," he told her, suddenly serious. "I never again want hurt…misunderstandings between us."

He paused for a moment to run one finger along the outline of her jaw, his dark eyes betraying clearly enough the anguish of bitter regrets, even before he said, "My behaviour towards you in the past has been, to say the least, less than just. I overreacted when I discovered that you—that I was not the first man you had—"

"Richard, there is something you should know," she interrupted gently, but he was determined to have his say, and placed his exploring finger over her lips.

"No, my darling, there's no need for you to explain. The fault was mine. I behaved like a damnable fool!" he rasped in violent self-reproach. "I loved you so much that when I discovered another man had known you, I felt bitterly hurt and resentful. My liaison with that woman in London meant nothing." The shadow of pain flitting over her features brought a further stab of self-disgust, but he forced himself to go on. "It was a cruel and heartless way of taking my revenge, I know. My only excuse is that I was consumed with rage and jealousy, and was still, even then, labouring under a heavy burden of guilt."

He saw a moment's puzzlement replace the sadness in her eyes, and knew he must explain everything if his callous behaviour towards her in the spring was ever to be truly forgiven and forgotten.

"You know that I was injured at Waterloo. The most frightening legacy of that terrible battle was my temporary blindness. I was nursed back to health by a young woman called Mary Smith. I truly don't believe I would have survived if it hadn't been for that blessed girl."

So wrapped was he in bittersweet memories that he failed to notice lips curled in a sweetly knowing smile. "One night I selfishly took her innocence. I was prepared to do the honourable thing and marry her, but Mary, ever giving, expected nothing in return, and started back for England the following day." He released his breath in a heartfelt sigh. "She must have suspected that my feelings for her were only deep affection, not love."

Elizabeth regarded him in silence for a moment, her expression unreadable. "Did you never attempt to find her?" she asked, rampant curiosity momentarily holding back her long-overdue confession.

"I fully intended to do so. She left me a letter, which I still retain to this day, but it contained no forwarding address. It was while I was awaiting the return of the owner of the house which she had hired in Brussels that I learned of her death."

"Death?" Elizabeth echoed, not attempting to hide her astonishment. "What on earth makes you suppose that she died? I mean,'' she amended when he regarded her searchingly, ''if you didn't know her whereabouts in England, how could you possibly have known that she had died?''

''She never reached England,'' he astounded her by responding. ''A Mrs and Miss Mary Smith were amongst those who took passage on *The Albatross*. It capsized in mid-Channel on its return to Southampton last summer.''

Lowering her eyes, she absently regarded the dark hairs at the base of his throat as memory flooded back. *The Albatross* had not departed when she had arrived at the port. There had been no earthly chance of her attaining passage back to England on that particular vessel, however, for not only was it fully booked, but her grandmother's health had deteriorated during the journey from Brussels to such an extent that they had been forced to put up at an inn for a few days before embarking on the sea voyage home. Naturally, she had learned of the terrible tragedy, but she had never seen a list of casualties. Not for an instant had she believed that he had tried to find her, for it would not have been an impossible task. When the weeks had passed without seeing him on her grandmother's doorstep in Bristol, or without receiving a letter from him, she had believed that her decision to leave him in total ignorance of her true identity had been justified. But he had tried to find her, and all this time he had believed that she, his Mary, had lost her life in that terrible tragedy at sea.

''Oh, God! If only I'd known,'' she murmured, and didn't realise she had spoken aloud until he responded with, ''How could you have known? I've never spoken of it before. Besides, I should never have allowed my feelings of guilt to interfere with our relationship. I wasn't in love with Mary, but I did fall in love with you. And never again will I risk losing you because of stupid pride, or thoughtless actions."

"Richard, you do not perfectly understand." She simply must tell him the truth now! "Richard, I have a confession to make. It concerns that man—that first time I—"

"No, Elizabeth!" he ground out. "I never wish to know his name!" Then, more gently, "I don't want to know who it was. It doesn't matter. Our marriage starts now. What has gone before is best forgotten. Let's away with recriminations and regrets. Let us, now, lay the past quietly to rest, and think only of the future."

"Yes, Richard, I know, but—"

She got no further, for he was determined to have his way, and the methods he adopted to achieve his aim were so sweetly pleasurable that she couldn't summon up further resistance. Some deep recess of her brain suggested that an opportunity would arise for her to broach the subject again, but now was hardly the most appropriate time, when it seemed that the only concern of the man she loved was to demonstrate the depth of his feelings in a peerless display of masculine passion.

After returning his pen to its position on the standish, Richard rose from his desk and stretched contentedly. He looked a man thoroughly satisfied with life, and his appearance was not deceptive. Since the evening of Caroline's eventful party he had experienced nothing short of perfect contentment: the fulfilling pleasures of his wife's lovely body lying beside him at nights; and long periods of her unrivalled company during the days. It had brought a whole new meaning to his life to know beyond a shadow of doubt that he was cherished in return by such a wonderfully caring young woman as Elizabeth: unique, unequalled; fulfilling the smallest requirement of a wife.

He turned as the door opened, hoping to see his perfect companion enter the room, and experienced more than just a twinge of disappointment when his butler walked into the library.

"There is a gentleman called to see you, sir, by name of Collingworth—a Captain Simon Collingworth to be precise."

"Good Lord!" Richard was surprised and didn't attempt to hide the fact. He hadn't set eyes on that young rogue since Waterloo. "Yes, Finch, show him in," he said, while moving over to the decanters in readiness for the entry of the man who had been affectionately christened "The Scourge of the Regiment'.

"Simon, this is an unexpected pleasure!" he remarked, genuinely delighted to see the tall, loose-limbed young man who strode with a swaggering gait into the room moments later. "What on earth brings you to this neck of the woods?"

"I'm paying a necessary visit to a favourite aunt of mine. Don't intend she should pop off and forget me in her will," he divulged with raffish honesty. "It's no joy being an officer on half-pay in peace time, I can tell you."

Richard accepted this with a knowing half-smile. The Collingworth family was a wealthy one and Simon, being the likeable rogue that he was, wouldn't think twice about approaching his elder brother to bail him out if he did find himself under the hatches.

"Trying times, indeed," he responded wryly, handing his incorrigible young guest a glass of Madeira before seating himself in the chair opposite. "Your unfortunate situation apart," he went on, serious for a moment, "it quite grieves me to see the plight of so many of those brave soldiers who fought with us. Unable to find work they are treated with less sympathy and compassion than lepers!"

"Very true. And that, Ricky, old boy, is precisely why I took the trouble of looking you up." Tossing the contents of his glass down his throat, the young captain took a moment or two to savour the taste. "Excellent wine! Nothing less than I would expect from your cellar... Now, where was I?"

"You haven't reached anywhere as yet, Simon. I'm still waiting to hear the reason why you chose to honour me with your company."

The younger man's eyes began to dance. Had the reason behind his visit not been so serious, his ever-lively sense of fun would certainly have prompted him to indulge in some harmless bantering with this gallant, one-time commanding officer.

"It's poor old Hawk that brings me here," he surprised Richard by announcing. "Came upon him quite by chance a few days ago when I was taking m'brother's new turnout for an airing in the park. Some silly clunch lost control of the high-spirited gelding he was riding, and who should come to the fop's aid but old Sergeant Hawker."

He shook his head sadly. "Didn't recognise him at first out of uniform. His clothes were tatty, little better than rags. He hasn't lost his knack with horses, though. Never known a man who has such a way with beasts as old Hawk. Had that gelding quietened down within seconds.''

Richard stared down into the contents of his glass wondering what his old sergeant was doing in the capital. Tobias Hawker had been born and raised in the country and hated large towns. He wouldn't have been in London unless he had no option but to be there.

''Did you get a chance to talk with him? Why didn't he return to his home in Nottinghamshire after the war?''

''He did, old chap. Apparently, though, his old master died last summer. The old man's eldest son turned Hawker's wife out of the cottage as soon as he had inherited the property, and told Hawk his services were no longer required on the estate when he eventually arrived back there. Mrs Hawker had come to live with her sister in London, and poor old Tobias followed as soon as he had discovered where she had gone. But London's like everywhere else. Times are hard. Hawk gets work when he can to earn a crust, but he's having a rough time of it—anyone can see that.''

Richard's feelings of sympathy were swept aside by a sudden surge of annoyance. ''Why the devil didn't the silly clunch get in touch with me? He knows where my house is in London. A message would have been sent on to me here.''

Captain Collingworth shrugged. ''Pride, I suppose. It would go against the grain for a man of Hawk's stamp to beg.''

''Stubborn fool!'' Richard muttered. ''Do you know where he's residing at present?''

"That I don't... Well, at least not precisely. We chatted for a bit. The poor chap looked all in after traipsing round the capital for hours looking for work, so I offered him a ride home. As soon as we were south of the river he didn't want me to take him any further, but I did manage to persuade him to join me in a tankard of ale."

"And where is this tavern to be found?"

"Green Street. It's called the Three Bells. You can't miss it. It's on the corner. Not one of the finest inns I've entered, I have to say. The landlord recognised Hawker, so I should imagine he can't live too far away from the place."

After a quick glance at the mantel-clock, Simon rose to his feet. "I'd better be making tracks if I'm to reach my relative's house in good time for dinner. I've still a fair way to travel," he announced, looking down at Richard's troubled face. "I would have helped old Hawk myself if I had been in a position to. I'll spread the word when I return to Horse Guards. Someone may be able to offer the poor devil employment. But I know you had a deal of respect for him, so I couldn't pass so close by without putting you in the picture."

"Yes, thank you. I'm glad you took the trouble." Richard rose to his feet and, with a promise to look his visitor up in London in the autumn, he escorted him to the door.

His thoughts were still very much on the plight of his sergeant when Elizabeth joined him a short time later. She had some concerns of her own, but couldn't mistake the look of disquiet on her husband's face, even though he did his best to conceal the fact behind a warm smile and a loving greeting.

Placing her hands on his upper arms, she held him away in order to study his features more closely. "What's wrong, Richard? Has something occurred to upset you whilst I've been out?"

"No—yes… Well, I'm not upset, precisely, just concerned over someone," he admitted, and then went on to relate the conversation he had had with his unexpected visitor earlier.

"There are old soldiers, unable to find work, begging on street corners in every town and city in the land," he went on bitterly. "It would be foolish to imagine that one could aid them all. But this particular man I would definitely help if he'd let me. He has a natural gift, Elizabeth. He can handle horseflesh better than any other person I know."

"You think there's a good chance he'd refuse your help, Richard?" she asked with her innate perspicacity, after seeing his brows snap together in an angry frown.

"Yes, stubborn fool!" Moving away, he began to pace the room in irritation. "I doubt he'd accept charity, especially from me."

"But it wouldn't be charity, now, would it, Richard?" she pointed out with a quizzical smile, as the most obvious solution to the problem had already occurred to her, even if it hadn't occurred to her very worried husband as yet. "It seems to me that he would be the ideal person to take charge of the stables here at Knightley Hall."

He stared across the few feet that separated them in blank amazement for several seconds, just as though she had suggested something so outlandishly foolish that she must have taken leave of her senses, then he uttered a triumphant shout of laughter.

"Elizabeth, my darling, you're a marvel!" Bridging the short distance between them in three giant strides, he took her in his arms again. "Now, why the deuce didn't that obvious solution occur to me at once?"

She didn't for a moment suspect that he required a response, but the fun-loving side of her nature decided to answer him nevertheless. "You've evidently a deal on your mind, Richard, and your wits have become addled somewhat under the pressure. You'll recover your natural thought processes given time, I dare say."

"I'll take leave to inform you, madam wife, that both mind and body have been under considerable pressure for quite some weeks, and the sole culprit for my continued disorderly state is right here next to my heart."

"In that case it is up to the wrongdoer to put matters right." The smile she cast him before taking the precaution of slipping out of his arms was a study in roguishness. "And you'll be forced to admit, Richard, that I have been doing my level best to effect a cure during these past few days."

A husky growl of well-remembered pleasure was sufficient to warn her, and she neatly avoided his outstretched hand as he made to pull her back into his arms. "Behave, Richard! This is neither the time nor the place to indulge in such conduct. Instead, channel your thoughts on how best to go about finding this old army acquaintance of yours."

"I have one small lead," he announced, reluctantly

doing as she asked. "Collingworth took him to a certain tavern. I'll begin my search there."

"When will you leave for London?"

"Tomorrow morning, if you think you can be ready by then." He watched a frown replace the smile. "What's wrong, Elizabeth? Don't you wish to accompany me?"

"I'd like to very much, Richard, but I feel I must forgo the pleasure this time. There is something I've promised to do for Caroline which concerns my sister."

She hadn't mentioned anything about that very enlightening conversation she had had with their neighbour on the evening of the ball. It wasn't that she wished to keep him in ignorance over her sister's behaviour. He was under no illusions, now, about Evadne's true character, so it would come as no surprise to him to learn of her appalling behaviour towards Caroline. But the issue was a sensitive one and the means by which she intended rescuing her neighbour from Evadne's clutches was equally so. Her sister deserved no consideration, she knew, but she refused to lower herself to Evadne's level and, therefore, would do her the undeserved courtesy of speaking to her in private.

"I must have a talk with my sister before she returns to Devonshire. That is why I went out this morning, as it happens. Unfortunately, Evadne had gone out somewhere and Caroline wasn't certain when she would return." Her frown grew more pronounced. "Caroline tells me my darling sister's been out and about a good deal during her visit. Apparently she's struck up a friendship with Lady Pentecost."

"Ha! That doesn't surprise me in the least. A well-matched pair!"

She couldn't prevent a chuckle at the scathing tone, but sobered almost at once. "Be that as it may, I still need to see her, and I'm not sure just how long she intends to inflict her company on poor Caroline, so I think in the circumstances I must stay here. Added to which, I'm rather concerned that Jenkins hasn't returned from Bristol with that small chest. He should have been back by now. If he hasn't returned by tomorrow evening I think I shall need to make a flying visit to Bristol."

"Well, you're not going by yourself!" he told her roundly, every inch the possessive, domineering husband. "I'll leave for London within the hour. I'll visit that tavern, but if I'm unsuccessful, then I'll pay a visit to an acquaintance of mine at Bow Street. I shall be back here tomorrow evening at the latest, and if Jenkins hasn't returned by then we can leave for Bristol the following day."

"How very kind you are to me, Richard." She went smilingly up to him and slid her arms about his waist with wifely familiarity, which seemed to please him immensely. "I shan't delay your departure by explaining things now, because it would take too long, but when you return I'll tell you precisely why the contents of that chest are so very important. In the meantime, I shall be counting the minutes until your return, and shall be on the doorstep, waiting to greet you with open arms, unless of course something, or someone, prevents my doing so."

Innocent enough words, but words that would return to torment him in the not-too-distant future.

Chapter Thirteen

Richard left Knightley Hall early in the afternoon. Driving himself in his racing curricle, he made excellent time. He kept several pairs of horses, all in prime condition, stabled at various inns along the main road to London. Changes were effected smoothly and he arrived at his town house in good time to begin his search for his old comrade early that evening.

After tooling the curricle round to the mews, he carried his small portmanteau to the front entrance of the house. His servants, not expecting their master's return, had put into effect the customary practices of protecting the delicate furnishings in holland covers, and removing the brass knocker from the door to indicate to any would-be caller that the master of the house was not in residence. It took Richard several minutes to attract someone's attention, but eventually Medway, busily working away in the butler's pantry, heard the pounding and came up from the nether regions to investigate the imperious hammering on the front door.

"Why, Sir Richard!" he exclaimed, not attempting

to hide his surprise at his master's unexpected return. "If I had known of your intention to come up to town, I would have put the house in order."

"Don't concern yourself, Medway," Richard responded, handing over the portmanteau as he stepped into the hall. "It's a flying visit. I intend staying for only one night. Just have my bedchamber made ready. There's no need to concern yourself with the other rooms, and I shall be dining at my club later, so inform Cook not to concern herself, either. Although we shall need a good breakfast in the morning before we leave."

Medway's ears pricked up at this as he followed his master up the stairs. "We, sir? Shall I be going somewhere with you."

"Yes. You'll be returning with me to Knightley Hall," his master explained, leading the way into his bedchamber. "I intended to send for you a couple of weeks ago, but, like so many other things of late, it slipped my mind. Finch is retiring and I should like you to take his place and accept full responsibility for both residences."

Medway's dearest wish had been granted, and it took several moments before he regained enough control of himself to stutter out his grateful thanks at being offered the opportunity to prove his worthiness. He had not, as yet, attained the age of thirty, and being offered such an exalted position at his young age in a respected peer of the realm's household was no mean achievement.

"There's absolutely no need for all this gratitude, Medway. You've worked hard and loyally for my family for many years, and have earned the promotion. Finch will be no easy act to follow, but I do not doubt you'll prove yourself a worthy successor. Now," he went on, collecting a clean shirt from the wardrobe, "do you consider young Frederick competent enough to look after this place in your absence?"

"He's conscientious, sir, and there's little enough to do here when you're not in residence. I think he deserves the chance."

"Very well. You can tell him he'll be starting his new duties from tomorrow." Richard shrugged himself out of his slightly travel-creased jacket and tossed it over a chair. "Whilst I'm changing I'd like you to go down into the street and hail me a hackney carriage. Find me one whose driver knows the area around the Three Bells on the corner of Green Street, which is situated somewhere south of the Thames."

By the time Richard had finished changing, Medway returned to say that a hackney awaited him at the door. The coachman knew the tavern's whereabouts, and the surrounding area like the back of his hand, or so he said, and Richard didn't delay in making use of the jarvey's knowledge.

As the rather musty smelling equipage headed in a southerly direction, Richard stared out of the window at the people going about their business. The Season had been over for several weeks and most of the *ton* had either followed the Regent to fashionable Brighton, or retired to their country estates to recuperate for a while before they returned to the capital and the next hectic round of social engagements. Life in London didn't stop, however, just because those most privileged persons in the land had left the heat and smells behind for the fresher country or sea air. The city was still bustling with life, though it was quite noticeable that there were far fewer fashionable carriages thronging the busy streets, and very few members of the *haut monde* wishing to parade in their finery for the edification of the populace.

As they crossed the river, the distinction between rich and poor became more marked. No fine mansions here, only streets and streets of tightly packed houses built in sentinel-like rows. There were no crossing boys to keep the streets clean and fit to stroll along and, apart from the occasional dilapidated private carriage, the only vehicles to be seen were lumbering carts, pulled by ill-nourished, work-weary horses.

It was rare for Richard to venture into this part of the city; after all, he had little reason ever to do so. He was not, however, completely ignorant of the misery of hardship. During his years in the army he had known what it was like to do without the basics of life; but his periods of privation had been short, whereas to the poor devils living here it was simply a way of life with little or no hope for improvement.

When the carriage drew to a halt, Richard alighted and, after requesting the jarvey to await his return, went striding towards the tavern. The instant he walked through the door, the smattering of patrons ceased their chattering abruptly, and he could not forbear a smile as all eyes, betraying blank astonishment, followed his progress to the counter.

It was safe to assume that a person of his evident means was a rare sight in this particular establishment. Which was in no way surprising, for Richard couldn't imagine any gentleman of his acquaintance, no matter how purse-pinched, demeaning himself by entering such a lowly place, where each worm-eaten table boasted a thick film of dust and all the walls were besmirched with large patches of black mould.

In fact, he was in two minds whether to chance a tankard of ale, but then decided it might be worthwhile taking the risk, as it was likely to make the landlord, who was eyeing him measuringly from his side of the counter, a little more forthcoming.

The ale, surprisingly, turned out to be very palatable, and Richard, ever polite, complimented mine host on the brew before asking outright if he was acquainted with Tobias Hawker.

''All depends on who be a-wanting 'im whether I be or no,'' was the surly response from the near-toothless and far from personable owner of the tavern.

''Perhaps this will help make up your mind.'' Richard drew out a shiny gold sovereign, holding it temptingly just out of reach of the landlord's eager fingers. ''It has always been my policy to pay for goods after they have been delivered.''

''I knows 'im right enough,'' the innkeeper growled, not taking his eyes off the glinting largesse.

''Does he reside nearby?''

''Ee may do.''

Richard's smile was not pleasant. ''My patience is not limitless, my friend. Either you tell me where he lives or—'' he cast a brief glance at the several interested onlookers ''—perhaps one of these other gentlemen might be more eager than yourself to earn some easy money.''

The threat lost nothing for all that it was softly spoken, and the reaction to it was not slow in coming. ''Ee lives in Brenner Street wi' 'is wife's sister and family. Don't know which 'ouse, though, but you'll find it no bother.''

"Thank you, my good man." He tossed the sovereign high into the air and had reached the door before it had been caught in the landlord's greasy palm.

"Brenner Street," he called up to the carriage driver. "Do you know where that is?"

The jarvey stared down at Sir Richard in amazement, wondering what a man of his undoubted quality could be wanting in such a run-down slum, but decided it might not be in his own best interests to enquire, and merely nodded. A few minutes later he drew the vehicle to a halt again at the entrance to one of the more noisome streets in the area, where the sun rarely managed to filter between the tightly packed buildings and the air was heavy and always foul-smelling.

"I don't know how long I shall be," Richard remarked, stepping down from the carriage and neatly avoiding a pile of filth in the road, "but I shall reward you handsomely if you do me the courtesy of once again awaiting my return."

"I wouldn't leave a dog alone round 'ere, sir," the jarvey announced, gazing about him in distaste. "I'll wait for you, don't you worry. And should you—er—be needing my services in any other way, then just you holler and I'll come a-running."

Richard cast a shrewd, assessing glance up at the small but sturdy individual perched on the box. "Yes, you look as though you'd give a good account of yourself if you were called upon to do so."

The jarvey didn't pretend to misunderstand and tapped the side of his broken nose in a meaningful way. "That I would, guv'nor. Not that I'm one to go looking for trouble, you understand, but there again I ain't never been known to turn tail and run, neiver."

He paid Richard the silent compliment of deciding that, for all he resembled some swaggering Bond Street beau, the body beneath the immaculate attire belonged to a man in fine physical condition, muscular and strong.

"I mind you'd handle yourself well enough if it came to a bout of fisticuffs, sir."

"I've been known to spar from time to time," Richard admitted with a ghost of a smile before turning and picking his way carefully along the narrow garbage-ridden street.

When he drew level with the group of children, who had all simultaneously abandoned their game in order to gape at the spectacle in their midst, he beckoned to one of the boys. Rampant curiosity quickly overcame the street urchin's innate mistrust of strangers, and a well-to-do stranger at that, an uncommon sight, indeed, in this rat-infested slum! He disengaged himself from his companions, his wide eyes and gaping mouth ample testament to his continued awestruck state.

"A shilling for you, boy, if you can point out the home of Mr Tobias Hawker," Richard offered temptingly, and then took the precaution of moving back a pace when the boy lifted his hand to his matted hair, and an alarming memory of an unwashed climbing-boy flashed before his mind's eye.

"I reckon ee be the one living wiv the Joneses, guv'nor. They lives there."

Richard glanced in the direction of the grimy pointing finger, tossed the boy the promised largesse and then went over to the house on the opposite end of the street. From the outside, at least, it looked as if the occupants had made some attempt to improve their lot. Brightly coloured curtains hung at the windows, and the area outside the front door had been recently swept.

The woman who came in answer to his summons was like a refreshing breath of fresh air in this less-than-wholesome place. Her mousy-brown hair was closely confined in a bun at the back of her head, and the apron that covered the front of her faded grey gown was as clean and well starched as any of those worn by the female servants in his own employ. For all that she was plainly attired in worn clothes and shoes, she was as much out of place in this locale as he was himself, and he had a suspicion of who she might be even before he introduced himself and she betrayed instant recognition of his name.

"Oh, sir! Do step inside, won't you? It isn't fitting for a gentleman like yourself to be standing outside in the street."

Mrs Hawker moved to one side to enable Richard to enter the small front parlour which, though shabbily furnished, was both clean and tidy, without so much as a speck of dust to be seen anywhere. Hawker had frequently remarked on the fact that, although his estate cottage might not be grand, one would need to travel a long way to find a cleaner abode.

"As you may have gathered, Mrs Hawker, I am here to see your husband. What time do you expect him home?"

Surprised that he should have known who she was, for they had never met before, as her husband hadn't approved of soldiers bringing their wives with them to Portugal and Spain, she silently gave herself a scold for forgetting her manners and not introducing herself to the man her husband had admired above any other during his years in the army. Determined not to be found lacking again, she politely invited the distinguished visitor to seat himself in the most comfortable chair, before offering him some refreshments.

"I have a bottle of brandy put by for medicinal purposes, sir, but you're most welcome to a glass while you're waiting for Toby. He shouldn't be too long now. Unlike my brother-in-law, he rarely goes to the tavern after he's finished work."

Richard was in two minds. He didn't wish to hurt this polite woman's feelings by refusing, but at the same time felt guilty at depriving her of something she could ill afford to replace, so he decided on a compromise. "That is most kind of you, madam, but just a small one, thank you."

Delving in a cupboard, she drew out a bottle and a clean glass and allowed him to help himself. "You say Hawker has found work?" he remarked, pouring himself a very small measure of the amber liquid.

"Until the end of the week, sir, yes." She betrayed her concern with a deep sigh. "It's difficult finding anything round here. Work is offered to the locals first, which I suppose is only fair. Coming from the country, Toby and me are considered outsiders, you see, although I did manage to find a few weeks' work during the spring, making gowns in one of the fashion houses in Bond Street."

Richard was only too well aware that that particular trade was nothing short of slave labour, with the poor women working up to sixteen hours a day in the cellars beneath the fashionable shops in poor light and airless conditions. "And you're not working now, I take it."

"I did manage to find work in one of the big

houses for a while, but the owners returned to the country. Perhaps I'll have more luck in the autumn when some folks return to the capital. I'm looking after my sister's baby at the moment. He's upstairs, sound asleep in his cot. My sister married a Londoner, you see, sir, so she's considered a local and has no trouble in earning a few days' pay now and then. This is their house. It was very good of them to take us in like they did,'' she finished, trying desperately to sound contented with her lot, but she didn't fool Richard for a moment.

She was a woman accustomed to better things and a woman, unless he was very much mistaken, who would be prepared to work all the hours God sent in order to have a home she could call her own again.

''I understand that you were evicted from the estate cottage you'd lived in for many years when the estate came into the hands of your old master's heir.''

She looked faintly surprised that he should have known this, but nodded in confirmation. ''I suppose in a way it was Toby's fault. He took a riding crop to young Master Roland several years ago, when he caught him one day whipping a horse. When the old master learned what had occurred he didn't dismiss Toby, as Master Roland had hoped, but carried on from where Toby had left off and beat his son. The young master never forgave us for that. As soon as his father died, he turned me out of the cottage. I wrote a letter to Tobias to tell him what had happened, but it must have gone astray. He returned to the estate after Waterloo to find strangers in our old home, but one of the estate workers told me where I had gone and he came to London to find me.''

''Why, then, did he not come and find me, too? It

is not, after all, such a distance to travel to my London residence from here.''

She looked faintly discomposed by this direct attack, but before she could offer an explanation the door opened and the subject of the discussion strode into the room, his expression suddenly changing to one of blank astonishment as his eyes fell upon the gentleman sprawled at his ease in the chair.

''Major, sir! You…here? But…'' His words faded and he slanted a decidedly disapproving look in his wife's direction. ''Is this your doing, Edith? I thought I told you—''

''No, it was not,'' Richard announced, coming to Mrs Hawker's defence, ''but it ought to have been yours.''

He rose to his feet and stared at his old sergeant in angry silence. They were both of a similar height and stature, and suddenly seemed to fill the small room, dwarfing everything else in it, including Mrs Hawker who, just for one dreadful moment, thought that blows might be exchanged, so belligerent did both men appear. Then, thankfully, her husband seemed to collect himself, and turned away, running impatient fingers through his short, curly black hair.

''You know why I couldn't do that, Major, sir,'' he said, almost brokenly, the unexpected sight of the man at whose side he had fought for so many years bringing him to the verge of tears. ''I've too much regard for you, that's why. You'd have found work for me—I know that. Then word would have got round that you were a soft touch, and you'd 'ave 'ad every raggedy ars—every poor devil in the regiment who hadn't been able to find work banging on your door looking for a hand-out.''

"You damned fool!" Richard returned mildly, touched by the depth of his old sergeant's regard.

"Aye, that I may be," Hawker countered, a spark of the old defiance returning, "but I've kept my self-respect. I've worked when I could find it, and when not I've gone without. Me and Edith will go on that way. We'll not accept charity."

"Who said I was offering you any, may I ask?" Richard responded suavely as he resumed his seat. "I am here to offer you employment. No, kindly allow me to finish," he went on when Hawker threatened to interrupt. "I have semi-retired my old head groom for reasons I shall not go in to now, and as yet have been unable to find a suitable replacement. Now, if you would like to be considered for the position, then kindly say so. If not, then I shall not take up any more of your time."

Hawker regarded him in silence for several moments, not knowing whether to believe him or not, and then echoed his thoughts aloud, but his wife experienced no such doubts.

"Sir Richard's in earnest, Toby. Anyone can see that. He ain't spinning no yarn. It's a real job, and one you were born to do."

"It would appear that your wife has far more wit than you have, Hawker. And, as further inducement, I should add that the position is at Knightley Hall, for the most part, and not here in town." He glanced from eyes betraying dawning wonder to those glowing with deep gratitude. "When can I expect you to take up your duties?"

"God damn you, sir!" Hawker cursed, but with all too evident gratitude seeping into his voice. "My life wouldn't be worth living if I refuse now." He cast tear-filled eyes in his wife's direction. "The country, Edith... We're going back where we belong, old girl."

"Excellent!" Richard announced with an approving half-smile, before tossing the meagre contents of his glass down his throat. "We'll take it as settled. Now, when can I expect your arrival at the Hall?"

"My brother-in-law managed to get me work in the docks until the end of the week, sir. It would show 'im in a pretty poor light with the folks round 'ere if I didn't turn up. So, if you've no objections, I'd like to do right by 'im, and then travel into Hampshire early next week. That'll give us time to collect our bits and pieces together, and settle everything nicely at this end."

"That's fine. I fully intend to return to my estates tomorrow. So, you'd better take this to tide you over." He tossed a leather purse in his ex-sergeant's direction. "And don't argue, Hawker," he added, checking the recipient's intention of doing just that. "I know precisely the amount contained in that purse and fully intend to deduct a little at a time from your wages for the next few weeks."

Richard then turned his attention to Mrs Hawker, who had sat silently regarding him as though he were some kind of saint. He swiftly disabused her. "I am not, sadly, in a position to offer you work, madam. There may be work in the house, but that is my wife's department and I have no intention of interfering in what is strictly her domain."

"There's no need to concern yourself on my account, sir. I'm quite capable of finding myself— Oh, heaven's above!" she broke off to exclaim. "Tobias, where are our manners? We haven't even congratulated Sir Richard on his marriage. We did read about it eventually, sir,'' she explained. ''The announcement was placed in one of the newspapers that came our way.''

''Taken to reading journals now, have we, Hawk?'' His smile was full of gentle humour. ''My, my! I have acquired an educated man as a head groom!''

Tobias took the gentle teasing in the spirit it had been intended. ''As you know, sir, it were Edith, here, who first started to teach me to read and write. She having been a tire-woman, she were taught by her mistress. You were kind enough to spare me a little time when you were able when we was in Spain. But it were Miss Mary that really made me see 'ow important it were to be able to read and write. Hours she spent with me, sir. Brought me on a treat, she did. God bless the darling girl!'' He glanced across at Richard. ''Do you ever think about her, sir?''

''Not so much now, no,'' he admitted softly, ''but I shall never forget her. I kept the letter she wrote to me, but…but I just wish I had something else to remember her by.''

Hawker exchanged a meaningful glance with his wife. ''Do you know where it is, Edith? Go fetch it. Miss Mary would have liked the Major to have it, I know. She were right fond of him.''

''Have what, Hawker?'' Richard enquired.

''She loaned me a book of poems, sir, belonging to her old lady, and what with one thing and another I never got round to giving it back. I never could bring myself to sell it, even though it would have brought us a shilling or two.''

He laughed suddenly, the first unforced rumble of laughter he had managed in many a long, unhappy month. "Snipped off a lock of her hair once, sir, so I did, when Miss Mary weren't looking. Mad as fire she were, but I wouldn't give it back. Placed it in the book for safe keeping. Pretty reddish hair it were too."

"Red?" Richard echoed. "But I thought her hair was blonde."

"Bless you no, sir! Why on earth did—? Oh, begging your pardon. I were forgetting your condition. You never saw her, did you, sir?"

"No, Hawk, I was denied that pleasure."

He turned his head as Mrs Hawker came back into the room holding a thin, leather-bound volume which she instantly placed in his outstretched hand. He raised the cover to see a very familiar shade of red-brown hair curled in an almost perfect circle. He gazed at the silken russet strands for several long and thoughtful moments before transferring his gaze to the faded writing on the inside front cover. The sentiment was too indistinct to read, but the names Mary and Smith were discernible enough. He studied the faded lettering more closely, turning the cover to the light, and the letters "s.o.n." tacked onto the surname were just legible. The surname was not Smith, but Smithson.

He looked across at his latest employee keenly, but managed to hide quite beautifully the deep-rooted suspicion which had firmly embedded itself in his brain and which was rapidly growing into an ever-increasing astounding conviction. "Mary's relative, Hawker— you always referred to her as 'the old lady'. I had assumed by this that she was Mary's mother. Might I have been incorrect in that assumption?"

"I only ever clapped eyes on her once, sir, but she looked more like Miss Mary's grandmother to me."

Richard, his eyes narrowing to slits, focused on the beautiful russet-coloured strands again. Blonde hair and blue eyes, indeed! he fumed inwardly, remembering clearly Mary's own description of her colouring. And that West Country accent she had perfected so well... After living in Bristol for so many years that had, evidently, been easy to imitate.

Experiencing a strange mixture of exultation, because there wasn't a doubt in his mind of who had taken his wife's innocence, and seething anger because she had kept the wonderful truth to herself for so long, he looked at his ex-sergeant again.

"And Miss Mary herself...? What was she like?" He didn't wait for a response, but, of course, there was absolutely no need to. "Were her eyes greenish-grey, one colour more prominent than the other depending on her mood? And did her mouth curl up slightly at the corners even when she was not actually smiling? And did she move with all the elegant ease of a thoroughbred filly, a floating, graceful motion?"

"Bless you, sir! Anyone would think you'd seen her yourself."

"Oh, but I have," he responded with a smile that would have frozen a desert oasis. "I most definitely have." He rose to his feet, clasping the book tightly in one hand. "I think it only fair to warn you, Hawker, that you are going to experience a rather severe shock when you reach Knightley Hall... But it is as nothing to what my darling wife shall experience when I reach my ancestral home!"

Chapter Fourteen

Elizabeth stared for several thoughtful moments at the small chest the young footman had just placed in front of her, before delving into the top drawer of her husband's desk and drawing out the small key which she had had the forethought to place there in readiness for just this auspicious moment.

"I'm sorry I were so long in returning," Jenkins apologised, watching his young mistress turn the key in the lock and open the lid. "I found the offices without no trouble, but Mr Ainsworthy weren't there and his clerk wouldn't hand over the box without Mr Ainsworthy's say-so. So I thought it best to await his return from Bath."

"You were right to do so," Elizabeth assured him, not in the least annoyed over the delay. "It would have been pointless your returning here. You would have needed to set out for Bristol again almost immediately. Did I give you sufficient funds for the extra nights' lodgings?"

"Yes, my lady," he answered delving into his pocket and drawing out a purse that was now woefully slim, "but I'm afraid there ain't much left."

''No. You keep that,'' Elizabeth ordered when he made to hand over the remaining few coins. ''You did very well, Jenkins, and deserve some recompense. It's the Melcham Fair in two weeks' time. I'm sure you'll be pleased to have a little extra money to spend on fairings.''

After taking out a pile of letters, neatly tied together with a thin strip of black ribbon, Elizabeth closed the lid of the box. ''Carry that up to my room. Aggie will know where to put it. Then take yourself down to the kitchen for some refreshments. You must be tired after the journey, so inform Finch that I have excused you your duties for the remainder of the day.''

Elizabeth waited until the touchingly grateful young footman had left the room before turning her attention to the pile of letters. As she untied the ribbon she couldn't help wondering just why her grandmother had retained the evidence of her wrongdoing. Perhaps she did so as a kind of self-enforced punishment, to bring out and read from time to time and torment herself with the only thing she had ever done in her life of which she had been ashamed.

''My disgrace,'' she had said to Elizabeth, handing over the yellowing bundle just a few days before she had died. ''Keep them or throw them away as you will, my dear, for you shall learn here and now what they contain from my own lips.''

Elizabeth recalled vividly that particular hour she had spent with her grandmother. When Mary Smithson had divulged the contents of the letters, Elizabeth had experienced no disgust or shame over her grandmother's actions, for she could not help wondering whether she would have acted any differently in a similar situation. After all, her grandmother had been prompted by motherly love only, and not out of any considerations for herself.

But Mrs Smithson had not been seeking forgiveness for actions she had been forced to take many years before, and had responded to her granddaughter's sympathetic utterances with, "Nothing anyone could say would ever ease my conscience, Elizabeth. It was all my fault that it happened in the first place. I'm only too well aware of that. When your grandfather died I transferred all my love on to your mother. I spoilt her, Elizabeth. Anything she craved, she was given, except that one thing. In preventing her from making such a foolish mistake, I unwittingly ruined her life. She never forgave me for forcing her into a loveless union with your father, and for that I cannot blame her."

"Does Evadne know the truth?" Elizabeth had asked.

"Your father would never have told her, of that I am certain. Your mother, however, was less considerate of her daughter's feelings. Yes, she told her. Perhaps she had hoped that it would increase the bond between them. From your own lips I have learned that your mother preferred your sister to you... But, then, my daughter never was very wise."

"And neither is Evadne, because her reprehensible behaviour has now forced my hand," Elizabeth murmured, returning to the present.

She turned her attention to the bundle of letters, and for the next hour meticulously studied the contents of each one in turn before tying them neatly together with the black ribbon once again and placing them in the top drawer of her husband's desk. She experienced no qualms over Richard's knowing the truth. He was a gentleman of honour, and she trusted him implicitly. He would never betray her family's secrets to any other living soul, unless she bid him do so.

It took some little time before Elizabeth could put the sad written confirmation of what her grandmother had told her to the back of her mind, but eventually she was able to channel her thoughts in a new direction. It was while she was engaged in the agreeable task of responding to a letter recently received from her dear friend Lady Dartwood that Aggie unexpectedly entered the library.

"Have you put that small chest away for safekeeping?" she asked, casting a brief glance at the person who would always be much more than just a trusted servant.

"Yes, Miss Elizabeth," she responded in the familiar way she always addressed her mistress when they were alone together. "But I really came to see you on a different matter. Miss Juliet is still troubled with that niggling cough. I'm not really worried, as I mentioned this morning, but the linctus I've been giving her is having no effect, and I was wondering whether you'd ask Tom to take a look at her?"

Elizabeth glanced at the mantel-clock. It was only a few minutes after three: time enough to ride over to Melcham to visit Tom and return to the Hall before Richard arrived home, surely?

"Lay out my habit, Aggie. I'll ride over myself. I could do with a bit of fresh air after being cooped up indoors all day."

Agatha turned, about to do as bidden, when the door opened and Finch came into the room. Before the butler had time to inform his mistress that Lady Chiltham had called, the lady herself, without waiting to be granted admittance, swept into the library, just as though she had been mistress of the house. Elizabeth, not in the least incensed by the imperious action, silently awarded her sister ten out of ten for sheer brass-faced impertinence; but Agatha betrayed her intense disapproval by a very unladylike snort.

"Something troubling you?" Evadne snapped out, more than matching the maid's far-from-kindly regard with her own look of avid dislike. She had never cared for the woman and was very well aware that the enmity was entirely mutual.

"I'll lay out your habit, *my lady*," Agatha said, and the deliberate emphasis on the polite form of address was not wasted on Evadne.

"Both my sister and I have earned the right to that particular title," she reminded the maid with honeyed sweetness.

"But there's only one lady in this room from where I'm standing," Agatha retorted, earning herself a dagger-look as she swept from the room, the wickedly grinning butler in her wake.

"That woman is excessively impertinent! I don't know why you put up with her, Elizabeth, really I don't."

"No, I don't suppose you do, and as I'm tolerably certain you would be completely uninterested in listening to the very long, long list of Aggie's many fine qualities, I suggest we don't waste each other's time, and that you come straight to the point of your visit."

My, my! Her dear little sister had changed over the years. Quite the self-assured lady of quality now! Evadne mused while thinking how infinitely satisfying it was going to be bringing about her downfall.

"I cannot stay. I'm in something of a hurry," she announced, completely ignoring her sister's polite request to take a seat. She moved nonchalantly to the side of the desk and, totally unobserved by her sister who, at that precise moment, happened to be delving into the drawer for a knife to sharpen her pen, dropped a folded sheet of paper into the wastepaper-basket. "I'm here merely to take my leave of you. I'm returning to Devon in the morning."

And what have I done to deserve such a courtesy? Elizabeth wondered, more than just a little surprised, but said in a tone that gave nothing away, "In that case, Evadne, you may expect a visit from me this evening. I have something rather important I wish to discuss with you."

Hiding a self-satisfied smirk, Evadne moved over to the door, but suddenly turned back to say, "Oh, by the by, Elizabeth. Whilst I was travelling back from Lady Pentecost's earlier, I came upon an accident just this side of... Oh, dear, what is the name of that wretched little hamlet a matter of only half a mile from dear Lady Pentecost's home?" She raised her shoulder in a negligent shrug. "Not that it matters. But the person who was being carried to that tumble-down old tavern there looked very like that young doctor friend of yours whose name for the moment escapes me. I can only assume he took a tumble from his horse. I certainly noticed someone leading a saddled mount towards that inn."

Elizabeth was suddenly alert. "Tom? Are you certain?"

"Not one hundred per cent, no. I should have stopped the carriage to offer assistance, I suppose, but I have had such a lot of errands to run today," she responded with such a complete lack of concern that Elizabeth for the first time in her life felt the strong compulsion to box her sister's ears soundly.

"Anyway, I mustn't stay. I'll see you later," and

with that she was gone, leaving Elizabeth with a positive vortex of emotions spiralling through her, not least of which was deep concern over the injured man who might possibly turn out to be Tom.

Leaving the half-finished letter on the top of the desk, she went straight up to her room to find Aggie there, placing some freshly laundered dresses in the wardrobe.

"Has that viper slithered away yet?"

Elizabeth frowned dourly at this rudely worded enquiry, but could not find it within herself to reproach her maid. Aggie had always had scant regard for Evadne, and she wasn't likely to change her very low opinion of her now. So she merely said, "Yes, she's gone, but not before she had imparted some rather disturbing news."

Agatha paused in her task, and looked searchingly at her young mistress's worried face. "What bad news, my lamb?"

"She came upon an accident on the outskirts of Eastlynch. She seems to think the injured man might well have been Tom. Needless to say, she didn't stop to offer assistance. If it was Tom, he has no doubt been taken back to his house by now, but I fully intend to make certain."

Knowing how concerned her young mistress must be, no matter how hard she tried not to show it, Agatha didn't waste a moment in helping Elizabeth to change into her habit, and then watched from the bedchamber window as her young mistress, a few minutes later, rode up the driveway out of sight.

She was not the only person to witness the departure. In an area of the park densely covered by trees, Evadne had ordered her coachman to pull off the driveway. From the vantage point she was able to watch, unobserved, Elizabeth ride out of the estate and take the road to Melcham.

"So far so good, Quimper," she remarked with feline satisfaction.

"But will she go to that inn, mistress?"

"Oh, yes, she'll go sure enough. I've learned from several sources just how very fond she is of young Dr Carrington. Her disposition is such that she could never rest easy until she had discovered what had befallen him. And if you have performed your tasks thoroughly, by six this evening, or thereabouts, the trap will be beautifully sprung."

"But supposing Sir Richard goes searching for his wife?"

"I learned from Mrs Westbridge that he's due to arrive home this evening. I doubt very much that he'll be in time to discover his wife's whereabouts before Lady Pentecost has looked her fill on the oh, so charming scene. Believe me, I've got that middle-aged tabby's measure. I chose her with particular care. She would never miss the chance of spreading such a monumental piece of scandal."

Quimper was not so certain of success. The plan was far from foolproof—too much left to chance for his liking. "What if Sir Richard arrives home earlier than expected and discovers that forged letter you wrote? Do you think he's likely to believe such a thing about his wife?"

"That, I'll admit, remains in the balance," she responded after several moments' intense thought. "If Elizabeth repeated what I had told her to anyone, then it would have been to that obnoxious maid of hers. Agatha Stigwell is devoted to Elizabeth, and Sir Richard must surely know this. Therefore, he might suppose that Agatha wouldn't hesitate to lie in order to protect her mistress.''

Evadne paused to remove a speck of fluff from her primrose-coloured carriage dress. ''Although he has professed deep love for Elizabeth, after further consideration, I still remain not wholly convinced of the depth of his affection. After all, Quimper, what man in love with his wife indulges in a sordid affair within a few short weeks of his marriage taking place? That apart, a person of Sir Richard's stamp could never withstand being branded a cuckold. And we can rely on dear Lady Pentecost to start labelling him just that. Oh, no, Quimper. No matter whether he personally believes his wife guilty of adultery or not, in the eyes of the world he will be made a laughing stock. Knightley's a proud man. The humiliation would be too much for him to bear. Believe me, the marriage will be over before the end of this day.''

Elizabeth arrived at Tom's house just as the church clock in the centre of the small market town chimed four. After looping the reins over the black painted railings, she hurried up the path, but, worried though she was, she still took the trouble to exchange a greeting with the boy Tom had engaged to do odd jobs about the place, as he busily worked in the front garden.

Mrs Middleton was prompt in answering the door, but not so speedy when it came to disclosing where her master had gone. ''To tell you the truth, my lady, I can't rightly remember whether he said exactly where he was bound or no. But he has been gone a fair time, so I shouldn't imagine he will be too much longer, if you would care to wait inside?''

"What time did he go out?" she asked, ignoring the request.

"Oh, it would have been about two hours ago."

Elizabeth was trying not to be pessimistic, but she couldn't help silently acknowledging that this would tie in with what Evadne had told her.

"Dr Carrington answered the door himself, as I was busy at the time in the kitchen when the caller arrived. Before he left the house he did say that he'd learned of a lady taken rather poorly, and that he would be out for some little time. So, I can only assume that whoever he was going to see doesn't live nearby."

"Was the name Eastlynch mentioned, do you recall?"

Elizabeth could see by the widening of the housekeeper's dark eyes that the name had struck a chord of memory even before she said, "Yes. Now you put me in mind of it, I do believe that was the name of the place where he was bound."

With a hurried farewell, Elizabeth sped down the path, leaving Mrs Middleton to watch the abrupt departure with surprised interest, before closing the door again and returning to her tasks in the kitchen.

Although the tiny village of Eastlynch was only a matter of three miles from Melcham, it was only accessible by a series of narrow and twisting high-hedged lanes. Once the market town was left behind, Elizabeth, riding her mare at a brisk trot, didn't catch sight of a single soul to enquire if a gentleman had met with an accident earlier that afternoon. Although Evadne had been rather sparing with details, her sister had surmised that the unfortunate man had taken a fall from his horse. Accidents happened to the best of riders. Tom was certainly not in Richard's class when it came to equestrian skills, but he was still a very competent horseman, and would certainly not risk proceeding at a gallop along winding lanes like these, where any obstacle blocking the road might be concealed round the next bend.

By the time she had arrived at the village inn, which was ill kept and uninviting, Elizabeth was still experiencing grave concern, and a deal of puzzlement too. Surely if the injured man had been Tom, someone would have sent word to his home long before now? She knew for a fact that Tom always carried an identity card on his person, so it would have been a simple matter to discover who he was.

Leaving her mare tied to a rough wooden stake, Elizabeth approached the front entrance. The cracked and decaying outside walls gave her a shrewd idea of what the interior would be like, and she wasn't in the least surprised to discover the deserted tap had been left in disorder, with several used tankards dotted about on the unpolished, ale-stained tables, and a liberal amount of dirt smeared over the unswept flagstone floor.

"What can I be doing for you?"

Startled, Elizabeth swung round to see a sparse, middle-aged woman step out from a shadowy corner of the tap. As there was no doorway in that area of the room, she could only surmise that the woman had been standing there all the time, her black, birdlike eyes watching her visitor's every move.

"I understand that a gentleman met with an accident not far from here earlier today." Suppressing the strong desire to back away as the woman slowly approached and the stench of an unwashed body hit her like a kick from a horse, Elizabeth took in every detail of the woman's unkempt appearance, from the filthy cap doing little to confine the matted, greying hair to the rough workman's boots on her feet. "I was informed he was carried to this inn. Is he still here now?"

"That ee be," the woman responded, peering at Elizabeth's features closely, before giving a near-toothless half-smile. "I put 'im in my own bedchamber, so I did, and he still be there now, sleeping like a babe."

"May I see him? It's just possible that I might be acquainted with the gentleman, and can arrange for his removal from this house so that you won't be inconvenienced further."

"Cause you can, m'deary. Just you come wi' me."

Keeping a discreet distance, Elizabeth followed the woman up a narrow, creaking staircase and into a low ceilinged bedchamber. Tom, lying in the large bed, had had his clothes removed and was sleeping soundly, a little too soundly for Elizabeth's peace of mind.

"What are the extent of his injuries?"

"He received a bit of a blow to 'is 'ead, as yer might say."

"And he hasn't regained consciousness at all?" Elizabeth frowned suspiciously as she studied the rhythmic rise and fall of Tom's bared chest. "Have you administered a potion of any kind?"

"That I did, m'deary. Just to keep 'im quiet, like…until you arrived."

Elizabeth swung round to find the grinning woman flanked by two burly men, one of whom held a small glass in one grimy hand. The resemblance was too marked for them not to be related. Mother and sons, she guessed, trying to control the rising panic at the men's lascivious expressions and the evil smile of triumph twisting the woman's thin-lipped mouth.

"And you're going to take a drop of the same," she added, taking the glass out of her younger offspring's massive hand.

Instinctively, Elizabeth backed away, but she realised there was no possible hope of escape even before the filthy old crone advised, "Now, deary, you be sensible and do as I say, and I'll see no 'arm comes to you, but if you tries anything foolish I'll be forced to let me boys at yer. And they'd like dealing with a pretty wench like you."

"Ain't you going to let us undress 'er fust?" the elder son asked hopefully and earned himself a resounding box round the ear from his mother. Although she was a dwarf by comparison, it was quite obvious she was more than equal to the task of keeping her progeny in order if she wished.

"No, I ain't, unless..." she looked back at Elizabeth in a meaningful way "...the little lady doesn't do as she's told."

What choice had she? It was in her own best interests to offer no resistance at the present time. The mere thought of those two filthy oafs laying hands on her brought a sudden surge of nausea to rise in her throat. "I shan't give you any trouble."

"There's a sensible girl!" The woman shooed her sons from the room, just as though they were two erring infants and, ordering them to see to the stabling of the lady's mount, closed the door firmly behind them before turning back to Elizabeth once more. "Take your clothes off, and get into bed!" she ordered. "And hurry up about it, I ain't got all day."

Elizabeth began to peel off her habit and placed it with Tom's apparel on the chair. When she had removed the last of her garments, she didn't delay in slipping between the far-from-clean sheets beside her friend. He didn't stir; he remained completely oblivious to what was happening. He was in no state to help himself, let alone aid her, and yet she found the warmth of his strong body strangely comforting.

"Now you drink this down," the woman ordered in a sickeningly coaxing way, handing over the glass. "I ain't giving you nearly as much as I gave 'im. Don't want you completely knocked out, just a trifle woozy, as yer might say." She tut-tutted as she glanced at Tom. "Gave 'im too strong a dose, I reckon, but then I ain't never done anything like this afore. So 'ow was I to know?"

Elizabeth, her mind working rapidly, placed the vessel to her mouth and allowed the milky-coloured liquid to seep between her slightly parted lips. Then, without being told, she laid her head on the pillow and after a few moments, during which the old woman continued to watch her closely, she lowered her eyelids. The bedchamber door opened and then closed again before she heard the grating sound of the key being turned in the lock, and the thud of retreating footsteps.

Sitting up abruptly, she quickly spat the liquid she had been holding in her mouth on to the floor, and then tiptoed across to the washstand, where she made good use of what remained of the contents of the pewter jug. After swilling her mouth out several times with the cold water, and spitting it out on to the floor, she was confident that she would suffer no ill effects, even if a drop of the nostrum had managed to find its way down her throat. This conviction was thankfully substantiated when she experienced no dizziness whatsoever as she tiptoed over to the chair.

How very fortunate it was that that dreadful woman hadn't considered it necessary to take their clothes away with her when she had left, Elizabeth mused, wasting no time in dressing again, and trying as she did so not to step about too much in case her movements could be detected below.

What on earth was going on? She stared down at Tom's pale face in some concern as she fastened the last tie on her skirt. Why, if Richard had walked in and had caught the pair of them naked in bed, heaven only knew what he would have thought... No, she amended silently. It was quite obvious what he would have thought—that she and Tom were having an affair...

Of course, that was it! She almost gasped as realisation hit her with lightning clarity. That was why this little charade had been planned! Tom had been merely the bait, lured here and no doubt attacked by those two ruffians in a wicked attempt to draw her to this out-of-the-way inn. And wasn't it obvious who was behind the despicable plot to ruin her reputation and destroy her marriage? Evadne!

The whole contemptible plot smacked of her sister's particular kind of malice. It wouldn't matter a whit to Evadne if Tom had to be hurt during the execution of the plan so long as she achieved her aim. Well, this time, Elizabeth decided, experiencing for the first time in her life a desire for revenge, Evadne had gone too far and would pay dearly for her evil-minded machinations. But before she could sample the sweet taste of justifiable retribution, she would need to get herself and Tom—for she had no intention of leaving him to the tender mercies of that trio below—well away from this place. Although it had to be faced that Tom, poor wretch, looked as if he would be of precious little assistance for some considerable time.

She began to examine him more closely and quickly detected a large lump on the back of his head, no doubt inflicted before the drug had been forced down his throat. She pulled back the sheet and saw to her horror that his hands and feet were bound so tightly that the cord was biting into his flesh. That, at least, she could remedy immediately, she thought, reaching for his bag which their obliging captors had evidently overlooked and had conveniently left beside the chair.

As she had suspected, the bag contained his small box of surgical instruments. Extracting the razor-sharp knife, she quickly had his hands and feet freed, but there was little else she could do for him until the effects of the drug had begun to wear off. Before that happened, though, she felt certain that someone would return to the room to ensure that they were both sleeping soundly in readiness for...what? Richard's arrival? She shook her head. No, that seemed most unlikely. Although he was due back at Knightley Hall today, there was always the possibility that he might be delayed. Besides which, Richard was no fool, and to alert him to his wife's presence in this inn would very likely have the opposite effect and merely make him suspicious, but not of his wife's possible infidelity. No, it was someone else who was supposed to catch Tom and herself *in flagrante delicto*, as one might say...but who? she wondered, going across to inspect the window.

This offered no means of escape. Not only had it been securely nailed shut, but from what she could see, even if she did manage to prise it open, there was nothing for her to climb down, not even a conveniently placed tree, and she certainly wouldn't trust those worn, threadbare sheets on the bed to bear her weight if she were to make the attempt and climb out. She turned and tiptoed across to the door but, as she had suspected, it had been securely locked.

Things were looking decidedly bleak for the pair of them, but she refused to give in without a fight, and went about the room picking up various objects which might prove useful weapons to add to the knife she had slipped into the pocket of her skirt. Whether she could bring herself to wield it with violent intent remained to be seen, and she was offered plenty of time to ponder over this rather morally disturbing issue before she became aware of a commotion below: low growls, a series of thuds and what sounded suspiciously like a table being overturned. Dear God! Surely those oafish sons weren't engaged in a drunken brawl?

Moments later she heard the sound of hurried footsteps mounting the stairs. Just one person, she felt certain. Quickly taking up a position behind the door, the heavy pewter water jug raised high above her head in readiness to strike the unsuspecting visitor, she waited, heart pounding beneath her ribcage, as the key turned in the lock and the door swung open.

Chapter Fifteen

Richard's elegant long-striding gait had not infrequently been admired by both men and women alike, but there seemed an extra spring in his step as he walked from the stables to the front entrance of Knightley Hall. After being informed that his wife had left the house a short while earlier, he took himself off to his library where he poured out a good measure of burgundy. Raising the glass to his lips, he sipped the rich red liquid and took a moment or two to savour its excellent taste, just as he fully intended to savour those delicious moments when he told that wickedly deceiving and adorable wife of his that he had discovered her outrageous deception during her time in Brussels the year before.

Taking his glass of wine across the room with him, he drew the thin, leather-bound volume, given to him by Sergeant Hawker, from his pocket and placed it for safekeeping in the top drawer of his oak desk. He noticed the pile of letters in there at once, but it was the half-finished missive on top of his desk which captured his attention, and he shook his head in disbelief.

Why on earth hadn't he realised long since? The clues had all been there right from the start, loads of them, but he had been too foolishly blind to recognise them for what they were and solve them. Elizabeth's reticence to discuss her time in Brussels had been the first, and the way she had neatly avoided discussing the subject for very long when he had happened to raise it. That distinctive smell of lavender-and-rose water he had detected in her hair on numerous occasions had been a complete giveaway and yet, fool that he was, he still hadn't realised. And then there was this, he mused, holding up the letter written in Elizabeth's beautiful flowing hand. He had seen numerous samples of his wife's handwriting during these past weeks, and yet not once had it dawned on him that it was the same hand that had penned that letter of farewell to him in Brussels.

Again he shook his head, marvelling at his own stupidity. His only excuse, he supposed, was that Mary had intruded in his thoughts only rarely during these past weeks, his mind having been totally focused on the lady he had married. He gave a sudden shout of laughter. Even now that he had been given irrefutable proof, he still looked upon Elizabeth and Mary as two separate people.

Having had nearly twenty-four hours to get over the initial shock, he found that he could no longer be angry with her for the diabolical way she had deceived him. He didn't doubt for a moment that she had had a very good reason for trying to keep her identity secret when she was in Brussels, although her motive for having done so still eluded him. She could, of course, have been trying to safeguard her reputation. After all, it was hardly deemed acceptable practice for a gently bred, unmarried young woman to take on the role of nurse to six British soldiers. He couldn't imagine Elizabeth worrying herself too much over any possible gossip arising from her actions, though. No, there had to have been some other reason, but just what continued to elude him, and it was fruitless, he knew, trying to speculate. He would no doubt get to the bottom of the enigma when she returned.

And where the deuce had she gone? he wondered, glancing at the mantel-clock whose hands told him it was half past four. The little wretch had promised faithfully to be here to greet him when he arrived home, and yet she had gone gallivanting off somewhere, forcing him to wait a while longer before extracting a suitable penance.

After taking a further fortifying mouthful of wine, he placed his glass down, and his eyes fell upon the neatly folded sheet of paper in the basket beside his desk. Was that supposed to be there? It wasn't, after all, screwed up. Had the letter been accidentally knocked off the edge of the desk? he wondered, bending to retrieve it.

Had anyone else been standing in the room he would have been unable to tell what was going through Richard's mind as he ran his eyes over the few boldly written lines, for his expression gave nothing away. He merely placed the missive down on his desk before going across to the door.

"Finch," he called, interrupting the conversation the ageing butler was having with his replacement in the hall, "do you happen to know precisely where your mistress has gone and what time she left the house?"

"Lady Knightley went out about an hour ago, sir,

but where she was bound I couldn't say. Perhaps Miss Agatha might know. Would you like me to fetch her?''

''Yes. Request her to come to the library.''

She entered the room a few minutes later, her thin-lipped mouth curled into a rare smile at her master's return. ''You wished to see me, sir?''

''Yes, Aggie. Come in and close the door.'' He waited until she had approached the desk before asking if she knew where her mistress had gone.

''To Melcham, sir, to see Dr Carrington. She was a little concerned about him.''

Richard handed her the note and watched her closely as she read,

My darling Elizabeth, I must see you today. Richard is not likely to be home until the evening, which will give us several precious hours alone together. Meet me at the usual rendezvous. I beg of you, don't fail me, my love. Tom.

''Would you say that that was Dr Carrington's handwriting?'' he asked when she raised puzzled eyes to his.

''It certainly looks like it, sir, yes. But—but Tom would never write Miss Elizabeth a letter like this. Why, it's—it's like a love letter!''

''Isn't it just!'' he quipped and Agatha looked up at him, aghast.

''Sir! You don't imagine for a moment that there's anything improper going on between—''

''No, Aggie, I don't,'' he interrupted reassuringly. ''But that, I should imagine, is what I was supposed to think.'' He moved across to the window and stared out at the sunlit park. ''Even if I did suspect that my wife's feelings for Tom went somewhat deeper than mere sisterly affection, which I don't, I certainly credit her with more sense than to leave damning evidence of an affair between them lying about for me to find. No, Aggie, I doubt your mistress has even read this letter. Someone planted it here.''

"Evadne!" the loyal maid spat, hard-eyed and disdainful. "Up to her old tricks again, I don't doubt. She was always trying to get my lamb into trouble when they were younger. She was here, sir. Here, in this very room, earlier this afternoon!"

"Was she now?" His voice betrayed nothing more than mild enquiry, but the look which sprang into his eyes was anything but gentle.

"Yes, sir, and it was shortly after her visit that Miss Elizabeth went out. She suspected that Master Tom had been involved in some kind of accident."

Richard turned to look at the very concerned maid once again. "I want you to tell me exactly what your mistress said to you, Aggie, before she left this house."

Once he had learned all, Richard was galvanised into action, issuing orders to his servants which were obeyed with lightning speed. Within a relatively short space of time, he, Medway and the estate worker who had temporarily taken on the duties as coachman were riding at the gallop towards Melcham.

Mrs Middleton betrayed a moment's surprise at seeing Sir Richard on the doorstep at this hour of the day, but didn't waste any time in relating the puzzling events of the afternoon, for she too, now, was rather concerned that Dr Carrington hadn't returned.

"And you, yourself, didn't see the person who came to the house requesting his assistance for the lady at Eastlynch."

"No, sir, I didn't."

"But I saw 'im," a voice from behind announced, and Richard turned to see Tom's odd-job boy, who had been tidying the front garden for most of the day, staring up at him.

"What was he like? Can you describe him?" Richard asked, and wondered why it was that every boy he happened to speak to these days had the rather alarming habit of raising a hand to scratch his head.

"He were small and thin and was wearing a black coat. Looked like a servant to me. Don't live in Melcham, sir. I never seen 'im round 'ere afore. Ee gets out of a carriage stopped further down the street. Ee spoke to Dr Carrington. Didn't 'ear what ee said, though, 'cause they goes inside."

"Did you see anyone else in the carriage?"

"No, sir. It were too far away. But it were a fine carriage, pulled by a right 'andsome team of 'orses, like the sort o' turnout you'd ride in, m'lord."

Worried though he was, Richard couldn't help smiling at this rather artless remark and tossed the boy a coin before remounting his horse. "I want you to return to the Hall to collect the carriage," he said, addressing his estate worker. "Bring Lady Knightley's maid and one of the footmen—Jenkins will do—to the inn at Eastlynch."

"Lord bless you, sir! You don't think anything's 'appened to the mistress, do you?" he asked, his tanned forehead furrowed by deep lines of concern. Like all the other servants, he had swiftly grown very fond of his young mistress.

"I sincerely hope not, Ben, but it's as well to make provisions for every eventuality. Be as quick as you can," and with that Richard turned his mount in the direction of Eastlynch, leaving an equally troubled Medway to follow in his wake.

Sir Richard uttered not a word during the time it took them to reach the small village, but the taut set of his mouth told its own tale. No matter how strange his master's behaviour had been in London during the spring, there was nothing puzzling in his conduct now: he was a man deeply worried, and it showed in every contour of his face.

Leaving their mounts tethered at the rear of the inn, Richard had a quick look inside the rundown old stable, and it told him much of what he needed to know. He delved into the left-hand pocket of his jacket and drew out a handsome silver-handled duelling pistol, one of a pair which he had had the forethought to collect from his gun room before leaving the house, and promptly handed it over to his new butler.

"I sincerely trust, Medway, that you are not completely ignorant in the use of firearms?"

"My experience isn't great, sir," he admitted, "but I believe nine times out of ten I could manage to hit what I was aiming at, providing my target wasn't moving too quickly."

"I hope you're not called upon to substantiate that statement, Medway, but it's as well to be prepared, for it's my belief that my wife is somewhere within that building, and I don't suppose for a moment that she is there of her own free will."

Medway grimaced as he entered the foul-smelling interior of the inn, but his master's face betrayed no emotion whatsoever as he made good use of a used tankard by hammering it down on the counter while setting up a shout for attention. It took some little time, but eventually the slatternly owner of the tavern, accompanied by an equally unkempt individual of the opposite sex, came in answer to the summons. A moment's surprise flickered in the woman's eyes as she surveyed the amazing sight of a top-of-the-trees Corinthian standing in her inn, but her hope that money would be coming her way was quickly dashed when he said,

"My wife is here. Kindly take me to her at once!"

It was abundantly obvious by the sudden panic that replaced the avaricious gleam in her eyes that Sir Richard was the last person she had been expecting to see.

"Don't waste my time, woman!" he ordered, cutting across her pathetic attempt to deny all knowledge of his wife's existence. "Either you take me to her at once, or I send my man, here, for the constable and magistrate, and have these premises searched from cellar to attic."

It was no idle threat. Richard, watching her closely, saw her eyes betraying the conflicting thoughts passing through her mercenary little brain before they suddenly focused on a spot somewhere behind him, and he swung round to see the third member of the obnoxious family moving stealthily towards him.

Both sons dived at him simultaneously, but Richard was more than equal to the combined attack. Within seconds he had the younger son writhing on his knees in agony, having received a well-aimed kick in the region of his groin, and he felled the elder brother with just one punishing blow to the jaw, the force of which sent him crashing against a table before crumpling, momentarily stunned, to the floor.

He then took the precaution of drawing the second pistol from his jacket pocket in case either man should foolishly attempt a further assault upon him. Medway, too, had drawn his weapon and had it levelled at the woman behind the counter, just in case she should foolishly make some sudden move.

"Well, madam, which is it to be—the magistrate, or an answer to my question?"

She cast a far-from-sympathetic glance at her incapacitated offspring, which boded ill for them later. "The lady be upstairs," she capitulated, drawing the key from the pocket of her grimy apron and tossing it to him. "First door along the passageway."

After handing his pistol to Medway, and urging him not to hesitate in using them both if necessary, Richard wasted no time in reaching the floor above. He turned the key in the lock and the first thing he saw after the door had swung open was Tom lying perfectly still in the bed. He took a step into the room, caught a sudden movement out of the corner of his eye and instinctively raised his right arm to ward off the blow aimed at his head. His elbow made accidental contact with a high cheekbone, sending his would-be assailant stumbling backwards on to the floor.

"God in heaven, Elizabeth! Are you all right?" He was kneeling down beside her in an instant, and could see clearly the livid red mark he had unintentionally inflicted just below her left eye.

"I think so," she answered weakly, still slightly stunned, but too deliriously happy to see him to worry too much over her hurts. "I never expected to see you," she admitted, allowing him to raise her gently to her feet. "I thought it was one of those brutish sons coming back into the room, and I had every intention of rendering him senseless."

The look he cast her betrayed his unholy amusement, but a deal of admiration, too.

"Oh, Richard; they were planning to ruin me. They've drugged poor Tom, but I managed to fool that odious woman and spat out what she had forced me to take the instant she had left the room."

"What charming habits you have acquired, my darling," he remarked lightly, going over to the bed to take a closer look at his friend.

"It's as well I did have my wits about me," she announced, slightly nettled by his frivolous attitude. "What would you have thought if you'd walked in here to discover Tom and myself stark naked in bed together, because that is what they had planned. At least," she amended, "I suspect someone was supposed to catch us that way."

"No doubt you're right," he agreed. "There's little we can do for our doctor friend, though, until the carriage arrives, so I suggest we return downstairs and see what we can discover from your oh, so charming captors. Our new butler is guarding them," he added, leading the way out of the room, "but I don't think it would be advisable to leave Medway alone with them for very much longer."

Elizabeth derived a deal of wicked satisfaction when she entered the tap and saw the two men nursing their hurts, and their mother paying not the least interest in either of them as she sat broodingly on one of the stools, no doubt cursing fickle fate for guiding Sir Richard Knightley to her hostelry. Elizabeth then transferred her gaze to the man who had successfully guarded the trio.

"How very brave it was of you, Medway, to come to my rescue! I shall be forever in your debt," she told him with such a glowing smile that he became her devoted slave from that moment in time.

After relieving his new butler of one of the pistols, Richard perched himself on the edge of a table and began to swing one booted leg to and fro as he surveyed the highly disgruntled woman. "It would be in your own best interests, madam," he advised her, "to explain precisely what has been going on this day. And you can begin by telling me the name of the woman who, no doubt, paid you handsomely to hold my wife and Dr Carrington hostage here."

"It weren't that much," she mumbled, "and it weren't a woman, neiver."

"Would the person who approached you offering financial rewards for the perpetration of this outrage be small and sparse and dressed in a coat of black cloth?" he asked, repeating the odd-job boy's description.

"Yes, that ud be 'im. Shifty-eyed little rodent! Comes in 'ere a few days back asking if we'd be interested in earning a few guineas." She cast a sorrowful look up at him in an attempt to gain his sympathy. "Well, I puts it to you, m'lord—what poor, 'ardworking woman wouldn't be willing to earn a bit extra?"

Richard's lip curled at this. "By the condition of this place, I'm given every reason to suppose that you haven't done a hard day's work in your life, but we'll let that pass for the moment. Did you gain the impression that this man was negotiating on behalf of someone else?" She looked totally bewildered at this, just as though he were speaking in some foreign language. "I'll rephrase the question," he continued with praiseworthy forbearance. "Did you think this man worked for someone who was willing to pay for your services?''

She nodded. ''When I told 'im I'd want more, he said as 'ow the person ee worked for wouldn't pay n' more. It were a case of take it or leave it, as yer might say…so I took it.''

''I think we both know who was behind this fiasco, Richard, don't we?'' Elizabeth announced, coming to stand beside him. ''The description of the go-between sounds suspiciously like a certain butler we saw in Devonshire. But what I should like to know,'' she went on, fixing her gaze on the landlady, ''is how long you intended keeping Dr Carrington and myself locked in that room?''

''Only until a certain person arrived. And I don't know who, neiver, so it ain't no good you asking me,'' she added when Elizabeth opened her mouth to do just that. ''All I knows is that someone was supposed to come 'ere, and I was to take 'em upstairs. And I was supposed to tell 'em that it weren't the first time you and the gentleman 'ad made use of my bedchamber.''

As if on cue the sound of a carriage could be heard pulling up at the door. After handing Medway the second pistol again, Richard wasted no time in going outside to investigate, and successfully thwarted the sole occupant of the elegant, but rather antiquated, vehicle from alighting, simply by positioning himself in front of the carriage doorway.

''Why, Lady Pentecost! What in the world brings you to this far-from-comfortable establishment?'' Elizabeth distinctly heard him say, and raised her eyes ceilingwards. Of course, Lady Pentecost! She might have known!

"I could ask you the same question, Sir Richard," the formidable matron responded, but he had been expecting that.

"We met with a slight accident and were forced to seek sanctuary here while waiting for the carriage to be repaired. I hope it won't take too much longer. I shouldn't like it to become common knowledge that I patronised such a place as this," he remarked with a look of distaste as he cast a glance over his shoulder at the dilapidated building.

He could not have said anything more likely to appeal to a person of Lady Pentecost's snobbish disposition. "Quite! I trust no one was hurt?"

"Lady Knightley suffered a slight facial bruise, but apart from that we came through unscathed."

Frowning slightly, Lady Pentecost tried to peer past him into the inn's rather gloomy interior. "Is there no one else here?"

"Only my new butler, ma'am. Why? What makes you ask? Were you expecting to see someone here? If so, I cannot say that I applaud your choice of a meeting place."

She hesitated for a moment before drawing out a letter from her reticule and handing it over to him. He cast his eyes over the brief note and looked back at her with raised brows.

"What on earth could you find intriguing in this place, I wonder? I can only assume that someone has been playing a practical joke on you, ma'am, for I cannot imagine that our slight misfortune with the carriage is of very much interest to you. When did you receive the letter?"

"My butler found it pushed under the door an hour ago, though just how long it had been there is anyone's guess. And I was forced to put back dinner an hour in order to be here,'' she finished, sounding decidedly nettled over the inconvenience of having to wait for her meal.

He tut-tutted sympathetically. ''It never ceases to amaze me what some people find amusing. Dragging you here for no purpose is unpardonable. Ha! My carriage at last!'' he announced, not without a certain amount of relief. The last thing he wanted was for her to insist on alighting and see the landlady and her progeny being held at gunpoint.

''Are you sure I cannot be of assistance, Sir Richard?''

''Thank you, ma'am, but we'll do very nicely now that our transport has arrived. I think what we all need is to get home to enjoy a good dinner,'' and with that he took up the steps and closed the carriage door, thereby giving her no reason to delay her departure further.

He remained outside until his own carriage had drawn up; after issuing instructions to Agatha and the footman to go upstairs and tend to Tom so that he could be carried out to the carriage, he rejoined his wife in the taproom, handing her the letter which had been sent to Lady Pentecost and which he had quite artfully retained.

''Recognise the handwriting?'' he asked after she had cast her eyes over the unsigned brief note which merely said, *If you wish to learn something of immense interest then go to the inn at Eastlynch at six o'clock this evening.* She shook her head, and he delved into his pocket. ''What about this one?''

''Why, this is Tom's handwriting. At least,'' she amended, studying the bold scrawl more closely, "very like. But he never sent this to me. I've never seen it before. Where did you find it?''

"In the wastepaper basket in the library."

"Evadne must have dropped it in there!'' Elizabeth responded, unable to keep her annoyance from creeping into her voice. Her eyes narrowed. "When Evadne was a child she used to practise forging other people's handwriting—she was very good at it, too. I don't for a moment doubt that this is her work. She must have got her hands on a sample of Tom's handwriting from somewhere. And, I suppose, she must have learnt during her stay here how very fond of Tom I am, and viewed him as the ideal candidate to carry out her despicable scheme to try to ruin me in the eyes of the world. She might have succeeded, too, if Lady Pentecost had discovered us together in that bedchamber.''

"Even if that had occurred, you don't suppose for a moment that I would have believed you guilty of adultery, do you? If I hadn't seen for myself that poor Tom is incapable of opening his eyes, let alone making a cuckold of me, I still wouldn't have suspected you two of being lovers,'' he assured her gently. "Evadne is incapable of comprehending that a man and a woman can love each other without any physical desires. She also very much underestimated my own depth of feeling. I may be a proud man, Elizabeth, but my love for you far outweighs my pride. I should have quashed any rumours very swiftly, believe me.''

She didn't doubt him for a moment, and smiled lovingly up at him before transferring her gaze to her erstwhile captors. "My sister has a great deal to answer for, Richard. But what do you intend to do about these three?''

''You have only to say the word and I shall summon the magistrate.''

''No, I don't want that,'' she answered, experiencing no desire whatsoever to see any one of them end up in prison. ''Their only real crime is wishing to earn some easy money. I truly don't believe they intended any lasting physical harm to either Tom or me. A few choice words from you and I don't think they'll get involved in anything like this again.''

''Very well. It shall be as you wish. But I must confess that it grieves me to think that that sister of yours will get away, scot-free, with what she tried to do to you.''

''Oh, she won't, Richard,'' Elizabeth assured him, her voice hard-edged and determined. ''You can safely leave Evadne's punishment to me... It is long overdue.''

Chapter Sixteen

Caroline Westbridge checked in the act of pouring her most unwelcome guest a cup of tea as the door opened, and her butler unexpectedly announced the arrival of Sir Richard and Lady Knightley. She didn't notice Evadne blanch slightly, nor did she see the sudden guarded look in her eyes, for it was as much as she could do to keep a firm grasp of the teapot's handle when she saw her friend's dishevelled state as she swept majestically into the room ahead of her husband.

"Heavens above! Elizabeth! Whatever has happened to you, my dear?" she demanded, aghast, when she noticed the purplish hue beneath the left eye. "Have you taken a tumble from your horse?"

"No, Caroline, nothing so dramatic, I assure you. I have merely been held against my will in one of the most disgusting taverns it has ever been my misfortune to enter."

"Whatever do you mean?"

The surprised enquiry was uttered by her sister, and Elizabeth fixed her eyes on Evadne with such a look of revulsion in their grey-green depths that Caroline could hardly believe that it was her young, kind-hearted friend whom she looked upon.

"Do sit down, my dear," she urged her, but Elizabeth declined the invitation. Richard, however, was not feeling quite so unsociable and accepted their very amiable neighbour's suggestion and seated himself beside her on the sofa, a rather odd smile playing about his mouth.

Although Elizabeth had hardly spoken more than a dozen words during the time it took them to ride here, he had the feeling that her taciturn frame of mind was rapidly coming to an end, and that he was about to witness a side to his wife's character he had never glimpsed before. On the surface she appeared perfectly composed; a little dishevelled after what she had been through, it was true, but that was only to be expected. Yet, beneath that calm exterior, he suspected her blood was flowing through her veins in a white-hot craving for revenge. And he wasn't wrong.

Moving towards her sister's chair, Elizabeth stared down at her, the look of disgust not diminishing from her eyes one iota. "You know very well what I mean, Evadne, so do not nauseate me further with any sickening protestations of ignorance or innocence. But for Caroline's benefit I shall explain what has taken place this day."

She turned her head to look at her friend and her expression softened at once. "My darling sister paid me a visit this afternoon and casually informed me that she believed Dr Carrington had been involved in an accident. She knew what my reaction would be, of course, and I must confess that in that one instance her judgement was not at fault. I do love Tom," she freely admitted, "but the love I bear him is purely platonic, like that of a sister. Which is something

Evadne could never comprehend. Richard, however, understands perfectly and wasn't fooled for an instant by that forged letter which you foolishly left for him to find,'' she went on, turning to look at her sister once again.

Evadne rose from the chair with panic-engendered swiftness. ''I don't intend to sit here listening to this farrago of lies a moment longer!'' she announced, but before she had taken more than a step towards the door, Elizabeth was in front of her, her slender, tapering fingers clenched in tight, angry fists.

''Sit down, Evadne, or so help me I shall knock you down,'' she warned in a voice that seemed all the more threatening because of its even timbre. ''Believe me, it would afford me the utmost pleasure to do so.''

Caroline, for one, didn't doubt for a moment the truth of this statement. She cast a fleeting glance in Richard's direction and suspected, by the hopeful gleam in his dark eyes, that he wished his wife would carry out her threat, but Evadne denied him the pleasure of seeing her receive a well-deserved slap in the face by doing precisely what her sister had ordered.

''I shan't bore you with all the details of my ordeal now, Caroline. I shall save that for another time,'' Elizabeth continued, turning her head to glance briefly at the two occupants of the sofa once again. ''Suffice it to say that my sister's intention was to have me discovered in a compromising situation with Dr Thomas Carrington. Fortunately, Richard discovered my whereabouts and my sister's foolish scheming was foiled. Had it not been for the fact that Evadne had involved Tom in her childish act of spite, I might well have attained satisfaction enough from the fact that she had not succeeded in her intention of ruining me in the eyes of the world. But she did involve Tom, without caring whether or not he might be harmed and, equally contemptible, without experiencing the least concern that his reputation might be irreparably damaged hereabouts if her vile plan had succeeded.

"Which brings me quite nicely to the point of my visit," she went on, keeping her eyes firmly glued on her sister's far-from-serene expression. "Dr Carrington isn't the only friend of mine to suffer from your pernicious activities, is he, Evadne?"

"I haven't the slightest idea what you're talking about," she countered, determined to brazen it out, even though she had a strong suspicion to whom Elizabeth referred. She cast a fleeting glance in Caroline's direction and couldn't imagine that she had divulged her heartbreaking secret to anyone, but Elizabeth swiftly disabused her by announcing quite calmly that she was very well aware that Giles Westbridge had committed suicide and, furthermore, that she knew precisely why he had done so.

"And you, Evadne, shall return the letter he wrote to Caroline before he died, which you quite heartlessly, and with malicious intent, purloined from this house."

For several moments no one spoke. Richard, pausing in the act of raising a pinch of snuff to one thin nostril, cast a disdainful glance in Evadne's direction; Caroline, looking remarkably composed in the circumstances, did the same; and Elizabeth, hard-eyed and resolute, waited silently for a response.

"Oh, very well," Evadne capitulated, before a trill of nervous laughter escaped her. "To be perfectly honest with you, I had forgotten that I still retained the wretched thing."

The blatantly false admission fooled no one, least

of all Richard who didn't attempt to suppress the deprecating sound that rose in his throat from passing his lips. Without waiting to be offered, he reached for the teapot and helped himself to a cup, which drew a genuine gurgle of amusement from his wife.

"Need to wash down a surfeit of bile, Richard?"

"Something of the sort, my love." Leaning back against the sofa, he peered up at Elizabeth above the rim of his cup. "Loath though I am to mention this, my darling, but are you perfectly certain you can trust Lady Chiltham to keep her word and return Caroline's property?"

"How well you have come to know her, Richard! Naturally, I cannot. She isn't in the least like me, as you and Caroline have remarked upon on more than one occasion." She looked from one to the other with an enquiring lift to one finely arched brow. "Has it never occurred to either of you to wonder why we should be so dissimilar, not the least alike, not even in looks?"

In truth, before that moment it had certainly never crossed Richard's mind to wonder, but now the reason positively screamed at him. "She is, perhaps, only your half-sister?"

She did not need to respond, for Evadne, after a horrified gasp and a feeble attempt at denial, buried her face in her hands and indulged in a bout of bitter weeping.

"I fully intended to speak to her in private this evening, Caroline," Elizabeth announced, deliberately raising her voice so that she could be heard above what had become hysterical sobbing. "But after her evil machinations of this day, she deserved no such consideration, and shall receive none from me from this day forward." As though to add credence to her words, she rounded on her sister with a merciless lack of pity. "Stop that infernal racket at once! You always could manage to burst into tears at the drop of a hat, and you're fooling no one, least of all me!"

"I—I don't know how you can be so—so cruel," Evadne responded in a pathetic whisper, having rapidly controlled what had threatened to be an inexhaustible flow.

"That's rich, coming from you!" was Elizabeth's forthright rejoinder. She felt tired after the events of the day, and discovered that the sympathy she had experienced for her sister when reading that pile of letters several hours earlier had long since ebbed away.

"Now, you listen to me, Evadne, and listen well. I have a number of letters in my possession which state clearly enough that you are the bastard daughter of a feckless and mercenary individual who was once in our grandmother's employ. No one will learn of this from me, unless you give me cause to reveal your unfortunate parentage. You *shall* leave this house first thing in the morning, and you shall *not* return here unless invited. When you reach Devonshire you *shall* return Caroline's property without delay. And you shall *never* divulge to another living soul what you know about Giles Westbridge's death.

"Should you be foolish enough to go against my expressed wishes, then I will not hesitate in making the contents of those letters widely known. I cannot imagine that Lord Chiltham, complacent though he is, could withstand the humiliation of being married to a bastard. You would be ruined in the eyes of the world, and could expect no help from me. I shall disown you entirely."

Richard waited until Evadne, earnestly sobbing this time, had fled the room before turning eyes, filled with admiration, up to his wife. "I think, my dear, we are likely to see a great change in Lady Chiltham in the future, thanks to you."

"You may be sure that I shall not repeat what I have just learned," Caroline assured them, still somewhat bemused by the startling revelations. "I cannot thank you enough, Elizabeth, for forcing her to return Giles's letter. You did, however, make me realise on the night of the ball how foolish I have been all these years in allowing Evadne to retain such a hold over me. I fully intend to disclose the sad truth about his father's death to my son when he returns next week. I had also decided to confide in my close friends, too, at least, those whom I knew I could trust. Which, of course, included you, Richard. But I shan't attempt to do so now. Elizabeth, poor girl, looks worn out, and your only desire at this moment must be to take her home."

It was true—Richard was most concerned about her, and had been doubly so since their departure from the inn. The events of the day had taken their toll, and the confrontation with Evadne seemed to have sapped the last of Elizabeth's strength. She had handled herself superbly and had come out the clear victor, but it was quite evident to any one with a modicum of sensitivity that the annihilation of her sister had brought her no pleasure whatsoever—quite the opposite, in fact.

Caroline, always so very considerate, offered to put her light carriage at their disposal, but Elizabeth, surprising them both, politely turned down the kind offer, declaring that she would much prefer to ride home in the fresh air. She surprised Richard further on their arrival back at the Hall by announcing her intention of joining him for supper, once she had rid her person of the unpleasant odour acquired at that obnoxious inn.

He awaited her in his library, occupying his time by reading the pile of letters she had left for his perusal in the top drawer of his desk. They made interesting, if rather sad, reading, for the events which had taken place thirty years before had had an adverse effect on several lives, not least of which had been Elizabeth's, whose childhood had been far from happy.

By placing the yellowing sheets in strict chronological order he was able to piece together what must have taken place. Louisa Smithson, at the tender age of seventeen, had come under the spell of a certain John Taverner, second in command on one of Mary Smithson's trading vessels. A devil-may-care, handsome rogue, he had seduced Mrs Smithson's daughter and then, in return for a generous remunerative consideration, and a captaincy on one of the sailing ships, he had agreed to have nothing further to do with his employer's daughter; but the damage, Mrs Smithson was to discover shortly after acquiescing to the demands, had already been done.

Louisa was with child, and Mrs Smithson had looked about in haste for a suitable husband for her daughter. Henry Beresford had been in Bristol at the time, staying with friends, and Mrs Smithson's eyes had fallen upon this younger son of an earl. The wedding, naturally, had had to be arranged swiftly, but it was only to be expected that the Honourable Henry Beresford would have become suspicious when his young bride had presented him with a perfectly formed child within seven months of their marriage taking place, even if he had never suspected anything before.

After reading the bitterly resentful letter Henry had written to his mother-in-law after Evadne's birth, Richard deduced that Elizabeth's father had considered the marriage at an end. Evidently, though, Mrs Smithson had somehow managed to change his mind, no doubt by digging deep into her purse once again, for he had not sought an annulment and, of course, seven years later Louisa had presented him with a second daughter, definitely his child this time. At some point after Elizabeth's birth Henry must have forgiven his mother-in-law totally, for he had visited her from time to time, occasionally taking his baby daughter with him.

From her letters it was quite obvious that Louisa had never forgiven her mother for forcing her into a loveless union. Learning of John Taverner's death at sea within a few short weeks of her marriage to Henry Beresford taking place certainly wouldn't have improved her attitude towards her mother, and Richard supposed that it had been only natural for Louisa to display such affection for her love-child, but her coolness towards her legitimate daughter had been unpardonable. After all, it had hardly been Elizabeth's fault that her mother had been denied the man she loved, but then, he reminded himself, it had hardly been Evadne's, either. No wonder Elizabeth had gained such little pleasure from their confrontation earlier. It was all so very, very sad for all concerned.

He had just placed the letters back in the drawer when Elizabeth, restored to her normally well-groomed self, came storming into the room, looking not in the least desirous of his sympathy. "Richard, I could quite cheerfully murder you!" she astonished him by announcing, and sounded as if she meant it, too. "What in the world do you mean by letting me go to Caroline's looking like a besom broom in a fit? And with a black eye, too! I was mortified when I caught sight of my reflection in my dressing-table mirror."

"My dear, you were determined to go," he reminded her soothingly, "and I am rather glad that I didn't attempt to dissuade you. I wouldn't have missed that performance for a king's ransom. You were magnificent!" he assured her, going across to the decanters and filling two glasses.

She accepted the Madeira with scant grace, but her resentment didn't last very long and she swiftly channelled her thoughts to more mundane matters. "I hope supper isn't too long. I'm absolutely famished. I've arranged for trays to be brought in here. I hope you don't mind."

"Not in the least, my darling. I can think of nothing I would enjoy more than a private supper with you, and then bed, I think, for both of us. I can only guess how you must be feeling after the events of this day, but I certainly feel exhausted. What with the journey from London, and all the excitement since, I feel I could quite happily sleep for a week."

Elizabeth was suddenly contrite. "Oh, Richard, I am sorry! It completely slipped my mind to ask before, but did you manage to locate your old army friend?"

At this artless enquiry the hand raising the glass to his lips checked for a moment. He had not intended broaching the subject of her reprehensible deception after what she had been through that day, but now the opening was there, was he gentlemanly enough to let it pass…? No, most assuredly not!

"Yes, I discovered his whereabouts, my sweet," he responded with such a wickedly smug grin that she ought instantly to have been suspicious, but she wasn't.

She asked eagerly, "And did you manage to persuade him to accept the position, here, as head groom?"

"Yes, my darling, I did. He'll be arriving here with his wife early next week." He paused to toss the Madeira down his throat and place the empty glass down by the side of his chair before adding, "Mrs Hawker is a very likeable woman. I'm certain you'll get along well with her. Perhaps you might find her work in the house?"

"Hawker, did you say?" Elizabeth frowned. The name struck a chord of memory, but where she had heard it before eluded her for the present.

"Yes. Sergeant Tobias Hawker's wife." He noted with immense satisfaction that she nearly choked on her Madeira before she placed the glass, with a hand that was far from steady, down on the table for safety. "He was my batman for many years. And—would you believe it!—we were both injured at Waterloo, and convalesced together in the same house. Now, isn't that a coincidence?" he finished, nailing down the final screw in her coffin.

She cast him a half-penitent, half-amused look. "You know, don't you?"

"Yes, you little baggage, I do now!" and before she could utter more than a startled gasp he had hauled her out of her chair and had her firmly imprisoned on his lap. "Why, if you had been there when Hawker handed me the book of poems you had loaned him in Brussels, and I saw that lock of your hair... Blonde, indeed! Now, what the deuce do you mean by keeping the truth from me all this time?''

"Were you very angry?'' she asked, suddenly finding the folds of his cravat of immense interest.

"Yes, I was. And still am, for that matter!'' he retorted, but a fleeting glance at his eyes was sufficient to inform her this was far from the truth.

"You would have married me, Richard, after what had taken place between us. I realised that at the time, but I also knew that you didn't love me. You've admitted as much, haven't you?''

"I would swiftly have come to love you,'' he responded without a moment's hesitation. ''After all, that is precisely what did happen when we met in Devon, remember?''

"Yes, I remember,'' she said, laying her head against his broad shoulder. ''But if I had stayed in Brussels I would always have carried the nagging doubt in the back of my mind that you had married me because I was Elizabeth Beresford and you had taken my innocence away.''

He could understand this, but was still far from satisfied. ''But why didn't you tell me shortly after I was brought to the house after the battle?'' he asked, not unreasonably.

"Because, my darling, I didn't want there to be any awkwardness between us. You wouldn't have felt comfortable being nursed back to health by a gently bred young woman whom you had known since she was a girl, now, would you?''

Recalling clearly the many tasks she had performed for him whilst he had been too weak to help himself, he couldn't help but agree wholeheartedly with this, but felt entirely justified for remarking, ''But you ought to have told me on the day we were married.''

''Yes, I know. And I hold myself entirely to blame for what happened between us shortly afterwards,'' she announced with a complete turnabout of her former opinion, and with a generosity of spirit that he considered did her great credit. ''It is little wonder you reacted as you did. And yet when I did try to explain on the night of our—er—reconciliation, you wouldn't let me, my darling,'' she reminded him with the most deliciously wicked feminine smile he had ever witnessed, but he couldn't find it within himself to be even remotely annoyed now, and betrayed the fact by kissing her in a way that left her in no doubt that he wasn't as tired as he had professed to be.

''Richard, it isn't the done thing, you know, to be discovered making love to your wife in the library!'' she told him roundly, managing eventually to extricate herself from his embrace and return to her own chair. ''What would poor Medway have thought if he had walked in with our supper and caught us?''

''Can't really say I give a damn what he might have thought!'' he returned bluntly, and consoled himself by pouring a second glass of his excellent Madeira.

''You might not, but I most certainly do. Why, he must have a very odd opinion of me already!'' she announced, growing quite pink with shame. ''The poor man hadn't been here above an hour before he was called upon to rescue me. And what he must have thought when he learned that his mistress had been lying naked in a bed beside the local practitioner is anyone's guess!''

''More to the point, what did Tom think about it?'' Richard countered, his shoulders shaking with suppressed laughter. ''I take it you have been in to check on him already?''

"Yes, though why I concern myself with such an ungrateful wretch, I'll never know! I hadn't been in the room above five seconds before he had the sheer effrontery to scold me for having had him brought here for Aggie to look after, instead of taking him to his own house. He's still a little woozy, but had certainly recovered sufficiently to notice my black eye. The callous monster seemed to find it highly amusing that you had done it! And not satisfied with that, he had the unmitigated gall to wonder why it had taken you so long to inflict such an injury on my person!"

Ignoring her highly amused husband's deep rumble of laughter, Elizabeth shook her head, genuinely troubled. "He worries me sometimes, Richard, really he does. When I explained to him what had been happening, and then mentioned that, for all of two minutes, we had been naked in a bed together, he didn't so much as bat an eyelid! No, truly he didn't even blink," she reiterated, decidedly piqued. "There is something wrong with him, so there is. I'm certain he looks upon the entire female race as nothing more than skin and bone and put together slightly differently than males."

Richard tactfully refrained from informing her that Dr Carrington had been seen on more than one occasion visiting the cottage of the delightful young widow whose son did odd jobs for him, and merely said, "I don't think you need concern yourself unduly on Tom's behalf. There's not much wrong with him."

"I wish I were as certain. I have never seen him look at any female twice, unless she happened to be one of his patients and then, of course, it was only from a medical standpoint. But I shan't give up hope!" she announced, brightening perceptibly. "What he needs is a good wife to humanise him. I'm positive that somewhere in the length and breadth of this land of ours there must be a girl just waiting to capture his attention. It's just a simple case of finding her, and bringing them together.''

''You can let Tom do his own finding, madam wife. I forbid you to interfere,'' he told her, his tone brooking no argument. ''Besides which, he isn't nearly ready for matrimony yet.''

''I am forced to agree with you on that point, at least,'' she conceded, conveniently forgetting propriety by sitting herself on his lap once more, and casting him one of her most captivating smiles. ''But if, in the future, he did happen to cross the path of a certain someone, you'd help me to give him a little push in the right direction, as it were, wouldn't you, Richard?''

''Most assuredly not!''

Elizabeth, her hopes not in the least dampened, smiled to herself as she laid her head upon his shoulder. It was not unheard of, after all, for a gentleman to change his mind.

And he did...

* * * * *

*Don't miss the conclusion to Anne Ashley's Regency duet in **Volume 8** of the The Regency Lords & Ladies Collection, available in February 2006*

MILLS & BOON®

Live the emotion

Historical
romance™

RANSOM BRIDE
by Anne Herries

Once a galley slave, now a Venetian merchant prince,
Lorenzo Santorini is driven to seek revenge. He spares
no time for emotions such as love. Yet when English
beauty Kathryn Rowlands appeals for help in finding
a friend lost to pirates, Lorenzo struggles to maintain
his cold detachment…

THE RAKE'S REVENGE
by Gail Ranstrom

Robert McHugh, Earl of Glenross, is out to avenge his
family's tragedy. He hasn't anticipated his reaction to
the alluring Miss Afton Lovejoy, and she, in turn, is
shocked by the passion she feels for this notorious
womaniser. Plunged into a world of intrigue and
desire, Robert begins to suspect that Afton is not
all she seems…

On sale 3rd February 2006

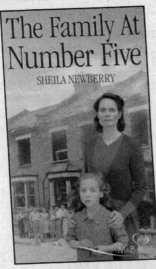

LONDON, 1932

Moving into Number Five, Kitchener Avenue, heralds the start of a new life for the Hope family...

Pregnant with her first child, Miriam knows it's a safe environment to bring up her family. For her fourteen-year-old sister Barbara, it means independence, boys and ballroom dancing. For Fred Hope, it's his chance to prove he can be a good husband and father. And with the birth of baby Glory, the Hope household is filled with joy.

But World War II is just around the corner and soon Number Five is more than a home – it becomes a life-line.

Can they survive the war and be reunited as a family once again?

On sale 20th January 2006

Available at most branches of WHSmith, Tesco, ASDA, Borders, Eason, Sainsbury's and most bookshops

Visit our website at www.millsandboon.co.uk

Be swept off your feet and into the past with award-winning authors Julia Justiss and Joanne Rock, and their stories of forbidden love…

Seductive Stranger by **Julia Justiss**

In Regency England, dashing Lord Brandon had been entrusted to help Lord Sudley's daughters find husbands. But now spirited Ailis had fallen prey to the charms of a notorious rake and Lord Brandon had become enraptured with Caragh's quiet beauty…

The Wedding Knight by **Joanne Rock**

The year was 1250 and Melissande Deverell, mere weeks before her final vows as a nun, found herself held fast in the arms of Lucian Barret, her childhood companion and now a warrior of great prowess…